Outstanding praise for Stephen Gr

“A deeply immersive and endlessly f
a true story I only thought I knew. C
with fresh perspectives and new insights as the story unfolded, seamlessly weaving together fact and fiction. An essential read for anyone fascinated by the fabulous life of famed writer Truman Capote and his complicated friendships with some of New York City’s most celebrated socialites. I was dazzled by the life of Lee Radziwill, wife of a Polish prince, sister to an American First Lady, and mother-in-law to a Real Housewife. A deeply personal portrait of a friendship between two unique people whose lives encompassed world travel, high society, popular culture, and human frailty.”

—Kim Van Alkemade, *New York Times* bestselling author of *Orphan # 8*

“A fascinating and effervescent portrayal of 1960s Manhattan high society and the complex friendship at its heart between legendary writer Truman Capote and Lee Radziwill, sister-in-law to President John F. Kennedy and one of Capote’s infamous ‘swans.’ Using a brilliant narrative overlay, author Stephen Greco brings the charismatic author of *Breakfast at Tiffany’s* and *In Cold Blood* to life with the type of biting wit, trenchant social commentary, and keen grasp of human nature for which he was celebrated. Insightful, intriguing and endlessly entertaining, *Such Good Friends* captures a platonic yet deeply passionate friendship that had all the fault lines of a doomed romance, and the seismic influence of Capote and Radziwill on their respective worlds, and each other.”

—Natalie Jenner, author of *The Jane Austen Society*

“*Such Good Friends* seamlessly blends high society glamour with human frailties in this vivid recreation of celebrated writer Truman Capote’s and New York socialite Lee Radziwill’s complicated friendship that spanned from the 1950s into the 1970s.”

—Mary Ellen Taylor, Amazon bestselling author

“A thoughtful examination of the precarious bonds of friendship, fame and fortune. Greco’s *Such Good Friends* stars two of the most notable personalities of their time, Truman Capote and Lee Radziwill, sister of Jackie Kennedy. Sweepingly detailed, with glamour and mystery woven throughout. Fans of Capote and the era of Camelot should be delighted.”

—Shana Abé, bestselling author of *The Second Mrs. Astor*

Books by Stephen Greco

NOW AND YESTERDAY

SUCH GOOD FRIENDS

Published by Kensington Publishing Corp.

SUCH GOOD FRIENDS

A Novel of

TRUMAN CAPOTE & LEE RADZIWILL

STEPHEN GRECO

John Scognamiglio Books
KENSINGTON BOOKS
www.kensingtonbooks.com

JOHN SCOGNAMIGLIO BOOKS are published by

Kensington Publishing Corp.
119 West 40th Street
New York, NY 10018

All Kensington titles, imprints, and distributed lines are available at special quantity discounts for bulk purchases for sales promotion, premiums, fund-raising, and educational or institutional use.

Special book excerpts or customized printings can also be created to fit specific needs. For details, write or phone the office of the Kensington Sales Manager: Kensington Publishing Corp., 119 West 40th Street, New York, NY 10018. Attn. Sales Department. Phone: 1-800-221-2647.

ISBN: 978-1-4967-3744-1

ISBN: 978-1-4967-3745-8 (ebook)

First Kensington Trade Paperback Edition: June 2023

10 9 8 7 6 5 4 3 2 1

Printed in the United States of America

In memory of Barry,
who moved smoothly in so many social circles

This novel is based on true events and the lives of real people. Some scenes have been created or modified for dramatic purposes, and some characters have been invented.

PART I

CHAPTER 1

TWO FUNERALS

My flight had been delayed. There was a mix-up over my seat assignment. My hip was acting up. But my friend Judy met me at JFK with a hired town car, which I thought a terribly sweet thing to do, and so typical of her. She was standing at the gate as I exited the baggage claim area: a perfectly put-together, upper-middle-class New York lady in her youngish-looking seventies, in a navy wool pea jacket and a pair of tidy jeans; her shoulder-length hair, which she kept dark, tucked into a youthful-looking, white cashmere beanie. It was almost the same look that her late mom, Sandy, might have been sporting thirty years before, on a similar errand, except that Sandy would also have been carrying a poppy-orange Hermès Kelly bag with an Hermès equestrian scarf tied around the handle.

"Oooh, welcome, welcome," said Judy as we hugged.

"Hello, hello," I said.

"Is that all you have?"

I was carrying a briefcase and pulling a small spinner-wheel suitcase.

"I travel light," I said.

"Good flight?"

I made a cheery-grim face.

"Like a long MRI," I said.

We headed for the terminal doors, comparing the February weather in New York with that in West Palm Beach, where I have lived since retirement.

"The last few days have been a bit gray," said Judy.

"Perfect for a requiem mass, no?" I said.

"I'm so sorry, Mar. I know how much she meant to you."

Judy and I had known each other for decades, since she was eighteen and I was nineteen, living in her family's home for a couple of years as the paid companion of her grandmother, a Park Avenue blue blood. Then we remained in touch after her grandmother went into a nursing home and Judy's mother recommended me for a staff position in the home of a friend of hers, Lee Radziwill—a position I held for fifty-five years. It was Lee's funeral bringing me back to New York, as Lee had become one of the two people in my life who were closest to being friends, souls I cared about greatly and who cared about me in some way—the other soul being Lee's former best friend Truman Capote, who had died thirty-five years before.

Outside the terminal, a security guard showed us where to cross the lanes of slow-moving traffic, to the pick-up zone where a black Lincoln SUV was waiting at the curb. The driver took my bag and stowed it in the tailgate, while Judy and I installed ourselves in the back seat. A tiny bar featured champagne, mineral water, and an assortment of sweet and salty snacks, none of which I had much stomach for.

"I wish you were staying with us," burbled Judy. "Our guest room is always there for you."

"I didn't want to bother you so soon after the wedding," I said.

"Burt is dying to meet you."

Judy had lost her first husband, John, two years before, after nearly fifty years of marriage.

"He's a lawyer?" I said.

"Another lawyer, yes," said Judy. "Go figure."

"How did you meet?"

"At a Philharmonic fundraiser."

Some women don't remarry at our age, but I wasn't surprised when Judy did. She seems to have a knack for domestic happiness, which I have always envied. I never married; my own family was a disaster, which is probably why, throughout the years, I've been so grateful to be included in the warmth of Judy's family. Actually, maybe Judy's knack is more specifically for mothering, which she undoubtedly learned from a loving mother and grandmother. It is a gift, this kind of motherliness, mystifying to someone like me, who'd had a rotten relationship with my own mother—though I have to admit that this gift can be shockingly lovely to see in action, as it was in so many tender moments I witnessed between Lee and her children, and between Lee's sister, Jackie, and hers. Except for Judy, I have benefited little, myself, from this supposedly essential life force, yet I have come through well enough. Good mothering is apparently not like food, water, and air. It's something you can live with or without.

"You seem very happy," I said.

"Burt is wonderful," said Judy. "You'll see. Though no one replaces the man you've spent a lifetime with."

She said this with a little exhalation that was almost a laugh. She has always had this way of half-smiling when making assertions—as if reflexively meaning to entertain and apologize at the same time.

"Some women wouldn't dive in again," I said. "Good for you."

I liked John and had thought him good for Judy since the day I met him, at a Washington Square Art Show, in the early '60s. I was probably one of the few people left, other than her children, with whom Judy could reminisce about him.

"He used to lecture us about Rauschenberg and Johns—remember?" she said. "He could be a bit pompous, but I was so impressed."

"Do you still have Marilyn?"

"The Warhol? Of course! You wouldn't believe what Kelly says it's worth now."

Sunday morning traffic was light. As the car sailed toward the Belt Parkway, heading ultimately for my hotel located only a few blocks from Judy's Upper East Side apartment, she and I caught up on the current events of our lives. Her new husband was a retired copyright lawyer, who was now investing in start-up ventures focused on cultural content. Judy's son James, a psychology professor, had been granted tenure at Yale, and her daughter Kelly, an auctioneer at Christie's, had just sold an Ingres drawing for a record sum. My news was less momentous, but Judy listened with characteristic pride and delight when I told her about the writing classes I have been teaching and the recent publication of a short story of mine in a literary journal. The latter led the conversation in a direction I hadn't expected.

"So exciting, to be a writer," said Judy. "But then, you had Truman as your mentor."

"I did, indeed," I said. "And I learned so much. I wanted to be like him. Though of course at a certain point, you have to find yourself and write like *that*."

"Interesting you say that, Mar. Tell me, do you think our stories make us who we are?"

It was an oddly philosophical question for an airport pick-up ride.

"How do you mean?" I said.

"Our stories, the histories we carry around—how important do you think they are? They *are* important, aren't they?"

"Well . . . of course."

"I mean, I know they are."

Though Judy knows that I've met several famous writers in my lifetime, we'd never talked seriously about the principles and craft of writing.

"Judy, are you in a class or something?" I said. "If this is for an exercise, I'd be happy to help, but . . ."

"No, no, I've just been thinking."

"Okay."

"We're both in our seventies now . . ."

"Are we?"

She laughed at my attempt to make light of the moment, but I saw that she had something to say.

"Listen, I don't mean to be coy," she said. "I want to share something with you—something that I don't think you know, that I should have told you a long time ago, except that Mother and Granny said I shouldn't. Only now that Mother's gone . . ."

"Uh-oh."

Was Judy a lesbian? That would be a neat surprise.

"No, it's nothing scary or anything like that," she said. "It's just about my mother finding you that job."

Had Lee been pressured to take me on or something? That was unlikely and, moreover, of no consequence now.

Judy and I have both led such conventional lives—me, a self-declared orphan who'd come through violence and wound up in domestic service; Judy, an upper-middle-class daughter and then wife; both of us circumscribed by basically the same set of cultural rules. Flashing back over the innocuous coffees and lunches that comprised the almost sixty years of our friendship, I doubted that Judy had anything of a skeleton-in-the-closet nature to divulge. It was probably just a nice story about her grandmother's final days at Shady Hill. Still, at that moment, I suddenly felt resistant. I'd been up early for my flight. I needed coffee. I was preoccupied with the funeral. If it were an historical footnote that Judy wanted to share, surely it could wait until the dinner we'd planned for two days hence.

"Sure," I said. "But maybe not right this very second? Can it keep until Tuesday?"

"No, no—sure, that's fine," said Judy. "You know me. I'm just a little . . ." She made a hand gesture that I believe translates as "impulsively high-spirited."

They say we tell ourselves stories in order to live. But that's not quite the full picture, is it? Surely it's better if the stories are accurate and complete. What I learned two days later, at dinner with Judy and Burt, was that I had reached the age of seventy-eight without knowing an important detail of my own story—a plot point, you might say, that once radically altered the flow of events in my life, that now puts a slightly different cast on my voice as a narrator and may influence the events unfolding as my narrative heads toward a close.

It had been ages since I'd last seen New York. I had returned only once since retiring in '05, to help Lee for a few days on the occasion of her being interviewed by Sofia Coppola for

The New York Times—shot on video in Lee's Lexington Avenue apartment, with a small complement of light and sound people for whom we provided coffee, lunch, and snacks. I saw Judy then, too—stayed with her and John—but otherwise, there was nothing else to bring me back. I have no family or other friends, really. Lee and I had remained in touch with a note now and then, and I knew that she'd been ill recently. And I wept a little when I heard on the news that "one of the world's most glamorous socialites" had died, thinking of all the kindness she showed me over the years, despite the ups and downs of her own life. I knew the funeral would be private, so I was surprised when Carole, Lee's daughter-in-law, called to see if I would be able to attend. Frankly, I was half-expecting Carole to ask if I would supervise the catering; but she was more gracious than I'm afraid I give her credit for.

The hotel I'd chosen for the visit was the Lowell, on East 63rd. I was staying for three nights, so that on the day after the funeral, I could meet with the producer who had shown interest in the pages I'd sent her and have an early dinner with Judy. Once installed in my room, I unpacked and hung up my black wool-crepe pants suit, which had a minimum of wrinkles because I always pack with layers of stiff paper, as Lee did. It was a bit of a splurge to stay at such an expensive place, but I can afford it, and I wanted to feel more than comfortable. After all this time away from New York, settled into the torpor of life in West Palm Beach, I wanted to feel protected from any assault by the city's more hectic energy. Truman used to remind me that "this glamorous city of ours" was also a "voluptuous opponent." Yet that fear of assault began dissolving into excitement, even on the ride into the city from the airport with Judy, on the expressway that runs along the bay, when we rounded a curve and I caught the first glimpse across the water of Manhattan's skyline, spiky with some of the new towers I'd read about—a next New York that had been constantly evolving, but which for me, away for fourteen years, was the sudden future. Even the Lowell, which I remembered as respectable but sleepy, now quietly embodied some fashion-forward fizz, the result of a recent overhaul that a conscientious bellboy in wire-rim glasses explained "takes the best of the traditional into the future . . ."

Lee was all about *the next*—in style and culture, certainly, but also in her search for fulfilling personal occupations. For a while, back in the early '80s, she was working away at interior design and even created a few hotel rooms herself, when she was seeing that charming real estate man that she was engaged to for a while, Newton Cope. I remember she said the rooms were meant to be pretty, but also to be based on "historical styles and ideas, not notions." There was no such style as "Orientalist," she insisted; that term was too imprecise. Instead, there was Persian, there was Mughal, there was Colonial Moroccan, and so on. She used to show me the sketches she was working with, the mood boards she was creating with chips of color and swatches of fabric. I learned so much from Lee about décor and the arts—about everything!—though her rooms turned out to be too expensive to maintain in a hotel's punishing daily service. She told me later she hadn't understood that hotel rooms had to be engineered as much as designed. She had simply been trying to follow the philosophy of her great friend, the architect and decorator Renzo Mongiardino, who had done her homes in England—Buckingham Place, in London, and Turville Grange, in the country. "Renzo always said he wanted to make his clients feel at home in the world," she told me once. "Isn't that a lovely idea—'at home in the world'? A room should be comfortable, of course, but he thought it should tell you something about the world, even about history—news about why life was so marvelous."

I thought about that idea later as I had a bite of lunch in one of the hotel's restaurants and then took a little stroll down to 57th Street and back. News of the world was on view in every shop window—well, news of marvelous parts of the world, anyway. And now that Valentine's Day was over, the theme was spring. Rather, early spring 2019, as window designers who work at this level are every bit as specific as journalists and fine artists. Thus *spring right now!* was bursting from the windows of Fendi and Prada, Hermès and Vuitton, Chopard and Fred

Leighton, Smythson and Montblanc; in the form of must-have items that we never knew we needed so much, that suddenly we wanted to inspect and think about more intently; items of sparkling jewels and lustrous precious metals, of sumptuous leathers, luminous silks, and lighthearted cottons; all displayed with bits of whimsy and touches of magnificence that subtly implied that material splendor might well point the way toward spiritual opulence. Especially here in the bosom of New York's most affluent audience, the onrush of *the next* is always presented in products and experiences that are amusing, seductive. And that's what fashion and style are for, aren't they?—to make the essential unknowableness of the future feel exciting, or at least less terrifying, for those who can afford such therapy.

Anyway, the stroll felt exciting to me. Even the air I was breathing in the chilly street, laced with that smell I remember fondly, of asphalt and metallic steam, was a refreshing change from South Florida's persistent swampiness. I'd read that New York was losing its soul, now that artists were being forced out by the high cost of living and foreign billionaires were buying up zillion-dollar floors in new apartment towers and leaving them empty. Yet to me, the city looked as good as ever.

In the creative writing classes I teach, I always ask my fellow senior citizens to think about what else is being shown them in a story besides the obvious plot points. Fred Leighton may be showing us sapphire and ruby brooches, but what else is going on when the brooches are popping up like flowers from miniature Fabergé-like flowerpots? Is *right now!* a time when ten-thousand-dollar brooches can be picked like springtime blooms? It was Truman who got me to question my view of the world this way—the world-famous author who was Lee's best friend for years; the provocative charmer who became my esteemed friend, too. Improbably, except in fiction like his, Truman made me a confidante and then even started sharing his trade secrets—which is why, even on a little stroll, part of me questioned the impressions I was getting of the world, this *moment* in New York. Was I, an old lady lucky enough to have witnessed close-up some of the most glamorous social goings-on of the late twentieth century, now truly seeing my old hometown for what it had become? Or was I compelled to observe it only through a lovely cloud of nostalgia?

Long after Truman died, years after Lee's anger over his betrayal had faded, she sometimes wondered aloud with me, about some event or person, "What would Truman think?" It is the same question I am asking myself now that Lee is gone: "What would she make of sapphire periwinkles in a little gold flowerpot?"

Lee's funeral, the next morning, took place under one of those gray, February New York skies that seem to accentuate the smug stateliness of the Upper East Side's prestigious, old apartment buildings. Those limestone façades impose most assuredly not in summer sunshine, but in winter's coldest light, when it's clear that the warmth they promise corresponds precisely to the metaphysical comfiness afforded by money and status. I walked the thirty or so blocks up Park Avenue from my hotel to the church. Even on such a sad day, I felt buoyed by the bustle of other pedestrians striding in and out of portals flanked by potted shrubs, stepping in and out of black town cars with tinted windows. So many wore black! It was a characteristic that had always been true of certain city sophisticates, I suppose, but it refocused itself for me now, after my years in a town where people looked splashier. Lee loved color, but always said that in the northern light of New York and London, black made everyone look "like Spanish royalty"—by which she meant the expensively tailored looks of the accomplished socialites and celebrities who were her friends.

The funeral took place amidst the restrained Gothic Revival grandeur of the church of St. Thomas More, on East 89th Street, between Park and Madison. It was the church where Lee's sister, Jacqueline Kennedy Onassis, was a parishioner until her death in 1994. I arrived ten minutes early and was greeted by one of a small team of elegant young women in black, who were discreetly making sure that anyone seeking entry had been invited. The women recognized celebrities and welcomed them in.

Of me, they would have asked for a name, but I offered it first, and they admitted me without consulting an iPad or conveying my name to someone else via headset, as might happen at a less solemn society event. Among the press, I recognized photographers from *People* and the *Daily Mail.* If there were security people around—well, there must have been—I didn't notice any.

It was a small congregation, even intimate. Whole rows at the back of the church were empty. I slipped into a spot at the edge of things, to a syrupy organ prelude incorporating themes of Puccini, one of Lee's favorite composers. Deployed tastefully around the church were masses of pink, green, and white flowers, no doubt courtesy of Renny or one of the other fashionable floral and event designers whom Lee knew. Above the altar, under a glorious stained glass window depicting the Resurrection, hung a crucifix of understated design. One doesn't gawk at an event like this, of course, but one does scan unobtrusively for friends—and I spotted several friends of Lee who had been decent enough over the years to remember my name and treat me more like an equal than a cook-housekeeper. Coppola, seated two rows ahead of me, managed to catch my eye when she twisted around to take stock of the crowd. The director flashed a little wave, and I was delighted to be recognized. She had not only been nice to me but revealed a few points about documentary storytelling during the interview with Lee, which I came to find useful in my subsequent work in writing and teaching. Sofia asked Lee all kinds of impertinent questions in a friendly way that day, about marriages and boyfriends and illnesses—though I noticed that the responses to many of those, curt and deflective, never made it into the finished video.

Truman, too, was unafraid of asking *all* the questions—though of course, that quality eventually became a parody of itself, as the drugs and the drinking and whatever else it was took him over. I was only a girl when I started working for Lee, so Lord knows I was susceptible not only to the glamour of both of them, but to their power . . . and genius, really. Genius and cheekiness. I remember serving lunch one day to the two of them in Lee's library—poached salmon with a dill sauce—and Truman asked me if I wanted to brush my teeth.

"Truman . . . !" exclaimed Lee, more amused than shocked. I'd served them often in her home by then, yet I suppose Lee was taken aback by Truman's familiarity. Even to the end, she never learned about the writing work that Truman and I did together secretly, which had already begun.

"Well, I'm sorry," said Truman, "but there's a little piece of dill stuck right there." He bared his own teeth and touched a tooth with his pinky. "I thought she should know."

"Still," said Lee. "Really."

"That's okay," said Truman, in that impish way of his. "Marlene and I, we have each other's backs, don't we . . . ?"

I smiled demurely. Lee knew I wasn't offended.

As the organ warbled on, I spotted several other prominent types who moved in Lee's circles: playwright William Ivey Long, fashion designer Carolina Herrera and her husband Reinaldo, magazine editor Richard David Story, author Hannah Pakula, author Meryl Gordon, and fashion guru André Leon Talley. Over the music hung a gauzy din of hushed conversations in French, Italian, Spanish, and Portuguese, as well as English. A sudden glimpse of a well-known doyenne revealed a familiar face that had been radically altered since I saw it last; I almost gasped, then brightened. It seemed right to behold this new face in a church, a place commemorating miracles and martyrdoms, unusual occurrences that were neither comic nor strictly tragic. Indeed, the lady's face now bore the expression of a plaster saint, her habitual poise and practiced grace newly hardened as if by the resolve of some unshakeable faith.

The organist concluded the Puccini and began a processional, as a trio of celebrants in white robes entered the sanctuary, accompanied by a flank of altar boys and girls, and the service began. I hadn't noticed the presence of a small vocal ensemble until they sounded their first offering, a Kyrie. It was a cappella, something modern and modestly scaled—Delius? Poulenc? Celestial strains soared joyously among arches pointing heavenward. The music's optimistic tone was so right for Lee, who always sought the best and brightest in life. And after so many bubbly lunches and parties that I know Lee and Truman enjoyed together, and so many frolics on yachts and private beaches that I heard about from each of them, so much affection and respect between them—after all that, I thought, and then those years of quiet acrimony—now both of them were gone; and sitting on the bookshelves of Rizzoli's, sixty blocks south, were several volumes devoted to each of them. An aphorism that Truman once confided to me came to mind as the mass went on: "God is happiest when he's playing with us."

After the service, on the steps of the church, I briefly chatted with several people. I approached Carole Radziwill just as she was saying goodbye to the Herreras.

"So good of you to come," said Carole, before instantly moving off to speak with Caroline Kennedy. A former star of *Real Housewives of New York City*, Carole was dressed in a conspicuously chic black suit and seven-inch black heels. I was never very close to Carole and am decidedly not a fan of America's real-housewives culture, yet I admired how deftly she was handling her post-service greetings—like the pro she is. I understand that by virtue of her marriage to the late Anthony Radziwill, the son of Lee and second husband Prince Stanislaus Radziwill, Carole sometimes refers to herself as "Princess"—though Polish titles no longer legally exist, and it is an open question about whether and how one might use a title socially in New York. Truman's affectionately waggish way of calling Lee "Princess, dear" neatly expressed this ambivalence, as well as his obvious awe of anything socially elevated.

Then I saw a neighbor of Lee's, from the Fifth Avenue building.

"Hello, Lily," I said. "Beautiful service, wasn't it?"

"So nice to see you," said Lily. Her manner was haughty as usual. "She appreciated all your support during those difficult times. And of course your marvelous way with those tiny vegetables."

"Yes," I said.

"See you back there."

As Lily turned away, I smirked. I had not been invited to the post-funeral reception, but I was amused that Lily still remembered a moment from a lunch I cooked and served years before, when she, Lee, Truman, and I shared a laugh over Truman's much-publicized statement that "rich people serve such marvelous little vegetables, scarcely out of the earth." I remember Truman at the table, which was set gaily with some of Lee's incredibly varied china and crystal, pretending to want some vegetables that were "even tinier" and commanding me to go fetch some.

"Hello, Marlene. Good to see you again."

Sofia Coppola was suddenly standing beside me, still looking like a twenty-something, with that lustrous brown hair.

"You, too," I said. "You're looking well."

When we met and Lee introduced me, the director had asked if I were German, like Marlene Dietrich. No, I explained. The name was Cuban, not German, though it is pronounced practically the same way.

"Still writing, I hope?" said Coppola.

"Oh yes—you remember!"

"Of course. We all have stories to tell."

I thought for a split second of telling her about the screenplay. Then I thought better of it. One of the most valuable things I learned from both Lee and Truman was when to impose upon friends and acquaintances, and when not to. Besides, the producer I was to meet with would have her own ideas, if she were interested.

"I loved *Marie Antoinette*," I blurted out. "Such elegant choices about what to show and what not to show at the end."

"Thank you so much," said the director. "I can't believe it was almost fifteen years ago."

I suppose it *was* fifteen years ago, I thought as I walked back to my hotel, yet *Marie Antoinette* still feels to me like "one of the new movies." By the same token, Truman's funeral, in 1984, still feels like yesterday. By the time he died, he and Lee had been estranged for years, because of a position Lee had taken that Truman felt supported Gore Vidal in a nasty public squabble that blew up between Truman and Vidal. But Lee knew I was still fond of Truman and was kind enough, when he died, to give me a few days off so I could fly out to L.A. and attend the funeral.

How different Truman's funeral was from the elegant little service at St. Thomas More's. My chief memory is of talking with Truman's great friend Joanne Carson as we stood before a niche reserved for Truman's "cremains" in a spare, space-agey, outdoor mausoleum wall at the Westwood Memorial Park. Near us, I spotted bronze markers in memory of child star Heather O'Rourke and crooner Mel Tormé. Joanne, formerly the wife of legendary *Tonight Show* star Johnny Carson, had given Truman shelter in her Bel Air home for the final months of his life. She dedicated a bedroom to him as well as a room to write in—not that the poor soul was producing much by then, his body and mind ravaged by booze, cocaine, and the five or six different kinds of pills he was popping regularly. Those last days were wretched for him, Joanne said. He was often confused, depressed; he'd severed ties with his longtime companion, Jack. Joanne said she was grateful for the opportunity to take care of him, partly in memory of the glorious times they'd spent together when Truman was living out there and went around to the starriest parties.

" 'Alcohol used to be fun,' he told me one day," said Joanne. " 'Pills used to help. When did they make me dead inside?' "

Joanne surprised me by asking about "a screenplay Truman said he'd been working on with your secretarial help." Did I know anything about its whereabouts?

I took special note of the word "secretarial," and wondered if that were Truman's word or hers. I deflected her query.

"We worked on a few things together . . ." I said.

She pressed.

"A story about the Cuban Revolution?"

I shook my head. I didn't know Joanne very well and thought it best not to say any more on the subject. But she continued.

"He showed me pages of notes that he was trying to reconstruct, but they were incomprehensible. I found him weeping one day, because he couldn't work as he used to."

"Dear Truman," I said. It was a sad state, his inability to work, and I'd seen it coming well before he left New York for the last time.

"Yet the desire to sit at his desk and do something stayed strong in him, somehow," said Joanne, "until the very end."

There is a welcoming hush when you enter the lobby of a small luxury hotel like the Lowell. Stepping through the hotel's modestly scaled, newly refreshed main entrance was like passing through a force field into a temple where the acoustics and lighting are as beautifully composed as the vases of lilies and tulips on display. Sitting at either end of the reception desk were elegant table lamps in the form of bronze kylikes mounted on marble pedestals carved with wreaths, Second Empire French in the Néo-Grec style, I guessed—again, based on knowledge I'd picked up from Lee. The lampshades were of pleated cream silk. Yet one thing I also learned from her is that there was such a thing as too exquisite. Thankfully, my room, though lavishly comfortable, was uncomplicated.

"God is happiest when he's playing with us."

I've always wondered whether Truman made up that phrase for me, on the spot, or was quoting someone, or was even quoting himself. I've read all his works and don't remember coming across that phrase—but it sounds like an article of faith that Truman, nominally an Episcopalian, might have held sacred. I do remember that he went on to say, with a silken giggle, that God also wanted us to play with each other. *That* was his credo, he said, and one reason why he was so keen on the secret writing project that he eventually involved me in, a screenplay for Lee—something to offer her that might make up for the failure of the TV movie he'd written and gotten produced for her, a remake of the 1944 noir classic *Laura*; something "that would really showcase her star quality." We worked on it off and on when he was in New York, depending on his other commitments, starting simply when he asked me one day about my own life and I began to tell an elaborate tale that he seemed to enjoy and wrote up afterwards, he said, as notes for himself, as he had often done when interviewing people for his books. We worked on the screenplay for several years, but things slowed up and he became less and less productive in the '70s, when he got deeper into cocaine and club-going and that whole crazy celebrity thing. Though by the time he left New York and died, we had actually done a fair bit of work.

Our time together was the making of me as a writer and a teacher of writing. I always knew I was not the genius Truman was, and could never produce anything like the brilliant works for which he is best known, even if I was exposed to some of his secrets and techniques and insights and literary wisdom. Yet I did continue to work on the screenplay after his death, and I must say, I think it is *something*—but what?

The funeral had been wearying, so I decided to take a short nap and then go downstairs for afternoon tea, which I'd heard that the Lowell does awfully well. First, though, I texted Vincent, one of the men in my class, who'd driven me to the airport, to say that the funeral had been lovely and I was enjoying my stay in New York. In the car, Judy had asked, "Is there anyone . . . ?", and I gave almost the same answer to this eager question that I'd been giving her for the last sixty years, "No," though I did mention Vincent.

"Oh?" she said.

"A man in my class. He asked me for a drink, just the other day."

"Very nice. Are you going to do it?"

"Maybe."

"How long have you known him?"

"He was in my class last year, and now this year."

"Well, I think you should do it, if you're even considering it."

"But we're student and teacher."

Judy made a skeptical face.

"He's around your age?" she said.

"He's sixty-nine."

"Oh, good for you . . ."

"But I have to think about ethics."

"Mar—you're in *adult* education."

"Still."

"You can put yourself first now—really. It's alright."

It was an odd thought—putting myself first. This was something that Judy had always encouraged me to do, but it was not so easily done, for someone with my background. I'd never had a model for it, certainly not from loving parents. And I suppose that was why I was happy to slip into a profession that pretty much guaranteed that I would never come first, at least until I retired, at which point, I found, the concept mattered less than it does when people are young.

Before I lay down, I set out on the desk the paper copy of the screenplay that I'd brought with me. After tea, I'd go over it again, just to keep the details fresh in my mind.

THE LADY OF THE WHITE ROSE [WORKING TITLE]
Written by Truman Capote
with Marlene Béatrice Marguerite Marie-Thérèse Barón y Gavito

When the producer emailed to say that she liked it, she admitted she wasn't sure that a family drama set against the Cuban Revolution was what the world was clamoring for right now, but she did want to hear how the project came about. Of course, there may also have been courtesy involved, since one of my writing students at the West Palm Beach Adult Education Center happened to be the producer's mother and had prevailed upon her daughter to meet with her "amazing teacher."

And maybe the producer would have some ideas about the looming issues of the byline. I generated most of the story's plot points; Truman always admitted that he was grateful for that. A cultivated young Cuban woman at school in Switzerland in 1959 is informed that the Revolution has driven her family into exile without a penny—everyone in the family, that is, except the woman's prideful mother, whose great-great-grandfather was deeded their property by the King of Spain. Now, since I wrote most of the screenplay, would it be all right to trade on the fact that Truman had something to do with it? Is it part of Truman's literary legacy? Truman did make the role of the mother, always planned for Lee, a hundred times more deliciously venal than I could ever have done. Is this a chance for me to begin the "real" writing career that Truman always said he wanted for me, which I have always shied away from? Is a career like that even possible for me, at this late date?

I had never told Judy about the screenplay—somehow, it always felt too immodest to say I was "working with" Truman Capote—and I hadn't said anything about my meeting with the producer. I drifted off to sleep thinking that I would just have to see where the meeting went.

CHAPTER 2

A BEVY OF SWANS

Lee told me several times that she and Truman first met "casually" at his place in Brooklyn Heights in the late 1950s, when he was living in the basement of the Willow Street mansion of his friend, scenic designer Oliver Smith. Actually, Truman preferred the term "ground floor" to "basement," and he was also likely to tell unwitting visitors that the whole house was his, if Smith were not in residence. Lots of prominent New Yorkers would cross the river to visit Truman there, have lunch, and then walk a block to the Brooklyn Heights Promenade to marvel at the view of lower Manhattan's skyline; and one of those prominent New Yorkers was Jackie Kennedy, who sometimes brought her sister along. But at that point, Jackie and Truman were the friends, and Lee was the tagalong. When Lee and Truman met "seriously," though, and when I think their friendship began, was at a holiday party hosted by Diana Vreeland, late in 1960. This was before the legendary style editor took the helm of *Vogue* and was still at *Harper's Bazaar*. Lee had worked for Vreeland at *Bazaar* years before, as a "special assistant" whose social graces, like speaking French, were more valuable to an anointed Vreeland girl than sharpening pencils and routine secretarial tasks.

The party took place at Vreeland's stylish, much-photographed Park Avenue apartment, with its riotously scarlet-on-scarlet living room, whose exotic décor she sometimes described as "a garden in hell." It was decorator Billy Baldwin at his most breathless, Lee said—draped chintz crawling with a Persian flower pattern, gilt-framed mirrors, crystal sconces, heaps of plants and flowers in porcelain cachepots, masses of pillows, collections of decorative objects like Scottish horns and Battersea boxes, endless photographs, and a vast painted-leather screen, in addition to overstuffed chairs and sofas of the standard Park Avenue variety. The first time I ever heard that quote of Vreeland's, "the eye has to travel," it was from Lee, who laughed when she said that during that holiday party "the eye traveled from here to Zanzibar and back again eighteen times."

The apartment was not huge, apparently, so parties there always felt pleasantly packed and lively.

"You two must know each other by now," said Vreeland, bringing Lee over to the tufted love seat where Truman was perched, surrounded by a clutch of partygoers buzzing about their holiday travel plans. The editor was dressed in a white silk blouse and long black skirt, her neck heaped with ropes of oversize glass beads and uncut semi-precious stones, her hair pulled back as usual and lacquered into a helmet.

"We've met once or twice," said Lee, who was wearing a little cream-color Givenchy with a tucked and belted waist.

"Yes, with Jackie," said Truman. He stood and took Lee's extended hand. He was conspicuously short and boy-like, with a silky, kittenish manner, Lee told me—in contrast with most of the other men there, who were "people's husbands" and comported themselves as the captains of industry they were.

"But we've yet to have a *real* conversation," added Truman with a wink.

"Now's your chance, kiddos," said Vreeland, as she stepped away to see to another guest.

Truman, when he eventually related the same meeting to me, described Vreeland's outfit in exactly the same way, complete with oversize beads, and he mentioned the tufted love seat, all of which confirmed the accuracy of the observation skills of both him and Lee, as well as the reliability of their reporting—though Truman could sometimes exaggerate and embellish wickedly (and sometimes quoted Mark Twain without naming him: "Never let the truth get in the way of a good story"); and Lee was known to omit an unpleasant detail or two from a story, more out of good taste than anything else.

In fact, once Lee saw that she could trust me, she told me lots about her life, past and present; and later on, when I got to know Truman, so did he, about his. And I paid attention to what both of them told me; and to the degree it was appropriate, I asked questions and got them to tell me details about the people and places involved, which they seemed to love to do, Truman in his literary way and Lee in more of a social insider way. Then, at some point after Truman and I started working together, he shared some of the secrets of his famously photographic memorization process, which he sometimes discussed on TV talk shows. When doing research for *In Cold Blood*, he told interviewers, he'd made it a point to talk to people without a tape recorder, to keep the conversation focused; then he'd go home and write up the notes, as close to verbatim as possible. He claimed great accuracy for the process. Truman's techniques are one reason why I can remember and describe details from his and Lee's lives so well—and why, if I may say so, I can make up things that sound real, if I have to. Which is something I try to teach my students.

And to a degree, I think this obsession for observing and describing things was something that drew Truman and me closer together. We both fancied ourselves as observers of society, fate having put us both inside the social center of things and slightly outside of it, too.

At the time of Vreeland's party, Lee and Truman were both on a roll. *Breakfast at Tiffany's* was still a best seller and had recently been sold to Hollywood. Everyone was talking about the film's star, Audrey Hepburn, and the *wunderkind* who'd written the novella that the film was based on. The year before, Lee had married Prince Stanislaus Radziwill, a Polish aristocrat living in London, and been featured in *Vogue* as one of the international set's new, young tastemakers. Now, in December, 1960, she was also the sister of America's next first lady. I, myself, was working then as a companion to my friend Judy's grandmother, Mrs. Madeleine Parrish Hawkins, a frail, elderly *grande dame* who'd retired from public life. Mrs. Hawkins was a kind, undemanding soul who loved reminiscing about high society life in the teens, '20s, and '30s, all of which I found completely fascinating. Eagerly, I would also read all about the contemporary New York goings-on in the "Cholly Knickerbocker" column of the *Journal-American* and the rival "Suzy" column of the *Mirror*; and later, of course, in Suzy's successor column to "Cholly" at the *Journal-American*, and then her own column, "Suzy Knickerbocker," at the *Daily News*, whose items were even cheekier and better informed than Cholly's. The authors of both columns moved among the folks they were writing about—unlike Lila North, whose "Don't Repeat This" column, at *Newsday*, was far less compelling, less well-connected, more on-the-outside-looking-in. Yet Lila did have her readers, and Truman used to say that "one looks at Lila *just in case*."

Vreeland's party, though, would have been entirely too *privée* to appear in print, even if Igor Cassini, who wrote as "Cholly," or Aileen Mehle, who wrote as "Suzy," had attended. It must have been such a glamorous soirée! According to Lee, a very nice twelve-page spread in *Bazaar* could have been based on the exquisite clothing worn by Vreeland's women guests that night—who included, by the way, two of Truman's famous "swans," Babe Paley and Slim Hayward. Babe was there in black Balenciaga, with her husband Bill Paley, the head of CBS. She was probably Truman's favorite swan—at least, until he and Lee became so very close, a couple of years later. Slim was there, too, in gray Adolfo, with British banker Kenneth Alexander Keith, Baron Keith of Castleacre, who would soon make her Slim Keith. Slim was a spirited California girl who'd once been chums with Gary Cooper and Clark Gable; the year before, she'd been gratified to receive support from so many of her friends when her then husband, producer Leland Hayward, ran off with Pamela Churchill, later known as Pamela Harriman.

The swans, as Truman nicknamed them, were the good-looking women of means whose iconic style simultaneously reflected and inspired the work of the best designers of the moment—like Givenchy in fashion, Kenneth in hair. They were an exclusive band of socialites, also including Gloria Guinness, C.Z. Guest, and Marella Agnelli, who were constantly jetting and/or sailing among the world's choicest destinations, lunching in the chicest restaurants, being written about and photographed constantly. And that moment, the dawn of the '60s, was important for women like that—reasonably intelligent and well-educated, more determined than their mothers were to move beyond the old-fashioned strictures governing how ladies were to function as pillars of society. They represented something fresh and new—not yet exactly feminist, but no longer so madamish—and their style reflected this, particularly in clothing and hair.

In fact, their style represented a new kind of classicism, and they all seemed to know that it was something different from the previous "next new things" that their mothers and grandmothers might have adopted. There was suddenly an unmistakable harmony between adornment and the human body, a consonance among line and shape and construction and proportion. That a hemline should be at the knee, rather than somewhere randomly between there and the floor (let alone somewhere above!) suddenly made more than sense: it felt like *the answer.* Did Givenchy's precise silhouettes and impeccably thought-out seaming reflect some new notion about the body? Who knows? Why did the volume and clarity of Kenneth's hair design—he called his style "uncontrived fullness"—suddenly feel like the fulfillment of a promise made decades before, at the dawn of modernism? Who knows? But Lee and other privileged women understood what this style meant and had the means to embody it. Givenchy did Audrey, and Kenneth did Marilyn and Jackie, and then everyone else understood and wanted to inhabit that world, too.

I hope I don't sound too loony when I talk about the style sense of Lee and her crowd. I was only twenty-one and quite impressionable when Lee hired me, the following year. I loved the way she and her friends looked. My own clothes at the time were from places like Saks Fifth Avenue and Lord & Taylor—basic things of good quality, like John Meyer of Norwich, but plain. I always had one good black dress in my closet—not too sexy—in case I needed to help Lee in a social role at some event, on which occasion she might lend me a lovely piece of jewelry to dress it up. But the revolution of the 1960s wasn't about me—and, believe me, I don't use the word "revolution" lightly. It was about the swans who helped the world really *see*—visually comprehend—the new era we were entering, which to my mind was as important as any social work they could have done or any other social upheaval they could have lived through.

"And you, princess—where are you headed for the holidays?" asked Truman, after Vreeland had introduced them.

"Oh, we're off to Palm Beach, and then the inauguration," said Lee. "Jamaica after that."

"Very sensible."

"Why sensible?"

"I meant the beaches—the sun and the water . . ."

If Truman noticed that Lee was looking a little tired that night, he never mentioned it to me. The truth is that it was only a few months after Tina was born, and Lee still felt physically worn out, yet was going mad with boredom and thought Vreeland's party was just the thing to cheer her up. Truman, I imagine, looked dapper that night, in a gray suit by a favorite Italian tailor of his at the time, Rubinacci, which both he and Lee made it a point to recount was accessorized with a lace-trimmed antique handkerchief in the breast pocket.

"We're taking the kids," said Lee. "And of course, the nanny."

At that point, Tina was just three months old and Anthony a year old.

"Oh that's right," said Truman, "you have little ones now! So quickly!"

"What I need now is some swimming and some good books."

"I've just done the Aegean again with the Guinnesses and the Agnellis. Fun, but . . . well, you know. Life on a yacht. Enough is enough. Now Jack and I are headed to Spain. We have a place there where I can work."

"Is Jack here tonight?" asked Lee.

Truman shook his head.

"He hates parties," he said. "Anyway, he's in Verbier. We'll meet in Palamós. And the prince?"

Lee cocked her head toward a banquette upholstered in bold stripes, on the other side of the room, where Radziwill was entertaining a small clump of guests.

"Telling funny stories," she said dryly.

"Sounds like you've heard them."

"By now, all of them."

"So what have you been doing in New York?"

"Looking for a house, actually—since we're going to be here more often now and in Washington. The place we've been renting on Fifth isn't nearly big enough."

Both took a crab puff and napkin from a passing butler's tray.

"A nanny!" said Truman. "How cozy."

"We brought her from London. We love her."

"And now Jackie again!"

A month earlier, Lee had been in Georgetown, where her sister had given birth to John Jr.—just two weeks after JFK was elected president.

"But the housekeeper here is *terrible*," said Lee. "I'm going crazy."

"Can't you bring one of your London people over?"

"We need them there. Besides, they'd never come."

"Where is the man with the drinks?" said Truman, scoping the room. "What do you say we go raid the bar?"

A bar had been set up at the back end of the spacious central hall, near the door to the kitchen. In the middle of the room was a table set sumptuously with platters of canapés and other hors d'oeuvres, compote dishes of nuts and fruit, and cake stands piled with teacakes and petits fours. Among those sampling the fare were a popular television entertainer, a reigning opera diva, and a young pop artist who, by the end of the decade, would be more famous than any of the other guests.

"New York is so much more exciting than London right now, don't you think?" said Truman, a fresh drink in hand.

"Oh, I don't know," said Lee. "We have the ballet, we have fashion . . ."

"And Paris feels stale, too—I mean in comparison, socially."

"What? With all those great writers?"

"New York feels more fluid. Different kinds of people can mix with others—rub elbows 'til they're worn slap out."

"Surely we don't want too much fluidity," said Lee.

"Of course we do," said Truman, "and I know that you understand this. New York is the future. London and Paris are both history."

Each finding the other more interesting to talk to than they remembered from those Brooklyn Heights visits, Lee and Truman gently resisted attempts by others to join them, speaking *à deux* for a few minutes longer than might have been usual for each of them at an A-list party like this. They spoke of the time Lee pulled hats for a fashion shoot Vreeland was directing (Vreeland: "They're absolutely dreamy, kiddo. Brava!") and the time Truman bought the very handkerchief he was then sporting (Truman: "Yes, madam, it's for me, and I do know this is Women's Accessories!"). When Lee took a cigarette out of the little bag she was carrying, Truman produced and flicked on a Cartier lighter. Like a 1940s movie star, Lee leaned elegantly into the light for an initial drag, then raised her eyes to Truman's before exhaling.

"Pure Dietrich!" said Truman as he pocketed the lighter. "And the lighting on your face is perfect, too."

Lee flashed half a smile.

"I don't think I've ever told you how much I adored *Breakfast at Tiffany's*," she said.

"You know, they've just started shooting it—the movie. Last month I was right there when they did the scene of Holly walking up Fifth Avenue. It was dawn, and we ended up right in front of Tiffany's."

"Marvelous."

"She's supposed to pull a Danish out of the bag and take a bite, and you know that sometimes you have to shoot a scene again and again, to get it right. Well, little Miss Audrey really did not like to keep eating bite after bite of Danish—she was afraid of getting fat!—and Lord knows they had a hundred of them there for her, just in case."

"I've heard you're working on something new."

"Two things, really. A true-crime book, and then something I've been working on for quite a while now, about society. As in Proust."

"Oh?"

"Actually, that one started out as a crime story, too," Truman said in a whisper, as if he were revealing an intimate secret. "It's about the aftermath of a society murder, but the book is becoming quite something else."

"Can you say what murder?"

"Mmm, better not, right now."

"Do you have a title for it—the Proust one? But wait—how could you? I suppose it's too early."

"Oh, but I do have a title," said Truman. "*Answered Prayers*."

He said that the quote was attributed to Saint Theresa of Avila: "More tears are shed over answered prayers than unanswered ones."

"I mean, look around this room," he said. "They all expect to get exactly what they want. And we all know what happens when they get it."

Truman punctuated this thought with a weary smirk.

"Then what about the other book—the other crime?" said Lee.

Truman explained that that was based on the sensational murder, the year before, of a Midwestern family of four, the Clutters, by two men. He was in the midst of researching and writing "an entirely different kind of book" about it, based on an idea that had recently started obsessing him: a "hyper-realistic nonfiction novel."

"Except for attending a party here and there, I'm actually in a monastic phase," said Truman, "since I am visiting Kansas quite a lot for research and interviews, and then retreating to Verbier to write."

Later that evening, Lee and Stas were in the lobby of Vreeland's building, where the coat check had been set up, when Truman stepped off the elevator, along with several other departing guests. Retrieving his coat, Truman asked the Radziwills if they were "going up to Eighty-first," as if they all had been invited to the same party.

"Oh, whose?" said Lee.

"I'm afraid it's home for us, old boy," said Stas, before Truman could answer.

Another couple were also getting their coats—a white-haired senior editor at a weekly newsmagazine and her escort, a conspicuously handsome, much younger man.

"Anyway, Stas," said Truman, "I'm sorry if I monopolized Lee."

"Not at all," said Stas.

"Truman, who is that?" asked Lee quietly, as the other couple were moving away.

Truman named the woman and her magazine, but said he didn't know who the young man was.

"Was that her son?" said Lee.

"Somehow, I doubt it," said Truman, trying to make his dubiousness as beguiling as possible.

"She couldn't bring a young thing to a party like this, could she?"

"Sure she could," purred Truman, a little louder than Lee would have liked. "And you could and I could too, that's who could."

"Don't Repeat This" —by Lila North
Friday, December 9, 1960

. . . One week in the life of the brilliant young Mr. Capote, it seems, includes not only lunches with Babe Paley and Gloria Guinness, but parties attended by Norman Mailer, Andy Warhol, Susan Sontag, Tennessee Williams, and Gore Vidal. He claims that the satisfaction he gets from his socialite friends is "distinctly non-literary"—but is it? Isn't "real life" where Capote's best stories have always come from? I have to wonder whether that writer crowd he hangs around with are truly friends, anyway, or something else. Friend and/or rival Vidal recently observed that "Truman has tried, with some success, to get into a world that I have tried, with some success, to get out of."

"Funny little guy," said Stas, as he and Lee walked over to Fifth, where their apartment was, fifteen blocks uptown. "I saw him mentioned the other day in some column."

"He's always in the columns," said Lee.

"Why?"

"He's a famous author, for one thing."

"Why?"

"Ha. You should read more, darling."

They were walking briskly. Stas knew that Lee hadn't been feeling one hundred percent before the party.

"How are you doing?" he said.

"I'm fine," said Lee. Her arm was linked tightly with his.

"What did you two talk about?" said Stas. "Books?"

"Yes, but also the Guinnesses and their antiques—he'd just been to an auction with Gloria—and their houses and their decorators, and other people's decorators and other great houses . . ."

"Talk about Renzo?"

"Of course. And I promised to show him the library the next time he's in London."

"He's friends with the Paleys, isn't he?"

"He and Babe have been friends for a thousand years. Bill seems to like him, too."

It was a cold, clear night, and Stas had not brought a coat, since he'd been in and out of chauffeur-driven cars all day. His shoulders were hunched, and he was holding Lee as close as possible.

"You poor thing," said Lee. "Should we get a taxi?"

"I'll be okay," said Stas. "Not unless you want. It's just a few blocks."

As they passed the entrance to an apartment building, a taxi stopped and discharged its passengers. With a gesture, Lee asked Stas if he wanted it, and with a facial expression, he answered no, and they kept walking at a brisk pace.

"Do you know how they met?" said Lee.

"Who?" said Stas.

"Truman and the Paleys. He told me—I'd never heard it before. It was an accident, I guess in Hollywood. Babe and Bill had offered David Selznick a ride to New York in the private CBS plane, and Selznick asked whether he could bring along his friend Truman, and Bill said yes, thinking Selznick meant the ex-president. Can you imagine—when this squeaky little creature shows up at the airport . . . ?"

"Funny."

They were walking quickly. Traffic seemed heavier than usual, probably because of all the parties taking place that night. Up and down the sidewalk were couples and groups whose attire or high spirits indicated that they were coming from or going to someplace festive.

"Remember, we're looking at that place tomorrow on Park," said Lee.

"Yes, yes, yes," said Stas. "But I thought you preferred Fifth?"

"Well, I do, but the realtor thought we should just have a look. It's a corner apartment, and there's more room for staff."

"What's the difference, then?"

"Between Park and Fifth?"

"The prices are all in the same neighborhood."

"It's a New York thing," said Lee. "I grew up on Park. Daddy built the building. There are some lovely places there, of course, but it can feel a little . . . *done*."

"And Fifth Avenue is *un*done?"

Lee laughed. Among the qualities that had attracted her to Stas was his sense of humor and general affability.

Pushing against them from Central Park, across the street, was a steady blast of frigid air.

"Two blocks!" said Stas.

"I love New York in winter," said Lee. "Except when my husband is freezing to death."

At home, they were greeted by Carla, the temporary live-in cook-housekeeper.

"Everything is fine," said Carla. "Mrs. Brown is with the children in their room."

"Thank you."

"Can I get anything for you or Mr. Radziwill?"

"Nothing, thank you, Carla. We're fine."

They were in the hall, and after a quick glance toward the library to confirm that Stas had gone in there, Carla stepped a bit closer to Lee.

"You had a call from London," she whispered. "Mr. Onassis."

Lee lowered her head.

"Anything important?" she whispered.

"Just to say hello. Please call back at your convenience. Tomorrow is fine."

"Thanks very much, Carla."

"I'll say good night, ma'am."

"Oh, Carla, before I forget." Lee's voice had returned to normal volume. "It turns out we will need you until April first, after all."

"Yes, ma'am."

"After the inauguration and Jamaica, we're back in London, then Mexico. I won't be able to start interviewing people until we're back in New York, probably in March."

"Very good."

Lee hadn't given Ari her New York number, but of course, he'd managed to get his hands on it. She'd been married for barely two years and had just had a second child, yet still Onassis was coming on to her with characteristically Olympian force. She'd been introduced to the shipping magnate before she was married, at a London dinner party; he was part of the moneyed crowd that she and Stas moved in, and had been instantly attracted to her; Ari and Stas could often be found anchoring the busy social scene at Claridge's Hotel, where Ari had a regular table. When Lee explained she was about to be married, he'd told her that "Radziwill is a good man, but he doesn't deserve a goddess like you." It was a corny line, but she marveled that Ari somehow made it work. In fact, she liked that in addition to all the money, Ari seemed to really know what power was. He was the only man she ever knew, she once told me, who had his own private army and navy. She remained extremely attracted to him, even after her marriage to Stas. I learned all this from her much later, since she vowed, after Ari's phone message that night, to keep her attraction to him secret—which included me, until Ari committed the sin of marrying Jackie, in 1968.

After looking in on Anthony and Tina, who were snug in their beds, Lee joined Stas in the library for a nightcap. He was in an armchair, looking over *The New York Times*. Next to him, on a little table, was a bottle of Balvenie and two cut-crystal glasses, one of which contained half an inch of whiskey.

"Did you see that O'Connell is going to take part in next year's Vatican Council?" said Stas, from behind the paper.

"No," said Lee. "Really?"

"It says he's been named a *peritus*—an expert—meant to be a sort of consultant to the Council."

"Golly."

Stas lowered the paper.

"Apparently, there are going to be hundreds of them—lay people, too. *Periti*, they're called."

"Well, O'Connell certainly knows his canon law."

Lee and Stas, both observant Roman Catholics, were in the process of petitioning the Vatican for an annulment of Lee's first marriage, to socialite and publishing executive Michael Canfield. When she and Stas were married, in 1959, both were legally divorced, but only Stas had obtained an annulment of his previous marriage by the Church, so the couple hadn't been married in a church wedding, something that Lee's mother, Janet Bouvier Auchincloss, wanted very much. I once overheard Mrs. Auchincloss tell Lee the situation was "distasteful as well as spiritually dangerous."

"He's a reformer," said Stas, "and that's apparently what this whole Council is going to be about."

"So this is good for us," said Lee.

"We'll see. I hope so. He says we're still at least a year off, in any case. And who knows what happens to the Sacred Rota when that convention is in town."

Lee, on the sofa opposite Stas, took a sip of the scotch she had poured for herself.

"So funny to think of us planning a church wedding at this point," she said.

"How are you holding up?" said Stas.

"I think tonight might have been a little too much."

"We should have grabbed a taxi."

Then they returned to the subject of Truman.

"He certainly has the presence of a big guy," he said.

"Yes, he does," said Lee. "With a pronounced desire to entertain. I think that's part of what makes a writer great—this desire to really get under people's skin."

"And am I right that he seemed to be flirting with that older woman's date, the one in the lobby? I swear he meant to be overheard."

"Did and didn't. I think that was more for us. He's the bad boy. We're supposed to observe the bad behavior and show that we don't mind."

"Is that it?"

"He's an original. I respect him for being who he is."

"He's plucky—I'll give him that."

"And Lord knows, we've certainly seen far worse from fags. Besides, he has a partner—a novelist who lives in Switzerland."

"When has having a partner ever stopped anyone from wanting another one?"

Lee shifted gracefully in her seat.

"It's a very settled relationship," she said. "Apparently, they have a discreet arrangement."

Stas laughed.

"Apparently not discreet enough," he said.

CHAPTER 3

PARTIES BIG AND SMALL

"Don't Repeat This" —by Lila North
Friday, January 20, 1961

> . . . Well, here it is: Inauguration Day! Our 35th president, John Fitzgerald Kennedy, will swear an oath of office on the steps of the Capitol, where Robert Frost is also slated to read a poem for the occasion! Then later it's balls, balls, balls—an unprecedented five of them, in fact! And what will Jackie be wearing? Here's what I hear: for day, at the Capitol, she will be in an Oleg Cassini coat in duck-egg blue and a "pillbox" hat made especially to match by a clever milliner who goes by the single moniker Halston. Then, for evening, she will be bedecked in an off-white sleeveless gown of silk chiffon, encrusted with brilliants and embroidered with silver thread, designed by Ethel Frankau of Bergdorf's Custom Salon, based on sketches made by Jackie herself! • In Washington for the festivities are luminaries from around the world, including four other First Ladies: Edith Wilson, Eleanor Roosevelt, Bess Truman, and of course Mamie Eisenhower—but not the new first lady's sister, Princess Lee Radziwill, and husband Stas. (It's pronounced "Stash," by the way!) What gives? . . .

Lila North had invited me to lunch once when I was working in my previous position. She knew very well that Mrs. Hawkins had become too old to go out much, but that she did contribute significantly to several arts organizations and served nominally on their boards. Though I was fairly green at that point and didn't quite know how it all worked, New York social life and surrounding publicity, I knew well enough that I was expected to be discreet about Mrs. Hawkins, her family, and myself. Still, I accepted the invitation, having received Mrs. Hawkins's approval on the condition that I mentioned the "terribly important" fundraising campaign she was helping to lead for the New York Philharmonic. And over a dowdy lunch at Schrafft's (Lila: ". . . the one on Fifth and 46th; it's right near my office . . ."), I dutifully named several of the campaign's donors and the amounts that they had given, yet Lila took no notes on any of it—all of which was public knowledge, anyway. She seemed instead to be more interested in me. I know now that she must have been probing to see if I were a rich somebody—a bright young thing who was playing at work for a year or two—or just a lucky nobody. If I had been the former, then any future indiscretions of my own or of my presumably rich young friends would have been useful to Lila, as she and I would already have opened a convenient line of communication. Naturally, I told her nothing about myself, except that I had no access to the kind of information that scoops were made of, for readers who clamored to know every little thing about Liz Taylor, Andy Warhol, and The Beatles.

I must say that I didn't find Lila too impressive that day.

"What do you think of this Peace Corps that President Kennedy is starting?" she asked.

"It sounds terrific," I said. "I don't know much about it."

"You volunteer after college, to go help people in the Third World."

"It sounds like a good idea."

"Would you go?"

"I have a job."

"I mean if you didn't."

"Don't you need to be a college graduate?"

"You didn't go to college?"

"Not yet, anyway."

"What about the Smith girl—the granddaughter."

"Judy? What about her?"

"Are you two friends?"

"We're . . . friendly."

"Aren't you the same age?"

"She's a year younger."

"Is she in college?

"Yes—Vassar. But as I say, I am not comfortable speaking about family details."

"It's your employer's family."

"Same thing."

Luckily, once Lila saw how little she would get from me, she started talking about herself. She referred to something that "Walter" had said, by whom she meant Walter Winchell, but only an item appearing in Winchell's column, which anyone could have read; though she made it sound like they were friends, and I learned later that they were not. Her nails were lacquered in what I knew even then was an old-fashioned shade of red, and they were chipped. Her hairdo was frumpy, and she was wearing too much perfume. When I said I was hesitant to ask for another piece of toast for my creamed shrimp and vegetables, she said "Nonsense!" and immediately turned to summon a waiter imperiously, telling me that she was well-known there, as if being known in a place like Schrafft's was some kind of honor.

Schrafft's, anyway, was becoming like a museum then—memorializing the way that genteel New York women used to lunch. Having long gotten together in places deemed safe and proper, in clubs and tearooms, or, if pocketbooks allowed, in bastions like the Colony, opened in 1919, stylish women now, in the early '60s, were becoming ladies who lunch, and they preferred the chic, new spots like La Côte Basque, opened in 1959, and La Caravelle, 1960. Lunch for those ladies was a growing scene that Truman told me later was "anything *but* safe." Even then, as naïve as I was, I knew that Lila should have taken a potential young source to one of those more up-to-date places.

I didn't speak to Lila again until I was working for Lee, when I was asked to parry a call from her during my first week there. Lee told me that she saw "no reason to talk to a creature like that."

It was the year before I started working for Lee when she and Truman really started getting to know each other, which I heard about later from Lee, after she'd begun talking to me about Truman and other friends. Her feelings about Truman were certainly many and complex, and her accounts of their adventures together were startlingly specific; I don't think she talked about him this way with too many other people—certainly not Stas, who wouldn't have been too interested in details about Truman's luxuriant wit. I doubt she spoke of him deeply with any of the boyfriends she started seeing, either, except maybe that Greek-god-of-an-artist, Peter Beard, who was as much a soulful devil as Truman was, in his own way. When Lee described meeting Truman at Vreeland's party, she repeated a lewd crack he made about the disappointing size of the three Kennedy brothers' "johnsons" combined—something she would never have shared with Stas, who wouldn't have found such a crack funny. She also told me she was feeling very weak that night—that entire season, in fact—having been depleted by the birth of Tina, just a few months before. Yet she went to Vreeland's party against her better judgment, because she was "going out of my mind with rest and recuperation."

The Radziwills were still spending most of their time in London, at the house they owned in Buckingham Place—not as fashionable as Mayfair or Belgravia, but near Stas's office and around the corner from the Queen—so Lee and Truman saw each other that year whenever they could arrange to be in the same place at the same time. First was in New York that spring, for lunch at the Fifth Avenue place that Lee and Stas were still using for their stays in the city. Still looking for something to buy, they had extended their lease there, so they could do a little "real" decorating, with the owner's eager assent; and since there were workmen that day in the library, where Lee would usually serve an intimate lunch for two or three, she'd asked Carla to set two places at one end of the grand Queen Anne table in the dining room.

"We're doing this room next," said Lee. "It's too formal. It needs to say more."

The walls were off-white and unadorned except for a pair of stern-looking ancestor portraits that, like most of the furniture, belonged to the owner. Window treatments were spartan.

"I agree," said Truman. "Right now, it's saying something *très* conventional."

"It's crying out for some color, some pattern, don't you think? Some details that tell a story."

"You know me—I love a story."

"Wait 'til you see the Indian paintings I'm putting in the library—a set of little portraits on glass. I've had them sent over from Buckingham Place."

"Speaking of stories, princess dear, I am very disappointed you don't have any juicy inauguration stories to share."

"I was so disappointed. Palm Beach was lovely, but there were so many Kennedys and so much Christmas. I relapsed. Stas insisted we head straight back to London. I wanted to be there so, for Jackie."

"You two are very close, aren't you?"

"Terribly close."

"But also rivals."

"Not really. Well, competitors—sometimes."

"Mmm."

"Jackie was always praised as the artistic one, the champion rider. Mother was awfully proud of her accomplishments, and always telling me I was too fat."

"No."

"So I developed my own interests. I learned to be independent. Once I was left alone at Merrywood, this enormous house of Stepfather's, in Virginia. They were off deep-sea fishing in Chile, and I couldn't stand it any longer, so I took my allowance, called a taxi, and went to a nearby orphanage. I told them my name and that I'd come to adopt an orphan, and said that I lived in a place where the girl would be terribly happy, with horses and dogs . . ."

"Oh, my!"

Lee loved to tell this story. It always amused her.

"The Mother Superior was absolutely stunned. 'I'm so sorry, my dear,' she said, 'but you're just too young to adopt a child.' My mother was furious when she heard about it. 'How could you torture me this way?' "

Truman already knew the basic story of Lee's life: a childhood of East Coast privilege, complete with the best schools and activities like sailing and horseback riding, as the daughter of a socially prominent mother, Janet Norton Lee, and a Wall Street broker father, John Vernou "Black Jack" Bouvier III, who claimed a lineage stretching back to a French soldier who'd fought on the American side in the Revolutionary War; and then as the stepdaughter of Janet's second husband, Hugh D. Auchincloss Jr., a Standard Oil heir. Her first marriage, between 1953 and 1958, to Michael Canfield, who was said to be the illegitimate son of the Duke of Windsor's brother, Prince George, Duke of Kent; and then, in 1959, her marriage to Stas, who inherited a princely title dating back to the Holy Roman Empire and had made a fortune in real estate.

"So we had to postpone Montego Bay until the fall," said Lee. "Maybe you'll be able to join us there."

"I'll see if I can," said Truman coyly, as if one of his very favorite things wasn't being invited to fun places by rich people.

As a hostess, Lee was flawless—witty, smooth, impeccably dressed, with everything under control. Dessert that day was poached peaches with raspberries, served on two of Lee's gaily colored antique Raynaud plates. She kept notes on all her entertaining, you see; I found these notebooks fascinating, and in fact, was responsible for studying them closely, once I was hired, to learn her preferences in menus and meal preparations, table settings, and service. Recounting the same lunch, Truman later told me that he knew instantly that Lee was going to be the most accomplished swan of all—not only stylish and fun to be with, but curious, well-traveled, and intelligent. She was even "learned," he said—"a real scholar of the things she cared about, including books and art." He couldn't imagine Babe Paley knowing the difference between Bernini and Borromini, as Lee did, Baroque architecture being among the topics that she and Truman touched on that day.

They also discussed Jackie, when the subject of the new presidency came up again.

"She's apparently adapting very well," said Lee.

"I'll bet she is," said Truman.

"But I am always grateful when people don't bring her up—people who aren't already friends, that is."

"No?"

"I live in dread of it."

"Mailer called her 'a prisoner of celebrity.' "

"Don't get me wrong. I love her. We adore each other, but . . ."

Truman giggled.

"You're hostage to a prisoner," he said.

"Don't put it like that."

"Maybe I can help. These things must be managed artistically."

"What things?"

"Your image. People should be focused on you for your own sake."

As Carla began to clear, they rose and headed for the living room, where coffee was served. A quick look into the library allowed Truman the opportunity to coo over a swatch of the blue-and-green–striped wallpaper that would be going up on the walls.

"One of the gossip columns even took note of the fact that I wasn't there at the Capitol," said Lee, after they had installed themselves in a light-filled corner of the living room.

"It was Lila North," said Truman with a sneer.

"None of the others mentioned it. They know how much I've been supporting my sister, how glad I am for her. I mean, this column made it look like I had skipped town in some kind of snit."

"I saw it. No one cares about that column. Don't let it worry you."

"And she called here!" said Lee.

"Who—Lila?!"

"I can't imagine how she got the number. Carla was ready to put her through!"

Truman grimaced.

"That's a no-no," he said.

"You know—I usually do my own secretarial," said Lee. "But now—well, that has to change." Lee lowered her voice. "I really need to replace Carla."

Truman mentioned that photography on the *Breakfast at Tiffany's* movie had wrapped. The movie was scheduled for an October release.

"You must be excited," said Lee.

"It's a very different beast," said Truman. "The writer and I are dear friends, and I did work with him, and I don't mind inventing a whole new character—that's fine. But it's not the same Holly."

"How so?"

"She's not a prostitute, for one thing," said Truman. "She's . . . an American geisha, a country girl turned café society girl. She has no job, but lives by socializing with wealthy men, who take her to clubs and restaurants, and give her money and expensive presents. She hopes to marry one of them. Like you did."

"Thank you, but I am no country girl."

"Holly's just like me. A po' Southerner with a few wits here and there," said Truman. "And frankly, I think Miss Hepburn is all wrong for the part. Holly is a blonde—'strands of albino-blond and yellow.' Marilyn would have been so much better."

"Didn't they consider her?"

"Oh yes, they did. They tried her and everything. I know Marilyn very well, of course. John Huston introduced us."

Lee offered a cigarette from a miniature silver urn on the coffee table and took one herself. Again, Truman was ready with his gold Cartier lighter. As usual, he was dressed impeccably that day—the poor Southerner in a cashmere sweater from Hermès, a paisley scarf from Charvet, and a gold Tank watch, also from Cartier.

"Were your parents storytellers?" asked Lee.

"Well, they told tales—that's for sure," said Truman. "And in the South, you know, everybody's a character."

Truman was born in New Orleans, as Truman Streckfus Persons. His parents, Archulus Persons and Lillie Mae Faulk, divorced when he was four, and he was raised in Alabama by an elderly cousin of his mother's, Nannie Rumbley Faulk, whom he called Sook.

"My mother hated my father the moment she married him," Truman told me. His mother's second husband, a Cuban businessman named Joe Capote, adopted Truman as his son and renamed him Truman García Capote; then he took Truman's mother to live in New York, leaving Truman with Sook. The boy later joined the Capotes in the big city, where they all lived for a while in an apartment on Park Avenue, right in the middle of things—until Joe Capote was convicted of embezzlement and they were forced to decamp for less expensive digs, more on the edge of things, in Greenwich, Connecticut.

"But we returned to Manhattan in 'forty-two," he said. "Instead of studying, I spent my nights at the clubs, making friends with people like Oona O'Neill, Eugene O'Neill's daughter, and her friend Gloria Vanderbilt. I was still a teenager when I got my first job working as a copyboy for *The New Yorker*. And the rest, as they say, is history."

Truman's once-doting mother evolved into someone quite different during her second marriage. Lillie Mae was now calling herself Nina, and could as easily be cruel to Truman as kind. She often picked on him for his precocious and effeminate ways—that is, for not being like other boys. With his mother, he said, he felt endangered, despite her stylish manner, which he adored; whereas with Sook, he felt loved, even when he was lonely, which was apparently often.

"Mothers!" he once exclaimed, when we were working on the screenplay, which involved a mother who was both monstrous and magnificent. "What does that term even mean anymore? Protecting someone? Instilling them with good values? Making them feel loved and safe? Nurturing them?"

After freshening Truman's cup, Lee asked Truman about his literary friends. Was it really a "circle," as it was sometimes described in the press, with him and Vidal and Williams and the like? Or did they just run into each other at dinner parties?

"Well, I guess it started in 1945," said Truman, "when I would hang out with George Davis and go to parties at his place on the Upper East Side. Did you know George? He died a couple of years ago."

"The editor—yes, I've heard of him." said Lee. "I believe he was at *Bazaar*."

"That's absolutely right. Well, I'd meet people like Auden and Cocteau and Dorothy Parker and Gypsy Rose Lee; and I was basically just a kid. So I met some of that crowd up there."

"And is that where this feud between you and Gore Vidal began?"

"That's an absolutely silly story," purred Truman. "There's no feud at all. If you ask me, it's about literary jealousy—*his*."

"I heard Gore at some party referring to this feud he had with Mr. Capote."

"Lee, it's all in his head. Ten years ago—more, 1947!—*Life* magazine did a big spread on young American writers. Gore was included, of course, but in a tiny photo that was quite awkward, I think, whereas they gave me three-quarters of the first page, a very glamorous shot. I had no say in that—it was the editors. But Mr. Vidal was disgruntled, and rightly so. Anyway, we're completely cordial when we see each other—except when he's accusing me of things like haughtiness and name-dropping."

"Well, Truman . . ." began Lee, but he interrupted.

"He claims that the 'instant lie' is my art form," said Truman. "Isn't that wonderful? I wish it *were* mine. 'Small but paradoxically authentic lies.' That sounds awfully good to me."

Lee laughed and shook her head, then took another drag on her cigarette.

"There's no one on earth like you," she said.

"You're cooking up a guest list in your head, aren't you, Miss

Princess?" said Truman. "Arranging your place cards, putting a lively mix together. I know how you gals operate."

It was Lee's curiosity as much as good form that prompted her to ask how the new book was going—the one about murder in the Midwest.

"It's going, thanks," said Truman. "I'm calling it a nonfiction novel."

"You mean like Zola?"

"Very good! But no, not exactly. The facts of the story are exactly the same as the facts of the true case. But I want to apply the machinery of a novel, so to speak."

This was a subject that Truman and I would discuss again and again in our subsequent work together, and the idea of telling a "true" story about someone's life has always fascinated me.

Added Truman, "I want this kind of writing to be more detached from the author."

"Why?" asked Lee.

Truman considered this for a second.

"I need to escape my own limits as a human being," he finally said. "Does that make sense? The artist in me likes to feel that if my creation is really successful, it's beyond little ol' me. It exists. It's the truth. I can't will it to be any different."

"Interesting," said Lee. "And what will you call this one?"

"I'm not sure," said Truman. "But maybe *In Cold Blood*."

"*In Cold Blood*—that's great. And what about the Proust?"

"Oh, I'm still gathering information about that one. That's why I like lunches like this!"

"Ha! To gather information?"

"You know it, sister."

"Information about what?"

"People, of course."

Truman was spending lots of time then holed up with his longtime companion Jack Dunphy at the place they owned in Verbier, an Alpine village in the French-speaking part of Switzerland. Truman loved the clean air, bright sun, and "all the delicious silence" there—a perfect place to write. A novelist and playwright, Jack had been trained as a dancer, and had married and divorced a dancer; he had also served in the Army during World War II. I came to know Jack quite well during those horrible final years when Truman was in and out of hospitals and we were both trying to keep him alive. The two had met in New York in 1948, at a party, and within weeks, they were sailing for France on the *Queen Mary*, ready to embrace the expatriate life together. After Paris, Venice, and Rome, it was on to more exotic playgrounds, like Ischia and Forio and Tangier, where they hung out with other artsy adventure-seekers like Tennessee Williams, Cecil Beaton, and Jane and Paul Bowles.

I believe that by the time I got to know Truman, he and Jack were no longer intimate with each other, their relationship having evolved, as many marriages do, into a partnership based more on inertia and habit than romance. Jack was spending most of the year in Verbier, except for summers with Truman in Spain, jaunts with him to London—once to attend a luncheon that Cecil Beaton hosted for the Queen Mother!—and occasional visits to New York for the opera, when Jack would stay with Truman in Brooklyn Heights and later at the place they bought out near the Hamptons. Jack always said that he kept hoping Truman would come to like the music at the opera as much as he liked the socializing during intermissions. The truth is that the two men were temperamentally quite different. Truman was often effusively social, and Jack was decidedly not. I think they loved each other in different ways, too. I *know* that Truman had been *in love* with Jack, while Jack, for his part, *adored* Truman, which is not necessarily the same thing. Jack had actually bought a place in Verbier by then, and Truman would go and spend long stretches of time there, concentrating on *In Cold Blood*, between research jaunts to Kansas with his childhood friend, author Harper Lee, who was helping him with research. Truman was a very diligent worker in those days, balancing his exuberant and wide-flung social life with long periods of monk-like seclusion.

Throughout the rest of the spring and most of the summer, Princess Lee kept inviting Truman to parties in London, but he declined.

"Gregariousness is the enemy of art," he wrote in a little note to her.

The next time they got to see each other was in Jamaica, early in the fall, at an exclusive resort called Round Hill. It was a place that Truman knew well, since the Paleys often invited him to join them at their place there.

I've never been to Jamaica, but I do know something of the Caribbean—that deceptively beautiful million-square-mile maritime domain where the pleasures of paradise are periodically smashed by wrathful storms. For at least ten thousand years, we're told, this collection of seven hundred islands, reefs, and cays has seen the mixing of cultures and civilizations, a carnival of colonizers, brigands, entrepreneurs, aristocrats, and slaves, and the evolution of language, religion, music, and food. Round Hill was built in 1953 on a lush, hundred-acre peninsula overlooking Montego Bay. A former sugarcane plantation, the resort comprises a hotel and a complement of private villas with pools, white-fenced porches, and green-and-white–striped awnings, all settled into lush, well-cared-for grounds boasting royal palms and Blue Mahoe trees, sea grape bushes, and lavish displays of hibiscus, frangipani, and tree-of-life blossoms. Lee always said that the cocktail-time breezes there were "spiked with the fragrance of tropical flowers and good cigars." She knew, avid historian that she was, exactly who among the world's rich and glamorous had visited the place over the years—Grace Kelly, Cole Porter, Frank Sinatra, Noël Coward, Ian Fleming, the Paleys, and of course, her own sister Jackie, who'd spent her honeymoon there with Jack Kennedy, in Villa 10.

Lee and Stas asked Truman to say at their villa. The children were left at home in London.

"Do you realize, Truman, that beyond the railing, the only straight line we see is the horizon?"

Lee and Truman were having coffee one morning on the

villa's main terrace, which faced a broad expanse of brilliant blue sea.

"Glorious," said Truman, in white shorts and nothing else. He was still in good physical shape then, he told me, and was never afraid of showing off his boyish figure. Lee was wearing a two-piece bathing suit over which she had thrown an open cotton blouse.

"All those straight lines in New York, in London," said Lee, "upright, somehow all saying, 'Me, me, me . . . ,' meaning civilization. 'We built this.' Yet here, we can actually see and hear and even smell something larger than that—something sacred."

"Yes," said Truman, slyly. "That's exactly why we come to expensive, luxurious resorts like this—to encounter the sacred."

"Where's the Paleys' villa?"

Truman twisted to his right a bit and pointed over his shoulder.

"Over there," he said.

"What's it like with them? Do you only talk with Babe?"

"Oh, no. It's very much a threesome. We're very simpatico; Bill and I like each other enormously. He gives me lots of insights about business, but I am always astonished by the extent and depth of his knowledge about absolutely everything. For instance, architecture. Did you know that he was personally responsible—speaking of 'me, me, me'—for getting Eero Saarinen to design the new CBS tower he's building on Sixth Avenue? Bill specified everything, even chose the doorknobs."

"Ah."

"Now that's no mean monument for the son of a Russian-Jewish immigrant who made a fortune in cigars."

"Oh."

"It's just always comfortable when I see them—down here, in New York, on friends' yachts . . . Babe, I adore. She has only one flaw—she's perfect. But I respect Bill, you know. He personifies all the power and glamour of being the head of an empire . . ."

I've always wondered whether Truman's friendship with the Paleys wasn't at least partly based on what people nowadays call a "man-crush." After hearing Truman talk about them so much—especially later, after he'd lost their friendship—he may have envied each of them the possession of the other. He had certainly fallen in a certain kind of love with Babe, as he would do subsequently with Lee. And I think Lee found a bit of wicked glee in thinking about the murkiness of Truman's friendship with the Paleys, jealous as she may have been at that point of Babe's close relationship with him.

"Sometimes I think she is too good for him," said Truman, his eyes closed, as if he were trying to nap. "She has a certain innocence and vulnerability. She is photographed all the time, but she's actually rather lonely. I suspect Bill takes her for granted, like a servant. Something in me wants to shock her out of it."

"Truman, I . . ."

"Of course, she entrusts me with all the scandalous secrets of their marriage," continued Truman.

"Let's get back to the sacred, shall we?" said Lee.

"Don't be shocked. It's an author's job to know and tell the truth. They were all trained, those Cushing girls, to secure good marriages. Their mother was called Gogsie—did you know that? Gogsie Cushing, the original social climber. And among them, they now have six—six good marriages. Isn't that great? Minnie married Vincent Astor, then Jim Fosburgh; Betsy married James Roosevelt, FDR's son, and then John Whitney. Babe's first marriage was to Stanley Mortimer Jr., whose family was one of the Four Hundred."

Lee, suddenly unwilling to learn any more about the Paleys, changed the subject. She noticed a scar on Truman's abdomen.

"What's that?" she said.

"Oh, that," said Truman. "I had appendicitis when I was a kid. Acute appendicitis, in a remote part of Alabama—can you imagine? There were no doctors for a hundred miles, and if they had had to bring me that far, I would have died. So they got a horse doctor to operate. Look at that terrible scar."

"I never noticed it before."

"Well, you aren't very observant, are you?"

"Truman, I was joking. I've never seen so much of your body before."

"Nor I yours, princess. And may I say, well done!"

They both laughed.

"And you paint your toenails!" said Truman. Lee's toenails shimmered faintly with the barely there pink of the inside of a seashell.

"I do when I am here," said Lee. "And only when I am here, where I won't be photographed."

"It's pretty."

"Mother thinks colored nails vulgar, so Jackie and I never do it. But the hotel's beauty girl suggested it one day, and I thought, why not? Stas never notices."

After a swim and a poolside lunch, they were sunning themselves on *chaises longues* and back to discussing the ways that Lee was different from Jackie. Lee liked hearing Truman attach language to feelings she'd always had but never articulated.

"She's cutthroat, isn't she?" says Truman. "You're the soulful one."

"That's a little harsh," said Lee. "She can certainly be stubborn."

"Babe said something interesting to me once. 'Jackie has something very great—more than poise. *She's* the real statesman, not Jack.' I happen to know that Babe envies any woman with ambitions and intentions beyond a husband and marriage. But that route is not for her."

Truman, on his *chaise*, shifted himself onto his side so he could face Lee.

"But you, you're determined, aren't you?" he said, shielding his eyes from the sun with his hand. "In your way, you're *very* independent. No prisoner of celebrity, you."

Truman told me that it was one evening on that visit to Round Hill when he began thinking about Lee as a "star"—as in a movie star of the Kate Hepburn variety. He'd been thinking much more about movies after recently writing the screenplay for a British-produced film called *The Innocents*, an adaptation of the Henry James novella *The Turn of the Screw*. The buzz around that project at the time was that everybody involved thought his work on the movie was great.

* * *

A month later, it was fall, and Lee and Stas were back in London. Truman came there from Verbier for a screening of *The Innocents*, to which he invited Lee and his old chum, photographer and designer Cecil Beaton. Lee loved the film and praised Deborah Kerr's performance as the neurotic and/or possessed governess, Miss Giddens.

"Yes, isn't she marvelous?" said Truman.

"She really captured that ambiguity between the natural and the supernatural," said Lee.

"Thank you," said Truman.

"Why thank *you*?" said Lee.

"Who do you think put it there, that ambiguity?"

"Henry James, I should have thought."

"James wrote a horror story, well and good," said Truman. "I went deeper into the psychology. Miss Kerr seized on that."

Cecil sniffed.

"What I'm afraid no one seized on was Miss Kerr's face," said Cecil. "I shot her in '44 and am quite familiar with it. The film's lighting made her look like a kabuki performer."

Truman and Cecil had been best friends for years, and had shared adventures at Hollywood parties, on Mediterranean beaches, and in bars on four continents. Each had his own kind of commanding, room-filling energy, and both revered great style. But Cecil, whom I met several times, was tall and imperious, twenty years older than Truman, and more of a snob. In fact, I suspect he was a model for Truman in this respect.

"So you're all signed up for *My Fair Lady*?" said Truman.

"Oh, yes," said Cecil. "Though Miss Cukor and I are argy-bargy over shooting in London. I believe we need some important exterior shots here, not on Hollywood sets. And she's complaining that British crews break too often for tea."

"Well, don't they?" said Truman.

"They do," said Cecil. "But we must sometimes suffer to make great art."

"Cecil, don't you think Lee would be terrific onstage or in a movie?"

"Oh, Truman . . ." said Lee.

"No, really," said Truman.

With marked theatricality, Cecil regarded Lee for a moment.

"All I can say, my dear," he said, "is that I would love to shoot you."

Truman had also come to England to accompany Lee to the renaming ceremony for the Royal Shakespeare Theatre in Stratford-upon-Avon, a follow-up to the previous year's establishment of the Royal Shakespeare Company, on whose board Lee and Stas both served. She and Truman were driven up to Stratford by Lee's chauffeur and would be staying the night there at the home of friends of hers and Stas's, also theatre board members. Stas, Lee told Truman, "had another engagement."

Stratford is a picturesque, old market town in the Midlands, with Tudor buildings and cobbled streets, famous as the birthplace of Shakespeare and thus often packed with tourists. Located on the western bank of the River Avon, the theatre is a stolid, red-brick pile with Deco-ish details, built in 1932—the design "more suitable than stylish," Lee once said, poking gentle fun at British middle-class tastes. The ceremony consisted of speeches and reminiscences, and a scene from *A Midsummer Night's Dream*, and then a reception on the terrace of the theatre's rooftop restaurant, overlooking the river and adjacent gardens.

"No Queen?" said Truman, as they sipped champagne and surveyed the crowd.

"Would we be dressed this way if she were here?" says Lee.

"And yet . . . there *is* an Elizabeth."

"How so?"

"Look over there."

Truman pointed out an imposing woman in a gray suit, her gray hair in a tight chignon, standing at the center of a group of some very important-looking gentlemen.

"That's Elisabeth Scott," said Truman. "She's the architect who designed this building. It was the first important public building to be built in Britain designed by a woman. I read about it yesterday in the paper."

"Extraordinary," said Lee. "How did you know which one she was?"

"Well, look at the way she's standing. That's the posture of a woman who could command a team of builders in 1932, don't you think? I pick up on these things, you see. Also, there was a photograph."

When the terrace became too chilly, most of the party moved inside. Lee didn't want to be late for the supper her friends were serving, so she made it a point to bring Truman directly over to RSC founder Peter Hall, for quick congratulations.

"Marvelous evening, Peter," she said, with a little kiss.

"We'd never be able to do it without good people like you and Stas," said Hall.

"Do you know Truman Capote?"

"Of course I do! Good to see you, Truman."

"Peter is one of the few people who saw my Broadway musical," said Truman. Based on a short story of Truman's, *House of Flowers* starred Pearl Bailey and Diahann Carroll, but closed to generally bad reviews after only four months.

"Well, maybe we'll get you to do something for us someday," said Hall.

"Peter's being very kind," said Truman. "The show was a flop. Besides, I know that Beckett is more your speed."

"Oh, that's right," said Lee. "Next season it's *Waiting for Lear*!"

Hall brightened to hear the informal nickname that was circulating in cultural circles.

"We're doing *Lear* here," he explained, for Truman's benefit, "and *Waiting for Godot* at the Aldwych, in London."

"Very exciting," said Lee. "We'll be there."

Half an hour later, Lee and Truman were ensconced in the back seat of her black Bentley. The tiny bar was stocked with a crystal decanter of Balvenie and a cold bottle of soda water.

"I thought it was Peter who directed your musical," said Lee.

"Oh my goodness, no. That was Peter Brooke. Get your Peters straight."

Gently, Lee slapped Truman's knee.

"Wait 'til you see Ginny's place," said Lee. "It's divine. She collects nineteenth-century dog portraits."

"What's the house like?"

"From the 1840s, built on the site of a 1450s manor house—her family's. It's passed all this way to her through the female line."

"Anything like the place you and Stas have your eye on?"

"Oh, no, no. Turville Grange is mid-eighteenth century."

"Where is it?"

"Between here and London, in Henley-on-Thames. Near Oxford. Actually, we passed the turnoff on the way up here, on the M40."

"I wasn't paying attention," said Truman, with a swig of whiskey from a crystal tumbler.

"You'll love it, Truman—the one we want. It's a so-called 'grade-listed' Queen Anne that was once owned by Henry Ford the second."

"Well, then, you simply must have it."

"Renzo and I are already discussing possibilities—though Lionel and Helena haven't even settled on selling yet! They're the owners. They know we love the place. That's Lionel Brett, the fourth Viscount Esher—since I know you like these little details."

"These details, Your Serene Highness, are not little," said Truman, using the princely style that was hers by way of her marriage to Stas. "Will your husband be joining us at Ginny's?"

Lee was silent for a bit, then spoke quietly.

"He's at a house party in Sussex," she said.

Truman put his hand over Lee's.

"It's fine," she said. She explained that the marriage was "good but not great." Stas was "solid and funny, but a little rough around the edges." He was "a great father and adores the kids, and they him." And she noted that the timing of the growing distance between them was ironic, since their petition of a Vatican annulment was moving forward and they might soon be able to "remarry" in a Catholic church. Truman agreed that this very European arrangement, which allowed Stas to go off by himself, also allowed Lee to discreetly pursue her own outside interests.

"I've seen Ari a few times," she whispered.

Truman nodded, with a sympathetic look.

"It's amazing the way you can whisper in a Bentley and still be heard," he said.

Just then, the telephone rang. Truman hadn't even noticed that the back seat was equipped with a phone—a device that looked like a chubby, black transistor radio with a colorless rotary dial, topped by a black plastic handset. Lee spoke for a while, without reference to the identity of her caller, but she looked exasperated and was finally, after several tries, able to hang up.

"My mother," she said, taking a breath. "Cocktail hour must have begun early today."

Lee and Truman laughed about it and went on to have a lovely cold supper and admire their host's newly acquired portrait of a King Charles spaniel named Bottoms, by the eighteenth-century animal painter George Stubbs. But Lee remained privately troubled, because the phone call had been about Truman. The next morning, on the drive back to London, she decided that she and Truman were good enough friends that she could be honest.

"It wasn't my mother last night in the car, it was Jackie," she said.

"Oh?" said Truman.

"She's throwing me a little dinner at the White House—upstairs in the Residence, family mostly—to thank me for keeping her company during the election."

"That's nice."

"I said I wanted to include you, because Stas can't come, and she loved the idea, she really did. But she said that she just can't do it this time."

"Why not?"

"I don't know. She has to be very particular about her guest lists now."

Truman's laugh expressed something between ire and disdain.

"It's not like I killed the Lindbergh baby," he said.

Lee explained that Jackie was under great pressure to maintain a certain "tone" for the White House social program, even the private gatherings. This one was to be strictly family.

"Tone!" said Truman. "Don't famous writers bring tone?"

What Lee didn't tell Truman was that Janet Auchincloss had repeatedly warned both Jackie and Lee against growing too close to flamboyant homosexuals; "it could always blow up in your face," she believed.

"I'll have a word with her," he said, leaning forward, picking up the phone as a joke and pretending to make a call. "Get me the White House!"

CHAPTER 4

THE PLEASURE OF YOUR COMPANY

"Thank you for speaking with me," said Lila.

"It's a pleasure," said Truman.

"I appreciate your making the time."

"Well, I want to do what I can to help the film."

They were speaking by phone, between New York and Verbier. Truman had agreed with the producers of *Breakfast at Tiffany's* to be available for print and television pre-publicity for the film, which was due to come out that fall. Giving interviews that were not focused directly on Truman or his writing were not his favorite thing, though he did want to see the film become a popular success, since that would likely increase the value of his next book deal.

"I know we have only ten minutes," said Lila, "so let's dive in, shall we?"

"By all means."

"Alright. Well, first of all, I'm curious to know how close the movie is to the novel."

"Novella."

"Sorry—novella."

"I assume you've read it."

"Of course I have."

"Good. Because you wouldn't be very well prepared for this interview if you hadn't read it, would you?"

"Well, then, how close is the movie to the novella?"

"Ha! Close enough. Of course, they're entirely different mediums, books and movies, and each has its own requirements. Also, a director does have his own vision and his own way of telling a story. Mainly, we added a character to the movie, to help intensify the relationship between Holly and Paul."

"What character did you add?"

"Mrs. Emily Eustace Failenson. She's a fancy but rather shady lady played by Patricia Neal."

"Why shady?"

"She's a married lady who's both sleeping with and supporting George Peppard, who's half her age. Shady enough?"

"But isn't that kind of thing one of the themes of the novella? Isn't Holly kind of a sugar baby?"

"Yes, she is, but all that was softened for the movie, to make Holly more appealing to American audiences. So we added back some shadiness in a character who is supposed to be deliciously unlikable."

"And does Patricia Neal pull that off?"

"Quite well, I think."

"So have you seen the movie yet?"

"It's not finished. They're still editing. But I have seen many of the rushes, because I was out in Hollywood several times when they were on set, shooting. It's going to be a wonderful film."

"I understand you were hoping Marilyn Monroe would play Holly Golightly."

"She was my first choice. We're good friends. Marilyn would have been terrific."

"I heard that Blake Edwards didn't want to work with her—because she can be difficult to work with."

"Is that a question?"

"Why didn't Marilyn get the part?"

"I don't want to get into any of that."

"Did you approve Audrey Hepburn?"

"Of course I did. They wouldn't have done anything without my approval."

"What do you think of Hepburn's performance?"

"She's lovely."

"Does she fulfill your vision of Holly Golightly?"

"Next question."

"You said that '*we* added a character.' Now, I see that George Axelrod is credited as screenwriter . . ."

"George and I are old friends. The word I would use to describe my role in the writing was 'collaborator.' "

"Not 'consultant'? It's not a co-write credit, is it?"

"Next question."

"Do you have any details about the premiere? Will it be in New York?"

"I haven't heard anything about it yet. Oh, but I should mention the song."

"What song?"

"Henry Mancini and Johnny Mercer wrote a perfectly lovely little song especially for the movie. It's called 'Moon River.' Holly plays the guitar, remember, and sings a little. So now we have this wonderful song for her. Johnny's from the South, too, you know, so the words express this very Georgia-Alabama mood."

"Did Hepburn do her own singing?"

"Oh, yes."

"How is it?"

"It's great—but you have to forgive me. I see that our time is up. I'm afraid I'm on a very tight schedule this evening."

"Thank you, Truman. Let me ask just one more thing, on a different subject. I keep hearing something about the Radziwills—that they are seeking to have her first marriage annulled and are not truly married in the eyes of the Catholic Church. Do you know anything about this?"

"It's nonsense," said Truman. "I haven't heard a thing about it. I can confirm, though, that Lee is a practicing Catholic. She and I attended a very fancy mass not long ago in Rome, and it was clear to me that the lady is quite devout. But may I say something to you, writer to writer, as it were?"

"Please do."

"I would expect someone with a byline in a respected newspaper to know the difference between a story worthy of a hundred thousand readers and the kind of salacious gossip that's not even worthy, as the French say, of a nosy concierge . . ."

"Thank you, Truman."

"Thank you."

"Don't Repeat This" —by Lila North
Monday, April 3, 1961

. . . Great news! Grimy old Penn Station is no longer slated to be renovated, as was announced a while back, but rather to be razed completely soon, to make way for a sparkling new station, paired with a new Madison Square Garden. The Garden complex will boast two main arenas, a convention center, shops, and a hotel. As they say, New York will be a great place if they ever finish it! • Our fair city, as you may have heard, is also the backdrop for *Breakfast at Tiffany's*, the new movie vehicle for *Roman Holiday* and *Sabrina* star Audrey Hepburn. Apparently, though, Truman Capote, author of the novella on which the movie is based, is unhappy with the choice of Hepburn as his free-spirited Holly Golightly character. Capote told me recently that he preferred his "good friend" Marilyn Monroe for the part. When asked if he liked Hepburn's performance, he said only, "Next question." • And speaking of Capote, which of his lovely swans may not even be truly married in the eyes of the church? Could it be the one who was seen canoodling recently in a swank London club with Greek journalist and man-about-town Taki Theodoracopulos . . . ?

I think that even by then, Lee and Truman understood that they had found a great friend in the other. Though they were both traveling a lot and spending time at multiple residences, they were making it a point to stay in touch, with letters and phone calls. Meetups in New York and London, Palm Beach and Palm Springs, were carefully coordinated, as jet-set life had to be for people in their social stratum. Truman was beginning to see as much of Lee as he had of Babe, though in a different way. He told me that he had fallen a little in love with Lee right away—that she was the kind of woman he would be attracted to if he were straight.

In fact, there was great depth to his close friendships with women. He had authentic respect and affection for his favorites, and was irked by the superficiality—and the frequency—of mentions of them in the press as "his swans." What about their individual characteristics, he'd say, their intentions and ambitions, their accomplishments? "It's not all about their goddamn poise!" He groaned when the press treated them as pretty puppets, whereas he—an artist wise in the ways of the human soul and spirit—couldn't help but see these women as the individuals they were, balancing the expectations of polite society with the realities of being space-age wives and mothers, let alone public goddesses. "Backwards and in heels," he used to observe, referencing Ginger Rogers, whose greatness was based on exactly the same kind of talent as Fred Astaire's—plus a little more.

Yet he knew well the benefits of being mentioned in newspaper columns and photographed for magazines. Social currency was becoming more than ever an actual commodity that could be profitized—a fact to which even rich people were hardly indifferent. Moreover, it was a moment, New York in the early '60s, when the boundary between public and private lives was fast disintegrating, when a generation of women who'd been raised to think their names should appear in the paper only thrice—at birth, marriage, and death—might themselves raise a daughter who'd see nothing wrong with squabbling like a jumped-up fishwife with blown-out hair on reality TV.

Lee and Truman happened to be in New York that spring, when they attended a spring gala together for American Ballet Theatre. The invitation came courtesy of Truman's "landlord," Oliver Smith, who was one of the company's directors and who knew that both Lee and Jackie loved ballet. Lee was thrilled, at the reception following the performance, to greet ballerina Nora Kaye, whom she admired, and Kaye's husband Herb Ross, the producer, director, and choreographer. I distinctly remember the wistful note in Lee's voice when she told me this story, which has a fateful side. While Lee was telling Kaye that night how much she'd loved her appearance in Antony Tudor's *Pillar of Fire*—a darkly dramatic ballet about a woman caught between love and licentiousness—she could hardly have known that Kaye's husband Ross would eventually, after Kaye's death, become Lee's third husband.

"He was so elegant—such an attractive man," said Lee. "It's funny, though. When we next met, at a dinner party in Bel Air, almost thirty years later, not long after Nora died, he didn't remember that night at the ballet. I did, of course, and we talked our heads off."

The ABT reception saw lots of festive chatting among the friends-of-the-arts types who'd paid hundreds or thousands of dollars for the pleasure of seeing some dancing and each other. Lee and Truman were standing with the Paleys and with producer and talk show host David Susskind and his wife Joyce, when two handsome principal dancer boys came over, each in a skinny-cut, Carnaby Street-style suit, and persuaded Babe and Joyce to be swept out onto the dance floor.

Truman took Lee's hand.

"Shall we give it a go, princess dear?" he asked cheerfully. "Or did you have your eye on one of the dancers?"

"Let's give it a go!" said Lee.

Lee already knew that Truman was a terrific dancer, having seen him at so many parties at which he was by far the most animated gentleman in the room, among a sea of stiff, tuxedoed husbands and generically smiling wives. "Effervescent" was the word Lee used to describe the physical sensation of dancing with Truman, his courtly but unfussy manner of holding and leading her—which is why, she said, she didn't care how they may have looked together—she was two or three inches taller than his 5'3"—or what anyone may have thought of a first lady's sister so plainly enjoying such vivacious company in public.

"You're a cool one," Lee said to Truman as they waltzed to the strains of "Love Makes the World Go 'Round," a song from one of that year's big Broadway musicals, *Carnival!*

"I assumed you would be an angel on your feet, and you are," said Truman.

"That would make you the smoothest devil I've ever met."

They stayed together for the next dance, a slow number, during which a fellow guest greeted Lee in passing and praised her for being with "the life of the party."

"I presume you know what *that* means," said Truman, as he and Lee danced on. Socially, Truman was never particularly "discreet," to use a term he found contemptible when applied to the men of his kind.

"Mm-hmm," said Lee.

"I'm used to it. But do you know how much I care?"

"I'm guessing not a jot!"

Later, after finding a quiet corner where they could sit, they were discussing the great balls of history. Truman was a big fan of balls and by this time had certainly been dreaming of throwing a big one of his own, along the lines of the Tsarina Alexandra's Winter Palace ball of 1903, or Salvador Dalí's Surrealist Ball of 1941, in Pebble Beach, or Count Carlos de Beistigui's Venetian costume ball of 1951. Though Truman's ball would be "modern, of the moment . . ."

"Just what we need!" said Lee.

"I can get some ideas from Cecil . . ."

"And you can put together the new Four Hundred . . ."

"Right? Something better than a piddlin' ol' bash like *this* . . ."

"Antenor Patiño keeps talking about doing something big 'for people like us,' as he puts it . . ."

"You mean the King of Tin?"

"He's created such a beautiful place for himself in Estoril. Have you been there?"

"I've heard about it."

"If he does throw a ball, that's got to be where it'll be."

But Truman was determined to do it first. And it delighted him to no end that the ball he wound up throwing a few years later came before the one Patiño eventually gave.

"Why doesn't Jackie do a big ball at the White House?" said Truman.

"There are several state dinners in the works, that I know of," said Lee.

"That's not the same thing."

"In fact, she wants Ballet Theatre to perform at one of them next year. She and Oliver are working it out."

On the dance floor, David Susskind was doing a free-form, rock-and-roll shimmy with one of the evening's young star ballerinas, now in a slinky yellow gown.

"Mr. Susskind looks like he is having fun," said Truman. "I wonder if she knows who he is."

"Those girls are remarkable, aren't they?" said Lee. "Onstage, they're goddesses. At a party, they're princesses. But in the street, on their way to or from class, they're just teenagers."

"They were a huge hit in Russia, weren't they, those kids?" said Truman.

"So I gather," said Lee. Ballet Theatre had toured the USSR the previous year, on a kind of cultural-diplomatic mission.

"It was the Van Cliburn effect all over again," said Truman. "The Russians are always so happy whenever a foreigner performs *their* art awfully well."

One of the things Truman taught me was to always keep the conversation light on social occasions. Religion and politics are fine, because after a brief exchange or two, someone will always deliver a laugh line, and then it's on to the next topic. But don't ask people about their work, though, because half of them won't want to talk about it, and the other half will want to say more than anyone wants to hear. It's all right to admire people's artworks, furniture, and decorative objects, but not to offer any additional information you may have about such things, because most people think they already know everything there is to know about their possessions. Recent performances are fine, as long as two or more people have seen them. Generally, Truman said, it's best to stick to food, gardening, and travel. He was conflicted when asked at a party what he was working on—wanting to avoid sanctimony but tempted to remind people that it was his responsibility as an artist to think deeply about the human condition all day, and, with *In Cold Blood*, murder, morality, and evil. In those instances, he'd make a quick, *outré* remark—"I personally know more murderers than there are guests in this room"—get a quick laugh, and then, if he felt he'd gotten enough attention, allow the conversation to move on.

Still, at a party, Truman liked to surprise people with zingers, often for the sheer devilish effect of it—which I think *he* thought was adorable, even long after he'd lost his famous boyishness.

"Lila North says that you and Stas are on the rocks," said Truman.

Lee hadn't expected such a sharp remark.

"Don't be vulgar," she said. "You know I never read that stuff."

"No. The point is that others do. And she's not always wrong—though she is always fifth-rate."

"The Taki thing? I try to have a little fun when I can, but I am a happily married woman. Anyway, isn't all gossip writing kind of fifth-rate?"

"Not at all. I find Suzy very readable."

"Stas is a very decent man, even if he isn't exactly . . . effervescent."

"Gore says he can be brusque."

"Can't they all? Can't any of us?"

"You know what I mean. Husbands."

"Truman, can't we dance more?"

As they were heading back out onto the dance floor, the band suddenly stopped playing, and for a second, the dancing gave way to hushed confusion, and then a wave of applause swept through the crowd, emanating from the room's main entrance.

"Oh, look," said Truman, "it's the Queen of America."

In a stunning gown of aqua, First Lady Jacqueline Kennedy was being shown the way over to the table where Oliver Smith and his American Ballet Theatre co-director Lucia Chase were seated. Everyone rose for greetings. With Jackie were White House social director Letitia Baldrige, in austere black and pearls, and four men in dark suits, who were obviously Secret Service.

"Did you know she was coming?" asked Truman, as the music started up again and he and Lee made their way over to Smith's table.

"No, I didn't," said Lee.

I would meet Jackie several times over the course of my employment with Lee. For many years, they lived within a few blocks of each other on Fifth Avenue. Sometimes Lee lent me to Jackie, for some bit of entertaining, and sometimes Jackie lent staff to Lee. Jackie's voice was a little higher and more breathless than Lee's, and Lee's manner of speaking could be markedly more theatrical than Jackie would ever be. Yet Jackie had what Truman described as "a magnificence." At that moment, he said, in the early 1960s, she was the only person alive who could go literally anywhere in the world—to embassies, palaces, private residences, rumored secret prisons, storerooms at the Louvre, ancient Cambodian temples that were closed to the public . . . He had it on good authority, he said, that every house manager of every theater and concert hall in the world now held a pair of "Jackie Kennedy seats" open until the last minute before curtain, just in case the First Lady of the Free World showed up.

". . . Let's just hope we can pull it off!" Jackie was saying to Oliver Smith, as she spotted Lee and Truman.

"I didn't know you were coming," said Lee, as the sisters shared a light kiss. "You should have told me."

"I didn't know myself until four o'clock," said Jackie. "I tried to reach you, but my schedule got away from me." To Truman, Jackie offered a gloved hand and a few nice words.

"What are you doing here?" said Lee.

"I'm giving a speech about human rights tomorrow morning at the UN. And I thought how marvelous to come early and look in on the gala."

Lee moved closer to Jackie so they could whisper.

"Did your sister slip your mind?" she said.

"Don't be silly," said Jackie. "Oliver knew I was coming, but I asked him not to say anything to you. I thought it would make a cute surprise."

" 'Cute' is one word for it. Are you going right back? I could arrange a little dinner . . ."

"I'm afraid I have to be back for a lunch."

Oliver and Lucia were holding back some of the Ballet board members who were determined to welcome the first lady, and Lee was too well-behaved to keep Jackie from the necessary greetings.

"Where are you staying . . . ?" asked Lee.

"The Waldorf," said Jackie, as she began to slide away. "Nice to see you, Truman."

Truman threw up an arm in a gesture toward the door.

"Any chance we can drag you along to the Peppermint Lounge?" he said.

"I wish," said Jackie, already offering her hand to the chairman of ABT's board and his wife.

Truman put his arm around Lee's waist.

"Now that was an entrance," he said.

"Debutante of the Year," said Lee. "Newport, 1951."

"Of course she was."

"Now, we're not really going to the Peppermint Lounge. Are we?"

"Well, you tell me, darlin.' Do you want to twist with me—twist 'til we tear the house down . . . ?"

And then I walked into Lee's life. It was like being an extra on the opera stage and then stepping in to play a small but essential role in a spectacle by Wagner. Sadly, my employer Mrs. Madeleine Parrish Hawkins suffered a stroke and had to be admitted to a full-care facility, probably for the rest of her life. I was no longer needed, and thought I would have to register with one of the staffing agencies that service New York's most affluent households. But then, Mrs. Hawkins's daughter Sandy—Mrs. Alexandra Hawkins Smith, Judy's mother—said that she knew that her friend Princess Radziwill was looking for someone and would be happy to put in a good word. Of course, I was thrilled. Which is how, at 10:25 in the morning on Thursday, May 4, I came to arrive at the main portal of Lee's Fifth Avenue apartment building. I smiled at the doorman, whom I would come to know well, and gave my name to the concierge, who was also to become a friend.

"Mrs. Radziwill is expecting me," I said. The lobby's walls were paneled in dark wood. Behind the concierge's desk was a large floral still life, on either side of which were brass sconces shaded in rose-colored silk. A massive arrangement of pink roses was positioned on one side of the counter.

"Of course," said the concierge. "The elevator to your right," he said, indicating the way with an open palm. "It's 17N."

The elevator operator was already pressing 17 when I entered the wood-paneled elevator. The operator seemed to be making it a point both to smile and to not look directly at me.

The elevator delivered me into a private landing that served only two apartments on that floor, 17N and 17S. Over a console table tastefully set with a small arrangement of white hydrangeas and peonies hung a mirror I later learned was of Venetian design. I was about to press the button for 17N when Carla opened the door, introduced herself, and welcomed me in. She showed me into the library and said that "Mrs. Radziwill will be with you in a moment. May I get you some coffee or sparkling water?" I declined.

Eagerly and with a little bit of awe, I took in the bookcases filled with books on a dazzling array of subjects; the lovely tabletop objects like bronze figurines, brass boxes, and crystal ashtrays; the Indian portraits painted on glass; classically elegant furniture upholstered in tastefully audacious patterns of blues, greens, and pinks; that richly striped wallpaper; and a large old painting depicting a family of tigers at rest in a tropical landscape. At the same time, I kept wondering how I was to address this woman I'd come to see. Some people called her "Mrs. Radziwill"; some, "Princess Radziwill" or "Princess Lee."

"Hi, I'm Lee," she said, gliding into the room in a pair of trim, parrot-green silk slacks and a white blouse. "You must be Marlene." She extended her hand, and we shook.

She already knew, of course, how to pronounce my name.

"Shall we sit? Sandy has said such nice things about you. Has Carla offered you some coffee?"

She was very kind to me that day—not haughty at all. We discussed her needs and requirements, and my skills and specialties. I was so young! There were already a nanny and part-time cleaners; the position I was applying for was cook-housekeeper, which included preparing and serving meals or supervising the service when there were large gatherings. Above all, she said, she needed someone completely trustworthy and discreet—two qualities that Mrs. Smith assured her I possessed.

After a brief tour of the kitchen, the service entrance, and the staff bedrooms and little sitting room, we reseated ourselves in the library. There were shelves and shelves of antique volumes bound in leather, a section of white paperbound books that I recognized as French, and a whole wall of modern and contemporary literature in English.

"I see you have the new Steinbeck," I said. *The Winter of Our Discontent* was one of a number of new-looking books displayed on a table.

"I have been meaning to get to that," said Lee. "Are you a Steinbeck fan?"

I nodded.

"I've read them all," I said.

"My goodness."

"I read everything I can get my hands on."

"The classics, too?"

"Of course. It's always been my way out of . . . some difficult times."

We talked a bit more about the way she liked her households to run.

"For the moment, my husband and I are still based in London," said Lee. "His business is there, but we both want to be near my sister, especially so her children and my children can know each other. So we'll be here part of the time, and part of the time you'll be here alone, keeping things going. This place, we're leasing. We're looking to buy in the neighborhood."

"I see."

"Sandy says you are . . . foreign-born."

"Uh, yes . . ." I said, but not instantaneously. In fact, Mrs. Smith had told Lee a bit of the story I had related to her mother over the years—that I was from an aristocratic Cuban family whose fortune was lost and sugar business was nationalized during the revolution. Mrs. Hawkins often said she felt delighted to be swept up in such an adventurous story, and I saw no harm in telling her more and more of it—she was such a dear soul who was rarely getting out at all. Over time, I gave her more and more details: school in Switzerland, jaunts to Paris and London, family troubles, a grand matriarch of a mother who either couldn't make it out of Cuba or chose to remain on inherited land, something about the mother's affair with a young Fidel Castro.

"But I don't usually like to talk about it," I told Lee.

"I understand," said Lee. "It must be painful. I can respect that."

"I hope it's not a problem."

"Not at all. I say we try it for a month or two and see how it goes."

"Thank you, Mrs.—I mean, Princess . . ."

Lee nodded modestly. "It's 'Mrs. Radziwill' here," she said. "But please call me Lee."

"Thank you."

"Can you start on Monday?"

"Yes . . . Lee."

I started on Monday, and within a week, I had met Truman.

I was just tidying up after dinner one night, when Lee came into the kitchen and announced that a "unique and very important author" would be joining her for lunch the following day, just the two of them. Of course, I recognized his name and knew something about him, so I wasn't surprised, the next day, by the exuberance of his arrival and jocular self-introduction to me as I served the entrée, which Lee seemed to find amusing.

"The fish was a poem," said Truman to me later, quietly, in the dining room, as I cleared and Lee was looking in one of the bookcases for a volume on Chinese export porcelain that she wanted Truman to see. "Do you know what that's from?"

"*The Lady Eve*," I said. "Preston Sturges."

Truman was surprised.

"My goodness, you don't seem like a servant to me," he said.

"Well, this is 1961, Mr. Capote," I said. "We don't exactly bow and scrape, do we?" It was impertinent of me to speak that way, but it was an instinct to do so—somehow, I knew Truman might find it amusing. "That kind of formality is not Mrs. Radziwill's style, anyway."

"Oh, is that what she's got you calling her?"

"She's asked me to call her Lee, at home."

"I understand you used to work for Mrs. Hawkins?"

"I did, yes."

"What was she like? I've never met her."

"She doesn't go out anymore. It was wonderful working for her."

"What did you do?"

"Secretarial things, mostly."

"Is that all? No cooking, cleaning . . . ?"

"No. She liked me to tell her stories."

"What kind of stories?"

"About people, about my life."

"About Cuba?"

"Well . . . yes. But I don't like to talk about that anymore."

"You seem more like the bright young people I know in publishing."

"I'm very happy here," I said, continuing to neaten the table. "Besides, all those publishing kids study in Europe and hang out in Marrakech with Genet and Cocteau. Me, I've been too busy learning how to fold napkins."

The cheeky remark seemed to startle Truman, as I'd hoped it might.

"Hmmm," he said, apparently trying to put me into focus, then putting a finger slyly to his lips as Lee returned to the table with the book. "To be continued."

Suddenly, a world-famous author and I shared a secret.

As I say, after Truman and I started working together, years later, and I learned more about his research methods, I would often take notes in a daily diary about the things that I'd seen and heard in their presence. But even before that, ever since I was a girl, I was just plain nosy about what I overheard, even if I didn't then know the difference between unimportant gossip and necessary truths.

Lee and Truman's world became the whole world to me—and my time with them was the biggest phenomenon of my life. If I had fallen in love along the way—been able to fall in love—maybe things would have been different, but that never happened. A life in service and then writing about it wasn't what I imagined for myself as a girl, but it was possibly my only path forward. I'd had violence in my background and was now perfectly happy to be part of someone else's calm—even if the calm between those two didn't last forever. Thank God it lasted long enough to supplant something darker and more destructive in my heart. Observing such charismatic people close-up was a great reward I was granted for sacrificing an early fantasy of a happy life of my own.

Chapter 5

Superheroes of Society

For a long time, all I could remember about that horrible night was waking up with him on top of me, the panic shooting up suddenly, the claustrophobic darkness, the stretching out of time in patches of dreadful what-ifs: What if I can't get his hand off my mouth? What if he's got a knife? What if nobody hears us?

He'd made the idea clear enough the day before at breakfast. I was plenty old enough, he said. I was only fifteen; he was six years older. Now he was breathing in my ear, telling me to stay still. He reeked of rum and fried onions, and was pulling at my underwear with his other hand, while I struggled to yank myself up. The bed jerked and scraped on the floor. "What if you like it?" he grunted with a laugh.

What if I could shift my body just enough to grab the lamp? What if this kind of stuff was all that adult life consisted of? What if I could get another life entirely?

Biting him wasn't a decision—only an instinct, involuntary. The taste was of salt and iron. And what if he hadn't yelped in pain, and his father, in the next room, hadn't heard him, and our mother, half-naked, hadn't stormed in, braying and beating us both with a shoe? What if that woman had actually cared something about me?

But I did know what would have happened if I had stayed in that house any longer. It would have happened again, and maybe again and again, until I had been murdered or maybe murdered someone myself . . .

* * *

"What's she like?" said Judy.

"Nice," I said. "Smart. Sophisticated."

"Mom says she's smart, too."

"Unpretentious—with me, anyway."

"No tiara?"

"Not around the house. Though I gather that out there in the world, she can be a bit grand."

Judy and I had gotten to know each other a fair bit when I was working for her grandmother, Mrs. Hawkins. Like her mother, Sandy, and indeed like Mrs. Hawkins herself, Judy was always warm and friendly, with not a bit of the social hauteur that I knew some prominent New Yorkers displayed with their staff. In fact, Sandy always said I was like family, and Judy and I did relate in some ways like sisters, sharing confidences and such. I think maybe because my past was described as "troubled," I was treated kindly by the family as something of a charity case, and that was fine with me. I needed charity. No one said so explicitly, but my going off to work for Lee was something of a graduation, and everyone seemed proud of me for it. And after I did so, Judy and I continued seeing a movie together every now and then, or going down to a Greenwich Village café for coffee and a sweet. We were speaking about my new position in the Peacock Café on West 4th Street, one day when Judy was in town on a break from Vassar and I had the afternoon off.

"So you like the job," said Judy.

"It could never be like working for your family."

"Granny misses you. She told me so yesterday. She'd love to see you, if you're willing."

"Of course I'm willing. I'd love to see her."

"She's still sharp as a tack. Shady Hill is only fifty minutes away. Mom says you can drive up with us sometime."

"I'd love to."

"Mom misses you. Even Hilda misses you."

"Thank God I kept asking Hilda to show me how to do things in the kitchen."

"You knew it might come in handy."

"I was just interested."

"Does she make you feel like a servant?"

"Not exactly. But it's clear that she is used to *having* servants—in contrast, let's say, to your mom, who thinks of it as having 'help.' "

"Yeah."

"I like the actual cooking. Turns out I'm pretty good at it. And there are two women who come in twice a week to do the actual cleaning. Though I have to make sure everything gets done, before anyone realizes it needs being done."

That visit to the Peacock was also when Judy shared the good news about meeting someone special.

"His name is John," she said, with obvious delight.

"This is great!" I said.

"He's at NYU Law. We're taking it slowly, and that's fine with me."

"How did you meet?"

"His sister's on my corridor. I knew her at Chapin, but we're not close-close."

"Nice."

"Turns out, his folks know my folks."

"Naturally."

"Anyway, he's not like the usual private school prince—as in, not as hungry for success as the poor boys, and insulated from the pain of failure by the safety net of family wealth."

"You did not just make that up."

"Sociology 101. But it's a real type."

Clucking over espressos about a new crush, dressed in our conservative-but-kicky outfits, we might have looked like two Park Avenue twenty-somethings—though of course, only one of us was a Chapin girl.

"Handsome in a non-Hollywood way." said Judy. "You were doubtless going to ask me next what he looks like, right? Dark hair and eyes; athletic but not muscle-bound. Quiet, sensitive—gentle. Almost homosexual."

"Almost *what* . . . ?"

"You know what I mean—intellectual, cultivated. He knows all about art and classical music."

The Peacock offered live music and poetry later in the day, but on the afternoon we were there, it was just recorded Renaissance guitar music. My first visit there with Judy, months before, had occasioned my first taste of espresso and my first encounter with God in cake form, a dessert called Venetian Rum Delight.

"I wonder why *Venetian*," I said. The slice was in four blond layers, each separated from the other by creamy custard filling, topped with golden meringue.

"Maybe the candied fruit bits?" said Judy. "You see that in a lot of Italian sweets."

I sampled a small, deliberate forkful—the custard was flecked with tiny shocks of unexpected joy. It was a revelation to me that sweet could be not just a taste but an array of specific flavors.

"What's in there?" I said.

"Oh—I imagine apricot, plum, pear, apple . . ." said Judy.

"Wow."

"Yeah. Quince, maybe. Ginger. I remember discovering candied fruit in Rome one summer. They put it in biscotti . . ."

This wasn't haute cuisine, exactly, but it was pure heaven—and a revelation that I automatically registered in terms of my employer's gastronomic preferences.

"She might like these bits in a bombe glacée," I said absently.

"You don't always have to think about her, you know," said Judy.

The café's décor was a Renaissance-Baroque mishmash, with shaky, mismatched tables and chairs; dark paintings and wrought-iron sconces on the walls; and at the center of the room, an eight-foot-tall statue of Pan in the style of Donatello. The boyish, barefoot Greek god stood on an orb, piping away on a double flute. Decades later, Janet and I learned that the statue of Pan was discovered to be "good"—the work of a distinguished nineteenth-century sculptor. It was bought by the Metropolitan Museum of Art and spirited away to their American wing, where we would sometimes later visit it. We would giggle to think that though the statue looked majestic in its new setting, it was somehow devoid of the companionability it possessed when it was eavesdropping discreetly on our café conversations.

"And you?" said Judy. "Is there anyone?"

I shook my head.

"You know me," I said. "I'm married to my work."

"You don't put yourself first. That's your problem."

"Oh, is that my problem?" I tried to look bright. "I always thought it was some kind of a solution."

Judy smiled with a wince, understanding the reference to my childhood traumas. She and her mom, Sandy, had always hoped I might meet someone in their orbit and fall into a relationship; and for a moment, I think, they were disappointed when I said I preferred another job in service after Mrs. Hawkins went off to Shady Hill.

"It's easier for me to devote myself to someone else's needs right now—do you see?" I explained.

"We never meant that for you forever," said Judy.

"I suppose there could be someone, someday," I said. "But right now . . . I can't. I just wasn't trained for it, as you were."

I explained that I was interested in men on an organic level, but not quite willing and able to pursue them in the romantic arena. When I used the phrase "too much baggage," to describe my fear that a boyfriend would unsettle my hard-won emotional independence, Judy nodded.

"Psychology 101," she said knowingly.

I guess you could say we were confidantes. And perhaps *confidante* is the word I'd use to describe what I became for both Lee and Truman, too, over the years. Certainly, I wasn't precisely a "friend" of either one of them. I worked *for* Lee, and later *with* Truman. I was lucky to have a modicum of respect from each of them, and was probably lucky not to have engendered undue affection in either, since I didn't want to test whether or not my heart had become as armored as I feared it might have.

Contact between Lee and Truman became more frequent in the next few years, and in addition to all the frolicking at parties, lying on beaches, and lunching at Orsini's, they were serious enough human beings to enjoy discovering more about each other's great strengths. Lee saw how scrupulous Truman was about writing, how dedicated he was to the art and traditions of literature. Truman saw what curiosity and insights Lee had about antiques and décor and fashion, let alone about books and history. In particular, Truman came to understand that Lee's interest in clothes and houses went deeper than the typical consumption mania of most so-called socialites. He saw that this interest expressed faith in the kind of elevated human existence once envisioned by enlightened French aristocrats; while Lee, for her part, came to believe that Truman's silliness was a sly critique of patriarchal power—a more engaging correlative of the gassy sociopolitical analysis that emanated from academic circles. In their way, Lee and Truman were philosophers for all to see.

Everything in Lee's life was reported publicly: what she wore, where she went, whom she was with, who was decorating her houses. Her fashion choices, and those of her sister and a host of other highly visible, stylish women of their class, coalesced into a broader pan-cultural style that mapped itself onto the new national moment of vitality and optimism, cued by the American presidency and, indeed, by shifts in global power. Columnists and commentators began calling this moment "Camelot," and so many of the visuals that people saw then in newspapers and magazines and on TV expressed what Lee called, in a fashion spread about her, a fresh, "modern-classic" style. The fearless simplicity of a dress by Ungaro; the imperial volume of a hairdo by Kenneth; the echoing neoclassicism of a façade by Philip Johnson—all this, as well as the movies and pop music that were coming out, seemed to reinforce the consequence of a new historical era that was suddenly upon us, an unexpected, almost mythical high point in our lives thus far.

Was it all due to a fresh balance between threat and security in the Cold War? Was it the fruition of a modernist impulse set in motion at the dawn of the new century? Alas, such questions rarely arose explicitly in the exquisite salons of those who were driving the era.

"I've been spending lots of time in Kansas with Harper, interviewing the murderers," said Truman.

"That must be fun," said Lee, dryly.

"I had already done what I thought was all the research on the murders before the culprits were found. And then they were found, and I saw that what I had was only half of what I needed. So now I've started interviewing the murderers, and let me tell you—it's interesting stuff . . ."

Truman and Lee were on the phone—him calling from the light-filled living room of his chalet in Verbier, in front of a window overlooking a broad, green valley that was bounded on the other side by snow-capped Alps; her from the elegant drawing room of her London home in Buckingham Place, whose Ottoman-meets-Mughal décor was both hip and sensuous.

"Isn't it scary?" said Lee.

"They're pussycats," said Truman. "It's completely safe."

"Where do you speak with them—in their cells?"

"In a terribly drab cinderblock room, with guards watching."

"Oh, Truman."

"And now I'm writing it all up."

"So you're working. Good."

"That's why we stay here. I can concentrate here. Verbier is so much less hectic than St. Moritz and Gstaad. I don't come to Switzerland for the commotion."

Truman described all the notes he'd been taking, and his method of processing them and painstakingly "designing" the novel's flow of information and narrative. Lovingly, he recounted his first interviews with murderer Perry Smith and his feeling that Smith was actually a hostage to his partner-in-crime, Richard Hickock, who, Truman said, was the evil mastermind.

"What's it like to speak with someone you absolutely know to be a killer?" asked Lee.

"Sister, I could ask you the same thing," cracked Truman. "I know for a fact that three or four times when we were at a party together, we were speaking with someone absolutely *known* to be a killer."

"Truman!"

"Well, absolutely *reputed* to be one."

Truman described Smith's sensitivity—his good looks, his artistic manner, the letters he'd begun sending Truman, "full of big words," but also full of thought and feeling.

"Letters!" exclaimed Lee.

"Oh, yes," said Truman, almost proudly. "He's very articulate and seems to want to impress me, which I find charming."

Lee noted that it sounded like Truman was falling "a little bit in love" with Smith, and Truman agreed. But he said that it was an author's duty to fall in love with all of his characters "at least a little bit," even if they were morally repugnant.

"*Especially* if they are," he added. "It helps you understand them." Truman paused for effect. "And what are you up to?"

Lee said that she was planning to accompany Jackie on a trip to India—"a big State Department thing."

"I can just imagine the clothes!" said Truman.

"Did you know that the State Department has someone advising Jackie on fashion protocol?"

"Our tax dollars at work."

"She says it's going to be lots of pink and orange."

Lee and Truman had been trying to find a time when they would be in New York together at the same time Jackie was there. The first lady had been coming to the city often to meet with antique collectors and dealers, and acquire furniture for the White House restoration project she was spearheading. She had proved extremely effective in raising the private funds necessary for the project, but the chairman of the White House Fine Arts Committee had also discovered not only the extent of Mrs. Kennedy's taste and knowledge of antiques, but her persuasive power in acquiring the objects she wanted at a price she thought fair.

"That sounds like fun," said Truman. "I'll be going back to Kansas several times in the next few months and stopping in New York."

As they spoke, Truman was looking out over the Bagnes valley toward the Grand Combin massif. Switzerland was safe for him, secure. Jack did all he could to make sure Truman's stays there were tranquil. Truman was absolutely dependent on retreats to Verbier, thankful for them as opportunities to work and also simply to recharge from the high-energy hot-dogging he did everywhere else in the world. As he became more and more a celebrity, he could still rely on Verbier as the place he could still be mostly an artist.

"It's shaping up to be a major work—capital M, capital W," Truman told Lee. "I'm so excited about it, I could burst."

"Good for you," said Lee. "I wish I felt like that about something."

"You'll find it, Lee. I'll help you find it."

A few months passed before Truman was back in New York. On the day before his outing with Lee and Jackie, Babe Paley threw a big "welcome back from Kansas" party for him at her and Bill's place, which was then a twenty-room palace at the St. Regis. Lee was invited, but came and went early with Stas, owing to another engagement.

The opulence of Babe's living room, designed by society darling Billy Baldwin, made a suitable spot to welcome a man who'd been stuck for days at Kansas State Penitentiary in a series of law enforcement offices. Tented in yards and yards of tobacco-colored Indian calico, block-printed in stylized pink flowers, the room boasted an elaborately patterned Bessarabian rug, an eclectic array of furniture and *objets de vertu*, and an aerial focal point of epic eccentricity: a chandelier-clock of so-called Orientalist design, depicting two men in apparent combat, one in robes and one with darker flesh, half-naked.

"Tenting is so convenient for people who don't want to repair their walls," said Cecil, who spent much of the party chatting with Truman, while other friends came and went. "And the chandelier! Are those . . . Turks?"

"It's an allegory," said Truman. "A Moor and an Ottoman, I think. I never know whether to stare or look away."

"Both, I should think. At least the time is correct. Seven twenty-three, and all is well in Tunis."

The guests were the usual boldface names, looking their

prosperous best and burbling amiably amidst a haze of cigarette smoke; moving among them, in flawless hostess style, was Babe, never particularly warm and touchy, but icily gracious—at least, said Truman, until she got to know and like you, in which case you might glimpse the sweetness underneath and even a childlike quality.

"I hope you're having fun," said Babe, who had joined Truman and Cecil, cigarette in hand.

"Immense fun," said Truman.

"Immense fun," said Cecil.

"Then again," continued Truman, "four days ago, I was in a prison."

"Was it hell?" said Babe solicitously.

"Why, this is hell nor are we out of it," said Cecil, quoting Marlowe's Mephistopheles.

A flicker of amusement brightened Babe's impeccably chiseled features.

"Well, at least the food here is better," she said, squeezing Truman's forearm and slipping away.

Truman confessed to Cecil that, improbably, he felt more remote here, among the fifty souls who'd shown up to welcome him, than he had on the road.

"Normally, I love a party, especially if it's for me," he said. "But I think Kansas is beginning to get to me."

"Steady on," said Cecil.

"Babe's a dear to do this, of course, but she once gave a dinner party for the blooming of an amaryllis."

Cecil, who was in the U.S. for pre-production on *My Fair Lady*, clucked over the bejeweled, double-blackamoor brooch that Babe was wearing.

"She carries it off rather well, I think," he said, "wearing little persons on her person."

"It's Fulco—one of her favorite pieces," said Truman, referring to Babe's great friend, jeweler Fulco di Verdura.

"Did you know he's a Sicilian duke?"

"So it's true, then?"

"And a cousin of Lampedusa."

"How marvelous you know these things."

"His career began with an introduction to Coco Chanel—by Cole Porter, no less."

Cecil remarked on the brooch's enormous pendant emerald and said he wondered what it was about blackamoor figures that made them so popular among their set.

"Think about it, Muzzy," said Cecil. "Don't we know of several blackamoor lamps and candelabra and torchères here and there, on both sides of the Atlantic?"

"Mmm."

"Yet I suppose a bauble like that will retain its value forever—the workmanship, the whimsy. I'll bet Babe's daughter and granddaughter will be wearing it proudly a hundred years from now."

"If that sort of thing is still in fashion," said Truman.

Cecil raised an eyebrow.

"But it's such a timeless theme," he said. "The non-European as the exotic *other* . . . !"

"Time will tell."

Coming from the next room were the comforting sounds of a pianist spinning out a stream of jazz and pop standards.

"I notice the Princess was in and out," said Cecil. "I thought she and Babe were friends."

"They are," said Truman. "Though I think that Lee really gets along better with Bill."

"The girls aren't rivals for your attention?"

"Everyone is a rival for my attention."

A gale of laughter erupted between them.

"I saw her with Onassis the other day, in Claridge's," said Cecil.

Truman nodded.

"I know."

"It looked *un peu* snoggy, so I wondered if we should be expecting *finito* any day now."

"Between us, I don't think Stas allows her the level of independence she needs, and I am hoping this doesn't become a crisis. Two nights ago at the White House, they were the perfect couple."

"Oh?"

Finally, as both a friend of Jackie's and a distinguished American artist, Truman had been invited to the White House. He had flown to Washington straight from Kansas City. It was an occasion with which Jackie's mother Janet was not involved—an "informal" family dinner in the residence, though not without butlers and ushers.

"It was lots of fun," said Truman, "even though I promised Lee to consume no more than three drinks."

"She's absolutely right," said Beaton. "Something always happens to you during the fourth one."

"Sure—I get happy. What's wrong with that?"

Cecil shot Truman an incredulous look.

"Tangier, 1948," he said. "Need I say more?"

"*Anyway*, Lee thanked me the next day for sticking to the promise and to say that the president had meant to ask me for book recommendations. She told me he might call."

"That man is always pestering me for stories of the Blitz," said Cecil.

"Very funny," said Truman. "Jack Kennedy happens to find me quite as amusing as Jackie does. And he'd already called me that day, before Lee, and we wound up talking about speechwriting."

"Ah."

"He happens to be a very smart guy. So is Bobby."

"Yes."

"Though I can't say too much for Ted."

They wound up giggling over the "ghastly" Eisenhower furniture that was still in use in the residence.

Running around New York with Jackie, the day after Babe's party, proved less fun than Truman thought it would be, because of the encumbrance of a Secret Service detail. Three agents traveled with Jackie and party in a black Lincoln; two agents led the way in a black van. Security considerations proved slightly inconvenient at Oleg Cassini's Seventh Avenue office, where two agents remained in the building's lobby and one stationed himself upstairs in Cassini's reception area, while Jackie, Lee, and Truman discussed the placement of a lone pocket on the jacket of a yellow bouclé wool suit. (Jackie: "You always find the balance in asymmetry, Oleg.") Security was awkward at the Madison Avenue showroom of an antiques dealer, where three agents stood outside keeping the sidewalk clear as Jackie bargained and charmed the gentleman into practically donating a table-desk that once belonged to Julia Grant, the wife of Ulysses S. Grant. (Jackie: "Generations of Americans will be grateful to you, Jacques.") And it was downright ridiculous at La Caravelle, where Jackie graciously accepted not one of the good, see-and-be-seen tables up front, but one way in the back, which was strategically more defensible against armed attack. (Jackie: "After all, this is a place where assassins come for lunch, whether or not there's a First Lady in the house.")

Both Lee and Truman cherished warm memories of that visit from Jackie, but for me, the visit was memorable chiefly for lunch the following day at Lee's place. For fun, and to honor Jackie, Lee chose an historic American menu, based on the simple one used at Lincoln's inaugural luncheon, almost exactly a hundred years before: mock turtle soup, corned beef and cabbage, parsley potatoes, and blackberry pie. I found it fun to prepare and serve this meal, and everybody seemed to get a kick out of eating it. Then at one point, Truman joked that it would have been thoughtful of Lee to have me dress up in 1861 garb—which made me feel oddly objectified but also automatically included in the whimsy of their costume-ball mentality. I played along when Truman tied a napkin around my head as some sort of cap that a nineteenth-century servant might have worn, and everybody laughed when I curtsied. It's a small point when compared with meeting a first lady, but the feeling of inclusion stuck with me and emboldened me even further, when I happened to find myself alone with Truman the following week.

He had only just arrived at Lee's place for a lunch *à deux*, when Lee called from Kenneth's salon to say that the hairdresser was hopelessly backed up and to go ahead and serve Truman lunch; she would join him in an hour or so for coffee. At first, Truman was delighted to lunch alone, like a pasha. Then, after the canapé, he said that he felt funny to be waited on this way and asked me to do him the honor of lunching with him—that is, actually joining him at the table after serving the entrée. So I thanked him, placed the fish on the table, removed my apron, and sat down at the place already set for Lee.

Truman poured some Albariño in my glass, refilled his glass, and we toasted.

"So what does she have you doing?" he asked.

"Cooking, which I love," I said.

"And which you are obviously good at," said Truman, indicating the plate before him.

I nodded.

"And light housekeeping," I said. "Usually she manages her own schedule."

"Do you like working for her?"

"I do. Very much."

"Are you comfortable putting her needs first?"

"Very."

"Does she confide in you?"

"I . . . don't know what to say."

"Good girl. If she did, you mustn't admit that to me—at once, anyway. Though perhaps, one day, at last . . ."

"She relies on my discretion, Mr. Capote."

"Of course. On the other hand, there is history to consider. And please call me Truman."

"What do you mean, history?"

"For one thing, some people say that she slept with JFK when she was still married to Canfield. Don't you want to know if that's true?"

"I don't know."

"You don't know if it's true, or you don't know whether or not you want to know?"

"Both."

"Well, my point is that some people do want to know. You must think of history, and also think of what's a good story. Now, what else? Do you do the shopping?"

"For the household, yes, sometimes. And I answer the phone and do triage."

"Very important—who she wants to talk to, who not . . ."

"The other day, Lila North called . . ."

"Oh, *her*."

"I announced the call, but Lee refused. She told me never to put Lila North through, ever."

"Very wise."

"But before she hung up, she asked *me* for information—if she was going to Greece, if she had been to a certain party . . ."

"And you didn't say anything."

"Of course not."

"You'll go far. She's fifth-rate, Lila. I mean, I talk to her sometimes, plant items when it suits me. But Lee has no need of someone like that."

"We changed the phone number. It was private before, but somehow reporters also started calling to ask about Mrs. Kennedy."

"Sad case, Lila North. I speak as a student of human nature, a seasoned observer of life in this crazy city. She's been writing her newspaper column for decades, but she's hardly the influential figure that she pretends to be. She has no other interests in life than appearing in print three times a week. I'm told that she shares an intern with a cultural stringer. She gets most of her so-called information from press releases. For a reputable newspaper, that's low in the pecking order. She's not married, has no friends, never goes out . . ."

"Sounds like she could be a character of yours."

"Well, she could be, couldn't she?"

"Only you'd make her more gothic."

"Hmm. So you've read some of my stuff?"

"All of it. I love it."

"*Other Rooms?*"

"Sure. Lee let me borrow her copy."

"You call her 'Lee'?"

"She asked me to. She said she prefers it from, you know, staff."

"Staff!"

"Well, that's what I am."

"As I said the last time, you seem . . . different."

"Though I have wondered whether the same first-name rule applies at the house in Buckingham Place. I imagine that things work differently in London because of class. And history."

"Ha—they certainly do! 'Servants' is what they have there. And it's even worse in Paris."

"Ah, but the French—they take their intellectuals more seriously."

"My thoughts exactly."

It was then that Truman, apparently intrigued, pressed a second glass of wine on me and asked to hear more. So after telling me about servants in the South, where he grew up in the care of his beloved Sook, he listened to a tale about a girl from a high-ranking Cuban family whose estate had been given them in 1830 by the King of Spain; about the girl's schooling in Switzerland, at Le Rosey, and the news she received from her father when the revolution broke out; about her confused and then bitter adjustment to a life with no school, no money, no clothes, no skiing in Cortina, no snorkeling in the Maldives, and no way of returning to her homeland; a tale about a mother who stayed behind, because it was her ancestor to whom the King had deeded the land, and a father who'd promptly died in Miami of a heart attack. It was a tale about a privileged girl with no more privilege but still in possession of her pride, who came to New York and gladly took a position on the staff of a classmate's prominent family and then another staff position and then another—because the girl had decided to forgo the sad cliché of the impoverished refugee aristocrat that was being peddled by so many of her former friends. A tale, in sum, about a girl who decided to be silent about her past and get on with the present.

"I feel it's important to reinvent yourself such as circumstances allow," I said.

"A true mark of aristocracy," said Truman. "Lee has that, too."

Since lunch was finished, I rose and began to clear. Truman thanked me for my company, and I told him I was grateful for the invitation.

"My stepfather was Cuban," he said. "Capote is a Cuban name. He was a rat, but of course, any culture has its share of *ratones*, doesn't it?"

"I suppose so."

I was in the passageway to the kitchen when I heard his next question.

"Your school is not very far from my place in Switzerland—well, the other side of the lake," he said. "Do you know Verbier . . . ?"

For a split second, I didn't know what to say. Then I put the things down and came back to the door.

"I miss the Alps," I said. "But I've been meaning to ask, before I start the coffee and Lee takes you away, what you are reading, what books you admire, what movies you admire . . . ?"

The conversation continued as I'd hoped.

"Oh, I'll tell you about a movie I love," said Truman, "that's based on a book that's only so-so: *Laura*. Do you know it? Gene Tierney?"

"I think so."

"Sort of a murder mystery, very chic. It was just on TV. It comes up now and then. Watch for it."

"I will."

"I want to do a new version of it and have Lee play the lead."

"Lee?"

"Reinvented as an actress."

"I didn't know she could act."

"I'm sure she can," said Truman. "She's a star, after all."

Chapter 6

Blind Items

"How was India?"

"Exhausting, but marvelous."

"I saw pictures of you two riding an elephant."

"Oh, yes. We saw everything there was to see, and then some."

The following June, Lee and Truman were about to converge in New York for a few days, so they were catching up by phone and making plans—Truman from Verbier, Lee from Cannes, where she was recovering from her busy week in India, on Jackie's "semi-official" visit there.

"Where did you stay?"

"That's the wonderful thing! After the first night at the embassy, we were Nehru's guests at his residence, a rather grand place called the Teen Murti Bhavan, which used to be the residence of the head of the British Indian Army."

"Is that the complex designed by Lutyens?"

"No, no—you're thinking of the capitol. But there were ceremonies at the capitol, an incredible, monstrously huge place—and at the U.S. Chancery, and the Gandhi Memorial, and a new hospital, and a new school. It went on and on. And of course, the Taj Mahal, and the Amber Palace, and the Palace of the Winds, and this perfect, little sixteenth-century Mughal city called Fatehpur Sikri."

"Lord!"

"I'm glued to a *chaise* by the pool right now."

"What is Nehru like?"

"Intelligent. Committed. Intriguing. Sensual."

"Sensual!"

"You know what I mean. He has a very soothing voice. And the crowds, Truman! Millions of people who wanted to see Jackie, absolutely everywhere. She's idolized."

"Did you feel eclipsed?"

"Ha. There were plenty of times when I knew enough to stay out of the way—the protocol people were ever so gentle with me—and then I'd be mobbed by reporters who wanted any shred of information about what Jackie ate for breakfast, what Jackie bought in Benares . . ."

"And you said nothing."

"I said nothing."

"Air Force One?"

"Oh, yes, of course. *Tout les conforts moderne.*"

They spoke about what peripatetic lives they led. After New York, for Lee it would be off to Mexico, where she was meeting up with Jackie again, this time with the president, for a state visit there; and for Truman, it would be off to Cap d'Antibes, where he was meeting up with some young, rich Russians he'd written about in an article, a few years before.

"Do you ever get tired of flying?" he asked Lee. "I don't mean tired of traveling, because you wind up in interesting places, and that's fine. But I mean the act of traveling itself—getting to the airport, getting on the plane, and then spending three hours or ten hours cooped up in a cramped seat, even in first class, breathing someone else's air."

"Oh, no," said Lee. "I always find it thrilling, I always look forward to it. Of course, we are lucky enough to not wait in the terminals with everyone else. There are VIP waiting rooms—*you* know—and we do often travel first class or in someone's plane, and there are cars waiting for us when we land. And for me, being suspended in the air, miles above the earth, captive only to rest and to contemplation, is a dream."

"I wish I shared that. Maybe I could learn it."

"But, Truman, here's what I do wonder about, sometimes: When we go here and there, there's always some good reason—

seeing friends, seeing great museums or legendary sights, resting, relaxing. But why do we do anything? What are we here for, ultimately? This is what I think about sometimes, when I'm thirty thousand feet above the planet and the cabin is flooded with that incredible light."

"Wow, that is a big question, sister."

"I know."

"I may be a writer, and it may be my job to think about such things, but I have no answer—yet, anyway. Though I feel I may be getting closer to at least understanding the question."

"Are you?"

"I sometimes ask the same question, in my world: why write anything? But it also occurs to me when I'm on the Guinnesses' yacht, having dinner on deck, and a great orange sun is going down over the Aegean."

"Good. So it's not all about ten hours in a cramped seat."

"Ha! Well, either way, it's an essential and quite terrifying question, if you ask me. And while the artist in me wants to wrestle with it, I must admit that the rest of me wants to just leave it alone."

"There's more to you than the artist, Truman?"

"Oh, yes," he said. "Much more. Part of me would be perfectly happy running a hardware store in Monroeville, Alabama, making sure we had enough round head nails in stock."

"That's a funny thought. Wouldn't the hardware store manager miss the Aegean?"

"Maybe, maybe not. But if you ever saw the Claiborne Reservoir, down the road a piece, you'd know that Alabama has its own special charms."

"See you in a week, Truman."

"Don't Repeat This" —by Lila North
Wednesday, June 13, 1962

. . . Ready for some controversy? The new film of that scandalous best seller *Lolita* opens tonight at Loew's State Theater—the tale of a 12-year-old girl who's seduced by a creepy middle-aged professor. After all the pressure on director Stanley Kubrick from the Hayes Code people and the Catholic Legion of Decency, it will be interesting to see how much of the steamy story made it to the screen. Slated to attend the premiere are stars Shelley Winters, James Mason, and newcomer Sue Lyon, and a host of other celebrities including Joan Fontaine, Hugh O'Brien, and Red Buttons. • What married jet-set lady was seen once again drinking bubbly with that married shipping magnate, this time in Paris? These two get around . . .

A week later, in New York, Lee caught Lila North's column and saw the blind item about her and Ari. Suddenly she panicked, wondering if photographs of the two of them might exist.

"Why does she even care about me?" asked Lee.

"Come on," said Truman, "you're news. Ari's news. Your life is public."

"Not all of it."

"Lord knows, you're not unhappy when publicity works *for* you."

"Can you do anything?"

"What's going on with you two, anyway? Should I be worried?"

"Oh, Truman, he's rich and owns the world. He's everybody's friend. Can you do anything?"

"With Miss North? Little ol' me?"

"You know her. Can you put her off the story?"

"I have *dealt with* her, but I don't know that I butter any hay with her. Besides, I don't want to owe her anything."

"Please, Truman."

"Let me see what I can do."

"Thank you."

"See you tonight for the movie?"

"Pick me up at 6:30."

Truman's next call was to Lila, whom he tried to bargain with.

"I'm calling as a friend, Lila, asking a favor for another friend," said Truman.

"One writer to another?" said Lila, not without a hint of irony.

"If you like. There's nothing to this story about Lee Radziwill and a Greek tycoon. I have it on good authority. You'll only look like a fool if you keep writing about it."

"I also have what I have on good authority."

"You don't and you couldn't, but that's not the important thing. The important thing is that an innocent party suffers when this kind of innuendo is thrown around."

"Call it what you like, Truman . . ."

"Look, Lila, lay off Lee Radziwill. In exchange, I promise to supply you with some juicy item about someone else."

"Let me think about it."

"Think about it."

"Before I let you go," said Lila, "is it true that you've been spending time in Palm Beach with Babe and Bill Paley?"

"Of course it is," said Truman. "That's hardly news. They're dear friends."

"Do you have a crush on Bill Paley?"

"Oh, Lila . . . ! Even if I did, I'd never tell you, and you could never print it."

"Couldn't I? I could blind it."

"What can I say? Bill likes me. All the husbands like me. I'm clever, I'm famous, and I'm as harmless as a baby. Anyway, Bill's not my type. He's a little too captain-of-industry for me. That last part is off the record, by the way. Though you can use the bit about husbands liking me."

Sue Lyon was fourteen when she was cast as twelve-year-old Lolita. Nabokov had said she looked like "the perfect nymphet," but the movie, to avoid negative public opinion, made her look several years older than twelve, and at the New York premiere, Lyon appeared very grown-up indeed, in a satin gown and a regal dome of blond hair, as befitting a freshly minted Hollywood star. At the reception afterwards, in the ballroom of the recently renovated grand old theater, all the talk was about how strong the performances were. Lee said she liked one line in particular, delivered by Shelley Winters as Lolita's mother Charlotte, when she is lying on a bed with James Mason's Humbert: "Hum baby, you know I love the way you smell. You do arouse the pagan in me. You just touch me and I go as limp as a noodle. It scares me." And Humbert responds, "Yes, I know the feeling."

"'You arouse the pagan in me'—isn't that immortal?" said Lee.

Truman marveled that Nabokov, who wrote the novel, wrote the screenplay, too.

"Maybe I should have written *Breakfast*," he said.

"Didn't you?" said Lee.

"George Axelrod. You know the phrase, 'loosely based on' . . . ?"

"Still, it's making you a lot of money."

"I like Nabokov's approach," continued Truman. "He shows us passion through the eyes of a criminal. Always the scientist, you know."

"He collects butterflies, doesn't he?"

"He *studies* them. He's a proper lepidopterist. He once said that he wants to explore 'not the genus or the species, but an aberrant variety.' Isn't that interesting? In a way, I try to do the same thing."

"Doesn't he live near you?"

"He and his wife are north of us, in Montreux. They live in a hotel. Isn't that chic?"

"Do you know them?"

"Not really, but I suppose I should invent some tale to tell at parties, about bumping into him at the local *pharmacie* when he's shopping for suppositories."

The ballroom was full of famous faces, all of which, it seemed, were destined to wind up in a photograph with Sue Lyon. Publicists were rushing around, trying to be unobtrusive as they engineered ninety-second meet-and-greets between the film's stars and celebrity guests.

"Everything's had to change, hasn't it—in movies, in books?" mused Truman. "Since Americans don't feel safe anymore, not even in their own houses. They might be attacked with a knife in their own showers. That's why Hitchcock isn't making *Strangers on a Train* anymore, and why Nabokov has gone darker and grittier. Exactly what I am doing with my Kansas murders."

They spotted Gore Vidal, who was there at the reception alone, approaching them.

"Be nice," said Lee.

"I'm always nice," said Truman.

Vidal greeted Lee with a little kiss.

"Looking gorgeous," he said.

"Thank you," said Lee.

"Thank you," said Truman.

"Did you like it?" Vidal asked Lee.

"Shelley Winters is marvelous, isn't she?"

"It's a nasty story."

"I see Nabokov all the time in Switzerland," announced Truman. "I asked him about the film and he told me—in that Russian-accented English of his, because I don't speak French, I won't speak French—he said, 'It is by Kubrick, it is not by Nabokov.' "

"You don't speak French?" said Lee. "How come I never knew that?"

"I speak menu French."

"But living in Verbier . . . ?"

"Jack's French is flawless. He takes care of everything. Last year, I was on a French talk show with a member of the Academie Française, and the man wouldn't address me in English, though in private he was perfectly fluent."

Vidal appeared uninterested in Truman's name-dropping, preferring to issue a statement of his own.

"No one enjoys a Nabokov book as much as Mr. Nabokov does," said Vidal.

When Lee asked how Vidal and Truman met, Vidal told a story he had clearly told often before.

"I first met Truman at Anaïs Nin's apartment," he said. "I wasn't wearing my glasses, and my first impression was that here was a colorful ottoman. When I sat down on it, it said 'I beg your pardon . . .' "

Truman rolled his eyes and exaggeratedly mouthed two silent words: "Not true."

And with that, Vidal glided away.

"Now, you wouldn't call that a conversation, would you?" said Truman.

"You know Gore."

"What was he doing here?"

"Same thing you and I are doing here. It's the hottest thing happening tonight in New York."

Nearby, Sue Lyon was posing for photographs in a pair of red sunglasses with heart-shaped lenses, like the pair she was wearing in the ubiquitous ads for her movie that showed Lolita sucking a lollipop.

"What do you say we say hello to Miss Lyon?" said Truman, setting down his drink. "Wouldn't you like to know how she's handling all this, how she prepared for the role? You'll note that there were neither sunglasses nor lollipops in the movie . . ."

"So we're thinking of Corsica this year, instead of Palamós," Truman was saying, on the sidewalk of West 55th Street, as he opened the restaurant door for Lee. They had been talking again about travel. "Jack's looking into it. We'd love to have you and Stas come to stay, and bring the kids if you like."

A few days after the premiere, Lee and Truman met for a look-in at Gucci and lunch at La Côte Basque. I must have heard bits of the story of this lunch several times from each of them. They seemed to remember it awfully well, and I think it meant something important to them because—maybe?—it was the first time they were ever together there as a lone pair, at home in their element, installed at a blue-chip table. And of course, the memory came to mean even more to them later, because the restaurant was the setting of that notorious excerpt of *Answered Prayers*, "La Côte Basque, 1965," that *Esquire* printed in 1975, which changed Truman's life so drastically.

The restaurant had been opened a few years before, by the well-known restaurateur Henri Soulé, as an alternative to his other New York restaurant, Le Pavillon, which was a more drop-dead formal spot where husbands might take their wives or their mistresses for a big evening. La Côte Basque was more a place where women took themselves, for lunch. Most of the swans frequented the place—Babe, Gloria, Slim, C.Z., Marella, Nan—as did other notable women like the Duchess of Windsor, philanthropist Mary Lasker, and First Lady Jackie Kennedy, along with the walkers and "extra men" these ladies liked, like Johnny Galliher and Jerry Zipkin, and the men they wanted to buy things from, like decorator Vincent Fourcade, designer Bill Blass, and costume jewelry maker Kenneth Jay Lane. Meant to be relaxed in a sophisticated way, the restaurant was more than a chic watering hole where you could show off your latest Gucci bag, or Givenchy suit, or Dr. Ivo Pitanguy facelift; it was more than a pit stop between getting your hair done and choosing a hat. At a time when café society was giving way to the jet set, this was ground zero for the ladies who tied their Hermès scarves to the handles of their bags, the way Babe Paley did. Yet seeing and being seen was only the mechanics of the place. Its function was to be *the* font of *the* most important information that a certain species of wealthy New York women wanted to know about their competitors.

As a social novelist, Truman felt he had to be there often—listening, observing, learning. And the merry party would sail on in that manner—a *caravelle*, a *cirque*—until a decade or so later, when ladies who were jet-set-eligible decided to become decorators and real estate agents, and lunchtime conversation might turn as much on contracts as on hemlines.

Lee and Truman arrived around one that day and were greeted warmly by Soulé, who walked them past the bar, with its little red-and-white–striped awning, to one of the best tables in the house: fourth on the left up front, in the passageway leading deep into the interior, which was Siberia. The restaurant was nearly full with people they knew—Truman spotted his friends Carole Matthau and Gloria Vanderbilt; Lee spotted her friend John Mack Carter, editor of *McCall's*, with designer André Courrèges—quietly chattering away amidst the rustic, faux-timber–framed décor, surrounded by murals of Basque-country harbors.

Ordering was simple business—a crabmeat salad for Lee and an omelet for Truman. So was the choice of champagne, Cristal. I would say more about the food and service at La Côte Basque, but the truth is I don't know more, except for what I read. Truman never told me much about it because, I gather, the sensory experience of the place—the smell of roasting beef and of steaming lobster, the bracingly salty bite of the Malassol caviar (a $24 surcharge on a $15.75 prix fixe lunch)—mattered less to him than the people who were eating the food. Lord knows that details of smell and taste figure hardly at all into the incendiary story he set in the restaurant. Though he did once note that Henri Soulé had to learn that his American customers expected to smell food cooking when they entered a restaurant, unlike the customers in the French restaurants where he'd trained, who expected to smell nothing. Apparently, this lesson had led to an expensive redoing of the heating, cooling, and ventilation systems at both Le Pavillon and La Côte Basque.

"I didn't know she was in town," said Lee, after waving to a mannish marchioness she knew from London.

"Diamonds at lunch?" said Truman, referring to a massive brooch the lady was wearing. "Indomitable."

"Very rich."

"Same thing."

"I remember an event at the Guggenheim, a cocktail thing," said Lee, "and there was a white-haired lady—a board member, I was told—in a tweed suit with thick wool stockings and sturdy shoes, like she was ready to go out stalking, and she was wearing what must have been every piece of diamond jewelry she owned: two brooches, a rather elaborate necklace, earrings, and a bracelet on each wrist."

"You can dress tweed up or down," said Truman.

"At six in the afternoon! It was marvelous!"

"If I had diamonds like that, I'd wear them to the grocery store."

"Truman, when was the last time you were in a grocery store?"

"Don't be ridiculous. There's a perfectly nice little mom-and-pop store on Henry Street in Brooklyn Heights where I go all the time."

"For cigarettes—not for food."

"That's a technicality."

Their lunchtime chatter was all about the latest plays, movies, and books. Various friends stopped by the table to say hello or goodbye. Then, over coffee—though they continued drinking champagne, too—they spoke of men and love and life.

"I've been thinking about what we were discussing the other day—the purpose of life," said Lee.

"Is that the way you remember we phrased it?" said Truman.

"There's at least one thing that keeps me going."

"Don't say motherhood."

"I wasn't going to."

"I'm sorry. Then what?"

"Wanting to try new things—things I might be good at. Maybe the artist in me! You said it's only one part of you. Maybe it's one part of me, too—or part of all of us, and it needs to be cultivated."

"But you're an active self-cultivator."

"I should be doing more. Jackie has her drawing and painting; even her role as first lady is an interesting, absorbing job that means something. I think I need something like that."

"Stas can't run for president, can he? What about prime minister?"

"Be serious. It's not about Stas, anyway. It's about me—what I can do or be, myself. I should be doing more with my photography. I've written articles—maybe I should try a book."

"Maybe."

"Help me."

"Maybe you could act."

Lee thought about this for a moment.

"Stas doesn't understand me," she said. "I thought that he did, but he doesn't—not really. I think I understand him, but what good is that?"

"Let's have another bottle," said Truman. "Do you have the time?"

Lee agreed, the Cristal arrived, and they lingered at the table, talking, while the crowd in the restaurant thinned out.

"You know so much," said Lee. "You know who you are. So all your effort can be spent being you. I have to spend time discovering who I am and then be it. I sometimes feel three years old."

"Thank goodness!" said Truman. "I thought you were ready to die or something."

"I go back and forth."

"Life is discovery—for all of us, isn't it?"

"Some people know just who they are and where they belong. Look at Marlene."

"What about her?"

"She doesn't have to wonder who she is or what she is going to become. She is already there."

"Who knows," said Truman. "I'm sure that she has to make up her story every day, like the rest of us—or retell it to herself. You know what I mean. Who was it who said, 'We tell ourselves stories in order to live'?"

"That's great."

"I think it was Joan Didion who told me something like that once, at a party in Malibu. Do you know Joan?"

"I don't."

"We are nothing but story factories—and it hardly matters whether the stories are fiction or nonfiction, or something in-between. I'm a big fan of in-between, as you well know. It's hard work, all this storytelling, making yourself up, but then there is the reward of having that to fall back on."

"You must be right."

"Stories last, princess. Things don't. Stories about this restaurant will undoubtedly last longer than the restaurant itself."

Monsieur Soulé passed the table several times as lunch service was quietly winding down, but he remained conspicuously gracious about making sure his lingering guests didn't feel rushed.

Lee asked Truman how "the new thing" was coming along.

"Fine," he said, and eagerly dove into greater detail about the nonfiction novel form he was using—a natural extension, he said, of the realism that Flaubert and others pioneered in fiction. Talking about these things, especially when under the influence of wine or liquor, Truman would always sound so professorial.

"I propose a narrative form that uses all the techniques of fiction but is nevertheless immaculately factual," he said. "And I am not talking about a documentary novel, or a historical novel. The difficulty is to choose the right subject—something that's both huge and obscure, like the murder of a family of four in a dreary little town. If you are going to spend three or four years of your life writing a book, you want to be reasonably sure that the material won't date, as it can in journalism."

"Fascinating," said Lee. "To hear the way you think about your work."

"And I hope to do the same thing for *Answered Prayers*—something almost realer than real life."

Lee asked about Truman's method of research.

"Do you interview? Do you tape?"

"I like to talk to people face-to-face," said Truman. "I don't tape. That's an entirely different experience. You might get truth that way, but not reality. Long ago I trained myself to transcribe conversations without a tape recorder. I did it by having a friend read passages from a book, and then later I'd write them down to see how close I came to the original. Turns out, I was a natural for it. After practicing for a year or two, I found I was close to absolute accuracy."

"Really?"

"Well, close enough."

"Fascinating."

"It is really a blessing to be able to work this way. Not long ago, a French critic interviewed me using a tape recorder, and in the middle of our talk, the thing broke down. The man was thrown for a loop, didn't know what to do, so I suggested we simply go on talking. 'No, no,' he said. 'It is so difficult to listen and remember at the same time.' "

"He halted the interview?"

"I had to give him pen and paper, and then it was no longer a conversation, but something . . . secretarial."

Truman described listening carefully to what accused murderer Perry Smith was telling him about his life, his crime, his relationship with the other murderer, Richard Hickock—and how Truman relived all that a second time, later, in his hotel room, when he wrote it all down.

"I had no idea your work was so laborious or so scrupulous," said Lee. "When it's also so poetic and soulful."

Truman smiled.

"I try," he said.

It was Truman the thinker that Lee was seeing that day, she told me—the Truman she respected, the Truman she wished more of her friends could understand, not simply the celebrity or the flamboyant homosexual. She used to worry in those days, too, that the media didn't see this side of Truman often enough.

"I was looking for the right subject matter for years before I found it," said Truman.

"Why murder?" asked Lee.

"Because it's exactly who we are. It's so human. And when true crime meets high society . . . !"

Truman silently mimed an explosion and the word *boom*.

"Can this form be applied to situations that are not crimes?" said Lee. "Crimes are so dark."

"All life is dark," said Truman. "*Dunkel is das leben, ist der tod*, princess. Li Po, the Chinese poet, via Mahler."

"So it can apply to life in general—*our* lives, for instance? This restaurant?"

Truman chuckled. "We'll see."

Outside, on the sidewalk, they were going in different directions, so Truman helped Lee find a taxi.

"Remember—Corsica," he said. "July, August, early September—somewhere in there . . ."

"Have you ever been there?"

"Nope. I have no idea what to expect. You?"

"Never."

"Jack's handling it. I suppose we'll find out."

CHAPTER 7

NO WAR IN HAVANA

I was now part of Lee's life, and that restored a sense of security to me that had been ripped away by past events. I had known that my position with Mrs. Hawkins was never going to last very long, because of the dear lady's age; and now, with Lee, if her needs remained the same, I felt I had a bit of a future, in a protected environment, surrounded by nice things but without the need to acquire and worry about them. Yes, I took care of Lee's things, but that was a comfort, really, because they belonged to someone else.

Truman once asked if I liked sweeping floors. I actually did very little sweeping for Lee. Occasional vacuuming, yes; we had two lovely women named Millie and Barb come in twice a week for the regular tasks. I made the beds; saw to the laundry, dry cleaning, and repairs; handled everything concerning the kitchen, and dining and entertaining. The household was quite well-organized when I got there, and I found that something soothing to fit into, rather than arduous.

Lee was so organized that she kept detailed notes on all her entertaining, in a series of wonderful Venetian notebooks with leather and marbleized blue paper bindings. Lee always kept the current volume with her, whether she were in London or New York or Turville Grange, or later, Paris. She saw many of the same people in all of these places and didn't want anyone to be bored by the experience of rote hospitality.

Here are some typical notes for a lunch she gave that year,

in London, before coming over to New York that June, from a notebook labeled 1962.

Lunch:	*Tues April 17—cool, dry*
Place:	*Buck Pl/garden room*
Guests:	*Margot and Rudy*
	Gloria and Truman
	L & S
Menu:	*Serrano-wrapped pears*
	Peruvian seviche
	Mixed green salad, crackers, cheeses
	"Watermelon" slices
Wine:	*Puligny-Montrachet Pucelles '55*
China:	*Ridgway*
Silver:	*Mixed*
Glass:	*Ruby Murano*
Flowers:	*Pink peonies*
Cloth:	*Orange Indian stripe*
Center:	*Brass censers*
Dress:	*Ochre Saint Laurent ('62)*
Jewelry:	*Hermès bangle (geometric)*

"L&S" were Lee and Stas, of course; "Margot and Rudy" were the ballet stars Margot Fonteyn and Rudolf Nureyev, who were great friends of Lee's. Nureyev had defected from the Soviet Union only the year before, and already he and Fonteyn were peerless as lovers onstage, as Giselle and Prince Albrecht, though he was then in his early twenties and she in her early forties. And "Gloria" was Gloria Guinness, who was in London for an estate auction, in pursuit of a set of eight Louis XVI chairs. The year before was also when Saint Laurent established his own fashion house, and Lee was among the first to start buying there. Funny, but I don't think she ever wore that ochre dress on this side of the Atlantic.

I asked Lee about serving watermelon slices for dessert. It

seemed like such a plain choice, in view of the fact that she would often ask me to prepare something more festive, like a small bombe glacée, for a luncheon dessert. She laughed and said the watermelon was practically the same thing. She'd gotten the idea from Jayne Wrightsman, who'd once served her a slice of watermelon sorbet with molded chocolate "seeds," edged with a band of cake that looked like a watermelon rind. I was thrilled when I was able to make this myself for Lee's lunches.

Truman, as usual, had an explanation for the watermelon dessert, which he shared once after I'd served it to him in New York and he later found me in the kitchen, to ask for some water.

"Rich people like being fooled in these little ways," he said. "That's why you see these baby bundles of caviar tied up in mini-crepes and called 'beggar's purses.' "

There was also a housekeeper's log in which I noted daily, weekly, bi-weekly, monthly, and seasonal tasks. Instructions for these tasks had all been specified in great detail long before, by a London housekeeper that Stas and his first wife had inherited from a minor royal. The instructions, Lee said, were the same that were followed for the household and royal collections of Buckingham Palace; and I found that all of them made great sense—starting with a simple walk-through of the premises every morning, to note any signs of damage, pests, mold, or other irregularities. Millie and Barb vacuumed the carpets and floors, and dusted and/or fluffed most of the basic furniture, in addition to cleaning the bathrooms and the kitchen, where the instructions specified "touch everything"—everything except for the artwork and objects, that is, and the more fragile antique furniture, which were all my responsibility. Indeed, all the apartment's artwork, precious objects, and books were mine, so like a curator, I inspected for minuscule signs of wear or damage whenever I cleaned or dusted anything—usually with a soft, extremely fine brush, or an extremely soft, damp cloth, or sometimes even a single, slightly moistened cotton swab: porcelain vases, gilded picture frames, inlaid boxes, and books, books, books. Needless to say, in an apartment so full of European antiques, I came to memorize every decorative scroll, flute, scallop, wreath, shield, cartouche, egg, and dart in the house.

Lee herself showed me how delicately the surface of an oil painting should be brushed, after inspecting carefully to confirm that the surface was still stable. She learned this from the minor royal housekeeper, whose notes, cribbed from an American museum, revealed that dust was a special enemy of hers: "Dust is inherently damaging as well as unsightly. It is abrasive, absorbs moisture and pollutants that can cause deterioration and corrosion, attracts insects, and encourages mold growth." Thus I oversaw the frequent replacement of the air filters of Lee's HVAC system, which reduced our exposure to the dangerous substance. Anyway, Truman said, rich people insisted on the best air.

Corsica did not work out for Truman and Jack, though the Agnellis, no less, thought well enough of the place to maintain a home there. Apparently, on his first day on the island, Truman decided that the tourists were animals and the Corsicans "combined the worse aspects of the wops and the frogs." Instantly, it was back to Palamós for him and Jack, where they found "an even better house than before"—after which Lee came for a visit, then the Paleys, and then Gloria Vanderbilt, who arrived not with the man she'd begun seeing, Wyatt Cooper, but with her friend, actress Tammy Grimes.

"Don't Repeat This" —by Lila North
Wednesday, June 20, 1962

. . . Liz and Dick just won't stop! Since meeting on the set of *Cleopatra* in Rome, the two stars have been inseparable, despite both being married—Taylor to her fourth husband, Eddie Fisher, whom she "stole" from Debbie Reynolds. That picture of Antony and Cleopatra relaxing on a speedboat in Ischia has been published everywhere! • We hear that fashion designer Yves Saint Laurent is taking a few days to relax in Marrakech, in the wake of his triumphant first runway show in Paris after leaving Dior. Among his clients are French movie star Catherine Deneuve, Hollywood legend Lauren Bacall, and socialite Lee Radziwill. • What heiress just showed up at Truman Capote's getaway place in Spain not with her third husband, a prominent director, producer, and screenwriter, but with a gal friend who happens to be a Broadway star . . . ?

Truman may have loathed Lila North, but he was as proud as a schoolboy with a gold star whenever he appeared in anyone's column. He drew my attention to his name being dropped in Lila's recent column when he showed up at Lee's apartment late one morning when Lee was out of town, to return a book.

"I thought she was going to stop mentioning Lee," I said.

"She agreed to stop talking about the affairs and rumored affairs," said Truman, "but you can't keep her from writing about fashion. Besides, that's good for Lee. The point is, she quashed a thing she had about Ari Onassis."

"Why did she quash it?"

Truman's Cheshire Cat grin appeared.

"Because I gave her Gloria Vanderbilt and Tammy Grimes," he said. "See how that works?"

"I see."

"She was so pleased, Lila was, though she was obviously too unconnected to know that Gloria is seeing Wyatt Cooper and *that's* the real story. Oh well—that's Lila North: unconnected." Then Truman grew more serious. "I'm afraid, though, that there's a far worse story out there now, and I don't think Miss Princess would be happy if it got out."

"What, may I ask?" By then, I knew several of Lee's secrets, though not the supposed one that Truman was about to tell me.

"That old thing," he said. "That when married to her previous husband, the lady slept with the current husband of her well-known sister."

"Oh."

"According to my source, who shall remain nameless, but whose initials are G.V., it is the lady's first husband himself who is spreading it around."

"I can't believe it."

"Can't you? Our free-spirited Lee? Apparently, it happened in the South of France, in a room next to the one my source was staying in."

"I suppose he had his ear to the wall."

"He may well have," said Truman with a giggle.

"You're so mean." I was half-serious.

"I am not mean," said Truman. "I observe people and listen to what they say, so I can do my job."

"Well, I wouldn't repeat that story even if it were true."

"There is truth and there is truth, my serene highness. If you're a writer, you've got to see it all and then decide which is which."

He'd started calling me "serene highness," a style connected to Lee's title but rarely used. He used it for me—affectionately, I think, and in reference to the idea of fallen nobility—the same way he called Lee "princess," or "Miss Princess," or "princess dear," always with a touch of sarcasm.

Since it was almost lunchtime, I offered to make him a sandwich, and he accepted.

"Join me," he said.

"I can't."

"Sure you can."

We ate in the kitchen, in the sunny, plaid-upholstered nook where Lee often took a little yogurt, fruit, and green tea for breakfast.

Knowing that I was turning into a good audience for his stories, Truman told me about some parties he'd been to in the previous few weeks, then mentioned that his "husband" was in town.

"When I say 'husband,' you know what I mean," said Truman. "Jack is my . . ."

"I understand," I said.

"I know you do. Don't think I don't know worldliness when I see it."

He told me that "that kind of sophistication can't be faked." And he seemed gleeful, even smug, to think that Lee hadn't paid enough attention to this quality in me. *He* was the one who recognized and valued it.

"Jack comes to town for the opera," he said. "He's a big fan of Anna Moffo. He used to be a dancer, you know. His wife was a famous dancer. Tonight he's staying at our place in Brooklyn Heights; then he's going out to Sagaponack. Did I tell you we got a place in Sagaponack? He doesn't accept too many invitations. He can be a little grumpy in social situations. Over the summer, when we stay on the Spanish coast, he usually forgets about manners entirely."

"I see."

"I say 'husband,' but it is turning into something else, which suits me fine. We never lived together, really—except those first few years. In Sagaponack, we have two separate houses on the same property, you see. I suppose you could say that it's like what Lee and Stas have—minus the kiddies."

"Mm-hmm."

"It's about a shared history, of course, and finally . . . stability."

"Everyone formulates a marriage in his or her own way."

"You're not married."

"No."

"Boyfriend?"

"No. Not yet."

"Never?"

"Not really."

"Not interested in men?"

"I'm not a lesbian, if that's what you're asking."

Truman laughed.

"Then not interested in love?" he said.

"I think that's it, yeah," I said.

It's true I had never been in love. I had not even been close to it then, nor have I been since—except for Peter Beard, whom I found extremely attractive from a distance, when Lee was seeing him, and maybe Vincent, this gentleman currently in my writing class in West Palm. When I told Truman that day at lunch that I had "not yet" had a boyfriend, that was as close to the truth as I was willing to get. I may have been attracted to men in some way, but my past experiences with the men in and around my family had not been good, and I was leery of falling for someone only because of a sexual attraction and then winding up, like so many others, in a bad relationship. Now, of course, who knows what I feel about men or love? Certainly not me. Until Vincent came along last year, when I was 77, I was in the habit of not thinking about all that too much. I had been alone for a long time, and that was a habit too nice to give up.

I am still not sure what to make of Vincent. He's nine years younger than I am, a widower with his own financial services company. He might have been handsome when he was younger, and is not unattractive now—though I don't chiefly think of people in terms of their physical attractiveness. He mixes more than I do with the folks of Palm Beach proper, with whom I have never felt quite at home. Vincent's writing shows lots of what Truman called *soul*—honesty, insight, passion—but he seems unsure, as yet, about what to write about, and that's what he and I are working on. As a teacher, I have enjoyed getting to know Vincent through his work, much as Truman and I developed our relationship through the writing work we did together. But just the other day, Vincent asked me after class if we might have a drink at Bradley's sometime. I was surprised. Though my first instinct was "no thanks," I told him that I would think about it. And I keep wondering, what would Truman think of him?

If I were uncomfortable discussing such personal matters with Truman over sandwiches in Lee's breakfast nook, I was also gratified to be getting closer to him. He was charming and magnetic in a nonsexual way—and I finally understood that day that this was an essential part of the relationship he had with his swans, this magnetism. It was a quality beyond all the wit and flamboyance and devilishness combined—a need to be loved, perhaps, plus a facility to use all the tricks at his disposal to earn it.

Perhaps emboldened by this new level of intimacy between us, Truman sprang a question about Cuba on me, and I decided to answer it. *What the hell?* I thought. *Why not go for it and give him more?*

"Truman, I am a child of revolution," I said, "so I'm fragile, emotionally."

"Fair enough," he said.

"My mother is a proud member of an old family whose fortune goes back at least a century and a half. I'm sure I've told you about the King of Spain. There was a plantation, a mill, a sugar business, a hundred-year-old mansion—until the revolution took it all away. My sister had already died of pneumonia by the time of the revolution. You know that my father died soon after relocating in Miami—the stress of his great loss, the doctors said. Many of that generation and class died for the same reason—sometimes they called it "a broken heart"—though of course, all the attention was on the middle-class refugees who came over. My mother is allowed to live in the house until she dies, which is one reason why she stayed behind. It is her family's. She is now in this empty, decaying mausoleum without staff, unable to communicate with anyone outside of Cuba."

"Lord."

"I was always a bit of a rebel with my mother. She had definite ideas about the kind of girl I was supposed to be and the kind of boy I was supposed to want—rich, white, aristocratic, straight. So now, here in New York, I have a lot to sort out. Maybe the revolution was good for me, in some way."

Truman nodded sympathetically. Eagerly, he listened—and, he told me later, made mental notes, as I thought he might!—as I described a thirty-two-room, neoclassical *palacete* in the Miramar district of Havana; a sprawling hacienda in Valle de los Ingenios, the so-called "Valley of the Sugar Mills"; the private, nine-mile train line to the hacienda, built in 1857, from the nearest city, Trinidad; the Escambray Mountains and the teak, mahogany, and flowering *majagua* trees, the lush ferns and eucalyptus . . . I told him of childhood visits to Miami, and Rio, and Paris, and New York; of skiing as a teenager in Gstaad and Portillo. And I cried a little and put up my hand to signal "Stop!

Too much!" when he began asking where I was when I heard the news of the revolution.

"Were you at school?"

I shook my head, without a word—though I instantly realized that I might already have told him that I *was* at school when I heard the news. Anyway, I made it clear I didn't want to continue this thread of the conversation, and got up to serve him a fresh cup of coffee.

Almost as a gesture meant to soothe me, Truman returned to his cozy comments about his partner Jack, whom he was meeting later for dinner.

"He's a writer, too," said Truman, "not just a dancer. When we met, in 1948, he had just published a very well-received novel called *John Fury*. In 1950, we settled in Taormina, Sicily, in a house where D.H. Lawrence once lived."

"I don't believe I've ever seen him here with you at any of Lee's parties," I said.

"Jack likes solitude. He's not such a great guest. I like being around people. I like charming them. He likes offending people."

"And you stick together for stability?" I asked. "Forgive me, but you make it sound unstable."

"Do I? Maybe *loyalty* is a better word."

"Loyalty."

"Loyalty to an idea. Jack gives me some ongoing memory of the quality of love."

Since the subject was personal connections, he couldn't resist telling me about "slumming"—cruising for sex—and I was relieved not to have to say more about Cuba. Slumming was good for the soul, he said. Before the success of *Breakfast at Tiffany's*, he had been picking up guys on the Promenade in Brooklyn Heights, a block from his house. There, in the small hours of almost any night of the year, he said, across the river from the glittering skyline of lower Manhattan, he'd join what he called the "silent pavane" of men of all ages and sexual orientations seeking to connect. Often, it was fun; sometimes, it was love;

now and then, it was violence. One time, a teenager he took home asked him for twenty dollars, and Truman laughed. There were tons of books and lots of artwork in the house, he said—which should have tipped the boy off that the short, effeminate, squeaky guy might have something greater to offer than money.

"Of all the things he could have asked for, that I could have given him," said Truman, "a book, some good advice, an introduction, a custom suit, a secret of the universe . . . he only wanted the twenty dollars. That made me sad for him."

Then Truman stopped picking up young men.

"I simply don't have time for all that now," he said. "The funny thing is, my lust wasn't even for the boys themselves. I think it was more for my own youth, which I feel draining away. Yet one does still want some excitement, some exhilaration . . . always, no?"

I agreed, but told Truman that I had to get back to work. He stood and thanked me for my company, and I thanked him for his.

"You should write up some of your stories," he said. "Revolution is an interesting theme. You're obviously sensitive. I'll bet you have some fascinating family stories to tell."

"Oh, I'm not that creative," I said.

"Everybody is creative, in one way or another. Though perhaps it's true that most people don't use their creativity very well. There are so many unsung geniuses who don't even know what great talent they have."

Thanksgiving seemed notably bright that year, as the month-long Cuban missile crisis was resolved in mid-November when the Russian missiles were removed from the island and President Kennedy lifted the naval blockade he'd put in place. Cold War tensions, while not eliminated, certainly did feel lighter, which fueled the season's festivity as New Yorkers shifted into higher gear with their holiday planning and shopping. I thought it would be nice to get a special gift for Lee, in gratitude for the pleasant year I'd spent working for her—and also to help cheer her up after the unfortunate worldwide publication of a photograph of her with Ari at a party for the opening of the newly built Athens Hilton. It would have been a harmless party picture, except for three things: Lee was married to Ari's friend Stas; Ari was more or less partnered with opera star Maria Callas; and the two of them are seated at a table very close to each other, Ari positively radiating his enjoyment while Lee is looking down at her folded hands, smiling softly as if tickled by a little secret.

I thought I might find something nice in a tiny shop on Lexington Avenue that sold vintage costume jewelry. I'd never been inside but had always been captivated by the densely crowded window displays. I called Judy, and we met in the lobby of her mom's building and walked over.

Lexington is where the Upper East Side finds a lot of its day-to-day goods and services—groceries, cosmetics, kids' shoes, secondhand books, dry cleaning, etc. Retailers, I'm told, say that on Lexington, you sell to Upper East Siders, whereas on Madison, you sell to New Yorkers, and on Fifth, to the world. And when I entered the jewelry shop, it did feel like a place that had served generations of neighborhood women who weren't necessarily rich, but were committed to always looking like a million dollars.

Inside, Judy and I found a garden of cheerfully mismatched glass cases as crammed with beautiful merchandise as the windows were. Yet, far from daunted, I found the sheer profusion of items thrilling, and was suddenly aware of a far greater desire for costume jewelry than I had ever been aware of having before. Impeccably dust-free and in as-new condition, basking under the warm glow of the shop's lighting, were hundreds of bracelets, rings, necklaces, and earrings of faceted gems, cabochons, rhinestones, and crystals; plastic and glass; pearls and beads; chains, links, and silk cords: things for day and for evening; things for town and for the country; things of all periods in all styles from the previous fifty or sixty years—all displayed in no obvious order, neither by period, nor color, nor material; though some special things, probably pricey, were displayed in a vitrine near the cash register.

Standing at the register was a distinguished-looking woman of a certain age, impeccably groomed, her gray hair swept up in a neat chignon.

"Good afternoon," I said.

"Good afternoon," said the lady.

"Beautiful shop."

"Thank you."

She was obviously the proprietor. I couldn't place her accent—was it Czech? Hungarian?

"I've always wanted to come in," I said.

"Please feel free to browse."

"I'm looking for a gift."

The lady stepped out from behind the counter. Dressed in a camel sweater set and low heels, she was wearing only a single piece of jewelry: a thick gold bangle that did not look costume to me.

"Let me know if you are looking for something specific."

"It's for my employer," I said as I started peering more closely into some of the cases.

"I'm just helping," said Judy.

"I understand," said the lady, immediately sizing me up, I knew, as household staff. She undoubtedly knew both me and the woman I worked for—our types, that is. And from Judy's three words, I sensed the lady was sizing her up, too: private-school girl.

"You want something just right," said the lady. Meaning tasteful—fun but not gaudy.

The lady and I chatted lightly about the approaching holidays, as I went from case to case. She didn't hover so much as remain at the ready, in case I asked for help. The shop had a dryly sweet, powdery smell—or was that her perfume?

So many ideas raced through my mind. A '30s deco bracelet in Bakelite? Maybe too common for Lee. A '50s rococo necklace of Venetian glass flowers? Maybe too ornate. A pair of copper and silver-plated clip-on earrings with faux-pearl drops? They were faintly Indian in design, which I thought Lee might like—

but too inexpensive, literally. The earrings cost only ten dollars, and my budget was fifty.

I held up a trio of glass bangles for Judy. She cocked her head and made a sour face.

Then I spotted a lovely brooch from the 1950s that I knew Lee would like, also with a vaguely Indian feeling—a double circle of aurora borealis crystals in a glorious array of blues and purples.

"May I see that?" I said.

"Very nice," said the lady.

She took the pin out and placed it in a little black velvet-lined tray on the counter. It glittered beautifully and did that ineffable thing that jewels of any price can do: usher you into a miniature theater of visual pleasure that somehow spreads to the whole body and spirit, stimulating some primal expectation that human life should be splendid, along with the sadness that we always get less splendor than we deserve.

"It's Gustav Sherman," she said. "Signed. Swarovski crystals. Probably 1955, '56."

"It's beautiful," I said, dazzled by all the glinting facets.

"Fantastic," said Judy.

"Fifty-five dollars," said the lady. "Mmm—for you, forty-five."

I was sold. At the counter, she placed the pin in a small white box, between two cushions of cotton gauze.

"There is something special about good costume jewelry, isn't there?" I said, after I had paid and tucked the box into my purse.

The lady produced a restrained smile. "Yes," she said, "but I prefer to call them 'vintage,' not 'costume.' "

"Oh. Why?"

"To be honest, I dislike that word *costume*. It makes me think of a clown costume, or a theater costume that's been worn by a hundred other actors. Ensembles are the way we should dress, my dear, no? It is so sad to see women today in costumes. I fear the next thing after costumes will be get-ups—and that would be almost as bad for the world as a nuclear war."

"How did we go from Austrian crystal to nuclear war?" I said to Judy after our visit to the shop, once she and I had settled into a booth at Neil's Coffee Shop, nearby, for a spot of lunch.

"My guess is that she is a victim of World War II," said Judy.

"So elegant, though."

"But wounded—didn't you feel that? Probably fled from someplace like Vienna or Budapest. Stepping over the ruins of bombed buildings to get to the station for the last train."

"That's awfully vivid."

"We're shaped by our histories, you know."

Judy well knew my own story.

"I prefer to choose the history that shapes me," I said.

"Rather like the Roman emperors who chose the gods they wanted to be descended from."

"How did you ever get so smart?"

"History 201."

After our burgers, we decided to go crazy and have dessert. We settled for the homemade rice pudding, but we giggled when we realized that what we really wanted was the Peacock Café's Venetian Rum Delight.

Lee soon arrived in town to attend a round of holiday parties before she and Stas met in Washington to spend Christmas at the White House. Then it would be off to Palm Beach with the Kennedys. I gave Lee the pin one evening when she was expecting Truman for a drink before they went off to a party together. She invited me into the library for a holiday toast with demitasse cups of eggnog that she had made herself and seemed very proud of.

"It's lovely," she said, examining the pin, her eyes bright.

"I'm glad you like it," I said.

"Where did you ever find it?"

"A little shop on Lexington."

"It's perfect. You'll have to tell me where."

I was surprised when she said she'd gotten me something. From a drawer of the writing desk, she took a small parcel and placed it in my hands. I undid the black ribbon and opened the tan wrapping to discover a volume of Spanish verse by the Cuban poet José Marti—a first edition of *Versos Sencillos—Simple Verses*—published in Havana in 1939. On the title page, in faded blue ink, was the inscription, *Para mí queridísima Fanny—¡No hay guerra aquí en La Habana!—Fausto, Navidad 1940.*

"Are you a fan?" Lee asked.

"Of course I am," I said.

Tenderly, I leafed through the volume, which was quite simply designed. Its short poems were printed in a sans-serif typeface, the quatrains floating within huge margins that spoke quietly of 1939 modernist chic.

"It's lovely," I said. "Thanks." But I had no further words of response, and Lee respected my reserve.

Truman clucked over the book when he arrived and I served the eggnog—which I realized later, when Truman told me about the evening, was more properly known by another name.

"Ready for the White House?" he asked her. She was leaving for Washington the next day.

"As ready as I'll ever be," she said.

"Where does she put you?"

"In what they're now calling the Queen's Bedroom. Stas is in the Lincoln Bedroom."

"Any word from her about this latest Ari thing? A couple of those rags alluded to the sanctity of the first lady's family and all that."

"I can't be bothered, and neither, I would imagine, can Jackie. We've both got better things to do."

"But you like him. It's not just him liking you."

Lee let out a slow exhale.

"Truman, you get to a point in your life where you're grateful for the attention—and yes, even for the lust—of a powerful man. I mean, the lust is very flattering."

"Of course. I understand. Even beautiful, rich people like to think they're good in the sack."

"And so many rich men aren't."

"Tell me about it, sister. But please tell me you don't use that phrase in public—'so many men.' It sounds wrong coming from a woman of your, shall we say, breeding."

"Ha," said Lee with a smirk.

"The wives are granted leeway for a little fling now and then," said Truman, "as long as it stays discreet and it doesn't endanger decorum, or honor, or the monetary value of the marriage—that is, if there is no danger of divorce."

"Oh, and here's the irony," said Lee. "We just heard from the Vatican that the annulment has been granted."

"That's terrific—congratulations."

"Two years we've been working on this!"

"Then I suppose you'll be getting married again, won't you? To Stas, I mean."

"We're already planning it. For June or July. Probably near Mother. Completely private."

"In a church."

"That's the whole point."

Lee poured more eggnog.

"This is wonderful stuff," said Truman, downing the whole cup in two sips. "Did Marlene make this?"

"I made it. It's called *coquito*. Like eggnog, but more tropical, with coconut milk. Isn't it fun?"

"Is it Cuban?"

"It's Puerto Rican. Jackie and I once spent the holidays in San Juan, when we were teenagers. We were wild for the stuff."

"It does make an evening very merry, doesn't it? You may have gone a little heavy on the rum."

"But they also drink it in Cuba, and I thought maybe Marlene might find it a nice reminder, but she didn't say a thing. Now I'm wondering if it was a faux pas."

Truman poured another cup for both Lee and himself and drank his immediately.

"I wouldn't worry about it," he said. "Hmm. You always think it's going to be heavier than it is. Though maybe we're just getting drunk."

Lee took a sip and was looking very thoughtful.

"But Truman, one thing I don't understand," she said. "Every newspaper in the world published that picture. Even *Newsday*. But your good friend Lila North didn't so much as mention it. I found that odd. Nice, but odd."

"Well, I took care of it."

"How?"

"She called me, and I gave her something nasty about Gore in exchange for her silence."

"What?"

"I said that he was secretly married to Lillian Hellman. And that Lillian was secretly a man."

"Is she?"

"Which one?"

Lee shook her head. "You fibbed," she said.

Truman giggled. "She's undoubtedly chewing on it right now," he said, "making a fool of herself by discreetly poking around to see who can confirm it."

"You're a terror," said Lee.

"Surely a holy terror, if one at all," said Truman.

"Tell me, Truman. Do you think love is very important? Could you live without it?"

"Uh-oh. So there *is* trouble in paradise."

"Seriously, Truman."

"Well, *I* could live without love, yes, but I think it would feel rather empty."

"Is sex very important to you?"

"I've never been without it, so I'm not exactly sure."

"Do you think that sex motivates people a lot?"

"What is this, anyway?"

"I'm curious. You're a great observer of human nature."

"Yes, I certainly do think sex motivates people. Don't you? Look at what's happening in the world! Revolution, social change. That's all caused by sex—or the lack of it. And its effects are as unstoppable as the glaciers melting at the end of the Ice Age. Whole cities are being drowned. New ones are being founded on higher ground. I think most people are very, very much motivated by sex—and also by greed and power, and by hunger and the cold."

"And money."

"Yes, but that's greed."

"Oh, right."

Lee had indeed put lots of rum in the eggnog, and it was getting to both of them.

"So how was Onassis?"

"Very solicitous."

"I mean later, upstairs in the Olympic Suite at the Athens Hilton."

"Truman, stop. Let's get out of here and go have some real fun."

Chapter 8

White Lies and Little Secrets

Lee always said that London cleaned up only in the 1980s. The city had been bombed horrifically during World War II, and Britain was drained financially, so griminess persisted until well into the postwar era, even as new construction began, making London's buildings and streets much dirtier and grungier in those days than those of un-bombed Paris and New York. Always clean and polished, however, was the affluent, private side of London that was Lee's primary turf, like the venerable Savoy Hotel, where she and Truman met for lunch one day the following March.

The weather was mild but unsettled, with patches of rain. The hotel's courtyard was busier than usual that day, with cars on slick pavement and people rushing about with umbrellas. All the bustle gave way to stately calm, though, as Lee and Truman stepped through the door to the Savoy Grill.

"Good afternoon, Princess Radziwill," said the maître d'. "Your table is ready."

"What's all the fuss about, Robert?" said Lee, as she and Truman followed the man through the wood-paneled and mirrored room.

"Another press conference, madam. For a film."

"Oh, which?"

"I'm afraid I don't know, madam. May I find out for you?"

"Oh, no. Please don't bother."

They were shown not to one of the window tables, which

were popular with people wanting to watch the comings and goings of the hotel courtyard, but to one of the more secluded tables toward the bar and side entrance, which were more the territory of power types—stars, moguls, royalty. Lee knew exactly which table Robert would have reserved for her, the one where she often sat when she was at the Savoy—Ari's table, the best in the house.

"We're expecting Dame Ninette and Mr. Beaton, Robert," said Lee.

"Very good, madam."

Ari was currently sailing—probably with Callas, Lee had told Truman.

"And yet the maître d' still puts you here?"

"He asked my housekeeper if the usual table was wanted," said Lee.

"And she knew that it was, and that he was out of town?"

Lee nodded and lit a cigarette.

"She knows everything," she said.

They'd come from Buckingham Place, where Lee gave Truman some coffee and showed him her latest acquisition, a Napoleon III writing table that her decorator Mongiardino had found for her. Truman had come over specially to see it from Verbier, where he was working constantly on *In Cold Blood*—a jaunt that was not unusual for him or for that whole crowd, really, since everybody was constantly in motion, darting about the globe, and the acquisition of a friend's new treasure made a perfectly good reason to spend a day or a week in another country. When Babe Paley gave her dinner party for the blooming of an amaryllis, after all, half of the guests had flown for hours to be present.

"I never liked learning so much as when Renzo is explaining something to me, like a cut-velvet writing surface," said Lee, "or showing me how he likes to mix periods. He always seems to know not just *what* I like, but what I *might* like—and he pushes me in that direction. Then I do some studies and really discover something."

"Imagine that—studying velvet."

"I mean discovering something about the world, Truman. And who I am *in* the world—at least in *my* world."

"What is he, a decorator or a psychiatrist?" said Truman.

Lee spotted their lunch companions being greeted by the maître d'.

"Oh, here they are," she said.

Joining them were Royal Ballet director and former ballerina Dame Ninette de Valois—born Edris Stannus in Ireland, at the end of the previous century—and Truman's old friend Cecil. Everybody knew everybody, so greetings were speedy and all were settled in a moment.

"Any luck with Romeo?" asked Lee of Dame Ninette. Lee and Stas served on the board of the Royal Ballet, and had agreed to help support a new production that Dame Ninette wanted to create for Nureyev and Fonteyn. The Ballet director had been talking for some time with choreographer Kenneth MacMillan about a new *Romeo and Juliet*, but Nureyev had also indicated that he was interested in choreographing the story.

"Afraid not," said Dame Ninette. "Kenneth is longing to do it, though Rudy has some wonderful ideas. You know—Russian storytelling."

"And the Ballet doesn't want a new *Romeo and Juliet* from Rudy?"

"Well, we can't," said Dame Ninette, "since we're already talking with Kenneth."

"I see."

"Besides, we want something that Rudy and Margot can do together, and Kenneth is not keen on Margot as Juliet."

"Ah."

"But Rudy does want to do our *Beauty*, and I must admit that he and Margot would be lovely in that. And it certainly would fill the house."

"He's absolutely marvelous."

Dame Ninette took a sip of water.

"We don't know how much longer Margot will be able to do these things," she said wistfully. "But we're boring the boys."

Truman and Cecil were clucking away about progress on

what Cecil referred to as *My Fair Laundress* and about the shoot he was doing on the movie for the December issue of *Vogue*. Lee and Dame Ninette listened, too, as Cecil spoke.

"The only thing is," he said, "that it's Audrey who's looking at us in costume, from underneath those enormous hats, not Shaw's latter-day Galatea, if you see what I mean. It's *Audrey* that *Vogue* wants, *Audrey* that Miss Hepburn wants."

"But not what Cecily wants," purred Truman.

Cecil made a face.

"I want a face that could launch a thousand ships," he said, "not one that's selling cold cream."

"Now you're mixing your myths," said Truman.

"You'll make it work," said Dame Ninette. "You always do. Did you know, children, that Cecil and I draped this entire hotel in swags and banners for the Coronation?"

Lee and Truman both seemed pleasantly astonished.

"Yes, my dears, it's true," said Cecil. "Well, maybe not the *whole* hotel . . ."

"It was the public rooms—all done up like a stage set," said Dame Ninette, with an elegant hand gesture that seemed to say *Behold!* "The Savoy gave a ball, you see. All the best hotels did. We made the restaurant into a domed tent with four thousand yards of fabric—pink and gray and turquoise."

"Nearly five thousand, Eddy dear," said Cecil.

"The theme was 'A New Elizabethan Era,'" said Dame Ninette.

"Someone had to do something fun, after the war," said Cecil.

"My sister was in town for the Coronation," said Lee.

"Really?" said Truman. "Did she attend?"

Lee giggled. "Hardly," she said. "This was just before she married Jack—one of her last assignments for the *Times Herald* as the Inquiring Camera Girl. She was part of the press corps. Can you imagine? Outside Buckingham Palace, asking people, 'Do you think Elizabeth will be England's last queen?'"

"How rude," said Cecil.

"Nonsense," said Truman. "It sounds like incisive journalism to me."

Lunch was light—salads, omelets, a bottle of Sancerre. Talk centered on the differences between lunch at a posh London eatery and one in New York.

"It's a little more ceremonial here—like tea," said Truman.

"Despite the décor," said Cecil, with a glance up at the dated Edwardian chic of the Savoy Grill's walls and ceiling. "One was glad to have covered it all up."

Truman spotted several notables in the Grill with them—a newspaper publisher, a television news presenter, a member of Parliament, a recording industry executive with a popular, young, boy-girl vocal duo sporting matching skinny suits and matching pageboy haircuts. Then an old friend of Cecil's, the film director Anthony Asquith, stopped at the table to say hello, in the glamorous company of the two biggest movie stars then on the planet, Richard Burton and Elizabeth Taylor.

"Forgive me," said Asquith, graciously. "How are you, Cecil?"

"Tony, delighted," said Cecil, standing. "Elizabeth, you look wonderful. Richard."

Cecil introduced everyone. Truman, who knew Taylor and Burton from Hollywood, rose and gave Elizabeth a little kiss. Both stars greeted Lee and Dame Ninette with quiet respect.

"Elizabeth and Richard just did a bang-up job in the ballroom, telling the press about our new film," said Anthony, who, like Cecil, was in his early sixties and retained more than a shadow of a youthful, poetic male beauty.

"So that's what all the fuss was about," said Truman.

"Not *Cleopatra*?" said Cecil.

"*The V.I.P.s*," said Taylor. "Very modern, very chic."

"That was fast," said Truman.

"It's Rattigan, you know," said Burton.

"Lots of Givenchy," said Taylor, with a wink toward Cecil. "And I get to wear some of the baubles Richard bought for me last year in Rome." She waggled a finger on which she was wearing an emerald the size of a matchbox—part of a suite of jewels purchased from what the star had told an interviewer was her "new favorite jeweler," Bulgari. On her wrist was a jangly bracelet of gold charms.

"Are you in London for long?" asked Truman.

"Good question," said Burton. "We've been living here while shooting both films. Though now, I suppose, we'll have to figure out what to do."

"We're gypsies," squawked Taylor. "We should be living in a caravan or on a boat."

Burton explained. "We had dinner last night on a friend's yacht, moored at Rotherhithe," he said.

"A boat is better when you have dogs," said Taylor. "All those quarantine rules!"

Years later, after Burton and Taylor were indeed living much of the time on their yacht, *Kalizma*, moored in the Thames at the Surrey Docks at Rotherhithe, Truman tried repeatedly but unsuccessfully to wangle an invitation to join them on a Mediterranean cruise.

Taylor was looking very much a style icon that day, in an off-white pants suit, whose matching turban sported a tail that reached to her waist in back and a sleek pair of goggle-like sunglasses pushed up to her just-visible hairline. The polished look was a change from the wanton Liz, emphasis on the curves, that tabloid editors usually placed next to headlines like "Is Liz being destroyed by love?" and "Mrs. Richard Burton says she'll never give up Richard!"

"We stay at the Dorchester," said Burton. "The Savoy is where Elizabeth likes to announce things."

"What can I tell you?" said Taylor, mugging. "People want to know things. Like when I get my throat cut open." The filming of *Cleopatra* had moved from London to Rome the year before, when Taylor developed pneumonia and required a tracheotomy to save her life.

"We're all glad you got through that safely," said Dame Ninette.

"Wanna see the scar?" said Taylor, pushing down the neckline of her off-white shell.

"When does the film open?" said Cecil.

"May," said Asquith. "My film does, that is. *Cleopatra* is in June, I think—Elizabeth?"

"If they finish cutting the goddamn thing," said Taylor.

"You were awfully quiet with Liz and Dick," said Truman after lunch, when he and Lee were in her car, on the way to an art gallery. As usual, they were smoking.

"I didn't have anything to add," said Lee. "She's so . . . *much*."

"That she is," said Truman. He once said how attracted he was to Taylor's "hectic allure."

"I can see how that would work on the screen."

"Cecil told me that Rex says Audrey has no fire. She works hard—and I know this very well, from *Breakfast*—and she's always prepared, but, well . . . Now Taylor, she may be slatternly—Cecil's word—but *quel* fire!"

"Maybe I need a little more fire, Truman," said Lee, half-seriously.

"Just stick with me, kid," said Truman. "We'll put a little heat under it."

By April, Truman was back in the U.S., comfortably installed in his place in Brooklyn Heights and ready for some fun. "I need a rest from my book," he told Lila North, who reported that the author's return to New York was "like emerging from a monastery." The emergence that spring included a stay at the Paleys' Long Island place, Kiluna Farm; visits with several other of his swans, either in New York or at their country places; dinner with Diana Vreeland, with Cole Porter, and with David and Joyce Susskind. And by June, he was back at work on the book—in Kansas, visiting "Perry and Dick" in prison, after a lengthy negotiation with law enforcement authorities there.

Lee, meanwhile, was making it a point to spend time in Washington with a very pregnant Jackie. Despite the nation's hunger for "Camelot"-style pageantry—large state dinners at which foreign leaders were visibly wowed by America's young queen—there was also immense national goodwill toward Jackie during her delicate period, while she continued to preside over lower-key events—like what Lee called "a small state dinner" in honor of the president of India, Dr. Sarvepalli Radhakrishnan, complete with excerpts of Mozart's *The Magic Flute* performed by the Opera Society of Washington.

"Mother was there, of course," said Lee from the White House, after the dinner, speaking to Truman, who was in a hotel room in Kansas. "She made it a point of saying that she'd seen a few references to us in the press."

"To *us*? You and me?" said Truman.

"Yes."

"What's the matter with that?"

"You know."

"We're not exactly naughty teenagers."

"We might as well be. 'Must you see that man?' she says."

"You sure she's not talking about Ari?"

"Ha."

"I'm a world-famous author, for goodness' sake. Doesn't she know you could do a lot worse?"

"'Can't you see him more discreetly?' she says. 'Why does everyone have to know about it?'"

"She's being absurd."

"Of course she is."

"The president certainly keeps his extracurricular life under wraps."

"I told her, 'I'm not Jackie.'"

"Nobody's Jackie."

"Exactly. And that was the expression on Mother's face."

"Are you speaking from the Queen's Bedroom?"

"I am."

"What does it look like?"

"It's all pink. They've made it quite pretty. It used to be called the Rose Bedroom."

"Are you speaking on a pretty pink telephone?"

"As it happens, I am."

"A princess phone?"

"Is that what they call it—the narrow oval one?"

"Mm-hmm."

"Then yes. And Truman, it's got push buttons instead of a dial. We don't have those yet in London."

"You will soon. That's precisely what we fought the war for."

"Stas is just saying good night."

"Good night, Stas."

"He says good night. Lots of wine for us both tonight."

"Tell me who was there."

"Oh, Bobby and Ethel. Sargent and Eunice. Lots of State Department people. Some people that Jackie and I met in India."

"Mm-hmm."

"And Gore."

"Gore was there? Back at the White House? With Bobby there?"

"He's family, Truman."

"I hear from Tennessee that Gore misbehaves himself and Jackie tolerates it. Apparently, there was an incident at some party when our friend touched Jackie in a manner that Bobby found too familiar . . ."

"I wasn't there, but I'm told that it was blown way out of proportion. Please don't repeat such things."

"Gore was apparently drunk and obnoxious, and got himself thrown out onto Pennsylvania Avenue by Bobby and some of the other menfolk."

"Everyone's agreed not to talk about it."

"Gore and I don't have much in common, but did you know, speaking of mothers, that both of ours were drunks?"

"Really, Truman."

"It's true. Now I suppose that Janet will want Gore banished, too."

"It sounds like we've all had a bit too much to drink tonight."

"The man is not a novelist. He's an essayist. Much too self-absorbed to create a character and give it life."

"I should say good night, Truman."

"Alright, princess, have it your way. But let me put a bee in your bonnet. I was just speaking with David Susskind, and I think we might have something here . . ."

Truman told Lee about having discussed with the producer a remake of *Laura*, with himself as writer and Lee as the star. Susskind suggested that Lee could do with some acting experience first, so Truman thought of Tracy Lord in *The Philadelphia Story*—a regional production somewhere. Woozily, he flattered Lee with words about her "star appeal" and "emotional depth," and said she'd make a "sensational" Laura. He liked the plot that novelist Vera Caspary invented but had some ideas about "punching up" the script. Moreover, he said, their version would be better than both the original and "that awful remake with Dana Wynter."

"You'd be so good, Lee," said Truman, whispering intently as if they were together in the Queen's Bedroom, speaking quietly so as not to disturb anyone.

"Would I?" said Lee, beguiled by the idea, but cautious.

"Of course you would. It would show the world that you are much more than a so-called swan, much more than somebody's sister. Cecil says that . . ."

Truman hesitated.

"Cecil says what . . . ?" said Lee.

"Cecil says that you'd be marvelous," said Truman. "And he knows about such things better than anyone." What Cecil had actually said to Truman, during a private moment at the Savoy, when Truman floated the idea, was that Truman would make "a fine Pygmalion" to Lee's Galatea.

"Me? Marvelous? I don't know," said Lee.

"I want us to show each other things," said Truman. "This I can show you—this aspect of your soul. You've shown so much to me. Let me return the favor."

"Maybe."

"Think about it."

Lee lit what she was determined would be the last cigarette of the day.

"My housekeeper said something interesting to me the other day . . ." she said.

"Marlene?"

"Yes."

"You can call the girl by her name. I *have* conversed with her, you know."

"Well, she asked me if anything could make me happier in life. Isn't that interesting?"

"Hmm."

"No: What would I need to make my life ideal? That's the way she put it. And she meant it perfectly innocently. Maybe she's a little starstruck . . ."

"And?"

"Well, no one's life is ideal, is it, so I told her I'd think about it."

"And did you?"

"Truman, I just turned thirty, in March. I'd really like to use whatever blessings I have been given—really *use* them. Before it's all over, you know? And then what? I become Janet—enforcing rules I had no hand in making up? I need to keep going."

"And so you shall, good princess."

It was around then, too, when I met my friend Judy and her new fiancé in the Village, for the Washington Square Art Show. Every year since the Great Depression, artists have come together for this outdoor show—some of them well-known or on their way to becoming so; some obscure and destined to remain that way. The public loved the show and came from all over the tri-state area to see it and maybe buy some art.

I must say that I felt a little trepidation beforehand. I wasn't comfortable at all having a life of my own then, meeting up with friends for fun times—and maybe I am still that way now, in my seventies. Fun and friends felt foreign to me. Having a big life of my own, with preferences and choices and peak experiences, was just something I wasn't taught to expect. It was never modeled for me, and I didn't have much of a talent for making it up. I'm not saying I was born to be a servant, but that kind of life did seem to suit me. And I was aware of this difference between Judy's and my points of view about life every time I was with her, especially now that we no longer lived in the same household. Yet she was family, in a way, and I was grateful for what I did have—safe harbor. I tried to stay focused on that, and on the glamorous human beings whom my safe harbor included.

I found the happy couple underneath the Washington Square arch at the appointed time. Judy and I hugged.

"And this is John," she said.

"Hi, John," I said.

"Nice to finally meet you," said John. "I've heard so much about you."

His hair was longer than I expected—it covered his ears—and he was wearing horn-rimmed glasses like Allen Ginsberg. Clearly John was something of what we'd now call a hipster. Good for Judy, I thought: indeed, no preppy prince. Instantly I saw that John was as sensitive and intellectual as Judy had described him. In his chinos and white shirt, he looked more like a grad student in English literature than a law student.

"I can't wait to see what we've got here," said John.

"I see some wonderful still lives over there," said Judy.

"I think we can say 'still lifes'—yeah, Jude?" said John.

We looked at the still lifes and then moved on, making our way past and around and through displays of paintings, drawings, sculpture, and other items; going forward in that wordless, wander-y way that small groups do in museums and galleries when everyone understands that no single person should constantly take the lead. The artists showing their creations were as varied as their offerings: a barefoot, white-haired woman in a purple silk caftan was showing some sort of woven wall-hanging to a woman in a crisp plaid shirtwaist; a beatnik in a paint-stained sweatshirt and black Keds with holes was trying to sell a green-splattered canvas to a man in an off-white summer suit and a woman in a pink shift.

"Judy says you know Truman Capote," said John, while Judy was a few steps ahead, examining some prints.

"We've met a few times, yes," I said.

"What's he like?"

"Very smart, very charming."

I had said little to Judy about getting to know Truman better. It felt presumptuous.

"I adore his writing," said John. "It's soulful, full of character. Does he come across that way in person?"

"Well, he *is* something of a character, so yeah, I guess. Are you a big reader?"

"Big. I think you have to be—especially right now in New York, where there are so many great writers around: Norman Mailer, Mary McCarthy, Saul Bellow . . . Same thing in art, I think. It's really kind of a great time in American culture."

"Is it?"

"Don't you think so?"

"I don't get out as much as you do."

John looked at me half-askance.

"You're joking, right?" he said.

"I am, yes," I said. "But I'm also serious, since I have a full-time, live-in job, and really only see the world through the eyes of my employer and her friends. I like it that way, to be honest."

"I gather that can be a pretty amazing view—when you're not polishing shoes, of course."

"Of course."

I could see John was a nice guy with a sense of humor—whatever else he might be. To be honest, I did get a homosexual vibe from him, but wasn't about to mention that to Judy. Anyway, what of it? I knew of lots of men in these Upper East Side circles who were loving souls with wives and children, and pursued any less conventional desires in a perfectly reasonable way. Lord knows, both Lee and Stas, and Truman and Jack, maintained relationships that were at least somewhat, shall we say, customized. If this was to be Judy's life, and it was based on love and respect, then so be it. I was predisposed, at any rate, to find for myself a successfully formulated life as satisfying as one steeped in primal passion. And that is what I feel, if anything, about Vincent—ready, perhaps, to customize something.

Now, it's not primal passion I feel—though I admit I do feel something for Vincent that I have never felt for another man. It's not too physical, except for the fact that I do like to look at his face, and enjoy all the micro-expressions it makes during conversations, as I know any of our faces normally do. Is it strange for me to find myself liking a man because his face is hugely entertaining? Anyway, a friendship with Vincent is something I may be inclined to pursue, because at the age of seventy-eight, there are so many things that one can no longer pursue; and also because at that age, certain mental programs designed for self-protection, that one has kept running for decades, are now out of steam and no longer even necessary. I don't dream about being in Vincent's arms, though every now and then, when he touches my shoulder, for emphasis or something, I feel a certain warmth that I attribute to gratitude for his approval. In class, I am an authority figure, and he accepts that, and I derive satisfaction from that kind of approval, too. Yet . . . I know there is more. Which is why I may well have that drink with him at Bradley's when I return from New York.

Truman told me all about his recent stays in London and Verbier and Kansas City, when he returned to New York. That was the year—'63—when we really started talking to each other. He said it was important to him, especially as he became more famous, to have a friend—"a good friend," he was kind enough to say—who wasn't famous. Though Lee and the family were off in Malta, and Truman and I could have met at the apartment, he thought that our friendship shouldn't be so dependent on Lee, so he invited me to lunch at one of his "new favorite" restaurants, the Four Seasons. It was in that still fairly new, bronze-and-glass modernist landmark on Park Avenue, the Seagram Building, designed by German architect Mies van der Rohe. The host was a little surprised when Truman declined his usual table in the soaring, light-filled Pool Room, among the rich and powerful, and said he preferred one in the more private-feeling Grill Room, among the merely notable, where he said that he and "Her Serene Highness" might converse undisturbed.

"I've never seen you in real clothes," said Truman, after we'd been seated.

"But I don't wear a uniform," I said.

"You've put yourself together—heels, pearls. You look great."

"So do you."

That made Truman laugh.

"They're costume," I said, slipping a finger under the modest strand I'd put on to accessorize my green linen suit. "There's a clever little shop I know on Lexington."

"I can understand that she'd rather see you . . . plain."

"There are no rules—nothing she's ever had to tell me. I just don't need to be fashionable."

"And you're how old?"

"Twenty-two."

"I don't believe I've ever heard a twenty-two-year-old girl say she wasn't interested in fashion."

"I didn't say I wasn't interested. I only said that I don't need to *be* fashionable myself. There's a difference. It's better to hang back and observe the fashionable world this way—from behind a sort of duck blind."

"Ha. Well, we have very different ideas about how to observe the fashionable world," said Truman.

"Do we?" I said.

"I like to be right in the middle of it. I feel it's my job. Although I must say I am intrigued by your intention to do this observing yourself."

"They are right in front of us, aren't they, Mr. Capote. We can observe them or ignore them."

"Hmm. Remember I asked you to call me Truman."

He described the Seagram Building as "an architectural poem of Cartesian clarity," which, along with Lever House, catty-corner across the avenue, showed New York how breathtaking the international corporate modern style could be, when it wasn't debased by cheap reproduction, as it would be in New York skyscrapers over subsequent decades. Of course, Truman knew the restaurant's interior designer, architect Philip Johnson—"that's his booth over there in the corner"—and he said that several times he'd met Pablo Picasso, whose monumental painted theater curtain *Le Tricorne* we'd passed in the restaurant's lobby. The whole place had a scale and grandeur I associated with museums and airport terminals, which would have been intimidating, except for luxurious details like rare wood paneling, soft but lively acoustics, and spot-lit flower arrangements, not to mention impeccable service that was far less fussy than that in the fancy restaurants whose names began with *Le* and *La*.

An imposing gentleman in a suit appeared at the table to ask if Mr. Capote wouldn't be more comfortable at his usual spot in the Pool Room.

"No, no. Thank you, Joe," said Truman. "We're fine here. This is what I asked for."

"Enjoy your lunch," said the gentleman, with a nod.

"What would Lee say if she walked in and saw us here?" I said.

"She wouldn't mind. She's very egalitarian."

"I guess you're right."

"She did ask me, the other day, though," he said, "if we were becoming friends, you and I, and I said 'Of course!' "

"That's nice of you."

"I had to stop myself from telling her all about you."

"Well—why didn't you?"

"Because I promised you I wouldn't. The question is, my dear, why *you* don't speak with her about it."

I had often thought about answering this question.

"There's no reason for me to talk about my personal life with her," I said. "At first I didn't, because I needed the work and didn't want the awkwardness of pity. Now I feel that dwelling on it like a soap opera would make things awkward."

I explained that many rich Cubans who arrived in the U.S. with manners but no financial support were too proud to accept charity. Their rich American friends didn't want to embarrass them. I said I knew several men who had gone into business and were rebuilding their family fortunes, but that was harder for women to do.

"My cousin Elisa was a doctor in Cuba, and couldn't afford to go back to medical school here and re-qualify," I said. "Now she's driving a taxi in Miami."

I said I was content to accept a different life now. Maybe one day I would write about my story. I said that I had lots to tell.

"It sounds like you do," said Truman. "I am all ears."

"Believe me, with an author of your stature, so am I."

When the waiter came for our order, Truman suggested I try the crab cakes.

"Alright," I said.

"They make them like quenelles," said Truman, as the waiter went off. "Lumps of crabmeat in a mousse of codfish."

"Wonderful," I said, though I didn't know what quenelles were at the time. "Do you cook?"

"Very funny. Now who are your friends, Marlene?"

"I have none, really. Well, maybe one—my friend Judy, the granddaughter of my former employer. We stay in touch. I guess we're friends."

"What do you do when you're not working?"

"I read, go to museums."

"What do you read?"

"Everything. Dickens, Faulkner, Balzac, Highsmith . . ."

"Balzac in French?"

"In translation."

"Still. Good for you."

"Lee lets me borrow anything."

"Well, of course."

"I feel that . . . maybe someday I could tell some of my stories . . . as a writer."

"I see no reason why not."

"Tell me, Mr. Capote—sorry, Truman—is it a calling, writing? Was it for you? Something you always knew you had to do?"

"Hmm. Well, it's something I *learned* I could do, early on. I was telling stories even before I could write them down. And then I did write them down and decided simply to leave out the things I thought were boring and put in only what I really liked. It was really no harder than that. It's about taste, really—what you like. Except that, yes, reading Dickens and Faulkner at least shows you where the bar is—how to structure things, how to make jokes work . . . it helps instill in you this very sensible panic about not wanting to bore a reader, any more than those writers did."

He looked almost like a child as he explained this to me—not the celebrated author who dined with the world's most famous and powerful people. Suddenly, I saw a small-town country boy from the South who'd decided to marshal the talents he had in an effort to get out of town and up to a city where people like him could thrive, somewhere where those talents would be recognized and cultivated, instead of ignored and neglected, until they shriveled into the front-porch rocking-chair habit of rehashing tales of neighbors with shotguns and lazy dogs.

"I think I always wanted to be loved through my writing," he said. "It was a trick I could do that no one else could do, like cartwheels on the lawn. But then I realized that beyond the charm of observing characters and telling about their little dilemmas was something deeper—the courage to face humanity, what it really is, including lust and greed and selfishness and murder. I could do that, too. And if no one else found it charming, at least I did. I guess what I'm saying is that I want to be loved for my ability to be heavy and light at the same time, you know?—which is why I joke about serious things sometimes."

"I see. Wow."

"And someday I hope to combine the heavy and the light into something even more hideous than murder but still . . . amusing."

"Is that *In Cold Blood*?"

"No. That one's just hideous. Though there is some humor in it—dry humor. If anyone will ever see that. No, it's something else that I've been working on for a long time, that started out as a murder story."

"What is that?"

"All in good time, my dear."

We talked and talked, as lunch plates came and went. By the time coffee arrived, we had become quite chatty.

"How were the crab cakes?" said Truman.

"Delicious," I said, almost asking what, exactly, a quenelle was, and then, foolishly, thinking better of it.

He lit a cigarette and sat back.

"Why do I like you, Marlene?" he asked.

"Well, I am no swan."

"But you do have some of the qualities that they do. You're smart, you're quick and interested. You have mystery."

"Swans have mystery?"

"Oh, you bet. They're swimming in it."

"I don't think Lee has too many mysteries."

"You don't? Did she sleep with Bobby? Did she sleep with Jack?"

"Now, Truman . . ."

"Relax. I'm just teasing you."

My repeated refusal to engage on Lee's love life seemed to reinforce the growing intimacy between Truman and me—as if my refusal were something adorably rude that he would only allow a friend to get away with.

When the waiter came with the check, Truman merely signed it. It was the first time I'd ever seen this gesture, and as we left the restaurant, I was trying to figure out how it worked. A monthly bill was sent, I supposed.

"Let me walk you up Park until your street," he said. "I'm off to the Carlyle."

The day was bright. The broadness of Park Avenue served to dampen the roar of traffic. On the sidewalk, as we strolled slowly uptown, the conversation shifted from chat between friends to more a discourse between master and student—which I very much welcomed. I asked him why he liked the Four Seasons so much, when places like La Côte Basque seemed to be such favorites of his.

"The Four Seasons is much more than a place to eat, Marlene, and more than a design story, which is what all the press has focused on. It represents a new idea about eating, about service, about *luxe*. It represents the rethinking of a stratum of upper-class life—possibly the end of the American habit of copying Continental manners, which we have done for two hundred years. It was the war that freed us from that, and it's taken until now to really see it happening. I mean, that crab cake of yours was American cuisine, based on American seasons, American products. This is where I expect restaurants to go, in the eighties and nineties—and, by extension, American society in the future."

Truman always said that unlike London and Paris, New York was about the future.

"I mean, we are in one future right now," he said. "The very pavement we're walking on is the future that Edith Wharton might have thought of."

He gestured broadly to take in the broad avenue, the median strip, the canyon of buildings we were walking through. He spoke about the development of Park Avenue's current form and the construction of Grand Central Terminal, back in the early part of the twentieth century. He spoke of the great apartment buildings going up in the '20s, and the imminent loss of the city's other great train station, Penn Station, despite the valiant efforts to save it by Philip Johnson, Eleanor Roosevelt, and others.

"I arrived in New York by train—did you know that?" he said. "It was just before my first book was published—*Other Voices, Other Rooms*. 1948. I took a bus to Montgomery, Alabama and got on a train to New York. It's a very civilized way to travel. You have time to think, to see the country—town by town. You think about your fellow citizens soul by soul. And when you arrive—grandeur. Well . . . it was grand then. Who knows what Penn Station will look like once they are done with it? They say it's going to be all underground. I have a friend, an art historian, who says he expects we'll be scuttling into town now like rats in drainpipes."

Truman laughed, amused at his own disgust.

"Marvelous," I said, making a point of using a word that Lee used so often, to mean *nice* or *very nice*—emphasizing the first syllable just a bit, the way her friends did, the way they emphasized the second syllable of the word *enormously* when they meant liking something *very much* or *very much indeed*.

"Train travel was something then," continued Truman. "At Grand Central, they used to roll out a red carpet every night, literally, when the Twentieth Century Limited pulled in, with all those Hollywood stars and moguls . . ."

We stopped at a corner.

"This is where we part, Marlenita," he said, giving my hand a squeeze. "It's been fun. Let's do it again sometime."

And it made sense to me, years later, on the day when I attended Lee's funeral, the day before my meeting with the producer, that I should dine that evening at the restaurant where Truman and I first met on our own. Of course, the Four Seasons was much changed by then, under new ownership, though obviously much care had been lavished on a refurbishment meant to be true to the original. But the whole world had changed; the eyes and ears and heart we bring into any place like that now, a historical landmark, are themselves changed. All history had shifted. My evening there was like walking through a shimmering dream. It was all so lovely, but there was no more Picasso. The server completely understood when she explained that the crab cake was no longer a quenelle, but a crab cake with a thin layer of potato on top, served on a bed of mustard seed aioli—which was fine, but different. And of course, there was no smoking. Friends whom we think will always be with us, dining and drinking at our table, laughing and smiling and squeezing our wrist, are suddenly no longer there; instead, they are more like marble statues in a museum, victims of a fate the reverse of Galatea's. But I will come to all that later.

CHAPTER 9

SLAVES OF HISTORY

Could the maître d' of the Four Seasons possibly have thought I was any kind of "Serene Highness," during that first lunch there with Truman? Was it just his good manners that kept him from cracking a smile, if he thought Truman was joking or that I, with my commoner's deportment and fake pearls, was pretending to be something I wasn't? Was it simply his years of greeting patrons of great importance that had made the man sanguine about people's various airs, affectations, and pretentions? In my forty-four years with Lee—from 1961 to 2005—I met plenty of titled individuals, and I would say they all did have a certain something that I obviously lack, something that even now I can't put my finger on, whether or not they had any money, manners, or breeding. Or does a title deliver to us no useful information about what the person bearing it is, only an invitation to think about them in a certain way, if we are so inclined?

Lee rarely spoke of her and Stas's titles and styles. I never once saw her correct someone who either used or misused or overused the title *princess* with her. It was Truman who told me gleefully, on several occasions, whose titles were legitimate and legal and attached to property, and whose were fake or dubious or used only as a courtesy. As a citizen of a nation whose constitution forbids the issuing of "titles of nobility or honor," and also, I think, as a dedicated humanist, Truman had an automatic skepticism of titles. And yet, like me, he felt something when in the presence of them. I saw him use titles obsequiously, though I think I heard the hint of a taunt when he did. When he called me "Serene Highness," I know it was with affection—but there was still that tinge of sarcasm.

Come to think of it, there may have been something about titles in Lee's blood. Her great-grandfather, Michel Bouvier, was a French cabinetmaker who immigrated to Philadelphia in 1815, after serving in the Napoleonic wars. Michel's son, Major John Vernou Bouvier, was apparently quite grand and had the family's genealogy recounted in a privately published treatise entitled *Our Forebears*, a copy of which was in Lee's library. The Major cites patents of nobility being granted to an ancestor at least as early as the fifteenth century, by King Louis the Prudent, and claims that "no less than twenty-four Bouviers companied the French forces to America and fought for this country's independence."

Stas's family too, I know, claims a figure who was made a prince of the Holy Roman Empire in the fifteenth century, by Maximilian I. There is certainly something compelling about titles for me. I have always been fascinated by what they represent. We all have ancestors. We all have some kind of history. I think everyone, deep down, wants to know and possess their specific histories, but only a few can do so—and even for them, the records are spotty, or dim, or half-true, and fail at any rate to go back as far as Adam and Eve. In some ideal world, the knowledge of our ancestors—all of them—would be ritually known, not in worship, as in China, but in gratitude. I have to imagine that forty thousand years ago, some ancestor of mine carved the bone of a gull into a flute or put a handprint on a cave wall, and I'd like to think that that ancestor and I have more in common than our genes. I'd like to believe in some continuity of character, of spirit, of soul . . .

When Jackie lost her baby, in August, it was something of a national tragedy. She received notes of condolence from all over the world. Truman, from the Agnellis' yacht, sent flowers with a short note, to which Jackie later responded with typical grace.

"I keep thinking what power a great writer has," she wrote. "It is a selfish thought, but if all you have written in your life was training for those seven lines that were seen only by me—and Jack—I am glad you became a writer."

"Don't Repeat This" —by Lila North
Friday, October 18, 1963

Jackie Kennedy was welcomed back to the White House yesterday by the president and their children, Caroline and John Jr. She had just returned from a trip to see friends in Greece, as part of the period of quiet grieving she was observing after the August death of baby Patrick Kennedy. We've all been praying for our first lady—it is good to see her back at home! • What's the matter with flicks today? It's nice to see a movie as wholesome and fun as *Bye Bye Birdie* among this season's Hollywood offerings. But sometimes it seems like Tinseltown is more determined than ever to peddle smut like *Tom Jones* and *Irma La Douce*. Both of those bow-wows take a lamentably lighthearted view of illegitimate sex. Are these the ideals we want to live by now? We should all be glad that the Vatican accused Liz Taylor of "erotic vagrancy . . ."

As usual, Lila North got only half the story of Jackie's stay in Greece. When Lee "flew to Jackie's side" in Boston after the death of baby Patrick, as Lila had rather fustily phrased it, she'd come straight from Ari's side, on his yacht in the Aegean. And though Lee and Stas had been secretly remarried in London in July, Lee returned to Ari right after Boston. Then, in October, Lee got Ari to invite Jackie to join both Radziwills and him aboard the Christina—"I was trying to do something nice for her," Lee said—which was when, Truman surmised, Ari's affections must have shifted from one sister to the other. Lee never let on—to me, anyway—that she had been so deeply involved with Ari and so bitter about his perfidiousness. Afterwards, the sisters were cooler to each other in a deeper way than their lingering childhood rivalry—despite their unity during a tragedy that was soon to come.

By November, both *Cleopatra* and *The V.I.P.s* had come out.

So had *The Birds*, *Charade*, *How the West Was Won*, *It's a Mad, Mad, Mad, Mad World*, and *Son of Flubber*. So had the Beatles' *Please Please Me*, James Brown's *Live at the Apollo*, and *The Freewheelin' Bob Dylan*. The British had clucked over the Profumo affair; American astronaut L. Gordon Cooper had orbited the earth twenty-two times and Russian cosmonaut Valentina Tereshkova had done so forty-eight times; people like Philip Roth and Andy Warhol and Leonard Bernstein were shaking up culture. Hemlines were above the knee and getting higher. Suddenly, all the girls were wearing white boots with low heels and calling them go-go boots. There is always change in the world, and sometimes there's more of it than usual, which some people find destabilizing. For me, though, the go-go moment felt wonderful, as though the huge changes that were happening so fast would probably be considered good ones, once the world got used to them.

It was early in November when Truman, in town for a few weeks with Jack, ran into Lila North at a mid-morning press screening of *Move Over, Darling*, a Doris Day remake of *My Favorite Wife*, the screwball comedy classic with Irene Dunne. Truman had promised *The New Yorker* to do a reminiscence of Marilyn Monroe, whose death the previous year had hit him quite hard. Marilyn had originally been cast as the star of the remake, which was originally called *Something's Got to Give*, but she was such a psychological mess in '62, when the movie was shooting, that her work on set was completely unreliable. She was often late or absent; she flubbed lines and missed marks. Eventually, she was fired. The movie, recast with Day, was now scheduled for a Christmas release.

Truman later said he took the encounter with Lila as a shot across the bow, since the columnist had recently elevated herself to the position of public scold, and Truman's unedited and unapologetic manner did not sit well with her.

"What did you think?" asked Lila after the movie, when she approached Truman in the screening room's tiny lounge, where coffee had been set up. The few other press people who attended the screening had rushed off.

"Oh, I think it's pretty good," said Truman. He told me he was surprised to see Lila "in the flesh," since when they communicated, it was usually by phone, but he went into what he called his "great-author mode" and dealt with her graciously.

"I was glad to see it didn't glorify bigamy," said Lila.

"Lord, when did you become so moral?"

"I'm a good Catholic girl, Truman."

"Hmm."

"Why—aren't you religious?"

"I am an Episcopalian but belong to no congregation and am not a believer in any formal sense, if that's what you mean. But God and I are on perfectly good terms. And now, if you'll excuse me . . ."

"It was a shame about Marilyn. Did you have a comment?"

"I think I'll save my comments for the *New Yorker* piece I'm doing."

"You knew her, though, didn't you?

"Yes, I did. She was a lovely girl—quite a gifted performer. Wonderful at comedy."

"Can I use that?"

"Help yourself, but it's not news."

"I heard that sometimes the movie crew had to sit around for days before she showed up to work."

"Well, I'm not going to comment on that. What you didn't hear, I'm sure, is that the rushes were delightful. It would have been one of the great comedies of all time. Right up there with *Some Like It Hot.*"

"You saw rushes?"

"I certainly did. George Cukor showed them to me, last year. I spend a lot of time in Hollywood."

"It seems to me you spend a lot of time everywhere."

Lila's column a few weeks before had reported that Truman was "a cavorting man-about-town in New York, Palm Springs, Bel Air, Palm Beach, and Portofino—as a good friend of the planet's most stylish ladies *and* their powerful husbands."

"None of what you've written about me is remotely news," he said.

"Then maybe I ought to be printing something about you and your kind that's more newsworthy."

"What's that supposed to mean? What is 'my kind'?"

Lila's way of holding the coffee cup and drinking from it, as she stood there, involved also still hanging on to her handbag, her tote bag, and a coat, though the lounge was otherwise empty and she could easily have put her things down. Truman also mentioned a detail that I remembered from my lunch with Lila: the chipped red nails.

"What I do know," said Lila, with evident self-righteousness, "is that I am now on the advisory board of the Catholic Legion of Decency, which will be expanding."

"Ugh."

"They are including distinguished people of faith from many fields. I intend to use my column now more in the service of decency, which has been eroding terribly in this country."

"Golly!" said Truman, mocking her with a trembly gesture of his right hand.

"Scoff if you want to, but there's a movement building to counter all this godlessness we see, all this reckless pursuit of fun and pleasure."

"And what's wrong with fun and pleasure?"

"There are higher values."

"It seems to me that it's rather old-fashioned forms of decency that have been eroding around the entire world."

"Then you agree?"

"I agree that society is changing, and that for the most part it's a very good thing."

"Then we don't agree."

"Of course we don't agree. I'm an artist. It's ludicrous to categorize works of art as 'morally objectionable' or 'morally objectionable in part,' let alone to condemn them. That's what your so-called legion does, doesn't it? It's so fifteenth-century. I understand that your inquisition condemned the latest Fellini and the latest Godard."

"They did."

"Good thing that nobody cares—except the ladies who attend seven o'clock mass in Astoria, Queens, and pick up that silly list every week at the door of the church."

"Those ladies are very important."

"I'm sure they are—to God."

Then, at the end of the month, the buoyancy reflected in space flights and rising hemlines lurched into shock and sadness, when President Kennedy was assassinated.

I was in the kitchen when I heard the news. Lee was in London, and I had just started to clean the oven. It was somewhere after one o'clock, on Friday the 22nd. The radio was on, the oven door was open, and I had covered the floor with newspaper. I was just starting to spray the oven's interior with Easy-Off when an announcer cut into Dan Ingram's program and said the president had been shot in Dallas. Suddenly, we were listening to a report from a Texas radio station:

"Everybody didn't know what happened there at the Trade Mart. I jumped in a police car and went to Parkland. When I got there I found that nobody knew too much about where he was hit, but they knew that the president was shot in the head. The president was shot in the head. Governor Connelly was shot in the chest . . ."

I found it hard to process the words I was hearing. I was instantly in a kind of shock. I went into the den and turned on the TV. The news was on all the channels, and I remember switching among them for a few minutes, to get as full a picture as I could of what was happening. I knew I must be having some kind of emotional response, but I wasn't exactly feeling it yet—shock and disbelief overriding, for the moment, sadness, fear, and concern for the Kennedys, for Lee and her family, and for the country.

For an hour or so, it was news flashes and somber commentary; grainy footage and details about shots fired at the Kennedy motorcade; reports of the president's death and then a contradiction from an aide who was waiting in the hospital corridor—the president was alive, and doctors were operating. And then there was Walter Cronkite on CBS:

"Regarding the probable assassin, a man twenty-five years old, we are—we just have a report from our correspondent Dan Rather, in Dallas, that he has confirmed that President Kennedy is dead. There is still no official confirmation of this, however . . ."

Then the death *was* confirmed, and it was reported that Jackie was okay.

I was in a daze, which is the way I remained all day, waiting for something to happen, perhaps for Lee to call, perhaps to hear from Truman, though why would anyone call me? I eventually went back to the kitchen and robotically finished cleaning the oven. I thought of trying to reach Lee, but there was no reason for me to do so. She would call me if she needed me or if anything special needed to be done at the apartment. Thinking of my job, I did prepare a little statement in case anyone should call the apartment—something about respecting the family's privacy during this time of grief—but no one did.

That night, there were photographs of the new president being sworn in on Air Force One, and Jackie standing next to him in her bloodstained suit. And then on Monday, as I watched the funeral along with millions all over the world—the flag-draped casket, the horse-drawn caisson, the immense composure of Jackie, the touching salute from John Jr.—came thoughts about what the world was like now that an American president had been assassinated. Would another power take advantage of the moment and start a nuclear war? Who were the assassin and the assassin's killer, and what did they want? After the glamour and sophistication of the Kennedy White House, would Lyndon and Lady Bird Johnson turn state dinners into barbecues?

And there in several of the television shots of the funeral was Lee, standing near her sister, both in black veils.

So soon after Patrick's death, I thought—*how awful for them. How awful for the kids.*

I learned later that Truman tried to reach Lee but couldn't get through, because she was traveling and then tending to Jackie. From Sagaponack, he and Jack watched the funeral on TV and found it "a model of dignity" that was obviously "written, produced, and stage-managed by Jackie": the widow attending her husband's body as it lay in state at the Capitol; escorting the body loyally, on foot, to the Cathedral of St. Matthew the Apostle; sitting stoically through the requiem mass; walking through the burial ceremonies at Arlington National Cemetery; leading the nation through a tragedy more effectively than any elected leader would have been capable of doing.

Truman liked and respected Jack Kennedy a lot—not least because the president found Truman almost as entertaining as Jackie did. Also, Truman may have had a crush on Kennedy, as the president had many of the qualities that Truman admired in the husbands of some of his swans. Kennedy too, said Truman, had "more power and brains than any of them." Truman wasn't necessarily one to fall for male beauty—preferring other qualities in men, like intelligence and unpretentiousness—but he once mentioned Kennedy's "museum-level torso," which he encountered early one morning in Palm Beach. Truman was staying in the guest cottage of Loel and Gloria Guinness's place, and Kennedy was running nude from his family's place, nearby, into the surf.

And then, six days after Dallas, the Macy's Thanksgiving Day Parade went ahead as scheduled, since the organizers wanted to bolster the national spirit and remind the world why capitalism was opposed to communism. The event was televised as usual, for an audience of millions, with Betty White and Lorne Greene doing their best to balance the festivity of a parade that featured giant balloons of Popeye, Donald Duck, and Bullwinkle with the fresh memory of a very different parade that included the riderless horse of America's slain leader.

PART II

CHAPTER 10

MORE STATELY MANSIONS

Even if the assassination revealed to us that we weren't living in the fairy-tale Camelot we thought we were living in, there was nowhere to go but forward—especially for people like Truman and Lee, whom I had begun to see as fearless pathfinders through society's newest frontiers. It felt like the pace of important events was accelerating, the number of them accumulating. Simply being alive demanded more stamina than ever. The future was demonstrably out there—on the moon!—and it was their self-appointed job to lead us there. Whether or not this unprecedented forward momentum was a lingering effect of social and mental shifts resulting from World War II, I can't say, nor whether or not this momentum helped produce the wave of cultural nostalgia that would arrive a decade later. I can only report what I saw, which is that the next few years saw an acceleration of everything that Truman and his swans did—partying and traveling, shopping and collecting, lunching and laughing.

I was no swan, of course, but I was on the edge of their momentum and felt the pull of it. Yet for me, anyway, there was the constant worry that the momentum was uncontrolled and would land us somewhere utterly foreign—which I found both exciting and scary. Other twenty-two-year-olds might love a joy ride, but I was craving safety and security. I suspect that for Truman and Lee, and others with money and power, it was sheer self-confidence that blunted any questions about where it would all lead. Everything would be fine, because they were in charge.

Confidence is essential to swanning. In my years with Lee, I learned that I lacked not only the social position and bank account for swanning, but something akin to what ballet people call *plastique*—the physical quality of the presence of a fully controlled human body. Maybe *bearing* is a better word. Are you born with bearing? Can you acquire it? Practice it? I was about the same height as Lee, but built more thickly, with facial features that were pleasant enough but not . . . captivating. My mother, who once had a flirtatious kind of bearing, invented her brand of it and sporadically tried to encourage it in me, which only made me less interested in it. In the era of Elvis Presley and Marilyn Monroe, bearing seemed old-fashioned. Yet Lee and the other swans embodied it in a sleek new way that I found admirable, even if it wasn't for me personally. Perhaps it was as codified as ballet, involving secrets of posture, gesture, movement, even eye contact—a glance given to suggest interest; a gaze averted to indicate dislike. Grooming was essential, too. I didn't need a note from a royal housekeeper to know that no matter what my natural blessings were—hazel eyes, thick black hair—I shouldn't groom myself in a way that might be seen as competition with my employer. A woman in my position should be well put-together but unobtrusive, with little makeup, and certainly no make-up *effects*. For my hair, I went to a little salon in the neighborhood where it was understood, for instance, that my hairstyle should be tasteful and up-to-date, but not as grand as my employer's—which, in those days, meant less volume.

Truman later said that he did see in me the equivalent of "a swan's confidence," through my writing—a remark that I will always treasure. Anyway, unlike the act of writing, social swanning requires an audience—those in whom the swan can excite some desire. I had no such audience and didn't want one. At that point in my life, my heart was fairly inert—the victim of assaults and indignities. I didn't talk about specifics, because I couldn't bear to think about them. Yes, I sometimes made up alternative memories for myself, in order to get by—and maybe that strategy worked, since my account of these memories was the basis of Truman's initial interest in me. And then, as I made up tales for him, his interest in my telling tales grew. All of which ultimately helped me get past the trauma and find myself, decades later, at least partly open to the interest of a man like Vincent.

For most of my life, I would never have been interested in anyone who was interested in me. I was envious of, but baffled by, the easy way my friend Judy and her boyfriend John took to each other—yet observing them, when I joined them for a movie or a museum visit, I never learned anything I could use, about human beings together. But today, chiefly because of the two larger-than-life human beings I was lucky enough to know, I have at least a chance. Vincent is a widower, a gentle soul with salt-and-pepper hair and a closely trimmed beard. Despite his moving among some of Palm Beach's toniest folks, he is quite a modest gentleman—assured and financially successful but unboastful. When I first settled on West Palm, I resolved not to have a social life. I didn't think I needed one, let alone a special friend. In a way, Truman had been the big relationship in my life, and that was enough. I had been grieving for him for twenty years, when I retired. For a long time after the move, I kept my head down, devoted to the good memories of my life in New York, while taking up once again the screenplay that Truman and I had started. Some of my writing students may have found me distant personally, yet most of them were seniors whom I knew had their own lives and friends. Vincent, however, now has me thinking about whether a special friend mightn't be nice. And since he doesn't push, I feel free to examine and develop my interest in him in my own time. No man had allowed me that, before—not even Truman, who was clearly a bit of a Pygmalion with me, too.

So I find myself suddenly open to knowing more about Vincent, aside from the things he writes about—his daughters, his boat, his childhood in Massapequa. Do I abuse my prerogative as a teacher when I ask for more, or is that my duty? How can I be so different now, at the age of seventy-eight, than I always have been? To use a concept that I hear a lot about from my students, it was the respect I got from Truman—simple respect—that helped restore my strength and resilience as a functioning human being. This was quite a gift, and it helped me let go of what I now recognize as fear—fear of the world, fear of others. Obviously, I keep wondering today what Truman and Lee would make of Vincent. They both knew so much about love and life and people! Lee might have asked astutely about Vincent's intelligence, his humor, his financial prospects. Truman might have laughed and advised me to remember, as he often did, that "God is happiest when he's playing with us."

After the assassination, Lee spent much of her time in the U.S., to be with Jackie—at first in Georgetown, and then, after Jackie's house there became a tourist attraction, in New York, in a thirteen-room penthouse apartment that Jackie bought at 1040 Fifth Avenue, directly across from Central Park and just above the Metropolitan Museum. In New York, Jackie could maintain more of the privacy that a famous widow wanted for herself and her young children, yet be part of the social and cultural circles she found most interesting. She was also speaking even then, Lee told me, of getting a job, perhaps something in book publishing.

"She invited so many writers to those state dinners," said Lee. "They always wound up upstairs afterwards, talking all night with her and Jack."

Bobby Kennedy, whom Jackie relied on greatly for emotional support after Jack's death, had helped her find the new apartment. Seven blocks north of the duplex that Lee and Stas had just bought on Fifth and were in the process of decorating, Jackie's seventeen-story, white-glove co-op had been built in 1930 by legendary architect Rosario Candela and featured a distinctively asymmetrical roofline of arches, terraces, and chimneys. It was the bluest of New York's blue-chip addresses.

Lee and Truman met Jackie there one morning soon after the deal had been closed, to discuss décor. Jackie had several rooms' worth of her own furniture ready to be shipped up from

Georgetown, and would not need too many new things to start. For the present, she wasn't going to need a *real* decorator, she said. Lee, who was already serving as her own decorator at her new place, with the help of a young decorator-contractor, volunteered to help Jackie with "the basic stuff."

"I asked my guy, and he can do it," said Lee. "He's a wonder, Jacks. Knows where to get all the best work."

"The bathrooms have just been renovated," said Jackie. "So I think they're fine."

"Great," said Lee, making notes in a little, leather-bound Smythson notebook. "So . . . windows and walls."

They were standing in the so-called conservatory of the still mostly empty apartment—a vast central hall as large as some museum lobbies, which was entered from a private elevator landing and gave directly onto the spacious living room and a passageway that led to the library and five bedrooms.

"We should probably see the kitchen first," said Lee. "Truman, we're heading to the kitchen."

Truman had stepped into the living room for a quick peek.

"*Alrighty*," he sang, reappearing. "Amazing view. The Reservoir, the Met, the Beresford . . ."

"Let's go through here," said Jackie, leading the group through the living room into the dining room.

"Then you probably saw the terrace, Truman," said Jackie, pointing to the windows. "It spans the library, too. And there's another one around on the street side, for two of the bedrooms."

"Mmm," said Truman, savoring the details of prime real estate. He had already been making sounds about moving into Manhattan from Brooklyn Heights, and if all went well with *In Cold Blood*, he might be able to afford to do so soon.

"Landscaping, gardener, terrace furniture . . ." said Lee, scribbling in her notebook.

"I have those Victorian lawn things . . ." said Jackie.

Lee looked dubious.

"Might be too garden-y," she said.

They passed through a little pantry-like room into the kitchen, where they stopped to let Lee take in the details.

"You'll want all new appliances," she said.

"I think so," said Jackie.

"Otherwise—a coat of paint," said Lee.

"Told you," said Jackie.

"René's not coming with you . . . ?" said Lee. The question was a gentle barb referring to White House chef René Verdon, who'd chosen to remain in place and serve the new president—and who, at any rate, was now famous enough to make it unlikely that he'd go into private service for anyone, even his favorite former first lady.

"Lee, guess what I heard!" exclaimed Jackie, with obvious glee. "René is unhappy with the Johnsons. Apparently, they brought in some kind of 'Texan food coordinator' who's ordering canned and frozen things."

"Cook . . ." said Lee, making a note.

"Barbecued ribs for ladies in white gloves," said Truman. "Now that's something I'd like to see."

Continuing the tour, they walked through a spacious servants' hall, at the back of the apartment, and a narrow hallway linking three small servants' bedrooms and a bathroom. Then they passed through a door and found themselves in the residents' bedroom wing, each of whose graciously scaled rooms featured an en suite bathroom. At the front of this wing, overlooking the corner of Fifth Avenue and 85th Street, was the master bedroom suite.

"Best light in the house," said Jackie, peering out one of the windows. "The museum, Central Park South . . ."

After a look into the library and a brief discussion about wall hangings and Jackie's collection of books, they were back in the conservatory.

"Such a lot to do," said Jackie.

"It'll be fun—you'll see," said Lee.

"Good. I could use some fun."

"You're in the right place for that," said Truman. "Fun City."

Describing this scene to me, Truman said that that the trio of their voices made an interesting bit of chamber music, as it echoed through the empty expanse: Jackie's hushed, breathless whispers; Lee's deep, lyrical drawl; and the cheeps and squawks that punctuated Truman's own androgynous, high-pitched Southern sing-song. He was anything but ashamed of his voice—though always sensitive about it. He judged people poorly if they were rude enough to express any reaction to it.

"It's painfully obvious, thus hardly worth mentioning, that I sound like a girl or an old woman," he said once, recalling an encounter with some crass husband or other. "The point is, do you want to speak with me about books and ideas, or don't you?"

Moreover, not once did I ever hear Truman deny or apologize for his homosexuality. It wasn't that he was strongly political, in the way that we mean identity politics today. The matter never came up *per se* in our talks together, though he was free about telling me stories about Jack Dunphy, Cecil Beaton, and the other men of his life. Even in the years before gay liberation, he simply knew who he was and knew there was nothing wrong with it. His self-esteem functioned on a level above pride and shame, masculine or feminine; then for years, when he commanded the power of best-selling books, he was above any judgment—a sacred monster. Even at the end, addled by drugs and alcohol, he was just a ruin, not necessarily a *gay* ruin.

While Lee and Jackie were discussing the move-in date and which of the bedrooms might be best for Caroline, John Jr., and the nanny, Truman was party planning.

"For small gatherings, you can do coats over there," he said, pointing to a closet at the far end of the conservatory. "For big wingdings, maybe set up the bar there and do the coats downstairs."

In the lobby, afterward, while Jackie stopped to talk with the building's head doorman and the captain of her Secret Service detail, Truman stepped aside with Lee.

"You're not going to give her what you would do in your own place, are you—Byzantium meets Biarritz?" said Truman.

"Heavens, no," said Lee. "Her taste is far less adventurous than mine."

"Speaking of taste, Babe told me the other night at Kitty's that she and Bill are looking for a new place."

"No."

"Yes."

"Why?"

"Space. Their new Picasso is too big for the St. Regis."

"Be serious."

"We're having lunch, so I'm sure I'll get the whole story."

"After all the work she put in—that tented oasis."

"She and Billy Baldwin are going to recreate it!"

"Why not just do something new?"

"You know Billy. Everything is a bond with his destiny."

They discussed the upcoming June wedding of Babe's daughter, Amanda, to a handsome young descendant of Cornelius Vanderbilt, Carter Burden. The wedding would take place at the Paleys' luxurious Long Island estate, Kiluna Farm, which featured grounds designed by Russell Page, the British landscape architect who'd done gardens for everyone from King Leopold III of Belgium to the PepsiCo corporation.

The security conference with Jackie was taking longer than the five minutes she promised. The three of them had a lunch reservation at Orsini's.

"Stas in town?" said Truman.

"London," said Lee, lighting her fourth cigarette of the day.

"Taki?"

"What about him?"

"He's *here*."

"So I heard."

"You heard?"

"I am trying to be discreet with you, Truman."

"How much does *she* know?" said Truman, tilting his head toward the security conference.

"She's no dummy."

"Does she know about Ari, too?"

"I suppose. We don't discuss it. You're awfully curious today."

"Always. It's my job."

"Sorry," said Jackie, rejoining them. "No kiosk out front."

"Oh, wouldn't your neighbors just love *that*?" said Lee.

"I don't know. They might," said Truman. "You see all manner of questionable types skulking up and down the avenue these days."

"What have you two been chattering about?" said Jackie, as the trio was escorted out of the co-op and into the back seat of a waiting limousine.

"A party we went to at Kitty Carlisle and Moss Hart's the other night," said Truman. "Do you know what Kitty said? She said that Lee would be 'a natural for the stage.' "

"Acting?" said Jackie.

"And I couldn't agree more," said Truman.

"Acting, Lee?" said Jackie.

"Possibly," said Lee.

"Have you thought about this?"

"Of course I have."

"Do you think it's wise?"

"Well, it could be, for me. Why? Do you have a problem with it?"

"No, but . . . have you discussed it with Mother?"

"I certainly have not. If she loves me, she will love anything that I do."

Jackie flashed a quizzical look.

"Are we talking about *our* mother?" she said.

Both sisters laughed.

"This is Truman's idea, isn't it?" said Jackie.

"I think she'd be marvelous," said Truman.

Lee defended her friend.

"He is very eager to help," she said, "and he knows David Susskind and lots of other people who could help make it work."

"Just be careful about exposing yourself to . . . you know."

"Exposing myself to what, Jacks?"

"Comment."

"What comment?" said Truman.

Jackie turned to Lee.

"Don't let him *expose* you to anything," she said playfully but with marked seriousness.

"I think we've all got a little too much security on our minds right now," said Truman. "What we need is some Veuve and escargots."

I was living at Lee's new Fifth Avenue duplex while the décor was being installed there. It wasn't too bad an experience, since my quarters were tucked away far from the main rooms, where most of the work was being done. I kept sandwiches, coffee, and fruit in the kitchen for the crew, as Lee instructed. She and Stas were living somewhat separate lives by then, a scheme that both of them appeared to find stable and satisfactory. As soon as the place was ready, Christina and Anthony would be living there, where they could be close to their cousins, Caroline and John Jr., while Lee and Stas would continue bouncing around the world, together and separately, with bases in New York and London.

Lee did a marvelous job supervising the decoration of both her and Jackie's places. The pressure didn't seem to faze her a bit. She was organized and clear with the workers about what she wanted, and was proud when Jackie was able to move in on schedule. I got to see Jackie's place for the first time that fall when she asked Lee to lend me to her, because Jackie hadn't found a cook she liked yet. It was for a small lunch she gave for Ari, ostensibly to thank him for his kindness after she lost her baby, when she spent a few days on his yacht. Ari was in town with his companion Maria Callas, but the foursome Jackie put together for lunch didn't include Callas. It was just her and Ari, and Lee and Truman. The diva was not invited, probably because, as Truman suggested, the get-together was to remain secret.

Onassis was, of course, one of the world's richest and most famous men—a shipping magnate who'd amassed the largest privately owned shipping fleet in the world. For people as rich and powerful as that, the physics of time and space seem to warp around them—and this is a phenomenon at least an order of magnitude greater than the regal bearing of swans. This was majesty—a rare quality to be found only in a handful of people on earth who have long since stopped fretting about the million-

and-one common things that occupy every other human mind, consciously or not. This is a mind free to pursue desires, appetites, and diversions, and all manner of self-service and sometimes even service to humanity.

Ari was dressed exquisitely that day in a well-tailored gray suit, with a white open-collared shirt and a white pocket square. As I served and cleared a meal that Jackie knew Ari would like—Spanish melon, lemon broiled chicken, baked tomatoes, a Bibb salad with some fresh herbs and lemon juice, and raspberries *à l'orange*—I saw two women deftly honoring and repaying the interest of such a majestic man by playing at equality with him, each desirable in her way, as they basked in his charm and savvy, each obviously eager to trigger that broad smile and hearty laugh. I found the man as handsome as the noble head on an ancient coin, and was particularly struck by the distinctly masculine beauty of his eyes, which seemed more expressively emotional than those of most of the other men of his stature that I'd encountered. In this, Ari was a good match not only for Jackie and Lee, but for Truman, who himself had no trouble expressing emotion.

Lunchtime chat about current books came to focus on the late Greek author Nikos Kazantzakis, whose novel *The Last Temptation of Christ* had been translated into English not long before.

"With no temptation, there is no resistance, and with no resistance, Jesus is just another man," said Ari. "A common mystic. The ancient world was full of them."

"The world still is," said Truman. "Especially Malibu."

Ari laughed.

"His humanity, his susceptibility is what made him great," said Ari. "I don't know why this is so hard for the Church to accept."

"Well, councils have been debating this precise point for nearly two thousand years, haven't they?" said Truman.

"I am glad the book was condemned," said Ari. "This attests to its power, its danger."

"This is what the Church does when it condemns something,"

said Truman, clenching a hand and then tightening it into a fist. "You tighten your grip. But you hold on to less."

"He's a marvelous writer," said Jackie. "So disappointing that he never got the Nobel."

"Nine times nominated," said Ari. "Nine! That's a prize in itself."

"Have you seen the English version?" said Jackie. "I'm wondering if it does justice to the Demotic Greek."

"Superb," said Ari. "Do you know what he said once, Kazantzakis? 'I hope for nothing. I fear nothing. I am free.' "

"Take that, Holy Fathers," said Truman.

"He was denied an orthodox burial—did you know that?" said Ari. "I sent a plane to take his coffin home to Crete."

When I served coffee, Caroline and John Jr. were brought in to say hello. Dressed neatly in blue-and-white sailor looks, both were treated to warm hugs from "Uncle Ari," though it was clear that Ari and John, who was only four, shared a special connection.

"Hey, sport, are you joining us?" Ari asked John.

John shook his head no.

"He's had his lunch—haven't you, darling?" said Jackie, brushing a lock of hair out of John's eyes.

Caroline, then seven, amused everyone by asking if they could go sailing on Ari's boat.

"Of course, of course—any time," said Ari. "Come to Greece. Or better yet, I will send it here to get you, whenever your mother wants."

I thought that perhaps even then it was visible to Jackie how good a stepfather Ari would be.

Truman had prepped me on what he was certain was an active rivalry between the sisters for Ari, but I didn't dare ask Lee later how she thought lunch went. Truman told me that Lee thought she had Ari "nailed down"—that if she could get him to promise marriage, she'd divorce Stas and "the angels would weep with joy." But Truman—who had been a guest on Ari's yacht himself and liked "observing men like him who run the world"—also saw that Ari was interested in Jackie, "the biggest prize in the world"—much bigger than the greatest opera singer of her generation. I never learned whether or not Ari and Lee got together alone, on that visit to New York. All I can say is that there were no nights when Lee didn't come home.

Needless to say, lunch that day was secret, not only from Maria Callas but from gossip columnists like Lila North. The paparazzi had yet to camp out across the street from Jackie's building, and the presence of two security details, Jackie's and Ari's, inside and outside the building's front door, attracted no particular notice. Nor did Lila know anything about my getting closer to Truman—meeting with him regularly to discuss families, mothers, revolutions—when she called me at Lee's, the following summer, to invite me to lunch.

"Why?" I said.

"Don't worry, I won't bite your head off," said Lila. "I'm just trying to stay in touch with some of the younger people I know."

"But—why? Why me?" I said.

"When people like Diana Vreeland start talking about a 'youthquake,' I pay attention."

It was an odd request, but Lee was out of town and I was curious, so I agreed on the condition that Lila wouldn't probe me for information about Lee or Jackie. Of course, she did wind up asking about all that, but I think I held my own.

She took me to a French restaurant called Larré's, on West 55th Street—hardly a Henry Soulé establishment, but an improvement over Schrafft's.

Most of lunch was simply idle talk about rock and roll and hip-hugger bell-bottoms. Then the conversation took a strange turn.

"I thought you might be interested to know that I spoke with your former employer the other day," said Lila.

"Mrs. Hawkins?"

"Yes."

"At Shady Hill?"

"Yes."

"How is she?"

"She seems fine. Her foundation is still making donations in her name, and she was kind enough to talk to me about a big bequest she's making to the Philharmonic."

"That's nice."

"It's a very lovely place."

"I'm sure it is."

"Anyway, she was telling me something very interesting—about you. She sends her regards, by the way."

"Thank you."

"She says that your family is an old one, aristocratic . . ."

"Well . . ."

She shook a red-nailed finger at me, in mock-scolding,

"No, no. I knew there was something about you!"

"I really don't like to talk about that, so if you don't . . ."

"I heard all about it—the fancy school in Switzerland, holidays in Rome and Paris, holding your own with Sartre and his crowd at the Café de Flore . . ."

"I don't talk about any of that. It's too painful."

"Why not? It could be good for you."

"Lila, I think I know what's good for me. Is this why you invited me to lunch?"

"Reporters always look for sources."

"Sources of what? I'm no source. I told you that. I'm a housekeeper."

"Of the sister of the most famous person in the world."

"Lila, look . . ."

"I know, I know. I'm not going to ask about that."

Half of my *poulet poêlé a l'estragon* was still on my plate, but I was suddenly not feeling very hungry.

"Sorry," continued Lila. "Finish your lunch."

Who was it who had lunch at Larré's, I wondered, glancing around the half-empty room. I saw no tables occupied by fashionable ladies. There were several couples and small groups who looked like they might be in some kind of business together—garment manufacturers? Broadway producers?

"You move in a certain world," said Lila. "You're from a certain world. Who knows? There might be a time when I could do you a favor—say, in print. I used to know writers, too, you know. In fact—I know you *don't* know *this*, but I knew Hemingway a bit, oh, twenty years ago, when he was between his third and fourth wives. That was in Miami. It was a little wild. That was before he won the Nobel Prize, of course."

Could this be true? Why was she telling me about it?

"That's nice," I said.

"But I have closed that chapter of my life. No more *wild* for me."

She pronounced the word *wild* with a little wink, as if it were a witticism. I think I may have disappointed her by not asking for details about Hemingway—though for a second, I did consider asking her to tell me more, as a way of deflecting more talk about myself.

"Some of us do have a literary side, even if we work in magazines and newspapers," said Lila.

"Absolutely," I said. "I'm afraid I am not too literary myself."

Which was a lie, since the conversations between Truman and me had been more frequent in the past year. We'd often meet for coffee, either at Lee's, if she were out of town, or at a coffee shop, and talk not just about my life, which he said was helping fuel his imagination, but about structuring stories and making characters come alive. He recommended books for me to read, told me what he liked about them. There was no need to tell Lila any of this, even if, against her promise, she did bring up my big literary friend.

"But you do know Truman Capote."

"We've met, yes. He's a wonderful writer."

Lila put down her fork.

"I would only offer a word," she said. "Some of us in the writing game take our responsibility seriously as . . . let's say guardians of morality, now more than ever. You seem like a sensible girl, not one of these beatniks. But you move in a larger world that thinks itself *so* sophisticated. I only suggest you keep your eyes open and protect yourself. Believe me, I know what I am talking about. And not to pressure you, but if you ever do see anything you think is wrong . . ."

"Wrong?"

". . . you can always talk to me."

When I had no response to this offer, Lila continued.

"I can shine the light of day on bad behavior, which can be very helpful, in the long run. Very cleansing."

I shook my head and smiled. It was all a bit funny.

"You should write a book, Lila."

She laughed—a bit too loud for a half-full restaurant. A couple from three tables away looked up to see what was happening.

"Better than that, Marlene," said Lila. "The Catholic Legion of Decency is expanding from movies into print media, and I am one of the columnists who is helping them do it. And believe me, here in New York, we have more than the usual amount of sin to keep our eye on."

"Sin," I said, incredulous. "That's an awfully strong word."

"That it is. That it is."

"You seem awfully eager to keep your eye on it."

"What—did Sartre teach you that sin was okay because it's nothingness or something . . . ?"

I was beginning to feel uncomfortable. I had thought lunch would be a chance to speak about youth-oriented fashions and music, and here we were talking about sin. It reminded me of a cab ride I'd taken a few years before, when the driver asked me if I had been "saved" or were interested in being "born again."

I tried to calm myself.

"Times are changing," I said quietly. "People like wearing hip-huggers right now. It feels good, and it looks good, and it's not a sin."

"No, dear," said Lila, leaning in. "But murdering a president is. Don't you see? It's all related. And I wouldn't be surprised if we saw more murders coming."

I sighed.

"That was terrible, of course," I said. "But there are always lunatics in the world."

Lila reached over and put a hand over my wrist.

"It was a sign," she said, and then she proposed we have some dessert.

"Don't Repeat This" —by Lila North
Monday, July 5, 1965

. . . Happy Fifth of July, New York! They said that the theme of yesterday's spectacular fireworks display was NASA's Project Gemini, but I didn't see any twins. Did you? Only sparkle. • Shouldn't Barbra Streisand be glad that fame has helped her clean up her act? In a recent magazine piece, the kooky-if-successful young songstress said, "I was happier as a beatnik." Really? Apparently, wearing all her great new clothes "gets to be a pain in the neck." • Maybe a more sensible singer to be watching is pretty Anita Bryant. The twenty-five-year old Oklahoman recently appeared with Bob Hope to entertain the sailors of the USS *Ticonderoga* in Viet Nam. I hear she's a sweety-pie . . .

Chapter 11

The Rite of Spring

I was alone in the house for most of the spring and summer. Lee was redoing the drawing room of Buckingham Place; then, it was over to Belgium and Holland, to look at paintings in museums and at auctions with Marella Agnelli; then to Portugal for some relaxation, and then back to England, for a look at Turville Grange, the country house she and Stas were soon to buy.

Truman also spent the summer bouncing around the globe, after completing *In Cold Blood*. At first, his account of finishing the book and visiting people's yachts and vacation homes was cheery enough, which made sense given that the product of five years' work was now at the printer and scheduled for a holiday release. The book was being described as "highly anticipated"—always a phrase that buoys an author's spirits. It wasn't until the fall, during one of our chats in the breakfast nook of Lee's kitchen, when she was away, that Truman told me a deeper story about how he had finished that spring; and he got so emotional about it that he nearly wept several times as we talked. This affected me deeply while also making me grateful that he had decided he could trust me enough to show me this side of himself.

On the night of April 14, Perry Smith and Richard Hickock were executed at the Kansas State Penitentiary. Truman had been a constant visitor there for years and came to know both murderers well, through a series of interviews and emotionally draining judicial appeals and stays of execution. And there was obviously the special fondness that developed between Truman and Perry, which produced all those warm letters between them—though Truman never told me whether or not he and Perry ever were lovers, as many have suspected. He was in Kansas on the day that the execution, now confirmed as definite, was to take place, but he was so shaken by his goodbyes to Perry and Dick, as he called them, that he knew he couldn't bear to watch them hang. He returned to his hotel and sent a message to Perry saying that he wasn't being permitted to attend the execution—which was a lie.

"Then I called Lee, blubbering like a baby," Truman told me. "I didn't know who else to call. I couldn't call Jack—that would have been too much for him, hearing me wail about Perry's death. Anyway, it was the middle of the night in London, and Lee said I should just go. She said I wouldn't forgive myself if I didn't go, and I knew she was right. Really, all the feelings I had for the boy, all the protection I wished he could have had instead of those orphanages and detention homes . . . We both had such similar childhoods. But my help with the stays, and my very public interest in his case, really couldn't protect him; and it certainly couldn't stop justice, let alone undo the terrible events he'd gotten drawn into.

"Lee said go, so I went. I was out there with my editor, Joe Fox, so Joe drove us back to the prison through the rain. It was like a movie, Marlene. They do it in a giant room like a truck garage. Nothing in it but a tall, wooden platform—which was built by other inmates, of course. Lots of officials in suits standing around, being very, very quiet. No chairs—which surprised me at first, but then I realized it was all supposed to be very, very quick. Dick was first. He was led up the stairs and was read the charges and verdict as they put the noose around his neck. A chaplain was reading a prayer. Then they put a hood over his head and pulled the lever."

I shook my head.

"Trapdoor," I said, automatically.

"Mm-hmm," said Truman.

He took a deep breath and exhaled slowly, then went on.

"They had him in some kind of harness that bound his arms, and his legs were bound, too—because, well, you don't want to make things any more horrible than they are. Anyway, I knew right then that I couldn't watch them do it to Perry. I just couldn't."

Truman described running out of the building and into a parking lot, crying in the rain, propping himself up against the side of a bus with bars on the windows, until Joe Fox found him and bundled him into the car. Truman had wanted to call Lee back immediately on reaching the hotel, but he was a wreck. Joe advised him to wait until morning, which would be afternoon in London.

"And Lee was right," continued Truman in a small voice. "I couldn't forgive myself. All summer long, I cried myself to sleep everywhere, in palazzos, on boats, wondering where I was when that trapdoor opened under Perry. Was I in the parking lot? Was I in the car? Was I back at the hotel? Was I mid-sentence with Joe, talking about a deadline for the book's final chapter? And I will probably go on wondering for the rest of my life.

"I told all this to Lee, and I will always be grateful to her for being so understanding. It was impossible for me to tell anyone about it but her. And now you, of course, my serene one."

After a moment of silence, he continued, weeping a bit.

"Do you know what he said, when we were saying goodbye? He said, 'Now your book will have an ending, Truman.' Just like that. Happy to be doing some good for someone else. It was like giving me . . . a beautiful gift.

"In fact, he did actually give me something . . ."

A little laugh accompanied Truman's blotting his tears with a plaid napkin, then folding the napkin neatly.

"When we said goodbye, he handed me an essay he wrote—beautifully typed in the prison library. Forty pages: *De Rebus Incognitis*. It's so like Perry to use a Latin title. We were always recommending things for each other to read—and, you know, he really did read what I suggested. He could have been . . . so *much*, if only he hadn't strayed from the path and wound up with that monster Hickock. Dick was the psychopath, you see."

"An essay?" I said.

"The title means 'Concerning Unknown Things,'" said Truman.

"What was it about?"

"Oh, it's quite a ramble. Mostly about all the other people any of us could have been, if circumstances hadn't made us what we are. Whether or not we can shift, in adulthood, from one potentiality to another—which he claims kids can do, but adults can't."

"Is it good?"

"It's not terrible."

"Can *people* make those shifts, do you think? I'd like to believe they can."

"Oh, I don't know. I just don't know. I read it on the plane and cried over it for days afterward—including at a concert that Lee took me to, a few days later."

To console Truman, Lee, who had been on her way to New York anyway, invited him to join her for a Stravinsky Festival concert that the New York Philharmonic was giving at their sleek, new concert hall at Lincoln Center. On the program was *The Rite of Spring*, along with pieces by Barber and Copland. The piece depicts, in terrifying symphonic intensity, the ritual sacrifice of a young maiden by her tribe, on the steppes of ancient Russia. She dies so the community may have a good harvest. The half-hour-long work was written as a ballet; its scenario, printed in the program book, contains scenes like "Ritual Abduction" and "Evocation of the Ancestors," all depicted with unprecedented orchestral power that unsettled audiences in 1914, when it premiered. It was during a particularly inflammatory burst of brass and percussion in "The Glorification of the Chosen One" that Truman uttered a scream, started bawling, and immediately covered his mouth and nose with a handkerchief, as if to muffle his reaction—which, by the way, was shushed by two well-dressed patrons in the row in front of him.

Lee put a hand on his knee, and Truman signaled he would be fine. They were sitting among the best seats of the orchestra section, which Lee said were close enough for her to notice that a violinist onstage had glanced in the direction of Truman's outburst, while continuing to play.

Afterwards, Lee and Truman joined the crush of admirers backstage and were allowed to squeeze decorously past those less celebrated, until they were spotted by the conductor and star of the evening, Leonard Bernstein.

"Lee, Truman, wonderful to see you," said the maestro, wiping a bit of sweat from his brow and kissing them both.

"Magnificent," said Lee.

"Thank you for coming," said Bernstein.

"The hall is beautiful."

"We're still tuning it up."

"Stravinsky certainly knows how to grab you," said Truman.

"That's what this whole festival is about," said Bernstein.

All in the murmuring crowd were observing that delicate, post-concert backstage etiquette that requires admirers to await their turn with the star, while trying to look both ready to be next but not ungraciously impatient. Bernstein remained focused on Lee.

"Truman was grabbed, anyway," she said.

"I'm afraid I yelped during the concert," said Truman.

"One of your violinists noticed," said Lee.

"That was you?" exclaimed Bernstein. "Marvelous!"

The conductor instantly enveloped Truman in a hug.

"You heard it?" said Truman.

"I hear *everything*. But it was no problem at all. You know me. I don't exactly just stand there when I conduct."

In the car, afterward, Truman told Lee that he was thinking of moving to Manhattan.

"Tired of Brooklyn?" said Lee.

"No, I love the Heights. But so much of my life is in Manhattan . . ." said Truman.

"Upper East?"

"Maybe. Jack's in charge of all that. He's looking around."

"Prices are insane."

"Princess, this po' Southern boy just sold the paperback rights *and* the movie rights."

"Good for you. I hear everyone talking about it."

"I'm very proud of it, of course, but . . . there's this idea rattling around in my brain that it's somehow built on human sacrifice."

"What do you mean? The family that was murdered?"

"Well, them, of course, but the murderers, too."

"Ah."

"They did what they did, Perry and Dick, and justice took its course. I am free that far."

"But?"

"But I got to know those boys very well. And it's no secret—I've talked about it on television—that I came to like Perry Smith a great deal. But no one was under any delusions."

"No?"

"I mean, I helped them with their appeals in good faith, but I think we all knew that their lives and my book would end the same way, with their execution."

"Uh-huh."

"There was never a chance of commutation, but of course, if there had been, and it had happened, it would have been a terrible obstacle for me."

"The author in you needed the execution. The friend in you feared it."

"Precisely. In that way, I was not free. I had my duty as an artist—but that had never felt like a sin before."

"Oh, Truman . . . how terrible for you. People should know."

"If the tribe had not taken those two lives, the book would have been far less—forgive me—satisfying."

"I see that."

"Joe Fox understood this. We discussed it openly, for years—though always, I hope, with some degree of respect for Perry and Dick."

"Of course."

"It's so painful, Lee, to hear, as I sometimes do, that I am 'glorifying murder,' or some such nonsense. Mind you, no one but my editor has read a page of this book yet."

"I think that you should explain to people what you are trying to do with this book—not just structurally, but morally."

"Maybe. Or maybe I just let it stand on its own and keep the rest to myself. Except for shrieking now and then during a concert."

I've often wondered whether Truman might have suffered some kind of mental injury from the terrible dilemma he faced, between loving Perry Smith and doing his duty to literature. It would be years before his talent for detriment really took hold and caused the sad rift between him and Lee—but was this the start of all that? Yet for all anyone could see, Truman was on the brink of a new level of fame and success. The novel was in production, and expectations about it were feverish. Indeed, the whole city was moving feverishly forward. A new New York was popping up everywhere, in projects like Lincoln Center, the Coliseum, the General Motors building, and FDR Drive, Robert Moses's express highway running up and down Manhattan's eastern edge, partly elevated, partly cantilevered. New architectural forms, like those on display at the World's Fair, which had been running out in Flushing Meadows that summer and the one before, suggested an exciting, fresh take on city living—which may be why Truman, instead of buying a place on Park or Fifth Avenues, chose a new apartment at the city's newest "it" address, UN Plaza.

A pair of thirty-nine-story, modernist bronze-and-glass towers, directly north of the United Nations campus, UN Plaza was designed by Wallace K. Harrison and Max Abramovitz, the architects responsible for the United Nations itself, as well as the Time-Life Building and the Metropolitan Opera House, the latter then nearing completion at Lincoln Center. UN Plaza offered an alternative to the Park-and-Fifth Avenue limestone-façade lifestyle, which was growing a little fusty around the edges. A few buyers in the new complex decided to drape or even panel over their floor-to-ceiling glass walls, but most embraced the complex's exhilarating brightness and transparency. The place was edgy at a time when the rich were beginning to discover it was fun to be edgy. That feeling of cool grandeur clobbered you quietly when you entered the vast lobby of UN Plaza, like the Met would do the following year, with icons of modern art, contemporary crystal lighting, and acres of red carpet.

It was chiefly well-to-do business and entertainment types who bought into UN Plaza—news anchor Walter Cronkite and movie star Yul Brynner, philanthropist Mary Lasker and television host Johnny Carson, Truman's friends producer David Susskind and *Washington Post* publisher Katharine Graham. Truman's apartment on the twenty-second floor offered spectacular views of the United Nations, the skyline of midtown and lower Manhattan, the East River and its bridges, and the borough of Queens, which at night was a tapestry of glitter laid out to the horizon. The apartment was as bright and exposed, Truman said, as his Brooklyn basement had been gloomy and secluded; and it was considerably larger, so to fill it, Truman wasted no time adding to his collection of furniture, artworks, and bibelots with new items purchased in East Side antique shops. I would visit the apartment often toward the end of Truman's life, when he was in and out of rehab.

Parts of *In Cold Blood* were scheduled to appear in the November and December issues of *The New Yorker*, and Truman took this as a perfect cue to host a "cocktail picnic" late one afternoon in his not-nearly-finished apartment. It was an intimate get-together for twenty or so "really close friends," including the Susskinds, the Paleys, the Bouvier sisters, and Katharine Graham, whom everyone called "Kay."

"It will be so much easier now to return to *Answered Prayers*," said Truman as the picnic began, his back to a glass wall that had yet to receive any window treatment. Beyond, the dusk overtaking midtown was punctuated by the illuminated spire of the Chrysler Building. "It will be so easy, by comparison. It's all in my head."

"I'll bet it will be a joy to get away from murder," said Joyce Susskind.

"Who said anything about getting away from murder?" said Truman.

"Uh-oh," said Lee.

As Truman explained to me later, and as Lee was to describe it, this cocktail picnic was a simple, impromptu get-together in advance of a proper housewarming—something akin to a construction party on a building site, which is why, though there was no actual construction taking place at the apartment, Truman had procured pristine, new white hard hats for each of the guests. The hats were set out neatly in rows on a table near the front door, like seating cards for a big party. The simple get-together also involved a caterer, a bartender, two butlers, and a dozen or so rented ballroom chairs, since the furniture from Truman's Brooklyn Heights place was inadequate to fill his new square footage.

Apparently, the make-do quality of the party—and its brevity, since it was meant to offer only a pre-dinner drink, in the traditional 5:00 to 7:00 p.m. cocktail slot—made everyone quite jolly.

"I only see Central Park at my place," said Jackie, gazing out the window, "but really, you see the world."

"I'm thinking about having no drapes at all," said Truman. "If someone out in Hunters Point has a telescope and wants to take a look, they're welcome to it." He threw open his arms, in a broad "look at me" gesture.

"You have such a flair for entertaining, Truman," said Kay Graham. "You should do more of it."

"You're going to have to now, won't you?" said Lee. "I mean, with the book and everything."

"We'll see," said Truman. "I may have something up my sleeve."

"Sit-down dinners for twelve?" said David Susskind, who was practically the only guest to have donned his hard hat.

Truman made a face.

"Not my style," he said. "I have something more fun in mind."

Truman didn't mention it then, but he had been continuing to think seriously about hosting a great ball, if for no other reason than all the lavish hospitality he wanted to pay back—to Babe, to Marella, to Gloria, and others. Though the choice of a guest of honor was stumping him. It shouldn't be one of the swans, or there'd be hell to pay with the others.

"We know you like to cruise, Truman," said Babe. "Maybe you'll charter the SS *France*?"

"Maybe," said Truman. "Or I'll have a ship built. I do know a shipbuilder."

"Now, don't let it get away from you, Truman," said Bill Paley, making a fist, to indicate holding money. He, too, was wearing his hard hat. "You've got plenty of friends with boats. Hang on to your earnings."

"Yes, Bill," said Truman, "but you of all people have to admit that there is pleasure in building something yourself, isn't there?"

"Of course . . ."

"Specifying all the details . . ."

"Things should be done right."

"Mr. Paley, I am told," announced Truman, "not only chose the architect for his beautiful, new black building, he even specified the door handles . . ."

"You know me," said Paley, smiling modestly.

"Even the kind of hot dogs that are sold in the little vest-pocket park next door," added Truman.

Everyone laughed. Paley kept smiling.

"Am I right?" said Truman.

"You're right," said Paley.

"His own recipe, no less," said Truman. "Seriously."

"This is why we admire you, Bill," said Kay. "Both the big picture *and* the important details."

A butler passed a tray of beef filet with mushroom-caper butter canapés among them.

"I tried to get the hot dogs for this occasion, but no dice," said Truman. "They're under contract."

"Will there be a book party?" asked Kay, after Truman had told the story of finding the caterer through restaurateur Henri Soulé.

"Random House is doing some industry events in January," said Truman. "And they've lined up a tour for me."

"What's this I hear about it being banned?" said David Susskind.

"Oh, someplace in Britain is objecting to it," said Truman. "Can you imagine—in 1965?"

"No, no, what I heard was something about California—the Glendale school system," said Susskind. "Savannah, too."

"It's absurd."

"It is, Truman, but it's nonetheless real. It exists."

"It's not the murder they're concerned about, it's the sex and profanity. That's the trouble with our society."

"Were you surprised?" said Lee. "You know very well what prudes some people are."

"Surprised, no. Annoyed, yes," said Truman. "This tendency to suppress what you don't know or don't like has been around for thousands of years. It's always called into play when new ideas are brought up, and I am in the habit of bringing up new ideas. That's part of what I do as an artist."

"Bravo!" said Jackie.

"Bravo!" said Kay.

"Frankly," said Truman, "I think it's more basic to human nature to pursue new ideas and put them into action, if they work for us. This is called growth. This is called progress. That's why I am so eager for certain people to stretch and play certain roles that they've never played before."

This was clearly an allusion to the idea of Lee playing Laura—which Lee caught, and which David Susskind caught, but which flew over the heads of the others. I knew Lee had been thinking about the idea for weeks, since the day I found a copy of the original Vera Caspary novel bookmarked on a table in the library.

"Okay—progress," said Susskind. "That's a fair point. But let me play devil's advocate for a moment . . ."

"Oh, David, this isn't TV . . ." said Truman.

"But hear me out," said Susskind. "I just asked the same thing of Robert Moses a week ago, on my show. Take Lincoln Center: four brand-new concert halls that can seat ten thousand people on any given night—but who are those people? Do they include any of the seven thousand families and eight hundred business-owners, mostly Black and Hispanic, who were displaced?"

There was a brief moment when no one said anything. Then Kay spoke up.

"We've commissioned a series on this exact subject," she said. "Title I of the 1949 Housing Act. That's what gave them eminent domain. But who is urban renewal for?"

"That sounds fascinating, Kay," said Jackie. "Who's writing it?"

Kay named the author, and no one was too disappointed when the subject of urban renewal gave way to party-friendlier chat.

Half of the guests were off to a museum dinner, so things broke up around 7:15.

"Fun party," said Lee, when Truman walked her and Jackie to the elevator. "Let me know if you can make Round Hill work."

"The calm before the storm," said Truman.

The three shared little air kisses and said good night. Both women were clutching their hard hats along with their handbags. Truman told me later that none of the women had actually donned their hats at the party, and he realized that this was because they didn't want to mess their hair. And he took this as a lesson that he said came in handy for him the following year, when he hosted his ball: guests like to be told what to do, but only up to a point. He laughed when he imagined why Lee and Jackie had taken the hats with them when leaving.

"Was it because it would have been rude to leave them? Would they treasure them as a memento of the absolutely smallest party they've attended in years? Was either of them possibly thinking that there could be a situation in their lives when a hard hat might be necessary . . . ?"

CHAPTER 12

THE NEXT BEST SELLER

Packed into a small storefront art gallery in the East Village, early on a February evening, were at least a hundred eager culture-seekers, including Lee and Truman, who'd been "secretly" invited to an unadvertised and untitled event that was neither the opening of an exhibition nor precisely a music or dance performance. It was a "happening," and for the previous few years, New York's most in-the-know people had been attending such events. It was well past the start time, and though it was cold outside and the gallery had no heat, everyone was getting hot, since there was no coat check and hardly any space for anyone even to take off a coat.

"I'm glad we got here when we did," said Lee.

"Hmm," said Truman.

"I see Lulu," said Lee, referring to a mutual friend, an art collector.

"I can't see anything," said Truman, who was conspicuously shorter than almost everyone surrounding him. Slowly, he and Lee were managing to shuffle farther toward the rear of the gallery, where the crowd seemed to think the happening would take place. Or was it already taking place?

"There's no room in here, anyway," said Lee. "Where could anything possibly happen?"

Occasionally, from the gallery's front door, came the sound of a heated exchange between the doorkeeper and one of the hundred other in-the-know people crowded outside on the sidewalk, unable to get in.

"This space can hold fifty or sixty, max," said Truman. "Why invite half of New York?"

Then there was activity at the rear of the gallery. A back door was opened, and the crowd began pushing forward into the gallery's backyard, which was loomed over by the back windows of surrounding five- and six-story apartment buildings. Respectfully, the crowd gathered around several individuals who were installed in different spots around the yard, crouched low or sitting on the ground, performing tasks. One was cutting out paper dolls; another was assembling sandwiches from a pile of sliced bread and cold cuts, then disassembling them, then reassembling them again; another was applying more and more makeup and examining herself in a mirror. There were six performers—three men and three women—and six different tasks in all, and twice, the performers robotically stopped, moved to each other's positions, and took up their predecessors' tasks.

"Welcome," said an amplified voice. "You're welcome to witness but encouraged to take part in any of the activities you find in the sculpture garden. Afterwards, please join us for a glass of wine in the gallery."

"Wine right now?" said Truman, able to see more and breathe more freely.

"We can't," said Lee. "Let's watch for a bit."

But the option of merely watching was reduced by the mimed encouragement of a mute master-of-ceremonies figure who began drawing guests into the performed activities. Soon a lady in fur was cutting out paper dolls, a man in a suit was making sandwiches, and a young woman in jeans and what looked like a secondhand men's army jacket was applying garish makeup to her face and admiring the result in a mirror.

Lee, wearing gloves, heels, and a designer overcoat, declined to get down on the ground with the paper-doll performer, but she did accept a pair of scissors and a sheet of paper, and managed, while remaining standing, to produce a very respectable set of paper dolls.

"Well done, princess," said Truman, who declined to make dolls himself.

At one point, one of the performers, a young man, stopped performing his task, stood up, and declaimed over and over again: "A time will come when Torvald is not as devoted to me." Then a young woman stopped and stood up in her spot and joined him in the same line: "A time will come when Torvald is not as devoted to me." Soon all the performers were standing throughout the yard and chanting: "A time will come when Torvald is not as devoted to me"—overlapping each other, in a cacophony. Then they halted abruptly and began waltzing in place with invisible partners, humming softly to themselves, after a minute of which they began wordlessly inviting guests to join them in a dance.

Lee smiled and shook her head *no* when a young man invited her to waltz. When the same young man then turned to Truman, Truman also declined and uttered in a low voice, "Back problems."

When the performers launched into a group dance in which each took turns walking joyously through an imaginary doorway embodied by other performers, Truman noticed that several guests were retreating into the gallery.

"Have you seen enough?" he whispered.

Lee took his arm, and they stepped inside.

"Torvald?" said Lee, holding both a lit cigarette and a plastic glass of wine in her gloved hand.

"I know!" said Truman. "*A Doll's House*. Did you know that that's what this was supposed to be?"

"Absolutely not."

"Ibsen, of all things."

"But everybody's talking about her," said Lee, referring to the happening's creator.

"You never know," said Truman. "My elderly cousin used to have a very wise saying for whenever some live attraction came to the local theater, that everyone was suddenly so hot to see. We would go, of course, but she would always remind me on the sidewalk beforehand, 'Remember, it could be nothing.' "

Lee smirked.

"Good advice to heed these days," she said. "But here's the thing, Truman. That girl with the dyed red hair . . . ?"

"Oh, yes, the one who was making the sandwiches. She was marvelous."

"*Marvelous*, wasn't she? She was the only one I believed."

"Me, too. She's obviously an actress, and a very good one."

"Her face alone—but the way she used her whole body . . . I found it so touching. The tedium of cooking and cleaning, all the effort involved in looking lovely, *hoping* to be lovely—but not having access to the outside world . . ."

"She captured it all."

"This is a secret fear so many of us have, women . . ."

"I know."

"To be Nora . . . to be no more than Nora . . ."

Lee's expression registered a flicker of real concern.

"*That*," said Truman, pointing at her.

"What?" said Lee.

"What you just said. And the way you said it."

"About Nora?"

"Yes. There is so much of *that* inside you, and that could be shared with the world, in theaters, on television, in the movies . . ."

"Please. That's what you keep saying," said Lee, taking a drag on her cigarette.

"Actresses would kill for that kind of depth."

"There's also technique."

"Technique can be learned, sister. What your soul understands is a whole 'nother matter."

They were standing near the bar—a card table dressed in a white paper tablecloth that was already half-soaked with wine. The bartender—a neat young woman in pearls—offered refills, and Lee and Truman accepted.

Their friend Lulu joined them at the bar, dressed very expensively in a radically asymmetrical black cloak and sculptural black hat worn at a rakish angle.

"What did you think?" said Lulu.

"Interesting," said Lee.

"Interesting," said Truman.

"Yes, I thought so," said Lulu. "Norton and I are thinking of collecting one of her works, but we've been talking about exactly how to do that."

"You could just sponsor her," said Lee.

"But we're *collectors*," said Lulu.

"Ha," said Truman. "Well, I suppose you could build a pavilion out at that beautiful place of yours in Greenwich and have the performers live there and do those dances every day, *ad infinitum*."

Lulu didn't know whether or not Truman was joking, but she laughed anyway.

"That would actually follow through with the themes of the play, wouldn't it," said Lee.

"What do you mean?" said Lulu.

"Well, love, marriage, entrapment, freedom . . ."

"Is *that* what *High Tor* is about?"

"What are you talking about?" said Truman.

"They were chanting something about Tor," said Lulu. "I assume it was a reference to the Maxwell Anderson play."

Lee and Truman shared a quietly astonished glance, yet registered nothing but their pleasure in Lulu's company.

"You know," continued the collector, "there really is a High Tor—it's a mountain—and it isn't very far from Greenwich. Just on the other side of the Hudson. Rockland County—not far from Mike and Lorraine. Oh, and Truman, congratulations on that book of yours . . ."

In Cold Blood had been released in January and was an instant hit. Truman was suddenly a celebrity of international proportions, pictured, interviewed, and talked about in all the media. The cover of the book, with that hatpin of blood stuck in the elegantly serifed title, delicate but chilling, was pictured everywhere. Within a week, the book's status as runaway best seller became official. It was a "masterpiece," declared Conrad Knickerbocker in *The New York Times*—"agonizing, terrible, possessed, proof that the times, so surfeited with disasters, are still capable of tragedy."

"Don't Repeat This" —by Lila North
Monday, February 28, 1966

> . . . Sunday night's appearance of that hot, hot girl group, the Supremes, on *What's My Line?* was a big hit. Clever Arlene Francis was the one to identify the group, which *Variety* calls "the greatest industry to hit Detroit since Henry Ford." You can catch the Supremes at the Copacabana until Wednesday. • Another big hit, apparently, is Truman Capote's new novel, *In Cold Blood*—though the book, a brutal blow-by-blow account of the murder of a Midwestern family, looks pretty ghastly to me. • We hear that steamy Italian star Sophia Loren and producer Carlo Ponti have decided to do the right thing and will head to the altar next month. On a very different road, Jayne Mansfield and new hubby, director Matt Cimber, seem headed for splitsville. Thank goodness the State's Catholic bishops are voicing objections to a proposed divorce reform bill, as you may have read elsewhere in this newspaper . . .

It was around this time that Lee mentioned to me that she thought Truman might be drinking more than usual. For lunch one day at home for the two of them, she had planned on one bottle of Verdelho to accompany their lobster salad, and Truman asked for another—that is, he asked *me* for it, as I poured the last few drops of the bottle into his glass, rather than suggesting to Lee seductively that lunch might be ever so much lovelier with another full glass. Lee, who was surprised that Truman asked for a second bottle at all, gestured to me that the request was fine—and luckily, we had the better part of a case of Verdelho in the back fridge.

She told me this after coming home late one afternoon that April, following an errand at Kenneth's salon and a two-bottle lunch with Truman at La Côte Basque. It was Kenneth's birthday, and Lee wanted to present the hairdresser with an inscribed copy of *In Cold Blood*, so she'd invited Truman to the restaurant and brought with her a pen and a copy of the book.

"What shall I say?" said Truman, after they settled into their seats. In front of him, on the table, he was holding the book open to its title page.

"Well, you know Kenneth . . ." said Lee. "It's his thirty-ninth birthday."

"Is it?" said Truman, with a chuckle. "His first one?"

"As a matter of fact, it is."

"Well, that's easy, then."

Truman scribbled some words into the book, closed the cover, and handed it to Lee.

"May I read it?" she said.

"You will anyway," said Truman.

"'To Kenneth,' " read Lee. 'Here's to staying thirty-nine forever! With fond regards, Truman.' He'll love it. Thank you, darling."

"Cristal?" said Truman, as the waiter approached.

They were halfway through the first bottle, and their food had not yet arrived, when they greeted Babe Paley, who entered the restaurant with Billy Baldwin.

"Hello, there," said Babe.

"Hello, hello," said Lee.

Truman stood, and the men shook hands.

"Truman."

"Billy."

Babe was carrying a small shopping bag containing a gift-wrapped box.

"I wonder, Babe," said Lee, indicating the bag, "whether we might have the same errand to do today."

"East Fifty-fourth Street?" said Babe.

Both women laughed conspiratorially.

"I'm heading that way right after lunch," said Lee.

"Let's go together?" said Babe.

"Lucky guy," said Truman, after Babe and Billy stepped away. "The city's most beautiful women, beating a path to his door."

"Sounds like you're pretty lucky too, Truman." He had just signed with Random House for *Answered Prayers* and received twenty-five thousand dollars, for a manuscript due in 1968. "Does this mean you'll have to cut down on your social life?"

"Far from it," said Truman. "I want to see even more people and places now. I don't want to miss a thing."

They compared the plans they had for the coming weeks and months. Both had several of the same parties on their calendars, in New York, in London, and in Paris. Truman and Jack would be in the south of France for a few weeks, then Truman would meet Lee and Stas in Portugal, before going back to Verbier and then on to cruise the Dalmatian coast with Gianni and Marella Agnelli. One of the upcoming New York parties was to be hosted by the Paleys.

"I guess they want to show off their new place," said Lee. "I can't wait to see what she's done."

"She's a funny one," said Truman, looking toward the table where Babe and Baldwin were sitting.

"How do you mean?" said Lee.

"Sometimes I feel Bill's instinct is to possess her."

"Mm-hmm."

"And I must say, I have felt it myself. I was out at a party with them last month, and people were saying all kinds of nice things about the book; and Bill seemed to go out of his way, in front of all his guests, to indicate what great friends he is with me. Arm around my shoulders—the whole thing."

"He can be quite warm."

"Horsefeathers. He was marking his territory."

"But both of them really like you."

"I know that. Honestly, though, at that moment, the friendship felt a little exploitative—as if he were claiming the return on an investment."

"I don't think they think of you in those terms."

"He does."

"Truman, this is the world you live in. It's a matter of balances. They like you and they like that you're a famous author. You like them and you like that they invite you to fly on Bill's jet. Nobody's being charged too high a price of admission."

Truman was philosophical, bordering on glum.

"I suppose I'm a trophy, just like she is," he mumbled. "And I suppose being a trophy doesn't mean you are loved any less."

"*Love . . . ?*" The word startled Lee.

"Well, I'm talking about *her.* I've always wondered if he really *knows* how lucky he is to have landed her. Otherwise, how can he truly deserve her?"

"It's between them, Truman."

"Honestly, I worry about their relationship. She says they have an 'understanding,' but I would call her position 'servitude.' You're so lucky that Stas is European. That's such a better model for a mature marriage—one that has a chance of enduring."

"You don't think Babe's marriage will endure?"

"Who knows? Bill would never give her up, and she's certainly not going anywhere. In their way, they are devoted to each other. Von Rothbart and Odette."

Lee smiled at the reference to *Swan Lake*—the evil sorcerer and the beautiful enthralled princess-turned-swan.

"Did you see Lila North the other day?" said Truman. She called Bill 'megalomaniacal' and Babe 'geisha-like.' I mean, it was a blind item, but we all knew who she was talking about."

"I try to avoid the columns."

"Unless you're in them."

It was Truman who was consuming most of the Cristal.

"I like a blind item, though," he continued. "Don't you? It's a hilarious little game."

Forty-five minutes later, after the plates had been cleared and they were halfway through the second bottle, Truman confessed that *this* was the life he wanted to depict in *Answered Prayers*, his Proustian novel.

"This?" said Lee, glancing over the lunchtime crowd.

"Well, not only this restaurant," said Truman, "but these people, these stories, these habits."

"How is it going? Lots of notes?"

"Oh, more than that, kiddo. I'm well into the writing—actually writing. Can't stop me, and why would anyone want to? Nobody's writing about this. Nobody else can. No one knows this life like I do. Certainly not Norman Mailer, Brooklyn boy. Maybe Gore, but that man has no heart, and you need heart to write about what's happening underneath all this. Two great social systems are disintegrating, Lee: East Coast Society and the Genteel South—you and me, baby! There's great sadness in it—fate; maybe tragedy. Certainly humor. I feel it's my duty to get it all down. Especially since that's all I know."

The side of Truman that Lee described as emerging by the end of lunch was one that I knew well: Truman could sound both as stupid as a drunk and as wise as a professor. Even when we met in the early afternoon for the "writing workshop" sessions that had recently become habitual for us, Truman seemed to be markedly tipsy.

"Yet how to make this book more than just gossip?" said Truman. "How to make it *tell* for the ages?"

Since Truman was rambling, Lee changed the subject, with an eye toward lightening the conversation so she might be able to leave the restaurant on time. She knew that Truman wouldn't become exactly *inconvenient*, yet tipsy people sometimes do need some special handling.

"Where are you and the Agnellis going to be sailing?" she asked.

"Adriatic," said Truman.

"Lovely. Dubrovnik?"

"Split. And those islands."

"Why do you like sailing so much, Truman? Surely it's not the luxury."

"Ha! Sailing is never luxurious, even when expensive. It's hard work—it's meant to be hard. Even on the Guinnesses' yacht. And they have a crew of thirty."

"Then why sailing?"

"I have the stomach for it."

"Oh, I see."

"Not everyone has, you see—this special knack for seafaring. The mind and the body function together, observation and intuition—it's all of a piece. You're in the middle of several elements at once—the sea, the wind, the stars . . ."

"Yes, that's true."

"It's a gift—to have the stomach for it. And it must be used, Lee; exercised—even if we're not off discovering new continents. Or maybe we *are* doing that—I don't know."

Truman was now rich enough on his own to be comfortable, yet was spending money wildly on clothes, accessories, antiques. And he was well-enough known as a best-selling author that people often stopped him in the street to say hello and offer a nice word about his books.

"Americans do not expect serious books to make money," he told me. "When they do, it becomes news in itself."

Throughout the spring and the previous fall, we'd been conducting our workshop sessions, at first at a Lexington Avenue coffee shop and then, when that proved inconvenient for all the note-taking we both did, at a branch of the Mercantile Library at Madison and 57th, in a private room that the library's director kindly provided for Truman's use. We met weekly when Truman was in town and simply talked. Ostensibly, we were exploring my family history and my experience surviving revolution, but Truman did also ask me to listen to passages of his writing and asked me for my opinion about them. And those discussions turned into a real master class for me in fiction writing—in which I saw more deeply into plot and character and voice and such than I had dreamed possible. Most of the time, honestly, I didn't know what he was reading to me—whether bits of a short story, or of a novel, or of one of the magazine articles he was always being asked to write. I never knew if any particular bit was part of *Answered Prayers*, and didn't feel I should pry into that without being invited. When I later read the excerpts published in *Esquire,* I realized that he'd read none of that material to me. And is it pride or presumption to say that I think I could have helped him improve the thing?

We did sometimes continue talking about the idea of a screenplay for Lee, and we came up with a few ideas, but he kept saying "I'm not ready for that yet. I'm not ready." We kept returning to my story and to what he referred to as "some literary *thing* in a form yet to be discussed," in which the central character experiences "privilege and youth, then social revolution, then the challenge of creating a new identity in a new land, in order to survive." And Truman explained that, as always, he went home after our session and wrote out notes of the entire conversation. But he kept saying that he was not yet ready to "synthesize."

"I have to be in the right frame of mind."

At one point, he asked if I wanted money for our sessions, since he was supposedly deriving value from them.

"I don't want to be stealing any material from you," he said.

"That's okay," I said. "Learning from you is more than a fair exchange."

"That's a very nice thing to say, Marlene, but I'd hate to be exploitative."

"Your interest in my story is an enormous validation. I learn so much from you; it is an honor to spend time with you."

And I meant that. Besides, Lee was paying me very well, and I didn't need more than that.

He also said that while he enjoyed our work together, he also expected his pride in having a rampant best seller to provide the momentum he was looking for to keep working. He made no secret—with me, anyway—about having been "a little dry" since writing the end of *In Cold Blood*.

Did he fear even then he was really going dry? I don't think so. He was simply doing what he'd always done when in doubt about the path forward: trying new things, seeing what worked. If anything, he was in danger of exploiting himself—pushing his talents and energies and appetites into new creative territories, with an eye toward the big spot in history that he now was convinced lay in wait for him. I later came to regret that I let Truman's interest in me deflect *my* concern about *him*; he sensed he was in trouble, and maybe I could have used the trust between us to help him diagnose this trouble more precisely, so he could have done something more about it than spin his wheels—which is an image I get when I re-read the published excerpts of *Answered Prayers*.

No, Truman's interest in me was flattering. His caring about my imagination constituted a great compliment, and turned my head. It made me feel if not exactly respected, then at least heard, for the first time. Without that, I'm not sure I could ever have gotten to where I am today—that is, relatively sane, about my writing, about my teaching, and about my evolving friendship with Vincent.

I told Truman so many tales about Havana, London, and Paris; Valetta and Malé; Rolle, the town in Switzerland where Le Rosey is located, and West New York, New Jersey, where a child of revolution could find refuge in a working-class enclave with the extended tribe of her family's trusted servant Benedict. I told him about singing "La Bayamesa" and eating *ropa vieja* and *picadillo*; about worshiping the Blessed Virgin as La Virgen de la Caridad del Cobre, before setting out for the big city across the river and seeking work as a servant myself.

Then one day at our vast oak table in the Mercantile Library, with a portrait of Ralph Waldo Emerson looking down on us from the wall, Truman announced that he needed to suspend our work together for a month or two, while he finished up some other projects.

"I am going crazy at the moment, Serene One. All these interviews, all the parties . . . Keep going without me, and we'll resume soon."

He described the harrowing volume of requests he was receiving—from magazines, television shows, universities, benefit committees . . . I was fine with taking a break. I had already absorbed so much from Truman that I was glad to have some time to process it all. For me, our sessions were always more about finding the artistic soul than learning a writer's tricks. It was about the intentions and hopes behind the impulse to write, itself. I knew that I had been afforded a privileged relationship with a great writer, and I was already eternally grateful.

It was during the same meeting that Truman confessed to me he loved Lee.

"I know you do," I said.

"No, I really do," said Truman. "It's not the same as with the others. Babe, I adore. Gloria, I adore. Lee is . . . somethin' else, as they say."

I was curious not so much why he was telling me this, but why he was feeling it *now*? I had an inkling that day—especially after all the talk about how busy he was—that money and fame had finally put him in a position to have what he'd always thought he should have, perhaps including the fairy-tale mate that an eight-year-old might have dreamed of.

It was more than wanting to help Lee further develop her independence, he explained. He wanted to possess her in the way Bill possessed Babe. He used that word, "possess"—a little ironically, a little comically, I think, but he also meant it. Truman didn't use words sloppily. Of course, he knew he couldn't possess Lee, he said, but that was the feeling he was now sure he had: love.

"What do you mean 'love,' Truman?" I wondered if he quietly resented all the successful husbands who "possessed" the amazing women who were his swans.

"If things were different with me, I would want her. Simple as that."

I dared not ask if he really meant physically, and if he would expect Lee to welcome this kind of love.

"I know she treasures you," I said.

"Well, yes, I *am* a treasure, aren't I?"

"Isn't that enough?" I knew I was being impertinent.

"Oh, now don't go and analyze me, Anna Freud. That would be boring, and you want to be anything but boring."

With a little extra free time on my hands, I read more voraciously than ever, finally getting around to *Bleak House* and then immediately re-reading it, to figure out exactly by what divine literary contraption Dickens could make me cry over the death of the crossing sweep, Jo. I could also say yes when Judy suggested I join her and John for some cultural outings: the opening of the Whitney Museum of Art's dramatic new fortress on Madison Avenue; a performance of a new play by Edward Albee, *A Delicate Balance*, that John called "an existential parlor drama"; a showing of *Variations V*, an informal but decidedly fascinating, so-called "mixed media" work by choreographer Merce Cunningham, with electronic sounds triggered by the dancers' movements. Judy and John were married by now, with a two-year-old child, James, installed in an apartment on East 78th Street, around the corner from the Park Avenue apartment where Judy had grown up and I had lived while working for Judy's grandmother. John's law practice was centered in the New York art world, with clients including major dealers like Leo Castelli and Ileana Sonnabend.

"He's a mama's boy," Judy told me, one day when we were having coffee alone, after taking in some art galleries on 57th Street.

"Oh, really?" I said, making a face.

"No, that's a good thing. I love it. It brings out the best in me."

"It does?"

"I love taking care of him, and it's usually on my terms. He was very well trained."

"That's a surprise. I thought mama's boys were supposed to be spoiled and selfish."

"Ha. Bad ones are. But the good ones—and my experience extends only to John, of course—they're communicative, cooperative, and kind to women. And you know how rare that is in today's world."

"So . . . you're living in a women's liberation paradise?"

"I wouldn't go that far," said Judy. "But it does work for us. Of course, it helps to have help."

Judy and John had engaged a full time *au pair* girl and were planning on having another child as soon as possible.

"Ulla is a lifesaver," continued Judy. "And do you know that James already knows a few words in Swedish?"

"That's wonderful! I wonder what Swedish for *wonderful* is . . ."

"She has James saying *fantastisk* a lot, for things he really likes, like his Liddle Kiddle dolls."

"I hope you're getting pictures of all this."

"Oh, yes. And John says he's not too young to start sketching, so he's got all the paper and pencils in the universe, and sometimes Ulla takes him into the park, where they always sketch the same tree. He tries his best, and she sketches, too, you see—so it's like a game. She went to art school. Oh, and Mar, once we all spent an hour in the park together, the four of us, sketching that darned tree. We must have looked like the oddest art class ever."

"Lee sketches too, sometimes. Botanical things. Watercolors, too. You know she has this wonderful collection of botanical art from various cultures. But she says she's terrible at figures—human figures. 'Jackie's the one who can do people,' she says."

"How's it going?"

"Well enough. Better than that, actually. Better than I had any right to expect it would be, back when I was a kid."

Judy reached over and put her hand on mine.

"Good," she said. "You've come through, and that's a wonderful thing to see."

"Your mom and grandmother were lifesavers," I said. "You know I'll always be grateful."

"All we wanted was to help. Because we like you so much."

"And now I'm learning so much from Truman."

"Really? Writing?"

I didn't want to say anything specific about a screenplay—that felt private, between Truman and me only—but I saw no harm in speaking generally.

"Writing, yes," I said. "All those devices and tricks and structures that writers use, for sure. He even helps me understand what I am reading—how an author doesn't necessarily have to *build* sympathy for a character but lets the reader unlock her own sympathy. There's that. Then there's some bigger view of culture, of life, that motivates a writer to write in the first place."

"Observation?"

"More like mania."

"Mania?"

"Writing to take care of one's self. Writing to take care of the world. By trying to entertain and enlighten, and thereby, oh, to *protect*. Do you know what I mean? Beyond all the prizes and accolades and movie deals. It's also a kind of deeply motherly act, I think—writing."

"Interesting."

"Anyway, I see this in Truman's work. The work he does, I mean—the application of his life to writing, day by day; not simply the work he creates, but the output of his soul . . ."

Sailing the Aegean and sailing the Adriatic are two different worlds. In the former, you are immersed in the afterglow of ancient Greek civilizations; in the latter, it's the lingering radiance of the Roman and Venetian empires that you feel. There is more sea between the Greek islands of the Aegean than between the islands along the Dalmatian coast, which also lie closer to the mainland. Whether or not there is much difference in the waters of each domain, and any domain-specific seafaring skills that might be required, I don't know. This is a detail that neither Lee nor Truman ever mentioned to me.

In July, Truman joined Gianni and Marella Agnelli for a cruise of the Adriatic along the Dalmatian coast, aboard their eighty-two-foot yawl *Agneta*—a sleek, regatta-worthy craft of teak and spruce, with exquisitely crafted, inlaid mahogany interiors and distinctive, maroon-colored sails. This was a sporty yacht, as befitting the manufacturer of sports cars and a race car driver himself. As yachts that Truman sailed on went, *Agneta* was relatively small—accommodating only its owners, in a relatively compact master suite; at most four guests, in two tiny cabins with tiny en suite heads; and a crew of two or three. The galley was no larger than what might be found in a camper, which meant that itineraries were often planned to accommodate overnight stops near towns with decent restaurants. By contrast, the Guinnesses' yacht was one hundred and forty feet long and had a statelier mien. It featured a proper saloon and dining room, and spacious decks for outdoor dining and dancing; a lavish owner's suite and five large guest suites; and crew quarters that accommodated twenty-seven. The Agnellis dressed casually to sail—well, elegantly and casually—while Gloria Guinness was known to emerge from her master suite to host an evening for twelve in a designer gown and jewels.

"Which yacht do you prefer?" I once asked Truman.

"Both are great in their way," said Truman. "I'm happy as long as there's good conversation. And by conversation, I mean gossip."

Both vessels were equipped with the latest electronic equipment, which included a ship-to-shore communications system that could patch into international telephone networks. Aboard the Agnellis' yacht, the phone was in the saloon, which for any privacy meant speaking on it after the Agnellis retired to their suite.

"We're in a little bay in Šolta," said Truman, a little drunk, his feet up on the blue-striped-canvas-upholstered banquette. He was in a pair of pastel plaid bathing shorts and an open, white Dunhill shirt with rolled-up sleeves. It was around ten at night, and he was speaking with Lee, who was an hour behind him, in the Algarve. It was a warm evening, and a peek out Truman's oblong, polished-brass-framed porthole revealed no lights at all, though they were close to shore.

"South of Split?" she said.

"Exactly. There's literally nothing here, no people or anything. It's an unspoiled bay. Apparently, to wake up in the morning and swim in the nude is the most wonderful thing."

"Does she cook? There's an absolutely minuscule crew, I believe."

"Only the skipper and his mate. No, we had an early dinner in a town a few miles away—mussels and black risotto—then we sailed here for the night. She picked up a few things for breakfast and lunch. I can't imagine anything more splendid. We're all reading. Gianni's got *A Thousand Days*—the Schlesinger—and Marella has *The Embezzler*—Louis Auchincloss."

"They've both read blah-blah."

"Of course they have."

"And you? What are you reading?"

"I have the July issue of *Town and Country*."

"Oh good. So you're relaxing."

"Well, yes, but I'm working, too—on two things. Can you hear me? I have to speak quietly."

"Everybody gone to bed?"

"It's just us. I'm the only guest."

"Well, it's good to hear you're working. Though I think you deserve a little rest."

"The thing is, Lee, I realize that I am desperate to write something for the ages. That's why I can't relax *too* much."

"What do you mean?"

"*Breakfast* was charming; *In Cold Blood*, incredibly successful. But *for the ages*?"

"Now, Truman . . ."

"*Answered Prayers* feels like what I was put on earth to do. I have become very aware in recent months—I can tell you this—aware of a need to get beyond this detestable satisfaction one takes in being lionized. Do you know what I mean? I realized I was defining myself more by my television appearances than by my writing, and that's not good. Jack helped me see this. We had quite a row about it before I left, but he's absolutely right."

"God bless Jack."

"Indeed. Though I drove from Verbier to Trieste, where I met up with Marella and Gianni, and I think they were glad to see that Jack didn't come, though they did invite him. He can be such a stick. And on a yacht, you really have to make an effort—you know?"

"You said you were working on two things."

"Oh, yes—the ball! I'm going to do it."

"Oh, Truman—how marvelous!"

"This fall, so get ready."

"So soon!"

"Why not?"

The bay was calm. The yacht was rocking gently, and a little breeze was slipping in through the open porthole. From outside came the sound of tiny waves lapping against the wooden hull.

"It will be a great masked ball in a beautiful room," continued Truman. "Cecil suggested it should be all black-and-white. I had been thinking about putting 'diamonds only' on the invitation . . ."

"I love it!"

"But I'm having second thoughts. See, originally I thought the presence of sapphires, rubies, and emeralds would spoil Cecil's black-and-white scheme. But then last month, I was sitting by Eleanor's pool—Eleanor Frieda, out in Bridgehampton—and she said that some of her friends had hocked their diamonds and wouldn't be able to come."

"They could always wear no jewelry. Or paste."

"Not at my ball, thank you. So there it is. I think the black-and-white attire will be strong enough to carry any jewels that night. And the masks, of course. Did I say masks?"

"Who will be invited?" asked Lee.

"I'm planning all that now—the guests, the food, the music," said Truman. "But I want it to be only people I like. Admission will be only by invitation with your name on it. No 'and guest' or 'plus one.' "

"So—very private?"

"No. Large and splashy, but definitely exclusive. I am thinking of the ballroom at the Plaza, something like that. But seriously—only people I like. If I like the wife but not the husband, then goodbye, Charlie."

"Good luck, Truman."

"It will all be done with grace. I want a mix of people—writers, actors, singers, artists, scientists, all that. I am thinking of asking some of my Kansas friends."

"Who?"

"Law enforcement in the Clutter case."

"Really."

"And I am going to ask Marlene."

"My Marlene?"

"Yes, why not? She's a charming girl. Maybe she'll meet someone."

"Are you sure she'll feel comfortable?"

"I'm sure."

"Alright."

Truman repositioned one of the throw pillows and curled up on the banquette.

"Now listen, I've been speaking to Susskind about *Laura*, and I think he is getting ready to talk to you," he said. "Please say you are still interested. Please say you are more interested than ever."

"I've been thinking about it."

"Don't be coy with me."

"I'm not being coy. It would be a big step for me, and I only want to make sure I'd be doing it for the right reasons. I know very well what you mean about the puny satisfaction of being lionized."

"Though of course that has its upside, too. Now that the book is a big success, Susskind has been calling *me*."

"Do you really think I can do it, Truman?"

"That's a given. And David knows it, too. Remember Babe's party?"

Back in April, they had all been together at a party in the Paleys' new apartment—Lee and Truman, Joyce and David Susskind, and fifty other movers and shakers.

"I did a little acting in school," said Lee, at the party.

"I'll bet you were brilliant," said Susskind.

"It's a great story, a great character," said Truman. "Someone *has* to remake it, and someone will make a bundle on it."

"What about the original author—Caspary?" said Susskind. "She's still alive, isn't she?"

"She'll be thrilled I'm adapting it."

"You sure about that?"

"She was thrilled with the original movie."

"She was not, Truman. I know Preminger, and he once told me she *hated* the script."

"Why should she hate it? The movie was a hit."

"Oh, Truman—because that's the way authors are."

"But David—you'll pay her well for the rights. Authors love *that*."

From the other end of the phone line, on his call with Lee, she laughed, to hear Truman recount his telling Susskind how much authors love money.

"What's happening in the Algarve?" said Truman.

"Well, the kids have been having a ball splashing around in the water. On Friday, we went for a beach walk in Albufeira with an oceanographer and learned all about tides and tide pools and animals that give birth in the sand."

"Oh, my."

"Then next week we go see the cathedral in Silves and learn all about earthquakes and architectural restoration."

"Lots to do."

"They're curious about everything, which is good to see. And I must say it's awfully nice to see Stas spending such a happy time with them. In spite of everything, the family is still so important to both of us."

"How cozy."

"And what do you all have planned?"

"Oh, Marella has some church she wants us to see in Hvar—particularly the bell tower. A travel writer is meeting us there, to tell us why we should like the thing."

"You don't sound very excited about it."

"Why are we always called upon to admire churches?"

"There's always a lot to learn, to think about . . ."

"The same can be said, princess, about a Cartier boutique. Except I don't think we'll find one of those in Hvar."

Chapter 13

The Ball of the Century

If you listen to what people of the comfortable class say about fall in New York, you will understand that the season means returning to the city after time spent at an ocean beach home, or a mountain lake retreat, or a country house not within view of any public road. It means new clothes and a full social schedule that requires them: Broadway premieres; opening nights at the opera, ballet, and symphony; benefit galas; private dinner parties . . . But if you listen to what the planet says about fall in New York, you may grasp something underlying all that social activity: a renewed clarity about the terms of life. The sun is actually closer to the earth during the Northern Hemisphere's winter, and its light is stronger, but it's the tilt of the earth on its axis that controls the seasons of both hemispheres. Because the sun is becoming lower in the sky during New York's fall, there is gradually more atmosphere for the sun's rays to pass through. Days grow cooler. Shadows begin to lengthen. The appearance of colors softens from glare to shimmer. Human beings have been in tune with these effects since the beginning of history, and each year, as our awareness of these changes pops from the subliminal into the conscious—*if* it does pop!—we shift between enjoying the season and enjoying our own enjoyment of it. It's a process analogous to what happens in the spring—only the enjoyment then stems from the possibility of Nature's taking care of Humanity, by renewing the earth, whereas the enjoyment of fall stems from humanity's habit of taking care of itself, by building shelter and storing food and fuel.

And then there is the way fall smells in New York, when there are fewer vegetal molecules in the air and the petrochemical ones become more noticeable. Moreover, New York's mass of stone, steel, glass, concrete, and asphalt breathes in its own way, inhaling and exhaling, with minuscule expansions and contractions. People who are paying attention can smell the city's breath. This respiration, mixed with those lengthening shadows and mapped onto busy social schedules—*that's* what quickens the pulse of people like Lee and Truman in the fall, especially if they are also wearing the season's newest clothes.

I was twenty-five in the fall of 1966 and feeling pretty good about my life.

My job was protecting and sustaining me as I had hoped it would, and I was beginning to feel I could afford to be a little more open about *finding myself*, to use the terminology of those times. I was beginning to *be* myself. I can hardly blame anyone but me for feeling *unseen* for many years. I showed myself to no one except a little bit to Lee and Truman—yet both of them died without ever knowing the truth about my past.

I kept the first seventeen years of my life to myself, not because I was ashamed of them, but because others were ashamed of them, and I unwittingly assimilated their attitude. Automatically, I adopted their habit of glossing over past horrors. Only recently, as a so-called senior citizen, have I realized that the world had moved on and no longer judged or blamed people for the kinds of things that happened to me—yet I was still stuck defending my icky shame. Now, perhaps, finally, it's begun to melt away and leave me some space for new feelings. Yes, I was an embarrassment to my mother; yes, I was treated violently by my half-brother and stepfather; yes, I was unloved by both so-called parents and couldn't wait to get away from them. And now all of that feels over.

The truth is I am illegitimate, the child of rape. It's the sort of thing that can happen in any family, Cuban or not, aristocratic or not, rich or not—right? My mother never loved me, but felt that because of the family's Catholic background, she had to keep me around. So I was resented and given second-class status that my mother's husband took as permission to abuse me. In fact, he abused all of us, my mother, my half-brother, and me. Over the years, I have heard stories of loving families and always found them slightly unbelievable. How could people possibly breathe, I wondered, when soaked in all that smothering love? Perhaps I was bitter without even realizing it, when puzzling over stories of children turning to parents for safety and protection. How could a parent's arms be safe? Perhaps watching Lee and Stas's family, which was far from ideal but still full of love, I felt a little envious—as I did watching Truman and Jack together, especially at the end, when a devoted Jack was helping care for his failing ex-partner. I have heard that lots of people with backgrounds like mine turn to violence and self-harm, or drinking and drugs. Me, I just kept walking away from the past, toward who-knows-what, telling myself a different story about the past in a purely instinctual effort to survive.

I wasn't playing around. This was a matter of life and death for me. My mother despised me, my father beat me, my half-brother tried to rape me more than once and then threatened to kill me if I told anyone about it, at which point I left home. For me, working for Lee was like being in a witness protection program—no, like having an important supporting role in the best movie ever! At close range were the most fascinating people, the most exciting parties, the most fashionable wardrobes, the most glamorous travel destinations ever, not to mention the great events of the age. *This* was a life I loved to watch, and I was both compelled and content to watch it, stuffed as it was with images of the kind that that canny Andy Warhol knew we wanted to stare at then—the Jackies and Marilyns and Maos and Lizzes and Elvises, the soup cans and astronauts and car crashes and electric chairs . . . It was the biggest blaze of images and messages yet in human history, and I had a front-row seat. Like a lot of movie junkies, I was convinced that this movie was better by far than my own so-called real life, and watching it became for me, for many years, Life Itself.

I am not qualified to judge Lee's marriage to Stas, or to know why it would end eight years later in divorce. My heart always went out to both of them—for their best hopes of formulating something that would work for them and for Tina and Anthony. I did witness little difficulties, though, and the memory of that continues to make me sad.

"So I heard from David Susskind about the screen test," said Lee.

"Yes?" said Stas.

"He liked it."

"Did he?"

"Yes, he did. He said I reminded him of Dina Merrill."

"So you're going through with this?"

"I'm leaning toward it."

It was an October evening, and they were having dinner alone, in the New York apartment. The children were in the nursery.

"I think you're making a mistake," said Stas.

"I know you do," said Lee. "Thanks for all the support."

"I . . . never mind. Why did you shoot it in London, anyway?"

That's where they'll be taping the film."

"For you?"

"It's cheaper there, apparently."

"Alright."

Between bits of conversation, the only sounds in the dining room were of knives and forks clinking on plates, and wine and water glasses being placed back on the table.

"By the way, the invitations arrived today for Truman's ball," said Lee.

"Ah, yes?" said Stas.

"One for you and one for me."

"Really? Not one for 'Mr. and Mrs.'?"

"That's not the way he's doing it. It's one person, one invitation."

"Odd, but then . . . so it won't be couples?"

"Not necessarily. I can think of wives he'll want whose husbands he won't."

"That's odd."

"It's next month."

"Fine."

"November twenty-eighth. It's a Monday."

"Right," said Stas, and then he paused for a second. "Oh, uh . . . you mean just after Thanksgiving?"

"That's right," said Lee.

"Well, Lee, as I mentioned, if you remember . . ."

"I do remember."

"I have that business in Palm Beach, the Worth Avenue property . . ."

"Stas, look, let's not have this conversation. You'll see her for a few days and then you'll get on a plane, and we'll attend Truman's ball together."

"I wish I could—I really do. Aren't you the guest of honor, anyway? Won't he want you at his side all night?"

"I am not the guest of honor. Kay Graham is."

"From Washington?"

"Yes."

"I didn't know they were such good friends."

"Well, they are. And he couldn't very well pick one of his New York gals."

"Why not?"

"How would the rest of us feel?"

"Ah."

"I ask very little of you, Stas. But there are certain requirements to making it work. We've talked about this. This ball will be the social event of the season, and I want us to be there together."

"I'll see what I can do."

"She will be fine."

Lee's tone of voice was firm. Stas sighed.

"If it means that much to you . . ." he said.

"It does," said Lee.

"Then I'll fly up on Monday morning."

"Thank you."

It was around the same time that Truman told me about an encounter he had with Lila North. She "accosted" him, he said, one afternoon in the lobby of UN Plaza.

"Truman, Truman . . ." she shouted, across the normally hushed, red-carpeted expanse.

She had been leaving the building and spotted Truman coming in after lunch, as he was heading for the elevator. She waddled over, barely managing her handbag, tote bag, and briefcase, in addition to a formless knitted hat that she hadn't yet put on.

"Yes?" said Truman. "Oh, it's you. Hello, Lila."

"Truman, do you have just a moment?" Lila seemed out of breath after crossing the lobby so quickly.

"A moment, yes," said Truman. He stepped away from the polished bronze elevator door and over to a glass wall, where he remained standing next to a pair of Barcelona chairs. "But I am expected upstairs. What are you doing here, anyway? Waiting for li'l ol' me?"

"I was interviewing Katharine Graham," said Lila, plopping her bags down on one of the chairs.

"Oh. Good for you."

"About your party."

"It's a ball, Lila. We call it a ball. And what did Mrs. Graham have to say about it?"

"She's very excited."

"As well she should be."

"Tell me, what does a guest of honor have to do?"

Lila had already produced a little, messy-looking tablet and was beginning to take notes with a ballpoint pen.

"What a question. My guest of honor has nothing to do but attend and enjoy herself."

"That's it?"

"That's a lot. One greets people and enjoys that. One dances a little and enjoys it."

"Will there be supper?"

"Oh Lord, Lila. Of course."

"What are you serving?"

"Are you serious?"

"I'm reporting."

"Chicken hash."

"And what about the guest list?"

"What about it? For the moment, it's an absolute secret. Rather, I am not publishing it, though people who have been invited are naturally free to talk about it themselves, if they like."

"The Duke and Duchess of Windsor?"

"I can't say."

"Mrs. Kennedy?"

"I can't say."

"Princess Radziwill?"

"Lila, I don't want to waste your time. If there is anything you want to know that I *can* tell you . . ."

"Are you inviting press?"

"Absolutely not."

"May I ask why not?"

"I can't see how their presence could possibly contribute to the atmosphere I am creating."

"But the buzz, Truman—the buzz! We buzz things up."

"Believe me, there is already plenty of buzz. I don't need to pay for any more of it from your lot."

"What do you mean, 'pay'?"

"I mean enduring the presence of nosy, badly dressed people who ask a lot of silly questions."

Lila was stymied and looked it.

"So there's no way you can work me in?"

"Ha! I'm afraid not."

"But I hear that Suzy Knickerbocker was invited."

"Mrs. Mehle, as you well know, enjoys a position in society quite apart from her column. She's coming as a friend."

"You may regret not inviting the press."

"Regret not inviting piece-workers to the ball of the century? I think not."

Lila closed her notebook and shoved it away in her tote bag.

"By the way, I saw you on *What's My Line?*," she said. "Part of your publicity program?"

"Bennett Cerf was kind enough to arrange that for me."

"I see. Is that why he wasn't on the show that night?"

"How did you like it—my appearance?"

"I think you made a smart choice by not using your real voice to answer questions. The clown horn really seemed to suit you."

Truman smirked.

"And now, if you'll excuse me, Lila," he said, "I really must get upstairs."

Truman walked back to the elevator and pressed UP.

"Good luck with your story," he said.

"Thank you," said Lila, tucking her hair into the knitted hat.

The elevator door opened.

"Please note," said Truman over his shoulder, as he walked in. "Chicken hash *and* spaghetti."

Central Park, in those days, though pretty to look at through Fifth Avenue windows, was neglected and run down. Plantings were overgrown, pathways were deteriorated, and litter was strewn all over the ground. Metropolitan Museum of Art director Thomas Hoving had recently been appointed as the city's Parks Commissioner and was promising a new Central Park program of concerts and festivals, but so far, the surveillance and maintenance necessary for such a program were not in place, and many New Yorkers felt that by day the park was still the territory of noisy gangs of skateboarders, and by night, of muggers, rapists, and murderers. A narrow band of park just inside its venerable stone walls along Fifth, though, was sometimes used by neighborhood residents for taking some sun on a nice day, as they sat on one of the benches that wasn't broken or soiled with bird droppings. The area in back of the Metropolitan Museum near the Egyptian obelisk, too, was relatively safe; Lee and Truman were sitting there one afternoon in early November, waiting to be met by Hoving, to be given a little "tour" of the obelisk and an overview—because Hoving was in fundraising mode—of the Museum's plans to build an extension on the park, to house a large art collection that had been promised to it.

"I almost feel sorry for her," said Truman.

"Why?" said Lee.

"She's a mess. She doesn't seem to understand how little power she has. She asks all the wrong questions, has no instinct for the real story. She's just not smart enough to command the position she has."

"Then why does she still have it? New York is supposed to be such a meritocracy. Why hasn't she been fired?"

They were talking about Lila North, who had recently reported that Truman was raking in upwards of two million dollars from new writing contracts and the sale of movie rights. Truman was conflicted about the mention—miffed to have his business affairs made public, but gratified that his business was being publicized as so successful.

The weather was cold but not frigid. Bundled in overcoats and huddled close together, they were smoking constantly while sharing one of those big, warm, doughy pretzels that are sold by the city's sidewalk vendors. Towering over them was the seventy-foot, pink granite monolith inscribed on four sides with hieroglyphics and cartouches.

"Journalism, dear princess, is not necessarily a meritocracy," said Truman. "I once heard something about her having slept with the paper's publisher."

"Still—that's not enough reason to keep someone on staff who's bringing down the quality of your publication," said Lee. "Is it?"

"No—you're right. It's got to be more than that."

"Though I suppose if what she writes is true . . ."

"What she writes may be true enough," said Truman. "The point is that it usually isn't news. Or particularly interesting."

"At least she's stopped writing about me."

"No, she seems more interested in me these days. She makes sounds about my 'male writer friends' as if she's uncovered a Russian plot. She's like a horsefly that won't leave you alone."

"So you're not planning to take over the world?"

"Lee, we already control the world. Haven't you heard?"

A pair of runners sped by, dressed in tracksuits.

"When did everybody start running?" said Truman.

"Jackie has started doing it. She loves it," said Lee.

"What are they running from? What are they running toward?"

"She says it clears her mind."

"She should be careful where she runs in this city."

"She seems to think the park can be revived. She's been talking to Tom about it."

"I wonder if New York can *be* revived. It's going to take more than Lincoln Center to make the city shine again."

"Did it ever actually shine? It's not that kind of city."

"Oh, yes, of course. 1902. Edith Wharton. Henry James."

Lee nodded and put a bite of pretzel in her mouth.

"Alright," she said.

"It *is* industry news—I'll give her that," said Truman.

"What is?" said Lee.

"My earnings."

"Are you still on that?"

"It's vulgar, but on second thought, it's valid."

"Truman . . ."

"I'm trying to be fair here. And I'm trying to be calm. I do have to deal with a lot of anxiety, you know—accepting all this money and promising publicly to deliver something big for it."

"Expectations can be frightening. I learned that with my mother."

"When I was a child, Lee, my mother would lock me up in a closet, and I didn't know when anybody was going to come and let me out. It created a tremendous sense of anxiety that I've never been able to shake."

"I know."

"I would spend hours and hours writing obsessively in longhand. Then when I was eight I was given a typewriter. That's when I learned to protect myself with the only means I had at my disposal—my mind."

"Self-protection. That's the key to survival. Jackie and I were always sailing on Narragansett Bay or riding on trails in the Blue Ridge Mountains—always competing on some level. My teachers at Miss Porter's seemed to find me bright and imaginative enough, but my grades were only average. Whereas my darling sister was the star."

"Have some more pretzel."

"I hated Miss Porter's," continued Lee. "It was so rah–rah-rah. And then at Chapin, I hated the sports, and was always the last one to be chosen for a team. Which made me feel pathetic."

"*You* are a star," said Truman. "And I have seen that knack you have for protecting yourself. It's a real talent."

"Thanks, Truman. That means a lot to me."

"And we're not kids anymore, remember."

"We certainly are not."

"All that is over. And we can take care of ourselves."

"We try to, anyway."

Truman laughed. "A smart, beautiful woman will never be at a loss."

"Don't be so sure. Look at poor Jackie."

"She'll come out okay. 'Poor Jackie,' indeed. Just you watch."

"So, about *Philadelphia Story* . . ." said Lee.

Truman and David Susskind had arranged for Lee to be offered the role of Tracy Lord in an upcoming production of *The Philadelphia Story* at Chicago's Ivanhoe Theater. It was more or less a dry run for Lee's participation in the *Laura* shoot, which was looking more and more likely, as both Lee and Susskind warmed to the idea.

"It's a great first step for you," said Truman. "And we can show David that you're serious."

"I've decided to do it."

Truman immediately stood and graciously bowed to Lee.

"That's the spirit," he said, and returned to his seat to give Lee a little hug. "I'm delighted to hear it!"

"I'll need help," said Lee.

"Of course you will, and we'll get help—the best acting coach there is. David is already onto someone he believes in for you."

"I thought, I'll regret it if I don't at least try."

"It's a natural for you, Lee. You *are* Tracy Lord. The writing is great. It will carry you, you'll see—as great writing for stage and screen always does. You discover . . . antigravity qualities in the words. They let you soar."

"Good. I'm excited."

"Turn to the left."

"What do you mean?"

"I'm looking at your face in this glorious daylight."

Lee turned.

"Now to the right, please," said Truman.

Lee turned again, then resumed her original position and took a drag on her cigarette.

"Even here, with only a single light source, our friend the sun, you look perfect—really. I can already see all that with my well-trained eyes."

"Can you, indeed?"

"You will need the coaching—lots of it. But everybody needs that—Hepburn, Marilyn, everyone. Lee, that's where you learn the tricks—what to do with your eyes, what to do with your hands. It's easy. You've just got to be shown. It will be fun. I'm so excited."

Truman checked his watch.

"It's five after," he said. "He's late. Are you okay? Do you want another pretzel?"

"I'm fine, thanks. Wait until you see the dress I got for the ball," said Lee.

"Givenchy?"

"No, no. I'm not going to tell you. I'll just say that I am very happy with it."

"Then I will be, too. White or black?"

"Wait and see. Maybe with my mask, you won't even recognize me."

Then Truman spotted Thomas Hoving, in a black overcoat

and homburg, walking toward them from the direction of the Museum's parking lot.

"Here he is now," said Truman.

"Greetings, greetings, you two," said Hoving, as he embraced Lee, then Truman. After a moment of apologies and pleasantries, the director led them closer to the obelisk and launched into a genial little lecture.

"It's called Cleopatra's Needle, but of course it dates from fifteen hundred years before that. As you probably know, it was a gift from the Khedive of Egypt, Mehmet Ali Pasha, and has stood on this spot since 1881, which was just one year after the Met moved into the original portion of our building here at this address . . ."

There had been resistance to Truman's "stag only" ball invitation strategy, especially from the ladies, who were not used to attending big affairs without a husband or favored escort at their side. One lady told Truman, "I'm not going to get dressed up and put on a mask only to arrive alone." So he had arranged for several small parties to be given beforehand, so guests could arrive at the ball in groups.

The choice of Katharine Graham as guest of honor was hailed as masterful, since she wasn't central to Truman's New York social orbit, as the swans were, yet she was powerful and well-connected. "She's been elevated to honorary swan-hood," said one of the many newspaper articles about "the party of the century." Years later, remembering the evening, Lee told me that she had indeed hoped for a while to be Truman's guest of honor, admitting that she'd wanted to cement her victory over Babe Paley as "head swan." She laughed as she recalled this venal desire and said she'd always nonetheless understood the strategic importance of Truman's putting a non-New Yorker like Mrs. Graham on his throne.

Early on the evening of the ball, before converging on the Grand Ballroom of the Plaza Hotel, Lee, Truman, and I were in three different locations, each of us on our own trajectory. Lee, after coming home that afternoon from Kenneth's, and dressing early, went off with Stas to the Paleys' place, for one of the eighteen pre-parties that Truman had more or less ordered his friends to host. Truman, whose apartment was in the same building, after all, as Kay Graham's New York *pied-à-terre*, looked in at the Paleys' with Mrs. Graham, then dashed with her over to the suite at the Plaza that he'd booked to make the evening as comfortable as possible for her and to give them a quiet place for a drink and a boxed dinner ordered from "21," before going downstairs. And I was at Lee's apartment, putting myself together in a long, plain black dress that I'd found on sale at Bloomingdale's, which I accessorized with a pair of diamond stud earrings that Lee had been kind enough to lend me.

Built in 1905 in the French Renaissance style, the twenty-one-story Plaza Hotel anchors the southeastern corner of Central Park at Fifth Avenue and 59th Street, on majestically broad Grand Army Plaza. Since opening in 1921, the hotel's Grand Ballroom has been a magnet for New York social elite, site of the city's most exclusive receptions, benefits, and debutante cotillions. The design and proportions of the white-and-gold room hum with neoclassical elegance. Bordered in round-arch colonnades of fluted, double-story Ionic columns, hung with two massive crystal chandeliers, and graced with all manner of painted cherubs, sculpted garlands, glittering mirrors, and gilded sconces, the ballroom is perhaps New York's most sanctified non-religious space, a high altar for those in the city devoted to the ritual enjoyment of wealth and privilege.

The evening was cold and rainy. From the back of my cab, I saw from even a block away that traffic at the intersection of Fifth and 59th was tied up. Leaving the cab at the curb of Fifth, near the fountain in front of the hotel, I had to make my way through police barricades holding back an exuberant throng of paparazzi, television cameramen, and umbrella-toting spectators eager for a glimpse of some of the celebrity guests who'd been mentioned in the press—a carefully curated mix of the twentieth century's most influential who's-whos: the Duke and

Duchess of Windsor, Lady Bird Johnson and Lynda Bird Johnson, Rose Kennedy, Harry Belafonte, Gloria Vanderbilt, Norman Mailer, Candice Bergen, Andy Warhol, Frank Sinatra and Mia Farrow . . . The ball was described by someone as "a tour de force of social engineering," and more than one commentator pointedly mentioned that only months before, a rally of two hundred thousand activists had taken place across the street, in Central Park, to protest America's involvement in Vietnam.

Judy had been so envious that I was going.

"Can you get me in?"

"Invitation only. It's very exclusive, you know."

"I just had to ask. John told me Andy Warhol is going."

"Of course *he's* going."

"What are you wearing?"

"Black."

"Mask?"

"Five-and-ten."

"Hair?"

"I dunno. Up? Back?"

I presented my admission card—which read MR. CAPOTE'S DANCE—checked my coat, and donned my mask—a simple, black-sequined, domino-type masquerade number. Mounting the broad staircase to the ballroom's palatial foyer, I heard the lush sound of Peter Duchin's orchestra playing inside, from the ballroom's stage—"I Have Dreamed," from *The King and I*. Within minutes, I had entered the ballroom, accepted a flute of Taittinger champagne, and was taking an initial stroll around, admiring the gowns and masks and the elaborate headdresses. Some of the men had pushed up or taken off their masks, but it looked to me like the women were taking the idea of disguise very seriously and were enjoying the game of *perhaps* not being immediately identifiable. The crowd was not too dense, allowing a proper amount of space for posing and preening. Truman had invited 540 people, and I guessed that the ballroom could accommodate twice that amount. The mood was unmistakably elevated, which is what every host wants for a party, but this gathering glowed with the added sheen of legend-in-the-making. Smiles radiated self-congratulation, as the status of "world's most fabulous" had been officially conferred by superstar author Truman Capote on every single person in attendance.

I spotted Truman at the head of the receiving line, alongside a very regal-looking Mrs. Graham, in a white cassock trimmed with black beads, that Lee told me later was Balmain. When it was my turn, a foursome glided away, and Truman instantly recognized me, despite my mask and the fact that I had put my hair up in a chignon for the first time in years.

"Good evening, Marlene," he said warmly. He was wearing a new Dunhill tuxedo that he'd had made for the occasion. "Kay, this is a great friend of mine, Marlene X. Her identity will be revealed anon, I trust. Marlene, this is Katharine Graham."

"It's a pleasure," I said.

Mrs. Graham said hello and extended her hand graciously, and then turned to greet the gentleman in back of me, author Ralph Ellison. Before Truman turned to Ellison, too, he squeezed my arm.

"Thanks for coming," he said. "You look spectacular. Have fun."

Before I was able to move off toward a more tranquil part of the room, I happened to overhear a bit of Truman's conversation with Mrs. Graham and Ellison.

". . . No. I didn't invite the president, because I didn't want all the extra security fuss, and the first lady agreed. We told him, 'Another time.' So it's just her and her daughter. Oh, and I'm expecting Alice Roosevelt Longworth and Margaret Truman . . ."

As I moved about smiling generically, trying to look like I was catching up with a date, I saw European aristocrats, Asian potentates, American bluebloods, and international industrialists mixing with novelists, scholars, musicians, dancers, and Hollywood and Broadway actors. Many I recognized from the pages of newsmagazines: poet Marianne Moore, literary swells Lionel and Diana Trilling, screen legend Claudette Colbert, and the

Italian princess Luciana Pignatelli, whose headdress featured an enormous diamond hanging between her eyes that Truman told me later was sixty carats and borrowed from Harry Winston.

Among those who had sent regrets were Audrey Hepburn, Nelson Rockefeller, and Jackie. Neither Lee nor Truman ever told me why Jackie didn't come. It may have been simply that she wanted neither to upstage anyone nor be upstaged herself. As the most famous woman in the world, Jackie may have been the only person on earth who was able to think of Truman's ball as just another party.

Lee and Stas arrived and were kind enough, when we spotted each other, to greet me as any other guest.

"You look beautiful," I told Lee.

"Thank you—so do you," said Lee. She was wearing a spectacular white-and-silver beaded shift by Italian designer Mila Schön, whose clients also included Imelda Marcos and the Empress of Iran. Lee told me—"if you're interested"—that Marella Agnelli was also wearing Schön that evening.

"It's quite a gorgeous, white embroidered caftan," said Lee. "You can't miss Marella. She's wearing an enormous headdress of white feathers."

I thought Stas was looking a little glum, until a gentleman stepped over to say hello to the Radziwills, accompanied by a woman in a gold sari—the only person I saw at the ball who wasn't wearing white or black. It was the Maharaja and Maharani of Jaipur, whispered Lee.

"Enjoy yourself," she said with a wink, before turning to the Maharaja.

In addition to all the VIPs, Truman had also invited Mrs. Graham's secretary, members of Jack Dunphy's family, one of his old schoolteachers, and a doorman from the UN Plaza. At one point, I found myself standing among a group of people from Garden City, Kansas, whom Truman had become friendly with during his investigations into the *In Cold Blood* murders. We were discussing the book and its success. I asked the group if, in their view, the book was accurate, and one of them ventured an answer.

"There is accuracy, and there is truth," said a stately older woman who looked as though she could have held her own in any gathering on the planet. "Truman was very accurate, but more importantly, he captured the truth."

The man next to me, who'd introduced himself as "a farmer named Odd Williams," told me quietly that the woman was the widow of Judge Roland Henry Tate, who'd presided over the murder trial of Perry Smith and Richard Hickock. The judge had died a few years before.

Among the recent hits and Broadway tunes played by the orchestra were a few that I gathered had been written by people in the room. After leading the orchestra in "Get Happy," Peter Duchin saluted, from the stage, a man standing in the crowd, whom someone next to me identified as composer Harold Arlen. And when the Duchin orchestra took a break, another jazzier ensemble took over—the Brothers of Soul. It was to a slowish number by this ensemble—"I Guess That Don't Make Me a Loser"—that I saw a round of sweetly prom-level dancing between Truman and Mrs. Graham, David and Joyce Susskind, Babe and Bill Paley, Lauren Bacall and choreographer Jerome Robbins, Henry Fonda and his fifth wife Shirlee Mae Adams, and Henry Ford II and his wife Anne McDonnell. As Suzy Knickerbocker would write a day or so later, "It was that kind of evening."

And then there was Truman dancing with Lee, to Duchin's upbeat rendition of Cole Porter's "Night and Day." It was such a perfect moment for them: the glamorous host and his glamorous best friend.

Whether near to me or far
It's no matter, darlin', where you are
I think of you night and day

They both knew well how to move on a dance floor. I thought Truman looked happier than I'd ever seen him and, now that I think of it, happier than I would ever see him again. And just as I registered his joy, standing there at the edge of the dance floor,

I realized that next to me was Mrs. Graham, also watching. We caught each other enjoying the sight of our dancing host.

"He's created such a magical evening, hasn't he?" said Mrs. Graham.

"It is wonderful," I said, thrilled to be sharing a word with the guest of honor. "I hope you're enjoying yourself. Truman was so eager to give you a nice party."

"Oh, I am—hugely. Ostensibly this is to pay me back for a little party I threw for him in Washington, when the book came out. But can you imagine?"

I smiled. Not knowing what to say, I came up with a cliché.

"He's terrific."

"That he is. If he weren't a great writer, he'd definitely be the best publicity director in the world."

I giggled.

"He once told me he was sure he could be the best car salesman in the world, too," I said.

"May I ask how you're connected to Truman?" asked Mrs. Graham. "I am guessing you're a writer, too, of some sort . . . ?"

"Well . . . no. I work for the Radziwills."

I presumed that Mrs. Graham was savvy enough to know I would have identified myself in another way had my position been grander. She was nice enough not to press the matter.

"That's nice," she said. "I saw Lee this afternoon at the salon."

"Kenneth's? That place must have been the busiest spot in New York today."

"A madhouse! And I was the last one in and the last one out."

"Oh?"

"You see, I simply don't know this town as well as I know Washington. I booked an appointment without specifying a stylist. I showed up, and the place was bonkers. The girl explained that it was because of a big party that was taking place. I told her I knew all about it, that I was the guest of honor; and she suddenly looked embarrassed. She disappeared and came back to say that Kenneth himself would take care of my hair."

"What a story!" I said.

"And now you must excuse me," said Mrs. Graham. The orchestra had launched into the next number, and Truman had come to lead her away.

"Marlene, you must let me steal Kay . . ."

"May I introduce myself?" said a man, before I felt too abandoned. I looked up and saw a soulful-looking gentleman in his fifties, with thinning hair and a crooked kind of half-smile.

"I'm Jack Dunphy," he said.

"Oh, Mr. Dunphy, good evening," I said, extending my hand, which he took.

"You're Marlene, right?"

"Yes."

"Please call me Jack. Truman's told me about you—said you'd be here, and I should introduce myself. I guessed which one you were."

I laughed, a little nervously.

"How?" I said. "Process of deduction? No jewels, no headdress, no maharaja?" I felt I could be jocular with him, as he seemed to want to put me at ease.

"Actually, no," said Jack. "He said he thought you'd be wearing black."

"Oh."

"As you see, most of the women here have opted for white."

"Making me . . . what—a dark horse?"

"A proper nonconformist. Just like our boy."

"Of course."

"Besides, unless I am mistaken, those are diamonds . . ."—he pointed to my ear studs—". . . so technically, that's jewels."

We decided to find the bar and soon had more champagne.

"He's very proud to be paying for this himself, you know," said Jack. "Any number of friends or corporate entities would have been happy to pay for it, if he'd asked. He's generous, in that way—wanted to do something nice for his friends."

"Oh, I know that side," I said. "He is very generous with me—his time, his thoughts—and I am so grateful."

"He likes to share his thoughts—that's for sure."

Jack and I chatted for a while—about Truman, about dance, about parties.

"I don't like parties so much myself, but this one I was ordered to attend," he said.

"Aren't you having a good time?"

"I am now."

I was flattered.

"How do you think it's going?" I said, as we looked out over the crowd.

"Very well," he said. "I imagine Truman is pleased. People seem to be playing nicely together. Although I am told that Pat Buckley threatened to strangle John Galbraith for writing something nasty about Bill—her husband, William Buckley—and Norman Mailer threatened to beat up McGeorge Bundy because of the Vietnam War. That's the former . . ."

". . . National Security Advisor—yes."

"Par for the course. And good for Suzy's column."

"Is Suzy the one who was standing with Truman . . . ?"

"Yup—right up there at the head of the receiving line, with Truman and Kay. Discreetly in back, of course, but filing away everything in her steel trap of a brain."

"Uh-huh."

"I have no doubt that she will also mention that there was a sixty-carat diamond in the room. Did you see it?"

"I think so."

"And did you spot the armed guard not four feet from the lady and her date?"

"Wow, no."

"That will make Truman happy—to read about that."

Jack and I must have talked for half an hour, alcohol having loosened both our tongues. My impression of him that night was of a man truly devoted to Truman, so I was surprised when Jack admitted that he was "no longer quite in love with him," though still "deeply loving and respectful."

"We stopped thinking of it that way a while back, though obviously at first—Taormina, the late forties, early fifties—it was more intense. He was in his twenties; I was ten years older. But still we abide today, because we're partners, and because, well, we need each other, in a way. At least I like to think he still needs me in some ways . . ."

I was touched by Jack's words—and by the fact that he felt he could trust me with them. It was more than the champagne talking. Jack and I were drawn to each other—perhaps partly because of our affection for Truman. And it does not escape me that Vincent has some of the same quiet dignity that Jack Dunphy had.

"And there's history," continued Jack. "That counts for a lot, when you have a lot of it."

Talking to Jack, I was able to glimpse the answer to a question about Truman that had been on my mind without my even knowing it: How can he do it? How can he keep it up? Why doesn't he spin out of control? Jack was Truman's rock, his secure base, as they say. Of course, later Truman *would* spin out of control, with drugs and alcohol. By then, Jack and I were, if not true friends, then partners in taking care of Truman as best we could. I felt responsible to a great friend and teacher; and Jack, obviously, was too good a human being to reject Truman, even after being treated shabbily, as Jack later would be.

We'd finished our champagne. The orchestra had started playing "I Don't Stand a Ghost of a Chance." Jack extended his hand.

"*On tente le coup . . . ?*" he said.

"I . . . beg your pardon," I said.

"Oh, sorry. Truman mentioned Le Rosey, so I thought . . . shall we have a dance?"

"Sure."

Jack led me out to the dance floor.

"I'd ask Truman," he said, "but I'm not sure society is quite ready for *that*."

Truman had told me that Jack was a superb dancer, and now I saw that this was true. For a second, I wondered where and when they might have danced together—on the beach at Taormina, alone at dawn, one summer day . . . ?

The arrangement was for luxuriant strings and a saxophone solo.

What's the good of scheming
I know I must be dreaming
For I don't stand a ghost of a chance with you

Getting a cab afterwards was easy. They were lined up for the opportunity of taking someone rich somewhere far. It was still rainy, but I only got a little wet. Lee and Stas must have come home much later than I did, after I was asleep. Lee had made it a point to say I need not be on duty until noon, but I was up and about at 8:30, in case coffee or breakfast were wanted. And sure enough, Stas appeared in the kitchen around 11:00 and was happy to be offered some eggs.

Chapter 14

Cover Stories

Truman told me later that in the days following the ball he received so many floral arrangements and bottles of champagne at his apartment that he had to have his concierge arrange to send most of the flowers on to a nearby nursing home. The champagne, of course, he kept.

"The Paleys sent over a case," he said. "Dom Perignon '59."

He mentioned, too, that Jack said he'd enjoyed meeting me and would like to see me again sometime. Though the sentiment was nice to hear, I didn't think that intimate dinners for three at UN Plaza would be on the calendar anytime soon, because Truman had gone from star to superstar.

The *Times* published the ball's guest list and a rather too unsensational account of the event, dryly dubbing it "social history." Of all the tabloid columnists who mentioned it, it was only Suzy who had the inside scoop on what really happened inside and who wore what. The others merely faked it.

"Don't Repeat This" —by Lila North
Wednesday, November 30, 1966

. . . "Utterly thrilled," is how *Washington Post* publisher Katharine Graham described her experience of being the guest of honor of Truman Capote's recent blowout at the Plaza. "Everyone [was] there, from European royalty to Hollywood stars." Kay, as she is known to friends, wore white Balmain. • Apparently, one

Italian princess sported a hundred-carat diamond to the ball and attended not with a date but with four bodyguards. • The inverts are at it again. Attempting to follow the example of civil rights sit-ins at American lunch counters, a loose-wristed group called the Mattachine Society has staged a "sip-in" at a bar in Greenwich Village. What's next? Rioting in the streets . . . ?

Truman confessed, in that devilish way of his, that the ball pleased him for deftly positioning Lee at the center of his social life, right under the noses of his Chief Swan Presumptive, Babe Paley, and his Featured Swan of the Evening, Kay Graham. Though he didn't say so in so many words, I saw that he took the ball as his coronation and Lee as a kind of royal consort. Suzy picked up on this when she joked in her column that "somebody has got to tell Truman that Lee Radziwill can't have him all the time."

Lee cackled when she saw the Suzy quote. She was obviously as delighted with the idea as Truman was. As Stas continued to fulfill his carefully programmed role, and Lee quietly saw Taki and Ari, Truman could be her ticket to carefree jaunts in the *nouvelle beau monde*. She said she trusted him completely, and that he was "the most loyal friend I've ever had and the best company I've ever known."

And Truman's stock rose even higher when Emmy Award buzz started around Christmastime, after the *ABC Stage 67* broadcast of his adaptation of his story "A Christmas Memory."

In January, Lee and Truman spent a leisurely week in Morocco, ambling from Rabat to Marrakesh to Taroudant with a car and driver, in search of pottery, rugs, and such. One afternoon, after a visit to the souk and a family-owned tannery, they were sipping iced mint tea and relaxing next to the pool in the bougainvillea-lined garden of Taroudant's hotel Palais Oumensour, a renovated former palace.

"I should be doing Chekhov," said Lee.

"Better to start with Philip Barry," said Truman.

"Maybe we should have looked for a play in London."

"Chicago makes perfect sense for you. New York and London are the deep end. The Ivanhoe is a very respectable regional theater but more . . . manageable."

They were lying in bathing suits on parallel *chaises longues*. Except for an extremely attractive young pool steward with black-black hair, they were alone.

"Are you learning your lines?" said Truman.

"Absolutely," said Lee. "You were right about the writing. It just works."

"I told you so. Writers who put words in the mouths of actors know that actors want fun things to say and do. There's the meaning of the line—the information it adds to the story—then there is the function of the line—the way it makes the actor feel while saying it. *That's* what a good actor has to find and *play*."

"Truman—nicely put!"

"Thank you."

"So was it hard for you to put Holly Golightly lines in the mouth of Audrey Hepburn?"

"Interesting you should ask that. This was exactly what George Axelrod and I talked about all the time: the behavior of a character on the screen, as opposed to the character on the page. Sure, there were lines on the page that no actress should have to utter. That's just reality. And by the way, I am very good at written dialogue."

"I know you are. You've even written lines for me."

Truman looked surprised. "Have I?"

"I should say you *created* a line for me—one. You didn't write it."

"When?"

"When Stas went back to Palm Beach, right after the ball."

"Ah."

"I was hoping he and I could go somewhere with the kids. Remember?"

"Of course I do."

"I wasn't heartbroken, exactly. I didn't feel betrayed, exactly. I was angry—and then guilty for being angry . . ."

'You sounded close to crying."

"I was. And remember what you told me to say?"

"What?"

"Stas," said Lee reservedly, recreating the scene, "I'm disappointed you can't spend more time with the children and me."

"Did you say it just that way?" said Truman.

"Just that way."

Truman thought about it for a moment.

"You'll be fine in Chicago," he said.

Lee laughed.

"I wouldn't ever have framed it as disappointment, but that's just what I wanted to say."

"I know," said Truman. "Anyway, David's keener than ever. His partners are impressed by the Emmy talk. And now that we have Milton Goldman on board . . ."

"He's an agent?"

"Lee, he's *the* agent. He represents Olivier and Gielgud."

"Oh, right."

"You're in good hands."

"So it's set?"

"It's going to be set. As soon as we get through Chicago."

After a moment, Truman sat up and noticed that his glass was almost empty. So was Lee's.

"More tea?" he said.

Lee looked up and said yes. Truman summoned the steward.

"Kadin, may we have some tea, please."

"Certainly, monsieur," said the boy, with a smile and little bow.

Lee watched as Kadin went off. The boy was in a sleek black tank suit.

"Truman, how old would you say something like that is?" she purred.

"Stop it," said Truman. "I doubt he has a title or a yacht to his name."

"No, I suppose not."

"You're not one for playthings, anyway—are you?"

"Not while I have you, darling."

* * *

In June, Lee met Truman in Los Angeles, and she accompanied him to the 19th Emmy Awards ceremony, at the Century Plaza Hotel. He had been nominated as writer in a special category, "Individual Achievements," for the "A Christmas Memory" adaptation. Largely autobiographical, the story centers on Truman's elderly cousin and boyhood best friend Sook, who helped raise him and, at Christmastime, made fruitcakes with him to give away as gifts. Featuring a touching performance as Sook by Geraldine Page, *A Christmas Memory* was up against stiff competition: *Brigadoon*; *Charlie Brown's All-Stars*; *Death of a Salesman*; *It's the Great Pumpkin, Charlie Brown*; *Perry Como's Kraft Music Hall*; and *The Jackie Gleason Show*.

The ceremony took place in the hotel's ballroom, and Truman and Lee were seated at a table not far from the stage. The awards were televised, and attracted an audience of stars and power players meant to be seen, which meant that the ballroom that night was one of the most brightly lit spots on earth. Lee's gown sparkled. Truman's horn-rimmed glasses gleamed. Lee was holding Truman's hand as the nominees were read.

"And the winner is . . . *A Christmas Memory*."

"Oh, terrific!" said Lee, as Truman rose, gave her a peck on the cheek, and squeezed past a table to the podium. The show's producers joined him there, but Truman did all the talking.

"People always said that Sook was a bit tetched," he said. "My parents always said so, though they did send me to go live with her in Monroeville, Alabama. But I could see the minute I walked in the door that this lady was some kind of genius. So I dedicate this to her memory."

After the ceremony, there was a party for fifty or so at Johnny Carson's house in Bel Air, hosted by Johnny's relatively new second wife Joanne. A former game- and talk-show host, Joanne had become good friends with Truman since being introduced to him not long before in New York, at a dinner party given by Bennett and Phyllis Cerf. Capote's newly fortified status as cultural superstar was due partly to the appearances he was making on Johnny Carson's *Tonight Show*.

"I wish I had had someone in my life as wonderful as Sook,"

said Joanne, among a small group who had gathered under a vine-covered pergola overlooking the pool terrace. The pool and grounds were subtly illuminated by hidden lights.

"She must have been quite special," said Lee.

"Truman and I were both wounded souls as children—weren't we, Truman?" said Joanne. "That's why I think we've taken to each other. Both of us from broken homes . . ."

"Did you run off to New York, too?" said Lee.

"I was sent to a convent school," said Joanne. "Then I came here."

"I loved my Sook," said Truman, "but she was batty, too. Mad as a chair. I told that to Geraldine, thinking she could do something with it. But she went in a different direction."

"And now aren't you glad she did?" said Joanne.

"Of course," said Truman.

"Lee, do you have any marvelous old bats in your family?" asked Joanne.

"Ha! Well, I don't know about 'marvelous,'" said Lee, "but I do have an extraordinarily eccentric aunt who lives with her eccentric daughter in an old house at the shore."

"Eccentric how?"

"Lots of cats, for one thing."

"Oh."

"You should write about them," said Truman playfully.

"They are very dear," said Lee, "and I have thought of making a film about them."

Conversation moved from aunts and cousins to children, and then Johnny joined the group.

"I hope Joanne's taking good care of you, Truman," he said.

"It's a wonderful party," said Truman.

"We'll have to get you back on the show sometime."

"You know me. Just invite me."

"The camera loves this guy," said Johnny.

"The feeling is entirely mutual," said Truman.

"We saw the *Life* cover last month—very powerful stuff."

"The cover of *Life* . . . ?" asked a young woman who had joined the group when Johnny did.

"It was Truman standing between the two murderers," said Johnny.

"Perry Smith and Richard Hickock," said Truman. "They have names, Johnny."

"Of course. Yes."

"The funny thing is that Gore Vidal was upset to see me getting such good press."

"No," said Johnny.

"Apparently he is still annoyed about a 1948 photo spread in *Life* that gave me much more space than him."

"Yes—I believe you've talked about this . . ." said Johnny.

"He keeps saying that I steal from Carson McCullers, with a bit of Eudora Welty and Flannery O'Connor thrown in. Which only goes to show you what a careless reader he is—lumping all these supposedly 'Southern' writers together. And notice they're all women . . ."

"Is that why you bear Gore such a grudge?" said Johnny.

"I bear him nothing of the kind," said Truman. "He's the one who bears the grudge. And I dare say that contemporary cover stories don't help the matter much."

Everyone laughed.

"And now these movie rights," said Johnny. "Twentieth Century Fox! You sold them the rights to *Answered Prayers* for what, three hundred thousand dollars?"

"Please," said Truman. "Three hundred fifty thousand dollars. And I didn't have to show them a page."

"When is the book due?"

"January 1971."

"Can you meet that deadline?"

"Johnny, that's four years away."

"How much of it is done?"

"Enough."

Later, after the party, Lee and Truman were driving back to the Beverly Hills Hotel, smoking and talking.

"Did it upset you that Johnny brought up that cover?" said Lee.

"Of course it did," said Truman. "I can't bear to see that

photograph. And to think that all of America saw it . . . I just hope we don't have to talk about it the next time I'm on the show."

"Can't you tell him you don't want to talk about it?"

"Mmm, not with Johnny; you don't want to do that. He likes to push buttons, but he also has your back. You kind of sign up to go through whatever he thinks America wants to see. That's the bargain."

It was late, and the streets between Bel Air and Beverly Hills were relatively quiet. Truman loved driving and enjoyed coming to Los Angeles because it gave him so much opportunity to do so.

"Truman, may I mention something—a small point," said Lee.

"Of course—anything," he said.

"I wish you wouldn't speak badly about Gore in public."

"Oh?"

"He's family, Truman. I have a certain loyalty."

"He's mean enough to me and quite often wrong."

"Sure. Of course he is. But I am fond of him, too. Please understand."

"Alright, princess. For you, anything."

Lee worked hard to prepare for *The Philadelphia Story*. She worked with coaches both in London and New York. Throughout the spring, an acting coach came to the Fifth Avenue apartment twice a week, with Truman often in attendance, to discuss scenes and run lines. I don't know that I ever heard of any breakthroughs taking place, but there was certainly progress. They worked in the library—as posh as that which the Lord family might have in their Philadelphia mansion, though undoubtedly more daring in décor.

"'Am I to be examined, undressed, and thoroughly humiliated at fifteen cents a copy?'" declaimed Lee, as Tracy. The script was in her hand, and she was doing her best to sound polished but breezy.

"Sorry to interrupt," said the coach. "The line is, 'I am to be examined . . .'"

Lee seemed puzzled. "Sorry?" she said.

"The script says, "*I am* to be examined . . .' You said, '*Am I* to be examined . . .' "

"But it's a question."

"It's a question in the form of a statement. She's indignant, but graciously so."

"Isn't it better to say, 'Am I to be examined'?"

The coach managed a patient smile.

"We'd better stick to the lines as written," he said.

"You did say I should take chances."

"I'm afraid we can't rewrite the play. Again, please."

Lee set aside the script for an even breezier approach.

" 'I am to be examined, undressed, and thoroughly humiliated at fifteen cents a copy?' "

"Mmm, better," said the coach. "But let's hear more of the indignation. She's just realizing what it will mean to have a writer and a photographer from *Spy* magazine poking around her wedding. Once again, please."

" 'I am to be examined, undressed, and thoroughly humiliated . . .' No, wait—that's terrible. Let me start again."

She repeated the line, and for a split second, it hung there in the air. Then the coach spoke.

"Lee, let's try it another way. Try facing away from Dexter for his line, and then, in response, turn to him in a bit of a huff."

Lee thought about this for a second.

"Okay," she said.

"I'll feed you the line," said the coach. " 'Well, it's tough, but that's the way it seems to be.' "

Lee delivered her line as suggested, and still, the result was fairly flat, if by now plenty breezy.

"I have an idea," said Truman, popping out of the chair where he'd been observing. "May I feed the line?"

"Go ahead," said the coach.

" 'Lee, think about Lila North—*right now.* That scabrous creature! You've just heard that she's going to do an item on your children—okay? 'It's tough, but that's the way it seems to be.' "

Lee immediately flashed ire.

" 'I am to be examined, undressed, and thoroughly humiliated at fifteen cents a copy?' "

Truman raised his eyebrows and glanced at the coach.

"Hmm," said the coach. "We'll get there."

Coinciding with the public announcement of the play's run was a cover story on Lee in *Life*, with the headline, "The Princess Goes On the Stage." Instantly, the four-week run of the play was sold out. Yves Saint Laurent was engaged to create Lee's costumes. Both she and Truman were conflicted about exploiting Lee's title and the Kennedy connection in the play's promotion, but Truman was more sanguine about it than Lee was.

"Cost of doing business," he told Lee, one June night in Chicago, in a plush upholstered booth in The Pump Room, at the Ambassador East hotel. It was a week before the opening.

"As long as they don't use *Princess* in the playbill and on posters," said Lee.

"Just stay focused on your character," said Truman. "I'll handle the Ivanhoe people."

On the table in front of them were two J&Bs, a pack of Newports, a crystal ashtray, and a small, silver Revere bowl with salted cashews.

"Stas and I were screaming at each other again last night."

"From London?"

"He doesn't want any part of this. He keeps saying it's undignified. Last night, he essentially called it a sin."

Truman snickered. "Listen, acting has nothing to do with dignity or sin," he said. "Stas is standing in the way of your creative development, and I, for one, think that's the sin."

"Thank you."

"Now Ari Onassis—*he* likes creative people, as we know . . ."

"Stop it."

"Look at his friendship with Madame Callas . . ."

"Ari I thought would come."

"He's not coming?"

"He said he would, but now he can't."

"Disappointing."

"He's been busy lately."

"Distant?"

"Busy."

Jackie wasn't attending, either. She said she'd long planned a trip abroad and sent a beautiful little enameled box to Lee instead.

"She's envious," said Truman. "Gore once told me that Jackie said she'd always wanted to act. She asked him if he thought it was too late."

"And what did he say?"

"That it didn't matter, since the Kennedys would never allow it."

"He was probably right."

But plenty of Lee and Truman's international friends, including Nureyev and Fonteyn, did come to see "Lee Bouvier," as she was billed. Yet despite all her hard work, and the rapturous applause, and the Saint Laurent dresses—and partly because, as Truman said, "people couldn't get Kate Hepburn out of their minds"—the reviews were disastrous. Miss Bouvier was a "lovely-looking amateur"; her performance "stayed on a consistently wooden level" and relied on "unmistakable Miss Porter's lockjaw"; the evening was "long and agonized."

"It is difficult for someone raised in my world to learn to express emotion," Lee had explained to Hollywood columnist Dorothy Manners. "We are taught early to hide our feelings publicly."

Truman had no illusions about Lee's performance, yet he remained cheerful and upbeat—partly, I think, because he loved Lee, and partly because he had his eye on a bigger goal: the production of *Laura* he was painstakingly putting together with David Susskind. Both men knew that cover stories and sold-out houses trumped even great reviews, at least in the short run—and that's what television was, after all: a very short run.

These were all people able to take things in stride—the arrival of vast amounts of money or sudden financial reversals; highly visible successes or public flops; fairy-tale marriages or splashy divorces. Unlike my life, which was steady-state, the lives of Lee and Truman were radically episodic though splendidly insulated, so that after a big bomb like *The Philadelphia Story*, they could simply sail on to the next adventure, distracted, with any regrets displaced by new thrills. From Chicago, Lee returned to London, where she had some house decoration issues to sort out with Renzo Mongiardino, and Truman met up with Jack in Amalfi, because "too much American Midwest was depressing."

A special delivery letter from Lee reached Truman on his third day in Amalfi. She was undefeated, she said, and looking forward to *Laura* more than ever.

"I wish we could begin tomorrow. I am possessed," she wrote. "Once in college I tried acting and it was a disaster. Not so much because of any talent I may or may not have. My confidence was absolutely shaken. Mother disapproved because 'that sort of thing just isn't done.' Yet I am an adult now and undeterred."

Truman also received a call from Susskind. They spoke as Truman sipped prosecco on the narrow terrace of the hillside house that he and Jack had rented, overlooking the Mediterranean.

"I saw that ABC dropped *Death Row USA*," said Susskind. It was a program about capital punishment that Truman had written and directed. "What happened?"

"Who can say?" said Truman.

"Didn't they like it?"

"They paid me for it."

"I heard they thought it was 'too grim.' "

"What were they expecting—*Rebecca of Sunnybrook Farm*? Anyway, I have the rights, and I'm going to screen it in New York soon. I'll invite you."

"You and ABC are still okay?"

"We're as peachy as can be, David. I've become a very profitable little sweatshop for them. In the past two years, my programs have won several Emmys and a Peabody. *Laura* will be fine."

"Despite Lee's reviews."

"Despite the reviews."

"I knew she couldn't do humor," said Susskind. "That's why I steered her away from *Turtle* when we first started talking, remember?" Truman had originally suggested Lee for a Susskind production of *The Voice of the Turtle*, a comedic play by John Van Druten about a single gal in New York during World War II.

"What can I say? You were right," said Truman.

"But I have to admit, you can't buy this kind of publicity."

"Of course you can, David, but the point is that now you don't have to. People want to see what she does next. It's the subtext that the public is clamoring for—don't you know that? How much it has to do with desire and *striving* . . . ?"

"The princess thing?"

"Not so much that. But the little girl raised so properly, finding her emotions in front of everyone."

David pondered this poetic thought.

"Truman, what's fueling this project for you?" he said.

"Good question," said Truman dreamily.

It was late afternoon in Amalfi, late morning in New York. Susskind's view, out the window of his office, was of midtown office buildings—steel, stone, and glass; on his mind were profit versus loss, the possibility of prestige versus susceptibility to risk. Truman's view extended halfway to Sicily, across an expanse of sea glistening in the afternoon sun. On Truman's mind was a story he'd wanted to write since first visiting Taormina, years before, as a young man, with Jack—set there in the late 1870s, about a fisherman's son who encounters an odd but kindly foreigner who asks to take photographs of him in the nude. It was a story he regretted he'd never be able to write, let alone publish. Yes, the world was changing, Truman admitted to me—but could *he*? Gore had published *The City and the Pillar* almost twenty years before, yet despite Truman's own unapologetic personal behavior, he felt that such professional plainness about homosexuality was ruinous.

When people called the Mediterranean a cradle of civilization, did they mean buggery or just the sun-bleached marble colonnades?

"I saw you two dancing—you and Lee," said Susskind. "Joyce noticed, too—at your ball. You two looked like the happiest couple in the room."

"We're very fond of each other, as you know," said Truman.

"Have you been to bed together?"

"David! Don't be vulgar."

"I'm serious."

"So am I. You know exactly who and what I am."

"I know that people have many sides."

"Of whom is that not true?"

"I heard something about Morocco—when you two were traveling alone together."

"Absolute nonsense."

"So what's the emotional investment in Lee? You've never tried to put Babe Paley on the stage."

"Oh, she wouldn't go," sniffed Truman. "And Bill wouldn't let her. Though she'd make a fine Mother Courage, don't you think? Can I interest you in some Brecht, David? With an offer from you, I might be able to persuade the Paleys . . ."

Susskind laughed.

"You're incorrigible," he said.

"I don't know," said Truman pensively. "With Lee, I feel I am more than a friend. I guess you could say I am a mentor. This is my way of giving her a gift of great value, worthy of her. Not just the role, but freedom from a straitjacket—a social straitjacket. And the release of artistic potential—that should never be choked, in anyone."

"I've never heard you speak that way about it."

"Well, what did you think? I'm a writer. I think about things deeply and I feel them deeply. Our whole world is changing, and women like Lee should be able to take advantage of the new opportunities; not for work or a job, necessarily—the feminists are always talking about jobs—but I'm talking about identity, self-esteem. There is only one high society now, and that's the society of achievement. What you yourself are and what you've done."

"Hear, hear."

The call ended with Susskind promising that by the end of the week, he'd have a definitive decision—yes or no—on his going ahead with *Laura*.

Chapter 15

An Actor Prepares

Truman was still in Amalfi when Susskind called back to say yes, and Truman immediately phoned Lee in London.

"It's a go," he said.

"That's wonderful," said Lee.

"A two-hour ABC movie-of-the-week, to air in January."

"Who else is in it?"

"He's working that out. First choice for the detective, I believe, is Robert Stack. Do you know him?"

"Not really. What's he been in?"

"*The Untouchables*, for one thing."

"Oh, *him*—the TV show. Do I have any say in this?"

"Not really."

"I guess I haven't been thinking too much about who I might be playing opposite."

"Lee, there's only one little kissing scene—that's it."

"I know."

"Anyway, it'll be fine. You're an actress now. You can make anything work."

"Alright. Well, thanks for making *this* work, Truman. You're an angel."

"I am, aren't I?"

"Mother will be so furious."

"Why? Doesn't Janet want her daughter to be a movie star?"

"You forget: she's already got one star in the family."

"Oh. Right. Well, don't you want to know how much they're paying you?"

"Oh, absolutely."

"Fifty thousand."

"Is that good?"

"It's exactly what it should be."

"Now, what's the next step?"

"I'm in New York for a few days next week; then I'll come straight to London. By then, I will have some schedule details for you. It will probably be rehearsals in September, shooting in October."

"Alright."

"David and I will line up some coaching for you, and we can start when I arrive. By then, we'll have settled on the script, and you and I can look over what we've got."

"This is exciting, Truman."

"I think so, too."

When Truman and I got together again, in Lee's kitchen, he told me that he missed Brooklyn Heights.

"Going back there at the end of the day really felt like coming home," he said. "Leaving the city, going across the bridge. At UN Plaza, until I get up to my place, I sometimes feel like I'm checking into a hotel. I know I'll get used to it. Still . . ."

But I think there was more going on with Truman than a change of address. He appeared to be spending less time with the people who'd long known him best, like Jack, who'd been an abiding partner, and Harper Lee, who'd been a constant friend, and more with rich-and-famous types who were entering his celebrity orbit. In a way, I felt like I was being groomed as a less-demanding substitute for the previous two, to help him process, as friends do, the commonplace trivia of daily life. He even missed the boys he'd encounter on the Brooklyn Heights Promenade late at night, because the "Whitman-like" intimacy he shared with them, too, was ordinary and everyday, the kind that's necessary for us all.

Missing Brooklyn was a tangent, though. Our session that day was about families—angry mothers, in particular. Both of us had had one. He asked why mine was so angry, and I said I didn't know. The angry blowups were simply a fact of nature, like hurricanes. They happened. But in my heart, I knew that part of my mother's soul had been destroyed by my biological father, an older man she knew only briefly, yet I shared none of this with Truman. He was so eager for my stories, and asked such probing questions about them, that I didn't want to present something new until I had worked out the details in my head.

"Have you always known what you are, Truman?" I asked.

If the question surprised him, he didn't show it.

"You mean about other men?" he said. "Yes, I have—always. The difference between me and a lot of other people is that I don't try to fake it, and I don't care who knows. Simple as that."

"You've always accepted it?"

"I did, even if others didn't. I've never felt guilty about it, even when I was very young. One day when we were driving into the city from Greenwich, my mother said that we were headed for a doctor's appointment where I was going to start getting so-called special shots to make me more of a man. And I said, 'I've got news for you. I'm not getting any shots.' I threw a fit, and she slapped me. Then I said, 'If you ever do that again, I'll break your nose.' After that, she kind of left me alone."

In September, Lee and Truman hosted a small dinner party at Lee's London townhouse in Buckingham Place, mainly for those already attached to the *Laura* project. In addition to the two of them, it was director John Llewellyn Moxey and a girlfriend who said nary a word throughout the entire evening; actress and *What's My Line?* panelist Arlene Francis, who was playing Laura's aunt, Ann Treadwell, with her husband, actor Martin Gabel; Lee's great friend and interior designer Renzo Mongiardino, who came alone; and Rudolf Nureyev, who was to have brought Margot Fonteyn but instead showed up with a young British danseur—"quite throwing off my table," said

Lee. Stas was off in the country with some of his friends from Divine Mercy, a school for boys of Polish descent that he helped support. Playwright and screenwriter Tommy Phipps, who had worked on the *Laura* screenplay with Truman, was also invited, but sent his regrets. And David Susskind, who was supervising the project from New York, would not be coming over to London until the taping.

With only a slightly larger staff than the New York apartment, Buckingham Place required a cook, a butler, a housekeeper, a maid, and a nanny. Published in *Vogue* the previous December, with photographs and text by Cecil Beaton, the house was one of Mongiardino's most magical creations—an "urban seraglio" that the designer described as "a place where the Orient resided more in the general atmosphere than in the actual composition." A courtly, soft-spoken man of around fifty, with a leonine mass of hair and a great beard, Mongiardino looked more like a professor or an Orthodox prelate than a society decorator. He had a background in film and stage design, so he always thought of rooms like sets, Lee told me once in New York, before my first encounter with the gentleman.

Cocktails were served in the drawing room, which Beaton had described as "a blaze of Turquerie." The walls were hung with inexpensive, woodblock-printed Indian bedspreads, in shades of apricot and pink, mounted inside rococo frames of plastic, painted gold. The divan was simply a mattress on a frame to which Mongiardino had added arms and bolsters—all beautifully upholstered, of course. Mixed into the décor were precious French, Italian, and Indian antiques.

"I feel the history of at least three continents in this room," said Arlene. "It's marvelous."

"Venice meets Baghdad meets Marrakesh," said Martin Gabel.

"Thank you," said Lee, taking Mongiardino's hand affectionately. "We tried, didn't we, Renzo?"

"Once we understood the circulation, everything fell into place," said Mongiardino.

"You wouldn't know it," said Lee, "but all these windows

and doorways were a huge challenge. Do you see how nothing lines up with anything else? There's no symmetry."

"We tried to create another kind of harmony," said the decorator.

"Our new place, Turville Grange, is the same way. So many tiny rooms here and there . . ."

"And who is in the place of honor?" asked Arlene. Hanging over the fireplace was an antique portrait of a young woman with a lace collar and golden necklaces.

"That's an ancestor of Stas's—Princess Louise of Prussia," said Lee. "I love that golden feather in her hair."

"*Charmante*," said Nureyev.

"It's Vigée-Le Brun—one of the few woman painters of the time."

"Stas must be very proud of his family," said Martin Gabel.

"We both are," said Lee.

Conversation touched on the weather, French politics, and transatlantic travel—everything but the movie, which wouldn't come up until dinner.

"Where is Stas, by the way?" asked Nureyev, who had arrived late.

"With some of his Polish friends," said Lee. "Countrymen. You must feel the same way, Rudy—for Russians."

"Russians are terrible," said Nureyev, who looked right at home in Lee's opulent drawing room, dressed in a white-and-gold brocade Nehru jacket. "They can't make anything that anybody wants, except ballets, books, and symphonies. They are lucky if they can keep themselves warm in the winter. Believe me, they don't want war, because they can't win a war. What they want, these big men, is prestige."

Nureyev seemed amused when the young man he was with piped up—a move that the girl who was with John Moxey was smart enough to avoid.

"Russians are great people, with great feeling," said the boy, whose face had an asymmetrical kind of beauty. "They make the best friends. It's the leaders who have this prehistoric view of power."

"I suppose you're right . . ." said Lee, more out of graciousness to Rudy than a desire to hear more from the boy. But the boy pressed on.

"The one good thing the Soviets are doing is the space program," he said. "It's the only thing they will be remembered for in a century. And you wouldn't believe how many women are involved! It's inspiring—though obviously not to the Americans, who won't even allow a woman into the control room of Cape Kennedy."

"Is that so?" mumbled Peter Gabel, after a second of silence in the room.

Then dinner was served.

"Stunning," said Arlene, as they entered the dining room, which was lined in panels of Cordovan leather that Mongiardino had recycled from one of his movie sets. Two brass lanterns with candles, and a low centerpiece of pink roses and orange and yellow dahlias, commanded the table. Delicate green Limoges plates with mousse of sole were already set at each place.

"Sorry Phipps couldn't make it," said Moxey.

"He's given me some awfully good lines," said Arlene. "Now, Truman, which are his, and which are yours, and which are Vera Caspary's?"

Truman shook his head.

"I'll never tell," he said.

"You both did an extraordinary job," said Moxey. "I think we can all have some fun with it."

The plot of *Laura* is simple. Laura Hunt is a glamorous New York advertising executive. A dead body is found in her apartment, shot in the face, and assumed to be Laura. Soon after detective Mark McPherson starts investigating the case, the living Laura comes home after a long weekend in the country, where she has been incommunicado. McPherson sets out to uncover the identities of both the corpse and the killer, all the while falling for the woman he determines was meant to be the victim. Any of Laura's sophisticated friends, he discovers, including her unctuous mentor, newspaper columnist Waldo Lydecker, might have had motive and/or opportunity.

"Lee, what do you think of the script?" said the director.

"I think it's terrific," said Lee.

"Do you know the movie?"

"Yes, I do."

"The novel?"

"I've just read it."

"And?"

"It's an interesting premise, isn't it? I only hope I can do justice to the character."

"David says that Lee will make the whole thing sparkle," said Truman.

A subtle glance by Arlene toward her husband did not escape Truman's notice, though he said nothing.

"Surely," said Moxey, "this is an ensemble cast if ever there was one."

"Tell me, do you have a Lydecker yet?" said Arlene.

"David's talking about George Sanders," said Truman.

"What about the other roles?" said Lee.

Moxey genially held up a palm.

"We're talking to several people," he said, "but I don't want to mention any names until we're farther along."

"But we do know about Stack," said Truman.

"Yes, we do know about Robert Stack. He's our McPherson," said the director.

"Arlene, have you ever worked with him?" asked Lee.

"Robert Stack? No," said Arlene. "But didn't he get an Oscar nomination for *Written on the Wind* . . . was it '58, darling?"

"Fifty-seven," said Gabel.

"Fifty-seven."

"Renzo's doing a new film," said Lee.

"Oh?" said Arlene.

"*The Taming of the Shrew*," said Mongiardino.

"With Zeffirelli," said Lee.

"Oh—Elizabeth Taylor!" said Nureyev.

"Yes, indeed," said Mongiardino.

"*Merveilleux!*" said Nureyev.

"Renzo, when do you ever find the time to do all this?" said Gabel.

The decorator shrugged, with a twinkle in his eye.

For the main course, the conversation broke into quiet little *tête-à-têtes.* Lee served a specialty of Mrs. Bly, her London cook: beef Wellington, with roasted potatoes and artichoke hearts, and an endive meunière. Wine for the course was a Mouton Rothschild '55.

Before dinner, Truman had arrived early for a drink.

"I'm glad he's not here, actually," said Lee, as she and Truman were served Suze-and-sodas in the drawing room. They were standing at one of the windows overlooking the house's small but elegant garden, talking about Stas.

"He's not happy?" said Truman.

"When he heard the movie was happening, he said that he'd had enough."

"Enough?"

"It's the children who are holding us together."

"*Poverina.*"

Both were holding cigarettes, and the window was partly open, for some ventilation. From the petite but thoughtfully laid out garden came a cool breeze tinged with mossy freshness. Edged in trellises and espaliered apple trees, the garden featured two old mulberries and some neat boxwoods, with two narrow, symmetrical paths converging on a postage-stamp-size piazza furnished with arbor-covered benches and a bronze sundial on a pedestal. At the back of the garden was a small guesthouse.

"I never noticed that before," said Truman, indicating the house. "It looks like a doll's house."

"John and Caroline stay there sometimes with the nanny," said Lee.

"It's tiny."

"Two up and two down, as they say. Apparently it's a bit smaller than full-scale."

"Ha! But Madame Jackie is always in the main house, right?"

"More like Claridge's."

"Ah."

"Stas takes women out there."

"What?"

"I try not to think about it."

"Surely not while you're here."

"No, but the housekeeper finds evidence."

"Lord."

"It's been bumpy, Truman. And now, he resents me for working like this and taking so much time away from the family."

Truman put his arm around Lee's waist, as they continued to smoke and look out the window.

"He knows he can't forbid me from working," she continued. "But he threatened to keep me from seeing the children."

"They're in London?"

"They're upstairs. But he'll back down. Anyway, he can't do it, legally."

They spoke quietly of the ramifications of divorce and of the best possibilities for making staying together work.

"Such a shame," says Truman. "I'm sorry."

"I have something for you," said Lee.

She stamped out her cigarette, stepped over to a little Florentine cabinet, and plucked a tiny gift-wrapped package from a shelf.

"A token," she said.

Truman unwrapped the package to find a black enamel cigarette box lined in gold, from the studio of master jeweler Schlumberger. Inside was an inscription:

To my Answered Prayer
With Love,
Lee
1967

"Dearest princess, thank you," said Truman, suddenly overcome with emotion. He took her hand and kissed it. "I'll treasure it always."

"It was never a so-called love affair," said Truman years

later, of his relationship with Lee. "Just an extremely emotional friendship."

Over dessert, a fruity bombe Caribbienne served with assorted petits fours, the party turned to the subject of the movie.

"John, how do you plan to approach a story like *Laura*?" asked Peter Gabel.

"Well," said the director, "Laura Hunt is meant to be strong and independent, so I suppose that the first thing I want to show is how indignant she is to have been thought even possibly dead."

Everyone laughed, and Moxey continued.

"And then, of course, she's as concerned as any of them about who was murdered and who the murderer is."

"Yes, of course, but I mean emotionally, who is she?" pressed Gabel.

"Well, she discovers she is grateful to McPherson for respecting her boundaries while proceeding with his inquiry."

"Boundaries?" said Lee.

"You can look at the first scene between them as a conflict between police procedure and the unfettered intentions of an independent woman," said Moxey.

"Hmm," said Lee.

"He doesn't want her to call her friends right away, but she does it anyway."

"Can you play that?" asked Arlene, brightly.

"Of course I can," said Lee. "She's glad to be alive. But still confident, composed."

"Good instinct," said Arlene.

It was an insight Truman had shared with Lee when they first went over the script.

"Other than that," said Moxey, "you're going to have to discover who she is psychically—make her who you think she should be."

"It's so interesting to me," said Arlene, "that she has been seeing a guy like Lydecker, if she is so independent—right? She is intelligent yet blind to the evil in his heart."

"*Potential* evil," said Moxey. "*Provisional* evil. But for McPherson, it might never have been activated."

"We are all provisionally evil, no?" said Nureyev. "This happens all the time in literature. The circumstances make it possible for evil to come out—necessary, even."

"Exactly," said Moxey.

"Except for those of us who already know we are all evil, through and through," said Truman, with a giggle.

"Very funny, Truman," said Moxey, "but to be serious, she has been seeing Lydecker socially, but not pretending to love him romantically. She knows *he* loves *her* and is content to let that be what it is, as long as he remains a gentleman. So that's one issue. Now, Lydecker loves her in a very specific, platonic way that ultimately Laura doesn't want as a substitute for real, romantic love . . ."

"Yes. I see that . . ." said Lee.

"Arlene, have you ever played this role?" asked Mongiardino.

"No, no," said the actress. "But it sure is a good one. Don't get me wrong—I love Ann Treadwell. She's both very strong and very weak. I mean, the fact that she knows she's weak gives her a kind of strength—or at least a kind of honor."

"Oh golly," said Lee. "You all know so much more about this . . ."

"Don't worry," said Arlene. "Just have fun with it. Learn the lines, wear the clothes, and don't look straight into the camera."

The rest of the casting for *Laura* went smoothly. In the following month, Farley Granger, of *Rope* and *Strangers on a Train* fame, was signed as the handsome gigolo Shelby Carpenter, and George Sanders—the incomparable Addison DeWitt from *All About Eve*—was signed as Lydecker. In advance of rehearsals, Truman arranged for a series of private sessions for Lee with a prestigious acting coach, who insisted that the best results would be achieved only if the sessions took place at his Bloomsbury studio rather than in the lady's home. Truman agreed, and happened to show up there on the first day a few minutes before Lee. Though the coach was being paid well, he knew about the *Philadelphia Story* reviews and had conferred with Susskind.

Moreover, he knew all about rich, beautiful socialites who take a notion to go on the stage or in front of the movie cameras.

"I can tell her how to move," he told Truman, "I can show her where the beats are, I can help her learn to modulate the voice. But I can't necessarily get her to slip into the pleasure of play-acting a fabulous character. That's a kind of trance, isn't it, and I am not a hypnotist."

"I know, I know," said Truman. "But I really do believe that she has a lot all locked up in that soul of hers, that we can get to and mold . . ."

"She has to find it herself, dear, and it's the only thing that makes an audience believe—seeing someone in that trance. I can only point the way."

"That's all we need."

"It's the same thing that game show producers look for in a contestant these days, you know—though of course, those performances are trivial, compared with a play."

"Sad, isn't it?" said Truman. "Sometimes I wonder what the world is coming to, when more people see me for seven minutes on *What's My Line?* than have read any of my books."

Even then, Truman told me, he wasn't really as shocked as others seemed to be about society's shift away from so-called "high culture" toward so-called "low culture." He and the coach lamented society's move toward the low, but it was a move that Truman had privately decided he liked. It was pulling him in opposite directions, both of which he valued: the serious and the trivial, the latter of which meant something noble to him—the "everyday," the "commonplace," that Flaubert was wise enough to cherish. Truman said he trusted his instinct to see if these supposedly opposite directions could be merged.

With the vigor of a steelworker, Lee threw herself into preparations for the role of Laura. With voice, body, and mind, she laboriously repeated lines, movements, scenes. She practiced feeling the screenplay's beats so she could embody them instead of just indicating them. She learned where to breathe, how to angle her head, when to look for the taped *X* spike marks on the floor that she had to hit precisely so her face would be in focus for the cameras. And what was fueling her vigor, I believe, was Truman's belief in her. Based not only on the passion to shape a swan into a great actress, but the love he had for her—an emotion he hardly suspected at the time could ever morph into its opposite.

Rehearsals started, and from the beginning, Lee had trouble getting her blocking right.

"Lee, the *X* is right there on the floor," said Moxey, indicating it with an open palm, when Lee had missed her mark by a foot, after moving from a doorway to a table and delivering a short line.

"But I wanted it to feel authentic," she said, "so we see why she decided to move."

"She doesn't *decide* to walk into the room," said Moxey. "She just does it, and she winds up here, okay? Let's do it again." The three other actors in this scene with Lee were waiting forbearingly for the next go.

Her scenes with Stack felt especially limp—like no more than an exchange of words. There was no chemistry between either the performers or the characters. One quality that Lee appeared to be relying on was "breezy yet warm in an aristocratic way"—yet, despite the fact that this was a generally likable quality in Lee herself, she couldn't seem to pull it off as an actress. In rehearsals, she came off as cold and shallow.

Unbeknownst to Lee, Truman and Moxey were quite closely aligned in coaxing the most credible performance out of her, so the production that Susskind was paying for would ultimately be successful.

"Her name is above the title," said Moxey. "I know it doesn't matter if she's good. I just have a duty to protect the other actors."

"But she *can* be good," said Truman. "That's what we have to help her with."

Except for Oscar winner George Sanders, who claimed roots in Russian nobility and was clearly curious about this titled creature, the actors never warmed to Lee. This was partly because of her lack of training and inability to do what they could do: subtly varying details of their performance to allow Moxey to experiment with different tonalities for a scene. Moreover, as Moxey complained to Truman, Lee appeared during the entire rehearsal process to think that she was different from the others "because she is a princess." She was frequently late to rehearsals, owing to the previous night's socializing, and came to be resented by both cast and crew as a dilettante.

For her part, Lee resented not being taken seriously—though she could see perfectly well all the skills and flexibility that the other actors brought to the rehearsal process.

"They think I'm not serious, and it kills me," she told Truman.

"One foot in front of the other," said Truman.

Soon, Moxey was riding her mercilessly—though always with that veneer of mutual respect used by most ladies and gentlemen of the stage. It turned out that the director was under orders to stay demanding, since Susskind was deeply frustrated by the reports he was receiving from Moxey. Because of his loyalty to the Kennedys, though, and his long-standing affection for the Radziwills, he couldn't bring himself to fire her.

"Maybe she'll quit," Susskind told Moxey. But Lee didn't quit. She managed to tough out the rough treatment and even refused to walk off the set in protest, when after a particularly humiliating dressing-down Truman advised her to do so, because, he said, "That is what an artist would do."

The taping sessions took place at the Intertel Studios in Wembley, thirteen miles northeast of London. Lee and Truman drove out and back every day in Lee's car, and frequently welcomed society friends as visitors to the set, much to the displeasure of Susskind and the actors, who merely tolerated the interruptions. Looking smart in costumes by television, movie, and Broadway veteran Donald Brooks, who also dressed Princess Grace, Barbra Streisand, and Liza Minnelli, Lee continued to flub lines, miss her marks, and improvise body movements that were not in sync with the set's lighting. What should have been a pleasant ensemble shoot for a little movie-of-the-week proved more grueling than anyone had anticipated, despite the professional behavior of the actors and the cascade of amusing quips from Sanders—or, if he was in character, from Waldo Lydecker.

And the wrap party that Susskind hosted at the Savoy was grueling, too, in its way—though practiced smiles and stiff-upper-lip got everyone through the evening. The producer had arrived in time to see the entire taping.

"The worst I've ever seen—and I was at Iwo Jima," said Susskind privately to Truman and Moxey, as the three men stood on the party's sidelines, watching the decorous revelry of cast, crew, and invited guests. On the other side of the room was a bar and buffet, and on a small stage was a jazz combo playing upbeat standards.

"Now, David, you're vastly overstating it, as always," said Truman, who had already had one too many drinks and was slurring his words.

"Stack told me he thought it resembled a high-school production," said Susskind.

"That wasn't me," said Moxey.

"Of course it wasn't you," said Susskind. "And it wasn't the lighting designer, or the set designer. And it wasn't our esteemed screenwriter, either."

"Thank you very much," said Truman.

"Rule Number One in this business: 'It's not all about you,'" said Moxey.

"But with a true star, it *is*, you see," said Truman.

Moxey demurred.

"She just adored sweeping around in those dresses and suits," he said. "For her, it was like being in a great big fashion shoot."

"Not true," said Truman. "I'll have you know that she loves the art in herself, not herself in the art."

"Oh, brother—Stanislavski, no less," mocked Susskind. "Look, ABC's committed. They're promoting the hell out of it. As a piece of business, it's a *fait accompli*—but I don't think it will have much of a life beyond January."

"I can think of several working actresses who wouldn't have been nearly as good," muttered Truman.

"Truman, man, I admire your loyalty," said Susskind, "but perhaps the lady's next move should be toward charitable work or something."

On the dance floor, Lee was doing the "loco-motion" with a particularly handsome young grip, who was dressed in full Carnaby Street finery. Truman excused himself and went to the bar for a refill, where he ran into Farley Granger, who was with his companion, Robert Calhoun. At the age of forty-two, Granger still commanded the dashing youthfulness he displayed in *Rope*, as one of two brilliant young aesthete-murderers who may or may not be lovers.

"Boys," said Truman.

"Truman," said Granger.

"Farley, you were marvelous as Shelby."

"Thank you, Truman."

"Lee told me you were very nice to her."

"I hope she can enjoy herself tonight," said Granger, also watching Lee on the dance floor. "I know she's had a rough time, poor thing."

Truman had met Granger some time before, through Patricia Highsmith, author of the novel on which Hitchcock had based the movie that became one of Granger's biggest hits, *Strangers on a Train*. Never particularly susceptible to exceptionally good-looking men, Truman had nevertheless been attracted to Granger as a good soul and solid fellow.

"I think she's quite something," said Calhoun. "Brave as the dickens."

The affection between Granger and Calhoun was unmistakable—and Truman enjoyed seeing how unembarrassed and unapologetic they were about being seen as a couple.

"Tell me, how long have you two been together?" asked Truman. It was a question he might not have asked if he weren't drunk. "Seems to me, Farley, you were single when we met."

"Yes, that's right," said Granger. "But Rob and I met in '63 and have been together ever since."

"Tell him the story, Far," said Calhoun.

"You tell him. You're better at it."

"We were on the road with Eva La Gallienne and the National Repertory Theater," said Calhoun. "Three plays: *The Crucible*, *Ring Around the Moon*, and *The Seagull* . . ."

"Light stuff," said Truman.

"You know how much I love the theater," said Granger.

"I was production supervisor," said Calhoun. "We had been talking and getting friendly . . ."

"I thought he was awfully nice—funny, not too Hollywood . . ." said Granger.

"We had drinks a few times, too, right?"

"Oh, yes."

"So we knew what was what," said Calhoun. "Anyway, it's November, 1963—we're in Philadelphia. November twenty-second, 1963 . . ."

"No," said Truman.

"Yes," said Calhoun.

"It was an emotional day, of course," said Granger. "We'd heard the news and were having a drink, more to steady our nerves than anything else. It was a few of us from the company, in the hotel bar, wasn't it? And then suddenly it was just us."

"Kind of surreal, actually," said Calhoun.

"They had the TV on in the bar—reports about the autopsy . . . it was just too gruesome," said Granger.

"So he said, 'Can I invite you upstairs?' "

"And he said yes."

Truman opened his mouth as if to say something, then closed it.

"Almost exactly four years ago," said Granger.

"That is the most interesting thing I have heard in weeks and weeks," said Truman. "Every word of that beautiful story will now be stuck in my brain forever."

"I was actually thinking of mentioning it to Lee, since she seems so comfortable with . . ." began Granger.

"Oh, no, no—don't, please," said Truman. "She's very sensitive about the assassination. It was family, after all."

"You're right."

Granger ordered them another round. By now, Lee was dancing a second dance with the handsome grip.

"Will she expect you to rescue her or something?" asked Granger.

"Lee? No. She's a big girl," said Truman. "I'll catch up with her in a bit and see that she gets home safely—or wherever she's going next."

"Are you going anywhere special, now that this is over?" said Granger.

Truman erupted into one of his Cheshire Cat grins.

"I am thinking of meeting my friend Jack in Paris, for some opera," he said. "Jack loves opera. Apparently, Birgit Nilsson is doing some Wagner that must be seen. Say, why hasn't anyone made an opera out of *Rope* yet? Don't you think it would be fabulous . . . ?"

Calhoun piped up, a bit apprehensive.

"Truman, you might have to think twice about Paris," he said.

"Really? Why?"

"We've just come from there. There have been protests galore, some of them violent—students, police. In the streets. Sometimes it's hard to get around. They say that there's a revolution brewing."

"It'll calm down," says Truman. "The French are so excitable. They're always talking revolution, then it's a carnival. Just you watch."

CHAPTER 16

LES ÉVÉNEMENTS

In December, a month before *Laura* was to be broadcast in the United States, it was previewed privately in the UK, and word of mouth about it spread fast. Everyone in the industry knew that the movie was dreadful. Susskind decided that there was no point in preventing the critics from seeing and reviewing it, as might have been usual for a television movie like this. They were going to say what they were going to say, Susskind reasoned; and to withhold *Laura* from them would have contradicted the producer's official stance, as expressed in marketing and publicity, that this was "an exciting movie event," based on the bold casting of a glamorous socialite in a glamorous leading role.

"The press were always going to be brutal to her, no matter what she did," Susskind reminded Truman. "A pretty rich girl who has everything—that's too good not to knock around, especially in this crazy climate of political protests."

And the reviews were as nasty as expected. One critic said that *Laura* was the "worst drama of this or any other season," that Lee was "unbelievably bad." Another called the remake "so labored and dull that it was just a walk-through." Said others: "Laura was reduced to a stunning clotheshorse upon whom no discernible thespian demands were made"; "The only slightly less animated aspect of the production than the portrait of Laura that hung over the fireplace was Laura herself."

Susskind was disappointed in the reviews but gracious to Lee. From New York, to which he'd returned, he sent her a telegram:

THANKS FOR BEING SUCH A TROUPER. NOT EVERYBODY COULD HAVE DONE WHAT YOU DID. LET'S TALK MORE ABOUT THIS 'OPEN MOUTH' IDEA.

A few days before the ABC broadcast in January, Susskind hosted a preview reception in New York, attended by friends and colleagues. Lee had hopped across the pond to be on hand, of course. Looking radiant, all smiles and wit, she greeted scores of enthusiastic guests before the actual screening and received congratulations from almost all of them. The enthusiasm reflected, I think, a typically American achiever-class tendency to give someone credit for stretching into a new endeavor, especially if someone else had invested money in it, since that meant that the stretch was likely a good move. At least two of Susskind's guests, though, may have thought more of artistic integrity than of financial validation, because sometime during the screening, both Ingrid Bergman and Johnny Carson slipped out, separately, possibly to avoid being in a position afterward to offer anyone, let alone Lee, an honest opinion.

On the night of the broadcast itself, Lee gave an intimate party at her place on Fifth, which is how I saw the thing—in bits, while managing the buffet and the bar. As much as I was watching for guests' reactions to the movie, I was also watching Lee—and found it curious the way she would wince in response to moments when she was particularly bad, but didn't seem particularly embarrassed or apologetic about it—as if it had all been a marvelous game, and she was a success in it simply by being willing to participate.

"I got that laugh in the second act," whispered Lee to Truman, as the others watched the movie.

"You certainly did," said Truman. "And now you should keep going. You could get very good at this. I have some ideas . . . and an original screenplay in mind . . ."

"Oh, I don't know, Tru. My destiny may lie elsewhere. Maybe writing, or television hosting."

"Hosting?"

"Didn't David tell you? He and I were speaking about it.

What about something like his show, *The Open Mind*—you know, where I sit and talk with people I know from all walks in life—accomplished people, charming . . . ?"

"Well, he didn't tell me, but do you know what? I think it's a fantastic idea. And do you know who your first guest should be?"

"Not Jackie."

"No, no—me!"

Jackie, in fact, did not attend Lee's viewing party, preferring, she said, to watch the movie at her place, on "a rare night home with the children." Maybe Lee didn't find it odd that her sister didn't walk a few blocks down to the party, but to tell the truth, *I* found it odd—as if Jackie were avoiding her sister for some reason other than the quality of her acting. And not long afterward, I came to conclude that I was right: Jackie was preparing for a development in her life that she knew would displease Lee, and felt that absence from the party was the better part of strategy.

From a business point of view, Susskind was ultimately not unhappy with *Laura*. The Nielsen ratings were unexpectedly high, and the production was on track to make a tidy profit. Conspicuously, from matriarch Janet Auchincloss, whose advice "not to make a spectacle of yourself" Lee had guiltlessly defied, came not one telephone call, telegram, or floral arrangement.

At the end of April, Lee and Truman managed to relax a bit together in the dry heat of Palm Springs—a place that Truman loved and where, for a while, he owned a house—then it was back to London and Verbier, respectively. They converged once again days later in France, where they had been invited to lunch by the Duke and Duchess of Windsor.

Lee and Stas knew the Duke and Duchess well, having seen them often at their Paris home, a nineteenth-century villa at 4, Rue du Champ d'Entraînement, in the Bois de Boulogne; or in London, when the couple came over to shop, or attend parties, or consult one of the Duke's doctors. The plan was lunch on Sunday, May 12, so Truman arrived in Paris on Thursday the 9th and checked into the five-star Hotel George V, where he and Jack usually stayed, not far from Lee and Stas's four-bedroom place on the snazzy Avenue Montaigne, with views of the Eiffel Tower. France had been roiling with social turmoil all that spring, with clashes between students and authorities, sometimes violent, resulting from the occupations and protests against capitalism, imperialism, and the like that were erupting all over the world. On Friday the 10th, as Truman was visiting the exclusive haberdashery Charvet, trying to decide between a moss green foulard pocket square and a lighter celadon green one, a noisy demonstration was taking place right outside in the Place Vendôme, with a mob of trade union supporters waving red flags and calling for a strike, barely contained by a massive police presence. Echoes of chanting filtered into the plush little shop.

Adieu, de Gaulle! Adieu, de Gaulle! Adieu, de Gaulle!

Mort aux vaches! Mort aux vaches! Mort aux vaches!

"Is the world coming to an end, Marcel?" asked Truman calmly, savoring the feel of silk between his fingers.

"I hope not, *monsieur*," said the salesperson.

"Such a lot of fuss. Is de Gaulle going somewhere?"

"I hope not, *monsieur*."

Also on Friday—after several French universities had shut down—word came from the Duke and Duchess saying that, given the unrest, they'd gathered up their pugs and decamped for their place in the country.

"Come see us in the forest. We'll have lunch there and then look at the garden," wrote the Duchess on one of her exquisite, off-white, informal note cards, engraved with her husband's coat of arms.

The Windsors' country place, known as Le Moulin de la Tuilerie, was a short drive from Paris, in the village of Gif-sur-Yvette, at the edge of the Chevreuse Forest. Truman wanted to drive, so on Sunday morning, he rented a Jaguar at the hotel and picked up Lee at her place. On the way out of Paris, they passed several gatherings that looked like they might swell into protests as the day went on, but the rest of the drive was quiet and uneventful.

Originally an eighteenth-century mill, the house had been beautifully restored and now boasted grounds designed by Russell Page. Truman and Lee were each given a room for the day—and reminded gently by the Duchess that they were welcome to stay the night, if they wished.

"We've had forty here for a weekend," said the Duchess. "Honorine always keeps two guest rooms ready, just in case."

"I didn't bring anything," said Lee.

"We have everything you might need," said the Duchess.

"Lunch was simple and light, at one end of a long, rustic wooden table in what they called the breakfast room," Lee would remember later, "though it took two servants to manage the four of us, and the silver and china—even for a little lunch in the country, at a home with 'mill' in the title—was an exacting as it might be in a palace."

Truman told them about navigating around barricades in the Place Vendôme, on his way back from Charvet.

"It's disgraceful," said the Duchess, "the way some of those students behave."

"I'm not at all for violence," said the Duke, in a measured way, "but there could be some improvements made to the system, you know . . ."

"Oh, David . . . !" said the Duchess.

"No, I mean it," said the Duke. "There are times when the people must speak up, and it is important for the rest of us to listen."

"Is that why you left Paris?" said Truman. "So you could hear better?"

The Duke chuckled.

"It was the dogs," he said.

"There was a *petite manifestation* even in the Bois, the other day," said the Duchess. "It was noisy, they were frightened. We thought we should come here for a while, for their sanity."

"I'd hate to think what an insane pug might be like," said Truman.

"They're talking revolution," said Lee.

"Nonsense," said the Duke.

"Still," said Lee, "will you stay in Paris? Stas says we should be careful, at the moment."

"They don't want anything from you and me," said the Duchess. "The workers want better wages, and the students want . . . well, what do students ever want?"

"A more just world," said the Duke.

"Well and good, but what has that to do with us?" said the Duchess. "We're relics."

The Duke chuckled again, and the rest joined him.

"Anyway," said the Duke, "we might go to Antibes for a while."

"Or Nassau," said the Duchess.

Lee and Truman did decide to spend the night, and it was on the drive back to Paris, on Monday the 13th, that they were given a real taste of revolution.

Conversation on the drive had focused on the "fantastic" work Renzo was doing at Turville Grange.

"We're refurbishing these marvelous wrought-iron gates," said Lee. "They were a gift from Queen Alexandra to the owner before Ford, Julia Caroline Stonor, also known as—are you ready for this?—the Marquise d'Hautpoul de Seyre."

Truman's eyes were fixed on the road.

"Wasn't Alexandra the one who was always taking pretty things from people?" he said.

"Was she? What do you mean?"

"She would visit some lord or lady and admire a pair of Jacobean chairs, which was basically a command to give them to her, because then the royal movers would arrive to take them away. Actually, no, I think it was Queen Mary . . ."

It was smoking and chatting for half an hour. Then, after entering the city, on the Avenue New York, as Truman was heading back to Lee's place, they encountered a massive demonstration blocking the road just before the Pont d'Iéna, which crosses the Seine between the Trocadero Gardens and the Eiffel Tower. Apparently, the demonstration was centered in the gardens and in the intersection itself.

"What's this?" said Lee.

Within seconds, it was the angry roar of thousands, in rhythmic chants. A horde of that extended perhaps all the way to the Tower. No, more like *tens* of thousands . . .

"Damn," said Truman.

He had been intending to pass the bridge and veer left onto the Avenue des Nations Unies, but in front of them were police barricades holding back the mass of protesters. Traffic was being re-routed.

"Oh, God," said Lee, slumping a bit in her seat.

Even inside the car, with windows closed, the roar was thunderous.

They were diverted leftward, across lanes, toward the avenue's underground bypass tunnel, which would mean a small detour at the other end, to get to the Nations Unies; and Truman was proceeding as slowly as the cars in front of him allowed, when all of a sudden there was a breach in the barricades and scores of angry protesters came rushing through, toward the cars, hurling epithets and chanting.

Cochons! Cochons! Cochons!

"Sweet Jesus!" said Truman.

Protesters were rocking cars, pounding them. Were these students? Workers? Stunned, Lee and Truman stared dumbfoundedly as three or four of them hurled themselves against their car's passenger-side door and window, and started pounding on the fender, door, and roof.

Cochons! Cochons! Cochons!

"We're American!" shouted Truman repeatedly, though there was no chance, amidst all the noise and confusion, that the protesters could hear him.

"Truman, that's half of what they're protesting against," cried Lee.

A loud blow to the roof on the passenger side sounded like it might break the car open, and sent Lee, with a shriek, into Truman's shoulder, her hair catching on the windshield-mounted rearview mirror. And then several police, with astonishing brutality, were pulling the protesters away from the cars, while one of the officers directing traffic was gesturing urgently for Truman to *keep going, right now, that way*, following the car in front of him, toward the underpass.

They inched forward toward the detour, and Lee recomposed herself in her seat, pushing her hair back in place as best she could.

"They don't want *us*," said Truman. "You heard Wallis."

"Are you mad?" said Lee. "What does Wallis know?"

"Let's try to stay calm. Traffic is moving."

The demonstration noise faded as they entered the tunnel.

"I've never seen anything like this," said Lee.

They would discover later that day that the economy and government of France had come to a halt, in a massive general strike. Fearing civil war or revolution, President Charles de Gaulle was rumored to be planning secretly to flee to Germany.

"Are you okay?" said Truman.

"I think so," said Lee.

"Let's get you home. We'll make sure your street is clear. If not, we'll go to the George V. Nothing bad ever happens at the George V."

For a few blocks, they drove in silence. The avenues were relatively empty.

"How do I look?" said Lee, checking herself in a compact mirror and trying to fix her hair, as they approached her block.

"In this season's Givenchy, you're fine," said Truman.

"Hmm. I don't like being called a pig."

"Is that what they were saying? You know me and French."

"*Cochon*. Pig."

Truman grimaced and shook his head.

"It's the car, baby," he said. "They tried to give me a plain black Mercedes, and I insisted on the yellow Jaguar. Story of my life."

* * *

Then in June, things went from bad to worse. Bobby Kennedy was assassinated in Los Angeles. It felt as if the world were coming apart.

Truman heard the news while sailing along the Turkish coast, on the Guinnesses' yacht with a small party that included Princess Luciana Pignatelli and Babe Paley, but not Bill. It was just before lunch when Gloria Guinness came to Truman's cabin to tell him privately that she had just heard the news by phone from her secretary. Truman instantly phoned Lee at Turville Grange and found her distraught. She'd heard the news while doing errands in the village that morning and had caused a fender bender while driving distractedly back to the house.

After the call, Truman joined the others for lunch.

"How is she?" asked Gloria, who'd already told everyone the news.

"Upset, of course," said Truman. "It was at the Ambassador Hotel. Some crazy Palestinian."

"Terrible," said Gloria.

"Poor thing," said Luciana.

"But so far, he's hanging on," said Truman. "The doctors are working on him. Apparently, there's hope."

"He'd just won the California primary," said Loel Guinness.

"Stas was in London and is already on his way to New York. He'll fetch Jackie and go straight to California."

"Not Lee?" said Babe.

"She was in the country, so she'll be on the next plane," said Truman.

"What's happening to the world?" said Loel.

They were in the Sea of Marmara, approaching Istanbul, having sailed from Antalya along Turkey's so-called Turquoise Coast, where they stopped to visit historic bazaars, local artist studios, ruins from the Greek, Persian, Roman, and Byzantine empires, and one super-luxurious thermal spa. Later that day, after passing Istanbul, they would be docking at the affluent little town of Bebek, on the western shore of the Bosporus, where a famous chef was preparing a special dinner for them. When the dome and minarets of the Hagia Sophia came into view,

Babe and Truman were sunning themselves and sipping iced tea in the outdoor lounge area on the rear of the yacht's main deck. Nearby, but off by herself, was Luciana, sunning herself too, topless, face down on a *chaise longue.*

"Luciana's out here more than any of us," said Truman. "Have you noticed?"

"She's testing a new sunscreen," said Babe. "For her line."

"Wouldn't it be easier just to stay out of the sun?"

"You don't sell products that way, Truman."

"Oh. Right. Everybody's selling something."

The sea was mildly choppy, though not enough to disturb the stability of the three-hundred-fifty tons of the Guinnesses' yacht. Conversation returned to Bobby Kennedy.

"Is it true that Jackie was having an affair with him?" said Babe.

"I don't know," said Truman.

"But I think you told me once that she was."

"I may have said that I heard something."

"Do you think it's true?"

"Who knows? It's an interesting thought."

"Somebody said recently that Jackie may be the bigger story than Lee, but Lee has the bigger life."

"Lee can certainly do more, can't she? It's hard for Jackie, what with being both a widow and a saint. I shudder to think what her adoring fans will say when she remarries and opens her thighs to any less a man than JFK."

"Have you heard anything?"

"Nope. Have you?"

"No."

"I suppose we'll see."

"And Truman, what about you and Lee? Are you going to marry her?"

Truman cackled. "Me and Lee?" he said.

"That's what people say," said Babe.

"What people?"

"People."

"People are silly."

"You make a great couple."

"Are you serious—or is this just a touch of sunstroke?" said Truman. "Shall we call for an umbrella? First of all, she's married. Second of all, she likes sex too much to be with the likes of me. Besides, as you well know, I saw the execution of someone very dear to me, and I will never be able to get over that. I think it's quite changed me—made me a little bit impatient for everyone else in the world, including swans."

"She might make a better partner for you than Jack."

Truman smirked. "I know that absolutely no one is disappointed when I show up on a boat without Jack," he said.

"He means well," said Babe.

"Don't tell me you're jealous of me and Lee, Miss Babe."

"Of course not."

"But it would be very nice of you if you were just the teeniest bit jealous."

"Don't be a child, Truman. You know that Bill and I have spoken to you about this."

Babe adjusted the headscarf she was wearing to protect her hair from the stiff sea breeze. Truman sighed and stretched. His white shirt and shorts incandesced in the late afternoon sunlight. As they approached the mouth of the Bosporus, the sea traffic was increasing—ferries, small pleasure craft, a few other big yachts. Now and then, the sound of a boat's horn echoed over the waves.

"Lord, how long have we been sailing," said Truman, languidly, his eyes closed, "a year?"

"Yes, we've been sailing for a year," said Babe, with gentle sarcasm.

"There's always this point when I just want off the boat, if you know what I mean."

"I never feel that."

"At cocktails, we talk about Fran and Dickie in Ravello, the Perettis at their lovely place in Malta, Honey and Saul and the sheep farm they just bought in New Zealand. Surely this vessel could make it to New Zealand. Blah, blah, blah."

"Maybe it's nap time."

"You know what they say: 'Anybody becomes a confidante on a yacht.' Which is just another way of saying that the small talk only gets smaller as the days go by. Meanwhile, in France, they're burning down the universities; in the States, they're killing presidential candidates. Sometimes I feel just like Jack. Sick of the small talk, sick of the same faces, sick of the wonders of past civilizations . . ."

"You seem wrought up, darling."

"What have we had to think about in the last five days—the last thirty-five-hundred years of history? More, if you believe that that prehistoric site we saw the other day was really twelve thousand years old. Just this morning, at—what was that town called? Çanakkale . . ."

"Troy."

"Right—the ruins of Troy. Layer upon layer—Bronze Age Troy, Hellenistic Troy, Roman Troy, unoccupied Troy. All I could think about was what kind of wars, and economic booms and busts, and plagues, and social upheavals forced one age to explode into the next one—until all the explosions came to a halt, and the place was buried. Meanwhile, those same forces are at work right now, this season, in our own world. Everybody in the States is protesting against the Vietnam War. The demonstrations are larger and bloodier. Ten million people are on strike in France—they're calling it "*les événements*." Doesn't that sound portentous? I picked up a copy of the *Herald Tribune* in Izmir. So much is going on. The Tet Offensive. Why are we out here floating? Somehow I want to be back in New York."

While Truman had been orating, a steward appeared briefly to make sure that he and Babe knew they were passing the sprawling Dolmabahçe Palace, home of the last Ottoman Sultans. Truman went right on, while Babe wordlessly acknowledged the information. Somehow, though, the yacht's passing under the July 15 Martyrs Bridge was what silenced Truman for a moment. Briefly the deck was plunged into shadow, far below thousands of suspended tons of steel and concrete. When the sun appeared again, Babe spoke.

"We're floating because we're lucky enough to be able to," she said.

Truman sat up.

"I'm sorry, Babe," he said. "I suppose we are. I'm terrible company. This thing about Bobby has really flattened me. I think a nap before cocktails might be a good idea."

The next day, they learned of Bobby's death. From his cabin, Truman called New York, looking for Lee, but she'd already left.

"She was here for only a few hours. Then went on to L.A.," I told him.

"How did she seem?" asked Truman.

"Upset, of course."

"Any word about Jackie?"

"None that I have been privy to."

"And you, Marlene? How are you doing? Scared by all this insanity?"

"What do you mean?"

"Well, you've lived through it—rebellion, revolution."

"Oh—yes. Well, sure."

"What's it like in New York?"

"Relatively calm. People are, you know, in denial, rather than up in arms."

"Here, too. We're in the Black Sea at the moment, heading to Trebizond. Do you know Trebizond? There are some Hellenistic bronzes there that Gloria wants us to look at."

And then in October, things went from worse to catastrophic.

"Don't Repeat This" —by Lila North
Monday, October 21, 1968

. . . Here we go, kids. Jacqueline Kennedy, America's favorite former first lady, wed shipping magnate Aristotle Onassis yesterday, in Greece. Did you know this was in the works? I certainly didn't. Under tight security, the ceremony took place in a small, private Greek Orthodox chapel on the island of Skorpios, which Onassis owns, in the Ionian Sea. Jackie's children, Caroline, ten, and John, seven, held candles during the ceremony. • Jackie's off-white, day-length chiffon gown was by Valentino, and the exclusive reception took place aboard Onassis's yacht, Christina, for only twenty or so invited guests—though we hear that reporters from around the world were chartering boats to Skorpios and crawling around the island's rocks with their telescopic lenses, hungry for good shots. • A fairy-tale marriage? You tell me. The groom is at least twenty years older than the bride, so nobody's exactly blushing here . . .

Lee told me that she thought the emotional distance she felt from Jackie after Bobby was shot—at the hospital in Los Angeles, at the funeral in New York, at the burial in Arlington National Cemetery—was attributable to the shock of another Kennedy's death. It was murder in Camelot all over again. But it was only four days before her sister's wedding that Lee found out what was really going on, when Jackie reached Lee in Tunisia with the news, by phone, at the same time that Ari was sharing it with a flock of reporters he'd assembled in Athens, in an impromptu media center he set up in the Hotel Grande Bretagne.

"She's talking about being rescued from 'engulfing shadows,' or some such business," said Lee spitefully to Truman, the first friend she thought of to call.

Truman was relieved to hear that Lee seemed resigned to the wedding—not particularly heartbroken, but outplayed once again by her longtime competitor.

"Things have been rough for her, of course—with the children and all," he said. "I'm sure she wants them to have a father."

"Yes, of course, I understand that. 'They're killing Kennedys, and my children are Kennedys.' That's exactly what she said."

"Well, there you are."

"But Truman, how did they get away with this? When did it happen? Why didn't I know? Why didn't Ari say something?"

She was sobbing off and on.

"C'mon, princess, what could he say? Or she, for that matter."

"They've both been distant . . ."

"Jacqueline Bouvier Kennedy Onassis. What a mouthful."

"The press are going to have a field day with this whole thing."

"Ari is a colorful figure."

"Stas has been absolutely splendid."

"Has he? That's good."

"Anyway, I'm leaving for Athens in a few hours. I'll meet Stas there and pick up some kind of dress."

"If there's anything I can do . . ."

"He could have let me know," said Lee, tearfully.

It was afternoon for Lee and morning for Truman, in New York, but both of them may well have been nursing a glass of wine at this point.

"You know, a few months ago he gave me some land in Athens and said it was a birthday present," she continued. "I thought it was odd, not least because it wasn't my birthday."

"Heavens—some kind of a consolation prize?" said Truman.

"And how could *she* do this to me?"

"It's crazy. They're both crazy."

"How could it happen?"

"It obviously has nothing to do with love. He's got an army—a private army—and I suppose that's what she needs."

"Is that what this is about—security?"

"He's better than the Secret Service."

"When I think of some of the things that that man has said to me . . ."

Truman hardly knew what to tell Lee, as she wept and sobbed. He said he thought that Onassis was acting like a possessive, entitled bully—like "all of those rich husbands."

"Yes," said Lee, calming down.

"It's all about their so-called achievements, their so-called possessions," he said, "I wonder if any of them was ever capable of loving a wife. I wonder if any was given a mother's love . . ."

Truman launched into one of his by-now predictable screeds about his own "rather terrible" mother, and the "horrible" man she married. When his mother committed suicide, he was thirty, Truman said—but he'd felt her loss long before and tried to fill the hole with writing.

"Truman . . . ?" said Lee, patiently, after a little pause.

"Yes, I'm sorry," said Truman, understanding his clumsiness. "This isn't about me, is it?"

"No, darling."

"So—you'll pick up a dress in Athens. What are you thinking about?"

"Oh, I don't know. Can I wear black? It *is* Greece, after all. Don't ladies there wear black to religious ceremonies?"

PART III

Chapter 17

Pillars of Society

That section of the museum was so jam-packed with viewers that we could barely move.

"So it's not an art show, is it?" I said.

"What do you mean?" said Judy.

"Well, look—it's just photographs, all blown up."

"Oh—I guess so."

"Where's the art?"

We were walking through "Harlem on My Mind," a new exhibition at the Metropolitan Museum of Art. Subtitled "Cultural Capital of Black America, 1900–1968," the exhibition seemed to consist only of floor-to-ceiling photomurals of Harlem, like some sort of anthropological installation at a world's fair.

"Harlem is supposed to be home to all these Black artists, isn't it?" I said. "Truman speaks of them all the time. Where are they?"

"Good question."

"Shouldn't there be tons of paintings and sculptures by Black artists?"

"I wonder why they didn't."

"Feels patronizing to me."

The show had been hyped as a must-see, but Judy and I found it unintentionally hollow, so we went off for a light lunch in the Museum's restaurant.

The place was a temple. Lounge-like arrangements of chairs

and tables bordered a skylit Roman peristyle court, with Doric columns framing a shallow fountain pool graced with bronze statues of naked boys surfing exuberantly on dolphins. Over the tables was a pageant of whimsical but majestically overscaled birdcage-shaped chandeliers.

"Granny used to call this place 'The Dorotheum,' " said Judy.

"Why?" I said.

"Her buddy Dorothy Draper designed it."

"Mrs. Hawkins knew Dorothy Draper?"

"Oh, yes. Dorothy did the gallery in our apartment for Granny—didn't you know that? During the Depression, no less. John loves it. We wouldn't touch it."

"I never wanted to ask, but I always wondered why your family didn't seem to suffer in The Crash."

"Grandfather got into aviation in the '20s, and was making tons of money when passenger service took off."

"Ah."

"Apparently, he was ruthless—or worse. He died when I was little."

Judy and John had switched homes with her mother. They and their two children now lived in the enormous Park Avenue apartment where Judy grew up, and where I lived for a year and a half; and Judy's mom, now a widow, was living in the East 78th Street apartment that John bought when he and Judy were married.

We both had the Atlantic Blue Crab Salad.

"We always see magazine pieces about Lee, Mom and I, and we think about you."

"That's nice."

"We were shocked by this whole Onassis thing."

"We all were. There's no telling about love and marriage, is there?"

"Uh-uh."

"To be honest, I feel lucky to be out of it."

I had long accepted I was going to remain alone, and if society was going to label that as *spinster* or *old maid*, that was society's problem, not mine. Being single was probably not ideal, but my awful childhood had robbed me of ideal options. Perhaps Judy's family had hoped to restore some options for me, but that process could go only so far. Unlike many people who'd been through the violence I went through, I was alive and not a drunk or a drug addict. That felt ideal enough.

"So here's something interesting, speaking of photographs," said Judy. "I found some pornography in a hatbox in John's closet."

"What?"

"You heard me."

"Pornography?"

"Homosexual pornography. Or should I say, pornography for homosexuals."

"Oh, Judy."

"Or should I say pornography for married men with children, who have never, ever betrayed even a hint of acting on that kind of desire in real life."

"Pictures of men?"

"Yes. But not in the act or anything. Just standing there, posing."

"Naked?"

"Some are naked. Some are draped or dressed, if there is a theme of some sort."

"A theme? Forgive me. I don't know much about this."

"A centurion with a sword. A fisherman with a net. A cowhand with a lasso. That sort of thing."

I could see that Judy wasn't presenting this discovery as too dark a tragedy, and I felt it my place to follow her cue.

"That actually sounds more like art than anything in the exhibition we just saw," I said.

"Ha. Some of the pictures were of Black men, too. Quite handsome."

"You looked through it?"

"Some of it. How could I not?"

"What are you going to do? Anything?"

"What can I do? There's no reason to confront him. He loves me and the children—of that I am absolutely sure. He's rarely out of town without me, and when he is, he calls me twice a day. He always comes home. Mar, I see him at parties and such. He never flirts with the waiters—you know, that sort of thing. A lot of his artist friends are homosexuals, and it's not like he's falling in love with any of them."

"Sometimes it's the ones who look the most normal."

Judy leaned forward a bit and lowered her voice.

"And if it's only to masturbate now and then, what's the harm?" she said. "That's what I say."

"Okay."

"Especially if, as a wife, you get all the benefits of a sensitive human being."

"And the love-making . . ."

"Listen to us—'love-making,' 'naked cowhands.' Anyway, it's as lovely and as frequent as it ever was."

"So that's good. You never suspected anything?"

"Never. And here's the thing. If these things are hidden, which they clearly are, then he has at least some issues around them, which I *sympathize* with!"

"You are such a good soul, Jude."

"And that's slightly maddening, since it's the one thing that I can't show him I understand and even support."

"Interesting."

"Human beings are such complicated things. We come in so many varieties."

"As do marriages."

"You don't think I'm weird, to be so tolerant?"

"Put the hatbox away and forget it's there."

"Funny. He's got a few hats that he never wears anymore. It was the fedora I was suddenly worried about, after reading a thing about moths and fur felt."

"Lord."

"A fedora from Tripler, no less. But way too bankerly for him. I don't know why he ever bought it."

"The hat was in good shape?"

"Perfect."

'Well, that's something."

"Don't Repeat This" —by Lila North
Monday, June 30, 1969

> . . . You may be scratching your head, as I am, about why the popular Oscar-nominated star of *The Graduate*, Dustin Hoffman, would be willing to skulk through a gritty, X-rated flick about a queer hustler. All I can say about *Midnight Cowboy*, which opened last month, is that the times they are a changin'—but not for the better. • Speaking of which, a brawl that took place at a Greenwich Village bar on Friday night was also X-rated—and gave shocking evidence of how fast society is decaying. Apparently, when police raided the bar, which is known for its fruity clientele, the fruits fought back! Who knew that limp wrists were even capable of such a thing? • On the plus side, pretty singer Anita Bryant was just hired by the Florida Citrus Commission as a booster for orange juice. How's that for wholesome? "It's not just for breakfast anymore," says Bryant. The singer, who participated in the Rally for Decency that took place last March at the Orange Bowl (to protest the Doors' front man Jim Morrison's disgusting onstage behavior), announced she is going nationwide not only with orange juice but with her decency campaign. Says Bryant, "I want to help bring America back to God and morality . . ."

In a way, I believe it was gay liberation and the social shifts that underlaid it that first began to pull apart the friendship between Lee and Truman. Before then, people knew how they fit into time-honored categories like "rich" and "creative" and "homosexual," and how people from those categories were supposed to relate to each other. After this well-publicized skirmish at the Stonewall bar—reported in the dailies with quotes mainly from the police, but nonetheless widely taken by liberals as more fuel for populist revolt—old-fashioned decorum among the social categories began dissolving. I believe that Truman, whose behavior was never particularly bound by decorum, took a sense of endorsement from the Stonewall skirmish—perhaps greater endorsement than he was ever aware of wanting; and *that*, distorted by fame, money, and intoxicants, pushed him from bad boy into something else. Lee had been trained by her class how to deal with bad boys who were fun, but she could have nothing to do with mad men who might be dangerous. Reflexively, she began withdrawing from Truman, which engendered an undertone in their friendship of irritation and regret.

At least, that's the way I see it now, all these years later. I watched it all unfold up-close—the devolution of a friendship and a way of life. By the end of the '60s, everything was different. And isn't that the way things sometimes happen in history—one little cue, a drag queen's push back, triggers a landslide of events that's been destined to happen sooner or later? I say "sometimes," because I believe that momentum for a Big Change had built up tectonically. It's rarely the assassination or the missile crisis that triggers the breach. More often, it's an initially obscure event that reveals itself as entirely subversive.

Lee's funeral brought a lot of this back to me. I recalled how eager Truman was to resume our writing sessions, as the fuss over *In Cold Blood* subsided and both he and his public refocused on *Answered Prayers*. More and more, at this time, he seemed interested in my life, so I continued telling him tales; and he listened, and took notes, and asked questions. And I marveled that he wanted to take so much time away from his *real* work to sit with me. He also recommended books for me to read, most of which I borrowed from Lee's library. I didn't quite realize then how desperately he hoped to be getting something out of me that he could use—specifics about childhood traumas, and adolescent seductions and abandonments—while casually sharing wisdom about writing and human nature. I only wish I could have made more of what I learned from Truman. I have come to see that I just don't possess at least one of the critical talents that made him a popular writer: this knack for breathing real life into a made-up world.

Surprisingly, he once referenced one of the books that he recommended to me, Boris Pasternak's *Doctor Zhivago*, as something he admired.

"Why?" I said. He more often referenced works by French and English authors.

"Well, for one thing, it's about great crimes," he said. "You know how interested I am in crime."

"But a *revolution* . . . ?"

"That's a crime, isn't it?"

"I suppose—against the ruling class."

"Exactly. But supposedly committed by and for the people. You remember the people, don't you? We live in a time of great crimes."

"Sure, but it's not 1917."

"No? Not yet, maybe. But you saw something of it, didn't you, before you went off to school?"

"So you are writing," I said, without hesitating. "That's good, Truman."

"Always," he said. "The story of some rich people in a world that's suddenly incomprehensively larger than they are."

"So that's what you want *Answered Prayers* to be?"

"I certainly do. Just like Pasternak."

"But isn't the plot of *Doctor Zhivago* a little contrived?"

"Please! If I could only contrive a plot half as good! Right now I'm trying to keep my eyes open—struggling to see how dangerous our little world really is. Because that will help me understand how to make a tale of lunch set in a fabulous restaurant feel like the warfare it is. Pasternak was lucky enough to have hordes of angry, noisy workers on the edge of every scene."

I knew Truman was having trouble going forward with *Answered Prayers*. It felt to me that his ramblings about Pasternak and Proust and a host of other authors were in inverse proportion to the amount of actual work he was doing on the book. And Lord knows, his delay in delivering it to his publisher was being discussed in the press. On *The Dick Cavett Show*, Truman referred facetiously to *Answered Prayers* as his "posthumous novel," explaining that "either I'm going to kill it or it's going to kill me." It came out after the show that because he missed his deadline with Twentieth Century Fox, he'd had to pay back the three-hundred-fifty-thousand-dollar rights fee they'd paid him for the book.

"It's okay to be stuck, you know, Truman," I said,

"No, it is not," he said. "All my life I have been like a turtle on its back. You see, I was so different from everyone, so much more intelligent and sensitive and perceptive. I was having fifty perceptions a minute to everyone else's five. I always felt that nobody was going to understand me, going to understand what I felt about things. I guess that's why I started writing. At least on paper I could put down what I thought."

I wanted to put my hand on his, to comfort him, but we'd hadn't shared a gesture like that before, so I just smiled.

"You needn't look as though you pity me, Highness. I'm a tough bird."

"Sorry, Truman."

"And I think it's time you called me Tru, like everyone else."

"Thank you, but I couldn't possibly."

Sure, it was revolution in the air at the dawn of the '70s. Most of us probably felt it, though, as an opportunity for personal reinvention, rather than an assault on the regime. Lee would be reborn several times during the coming decade, with new careers like interior decorating and public relations, and new boyfriends like British politician Roy Jenkins, New York politician Peter Tufo, hotelier Newton Cope, and the fabulously handsome and multitalented photographer Peter Beard. Lee's reinventions had much to do with her stepping out—or being pushed out—of her sister's shadow. After Jackie's wedding, I heard Lee speak about her sister far less frequently. As for Truman, as his reinvention from writer to celebrity writer jolted onward, he started obsessing on a series of boyfriends who were conspicuously unworthy of him, as his standards were being disintegrated by drink, drugs, and manic socializing. There was Danny, a Korean war vet with a wife and two kids; Rick, an ex-Navy guy who had a son and an ex-wife, and worked as a bartender; and a few others who were attracted chiefly by the money and the parties.

At the time, Truman was raking in tons of money, for speaking engagements and for work both delivered, like magazine articles, and promised. He and his lawyer had renegotiated the now-outdated 1966 contract for *Answered Prayers* and had obtained a substantially larger advance than previously—seven hundred fifty thousand dollars—for a trilogy of novels including *Answered Prayers*, now to be delivered in January, 1973. Random House was eager to have another Capote best seller, and authors capable of producing best sellers were cosseted. Like a mining or oil company, the publisher had little choice but to keep drilling until it struck something. But Truman was also spending tons of money—on property, travel, dining, entertainment, and expensive trinkets like Dunhill lighters and Gucci bags. So for him, the '70s was a decade when he might also be in debt for a while and desperate for the next paycheck. He confessed this up-and-down condition to Lee one day at the Cartier shop on Fifth Avenue, where he was shopping for a watch.

"Jack says that I should write more and socialize less," he says. "He has some kind of formula for me—how much I should write, how much I should earn, how much I should party. But I can't look at it that way. I'm an artist, and I have a right to my impulses."

"I suppose you have a right to buy a second Cartier watch?" said Lee playfully.

Truman shot her a look of mock disappointment.

"You know perfectly well that this is my fifth," he said. "You were with me when I bought the Panthère, weren't you, in Nassau?"

"Was I?"

"Maybe it was Babe . . ."

They were seated at a tiny desk in a small, private area in the back of the shop. As usual, they were the best-dressed couple on Fifth Avenue that day—Lee in a tailored, cream-colored coat by Bill Blass and matching slacks, Truman in a gray Dunhill suit. On his right hand he was wearing the classic, rectangular-shaped Cartier Tank watch, in gold. A salesperson brought over a small velvet-lined tray of oval-shaped Baignoire watches, in various shades of gold, some with elongated faces.

"I saw one of these on Loel's wrist, and I had to have it," said

Truman, taking several of the watches from the tray. “Not too masculine, not too feminine, no?”

He selected one of them and modeled it for Lee.

“Very handsome,” she said.

“”I’ll take it,” said Truman. “Send it to my home, please.”

“Did you want to know the price, Mr. Capote?” asked the salesperson.

“Oh, I know the price,” said Truman. “It’s as much as a Chevy, right?”

Outside the shop, heading to La Côte Basque for lunch, Truman stopped suddenly, almost like a child on the brink of a tantrum.

“Oh, I wanted to show you—well, next time,” he said.

“Show me what?” said Lee.

“The Cartier Dalí watch—do you know it? I think they call it the Crash. The shape is like the Baignoire, but twisted—melted, like the clock in the Dalí painting. I’ll show you next time. They say a Cartier executive was wearing a Baignoire when he died in a car crash, and they recreated what they found on his wrist in the wreckage.”

As they stood there speaking, passersby recognized either the impeccably dressed lady or the very short gentleman, but kept on walking.

“What a story,” said Lee.

“You see? From the wrist of a dead man to a chic Fifth Avenue shop. Now *that* is what money can do.”

It was around this time that Lee seemed to become more comfortable sharing comments on some of her day-to-day doings with me. Nothing profound, and I don’t use the word *confide*, because I can well imagine how many more important things she would share only with Jackie, whom she still loved and trusted, of course, despite everything, and with Truman. But I had been working for Lee for around a decade at that point and, I think, had proven my trustworthiness, so it wasn’t unusual for her, later on the day of her visit to Cartier with Truman, to tell me how embarrassed she was to see Truman’s flamboyant effeminacy on display on a Fifth Avenue sidewalk.

When she told me this, it was cocktail hour, and she was home alone, in the library, with a Suze and tonic. Stas and the children were in London. When I came in with a small plate of the crab puffs she liked me to make for her, she asked me to sit and have a drink with her.

"'That's what money is for,' he said—just like that," said Lee, recreating Truman's extravagant arm gesture. It was certainly a more effeminate gesture than I'd ever seen even Lee or any of her friends make. "It's almost like he's making himself a target. But I guess that's something fags do sometimes."

I'd heard Lee use that word before, privately, and I don't think she meant it in a particularly hateful way. It was simply a term for what was called "sexual preference" back then that sounded less clinical and academic than "homosexual," while the word "gay" had not yet come into general use. She had first used the term in conversation with me only a few weeks before, when describing a dinner for some very fancy people that she and Stas hosted in London, to which Truman brought his momentary boyfriend Danny. She said with naughty sharpness that she had been "no more impressed by that young fag than anyone else was—and no more than he was with me." She also used the term when telling me how surprised she was that Truman had made Waldo Lydecker so obviously "a fag" in his script for *Laura*, where novelist Caspary had been more concerned, Truman told her, with the character's "impotence and destructiveness," and director Preminger had been pressured by the studio to "blunt it a bit." Lee said that Truman told her he wanted to show that Laura had no problem with "fags" if they are clever and useful enough.

"He uses the word himself," she added, not wanting, I think, to appear unliberal.

While never quite a political crusader, Truman was something of a pioneer about being himself, whether at a dinner party, or on a Fifth Avenue sidewalk, or on television. In fact, some of the rivalry between him and Gore Vidal stemmed from the fact that each expressed his sexual identity in his own way. Truman purred and seduced, which I think helped the public align him with women writers like Flannery O'Connor and Eudora Welty. In public, on the air, at a party, he might wield the camp put-down, whereas Vidal was a more pugilistic figure. Decidedly more masculinist in his bearing and literary style, Vidal seemed to identify more with figures like Hemingway and Mailer. All his life, Vidal made it a point of saying that everyone, including himself, was bisexual; and he always expressed contempt for the gay scene in the New York of the 1940s and '50s, where Truman had been quite at home. I know that Lee, on some level, understood the differences between these two, even if she didn't necessarily grasp at the time that history was lining up in back of her friend, the po' Southern nobody, and not behind her relative, the rich patrician whose grandfather had been a senator.

The turbulent times played a part, too, in adding to the jealousy Truman came to feel for Peter Beard, after Lee started seeing him. Whatever romantic connection Truman might have imagined possible between him and Lee, based on the long-established conventions of their respective classes, became more ludicrous as the '70s wore on. Besides, even if there were still ways for homosexually inclined men to marry heterosexual women, in consideration of family names, high positions, inherited property, or sometimes even love, this was never the kind of relationship that Lee was looking for. Except for the fact that Peter had no money, it was someone like him, dashing and creative and horny, that she was looking for, now that her marriage to Stas was winding down.

Without Stas, and often without Truman, Lee was traveling a lot in those years—Acapulco, Capri, Mykonos, Marrakech, Palm Springs. It was during a long summer stay at a big house in Montauk that she leased from Andy Warhol that she began her affair with Peter Beard, who at the time was a fellow Montauker. She already knew Peter fairly well. He had just divorced his first wife, Minnie, and years before had had an affair with Jackie. Five years younger than Lee, he was known as something of an adventurer and a party boy. Moreover, he had been invited to join Jackie and Lee and their children on Skorpios the previous summer, where he was expected to keep the house littered with stimulating debris from his paintings and collages in progress, and to amuse the children by involving them in art-making. It was a time, described Lee once, dreamily, that was "devoted purely to creativity and the imagination, to sun and the sea," when everyone wore shorts and bathing suits and as little else as possible.

When Peter arrived in New York in the fall, after Montauk, he alternated between staying with rich friends and sleeping in an old, beat-up station wagon he owned.

"Though he does have a place on Central Park West," explained Lee.

"Cozy," said Truman.

"I think his sister lives there."

"A family place."

"I think so—yes. And full of ideas and interests. He seems to have endless curiosity about everything. And Truman—the body of a Greek god, always so tan."

"Isn't that nice?"

Lee knew well when Truman's silkiness was blossoming into sarcasm.

"Don't be jealous, darling," she said.

"I'm not jealous in the slightest," purred Truman. "I'm just observing."

Truman knew Peter's background well. One of the heirs to an old railway fortune, Peter was born into social prominence, part of a family whose seasonal wanderings included both Tuxedo Park and Southampton. Though it turned out his inheritance yielded an income far too modest for Lee, who was always very clear about the kind of life she was accustomed to, it was Peter's energy and style, not to mention his good looks, that kept her interested.

At a small dinner at Lee's house, that first year that Peter was around, Truman and Peter sparred playfully about the state of modern literature.

"At least your books are readable, Truman," said Peter. "Some these days, you can't even read."

"What a lovely compliment—'readable,'" said Truman. He

pretended to be slighted, but a hint of coquettishness betrayed the truth: Truman was also struck by Peter's star quality.

"You know what I mean," said Peter. "You're a natural storyteller. You can see people's souls and have a talent for sharing that vision with others."

"Isn't that nicely said, Truman?" said Lee, clearly proud of her new boyfriend.

"Better keep close tabs on this one, Lee," said Truman. "He's too much."

After dinner, Truman had a word with me, since I had witnessed much of the merriment in my role as server.

"What do you think of your boss's new beau?" he whispered.

"Nice," I said. "He asked to photograph me."

"What? You?"

"Mm-hmm."

"I hardly know what to say. He asked you tonight?"

"No—a few days ago, when he was here. He was showing me some photographs he gave Lee. He paints over them. It's really interesting."

"He collects people like specimens. He's a child, really—a bug collector. Well, Serene One, do what you want. Just be sure to tell me all about it."

"Don't Repeat This" —by Lila North
Friday, February 5, 1971

> . . . Our beloved former first lady, Jacqueline Kennedy Onassis, returned to the White House for the first time on Wednesday at the invitation of Pat Nixon, to view the newly painted and installed portraits of Jackie and JFK by artist Aaron Shikler. My sources say that Jackie had been dreading the visit, but that the Nixons made it a positive experience • Apparently, paparazzo photographer Ron Galella has been pursuing Jackie more fervently than ever—as she walks down New York sidewalks, enters and exits restaurants, etc. Candid snaps of her, as you know, can go for hundreds of dollars—more if Caroline and John Jr. are involved. But the lady is fighting back, seeking a restraining

order against Galella. • The only thing in Christendom more terrifying than last-year's Beatles break-up is a report that the elderly aunt of Jackie and her sister Lee Radziwill is living in squalor in a formerly lavish, twenty-eight-room mansion in East Hampton, Long Island, along with her unmarried adult daughter and dozens of cats. I hear that "steps are being taken" to rectify the sad matter . . .

The revelation that Lee's cousin, "Little Edie" Beale, and aunt, "Big Edie" Beale, were living in squalor in East Hampton was a real trigger for Lee. I think it played simply to her decency and kindness as well as to her family loyalty. She felt a certain pity, too, that, poverty aside, the Beales just couldn't manage to keep up with the evolution of old guard society as gracefully as the Bouvier sisters were managing to do. Lee and I had more than one conversation about "that generation" of women, meaning Big Edie and Lee's mother Janet—what was expected of them and what they expected of themselves and their daughters. I confided to Lee—for the first time—that my own mother was a nut case who had been made so by some very nasty forces both in and outside the family; and Lee seemed to identify when I explained how little my mother ever approved of me.

When the headlines about the East Hamptons house, known as Grey Gardens, were published—FORMER FIRST LADY'S AUNT LIVING IN SQUALOR!—Lee garnered great sympathy from friends. Peter suggested that he and Lee should visit and help the eccentric Beales, but Lee said that "they'll never let us in there." It was Peter's idea to get the filmmakers Albert and David Maysles, whom they knew well from Montauk, to help by bringing cameras and saying they wanted to shoot a movie.

When Truman heard that Lee had hired the brothers to make the film that turned out to be *Grey Gardens,* he was delighted.

"That was your artistic instinct at work," he said.

"I don't know about that," said Lee. "I just want to help the poor dears."

"Of course you do."

"Only how to get them to accept the help . . . ?"

"Easy! Appeal to their inner movie stars," said Truman.

"Isn't that exactly what you did with me?" said Lee.

"Well—uh, no, not exactly . . . Oh—you're being funny. Ha ha."

But Lee was happy to claim that it was her artistic instinct at work in an offer she had just received from the Rizzoli publishing house, to write a memoir about a summer trip to Europe she took with her sister Jackie in 1951, when Lee was eighteen. It was to be a picture book with commentary. Lee would help design it, as well as write it.

"Do it," said Truman. "It sounds heavenly."

"Of course, I'm sure it's partly because Jackie's in it," said Lee.

"Just do it, and do a fabulous job. If you need help, I'm here. I could help you flesh out your stories."

"What do you mean 'flesh out'?"

"Just that. What does Pooh-Bah say in *The Mikado*? 'Merely corroborative detail, intended to give artistic verisimilitude to an otherwise bald and unconvincing narrative.' "

"My narrative is not bald and unconvincing, thank you."

"Anybody's is, princess. Beef it up. Let's see—1951, did you say? Did you visit Venice? Of course you did . . ."

"Well, yes . . ."

"Good! Then you and Jackie attended the Beistegui Ball—done, *perfetto*. She went as the Empress Theodora and you were Antonina, the wife of Belisarius."

"Truman . . ."

"Oh, forgive me. *You* were the Empress and *she* was the attendant."

"We didn't go. We weren't invited."

"There you go—messing with history."

It was interesting to me that Truman's interest in helping Lee amplify tales about herself came at the same time as he was once again accepting movie studio money for the rights to *Answered Prayers*, though he had basically nothing to show for the book. Jokingly, he blamed Lee, of all people, for his lack of writing inspiration.

"She makes me lazy," he complained—only somewhat tongue-in-cheek. "She's draining me like a vampire, as she becomes more creative."

Openly he admitted—at least to me—that he'd run out of his own ideas, except for the beginnings of *Answered Prayers*, which were the product of "a much younger mind and maybe no longer applicable." He turned to the idea of "co-creating" and thought that a screenplay might be best for this. Again, he had his need for money in mind at least as much as his identity and agenda as an artist. He wanted to know more and more about my family, their hopes and dreams, their fall from grace and riches, their relationship with the Cuban soul. He loved the centuries-long tale of fortune and aristocracy; he wanted to hear ever more about the cultivated, international life that I once led as a child and teenager. It's almost as if he were pivoting from Lee as a protégée to me.

"You've come to mean so much to me," he told me once, during one of our Mercantile Library sessions.

"How so?"

"My friends are . . . well, I have no friends. No real ones."

"You have Jack."

"I've been terrible to Jack—running around on him too much. He's withdrawing, and I don't wonder."

"What about Lee?"

"*Is* she a friend? Or an ally? Or a partner—a henchman. Or, I suppose, a trophy—though that's terrible to say. Now you, Serenity, you're what I had when I was a kid with a very few special friends, like Harper—whom I can relax and simply co-exist with."

I thanked him for that nice thought with a little nod. Looking down on us from the wall, as usual, was Ralph Waldo Emerson. We were seated, as usual, in venerable Boston chairs, on opposite sides of the room's massive French Renaissance–style table. Off-limits to day-to-day patrons, the room housed a collection of what a well-read gentleman of business would have had in his library in the first few decades of the nineteenth century—

volumes of Homer, Cicero, Dante, Cervantes, Shakespeare; of history, geography, anatomy; several collections of sermons—mostly leather-bound, all in excellent shape.

Libraries, Lee once told me, were lenses through which we could behold humanity in its entirety—not historically, observable during age after age, marching along some destined path from the past toward the future, but discernable all at once, as in a crystal whose vertex points represent all the ages simultaneously. In a library, all those other "present days" represented in words from the last three millennia were mapped onto the present moment. This timelessness—or is it the opposite of timelessness: the confluence of all epochs?—was palpable to Lee. It excited her. It was one reason why, I think, she liked to entertain in her libraries, as well as read and write in them. For her, they were mystical places—practically like something out of fantasy and science fiction. In fact, I'd say that this experience of timelessness underlaid the thrill Lee took in everything she did—decorating, dressing, probably even dating. Peter wasn't simply the next boyfriend; he was one of those glittering vertices.

Truman was slumped at the library table, looking glum, an open notebook and a black Montblanc ballpoint pen in front of him, but not writing.

"I'm afraid of what may be coming," he said.

I was afraid of what was coming, too—for him, since he'd begun showing up for our afternoon sessions in various states of inebriation and mental abstraction—but I told him that I knew he was going to be okay.

"It's a time of revolution," I said. "You said so yourself. No one knows what's coming. You just have to hang on. It's just that . . . you're so sensitive . . ."

He looked at me with an unusually beneficent quality.

"So are you," he said.

"No—I am numb. But that does give me an advantage."

"Ha! What did Candide say when Cunegonde asks, 'Weren't you clever, dear, to survive?' He says, 'I've a sorry tale to tell. I escaped more dead than alive.' "

"Is that Voltaire?"

"Not exactly. It's a man named John La Touche, with a little help from a man named Richard Wilbur."

"Who?"

"Lyricists, darling."

"Well, you certainly will survive."

"I'd like to believe I will."

He straightened in his seat and picked up the pen.

"I'll tell you what's on my mind," he said. "I'm thinking of this story of yours as a screenplay. For Lee."

"I know."

"Oh. Okay. I'm thinking of Lee for the mother."

"Right."

"I was wrong to think of Lee as an Audrey Hepburn type. She's more of an Anne Bancroft type. She can go darker, more dangerous—sexy if she needs to."

"I suppose so."

"Tell me, were there any ghosts in your family?" he asked.

"Ghosts?"

"Ghosts of the Caribbean can be good for a story line."

I was mystified but game. I looked at everything that came out of his mouth as oracular and potentially important.

"Maybe my mother's brother, who died young?" I said tentatively. "He was the last one to have the title *marqués*," I said. "It passes on the male side. He had no children. My mother has no title, really—though she didn't correct people when they called her *marquesa*."

"So that was your uncle . . ."

"He is buried in the garden next to our house," I said. "There's a beautiful monument. That was the only land my mother was allowed to keep—that and the house itself. The rest—the gardens, the grove of banyan trees—is now all the property of the state, along with the mills and the hacienda in the mountains. It was hard to lose the hacienda."

"Tell me about that."

Chapter 18

What Is There to Remember?

The floor was spread with sheets of newspaper. Scattered over them was a riot of photographs and collages made from photographs, many of the latter works in progress. The main themes were bush and grassland terrains; giraffe, rhinos, and other wildlife; and dark-skinned women in fancy headdresses and massive beaded chokers. Around the edges of the collages were clumps of glued-on twigs or grass, and tiny, primitive but animated drawings and paintings of people and animals, trees, and flowers. Here and there, a collage was overlain with a human hand-print or footprint, in ink, or paint, or what looked like blood.

"Wow," said Truman.

"He's working with material from a trip to Kenya," said Lee.

"Wild. Is that real blood?"

"I think so. It's a reference to swimming in a river infested with crocodiles."

"Did they get him?"

"No. Though once he was gored by an elephant. The scar is dreadful."

They were on the ground floor of Lee's Buckingham Place guesthouse, across the garden from the main house. Peter Beard, who was visiting London and staying with Lee, had set up a makeshift studio in the guesthouse, where he spent long hours, when the two of them were not out among London's most progressive and creative types. On the dining table, the surface of which was protected by a plastic drop cloth, were pots and tubes of paint, bottles of ink and glue, boxes and cans of assorted brushes, pens, and palette knives, and a pile of mismatched notebooks. Hooked to the back of a dining chair was a spattered workman's apron. On the floor next to the chair was a pair of well-worn leather sandals.

Also on the floor were several photographs of Mick Jagger's head, in different poses.

"Those are very recent," said Lee. "They're studies. Did I tell you he's going to be touring with the Stones?"

"Is he? Don't tell me the man plays the guitar, too?"

"He'll be taking pictures, making art. Just like on safari."

"When?"

"Starting in June—New York, L.A., Chicago, Kansas City, Houston . . . I am thinking of going along."

"On the road with the Stones? Now that sounds like an article, if not a major motion picture."

"It does, doesn't it?"

"Quite coincidentally, the magazine *Rolling Stone* has been after me to write something. Maybe I should join you two. If that wouldn't cramp your style."

The occasion was a little dinner for just the three of them—Lee, Peter, and Truman. Peter was in London to finalize details of a gallery show there. Lee and Stas were by now living fairly separate lives.

"I've got a secret," said Truman, when they were back in the drawing room of the main house.

"Oh, Truman, so do most people. Their secrets are usually small and ridiculous."

"Mine's a good secret."

"Don't be coy. You're going to tell me, so why not just tell me?"

"I have the next role for you—a screenplay I'm working on."

"No."

"Lee, but this one will be original, so no one will be comparing you to anyone."

"No."

She was checking to see that the cigarette boxes were full and the ashtrays empty and positioned correctly.

"And you will play older, not younger," said Truman, "which everyone will think is brilliant of you."

"I have Peter now," said Lee.

"Since when does having a boyfriend preclude your being a movie star?"

"I haven't the time. And now Rizzoli has asked me to write this memoir . . ."

"Peter doesn't want a movie star for a girlfriend?"

"He'll be back soon. Mix us some martinis."

"Notice I'm alone," said Truman, heading to the bar.

"Thank God," said Lee. "Honestly, you could do much better than with most of these creatures."

A few months before, Truman had met Lee for dinner with another of his provisional boyfriends, Rick, in tow. It was another case in which the young man failed the social graces test, made a nasty crack about Lee afterwards to Truman, and was summarily dropped from Truman's social rotation.

"How come you haven't asked me what Peter is like in bed?" asked Lee, after seating herself on the orange silk-covered settee and lighting a cigarette.

"Because I know," said Truman.

"Now, *that* I will never believe. None of your tall tales, please, Mr. Capote."

"Of course I haven't slept with him, but I know all about what privileged, pretty, WASP boys do in bed. Ardent but unskilled. Besides, if I asked you that, then I might also have to hear what *you* are like in bed, and I am not ready to know that."

Peter arrived, gave Lee a kiss, and gratefully took a martini from Truman.

"Fascinating to be the one posing," said Peter, joining Lee on the settee. He was wearing a tweed sport jacket with a blue chambray shirt.

"Posing undraped at the Royal Academy again, Peter?" quipped Truman. "What some people won't do for a little pocket money."

"Ha—no," said Peter. "My friend Francis Bacon—do you know Eggsy . . . ?"

" 'Eggsy'? Do you mean the painter?"

"Yeah, that's what I call him—Eggsy. Actually, that's what his, uh, lover calls him, and it's kind of caught on. Anyway, he asked me to pose for him."

"A portrait," interjected Lee.

"Well," said Peter, "he'd say it's not a portrait *per se*, because of the historical baggage that comes with that term. A picture of my head, is how he describes what he's doing—studies so far, in the most remarkable shades of blue."

"I adore his work," said Lee. "Truman just had a portrait done, Peter."

"Did you?"

"Yes," said Truman. "By Jim Fosburgh—Babe's brother-in-law and a good friend of Jackie's. He and I have known each other forever."

"Are you happy with it?"

"Interesting that you should ask that, Peter," said Truman thoughtfully, "but you are perhaps the ideal person to be discussing it with, since you are an artist and now have this experience of being looked at by an artist. To be honest, I don't know if I like it, or if I need to like it. He's a great painter, and the picture is very good, in terms of likeness. In fact, he's made me a look a good deal younger and more handsome than perhaps I am, and I have found myself embarrassed to be enjoying that quality. The picture hangs in my home now, and I see it every day, so I can enjoy that quality every day if I want to. But I'm not sure what it *means* . . ."

"I know what you're talking about," said Peter. "You absolutely give yourself over to an artist, you agree to that, and it's a brave thing to do . . ."

"Right. Because I feel there is *more* than likeness in it—more than I am seeing right now; more, perhaps, than I am capable of seeing. And that makes me uneasy."

"You're wearing a very nice Panama hat in it," said Lee, "which is very you and gives the portrait such warmth and character."

"Truman, let me photograph you sometime," said Peter, brightly. "I know exactly how to solve the likeness problem in a way that will also capture some of your spirit."

"How?"

"I'll make a mask for you to wear and photograph you in that."

Truman cackled in delight.

"Perfect," he said.

"An echo of your famous ball," said Peter.

"Indeed," said Truman.

"Listen to us," said Lee. "So concerned about our images! I'll bet each one of us has been somehow mentioned in the press in the past week or so—am I right? Doesn't that mean that the press has gone crazy, or that we've reached the absolute pinnacle of narcissism?"

The words hung there in the air for a few seconds, until Truman spoke.

"Oh, I don't know about a pinnacle, princess," he said. "I'll bet things could get worse. Perhaps someday soon it will be possible for each of us to be our own, little individual publicity factories—manufacturing very flattering items about ourselves five times a day, and sharing them with each other, all the while hoping that the rest of the world will see them and like them."

Dinner chat was about recent and upcoming travels—Peter had come from New York, where he'd been palling around with Andy Warhol; Lee from Paris, where she'd been fitted for some clothes; and Truman from Verbier, where he was "doing battle with my book." It was agreed that Truman would join Lee and Peter on the road with the Rolling Stones, if Truman's magazine assignment could be arranged.

"I always see you in New York, Truman," said Peter. "How much time do you spend in Switzerland?"

"Enough," said Truman. "Do you know Switzerland?"

"Sure—skiing and such," said Peter. "Last year I did a shoot in Gstaad for *Vogue*."

'That's the German part of Switzerland. I'm in the French part."

"Are they so different?"

"Very different. Alps and tax havens may be all alike, but the German-speaking Swiss are awfully buttoned-up, compared to the French."

"And the Italian speakers?"

"Let's not speak of them."

Laughter.

"I assume you're fluent in French?" said Peter.

"Not at all," said Truman. "I do have to say 'I'm sorry' a lot—*Je suis désolé.*"

"But you must like it there."

"We have a place on a hillside, overlooking a beautiful valley. Lots of light. I literally would not survive if I couldn't return there frequently, to organize my thoughts and get some real work done. Jack takes care of everything—*he* speaks French—and I just work, work, work. They produce a very nice white wine there that I am very fond of, called Chasselas, and they pull trout out of those gorgeous streams and smoke them, which is obviously a very clever thing to do, that's been going on for centuries. And then there's that marvelous raclette."

"Cheese."

"Cheese."

"Living there sounds like a recipe for a long and happy life."

"Peter, my life will not be long, in any case," said Truman.

"What makes you say that?" said Lee.

"I've always known that," said Truman.

"How can you say that?" Lee sounded genuinely alarmed.

"Anyway," said Truman, "I travel so much. That's bound to increase my chances of an early death, isn't it?"

Peter instinctively took Lee's hand, across the table. And Truman later told me that that's when he understood the depth of their mutual affection—deeper, he said, than anything he'd ever seen between her and Stas. So this was the new Lee, he thought; and would this mean less Lee for Truman? He said, though, that he wasn't feeling jealousy so much as guilt, because he knew he wasn't as happy for her as he should have been.

"That's what I'm after in my life, that kind of balance," said

Peter. "Between being out in the world, seeing and touching everything, and then in the studio, putting things together."

"You're lucky not to be afraid of making a mess," said Lee. "Now, don't take that the wrong way."

"Don't worry," said Peter.

"But I do. I am definitely too neat for my own good. I thought I could be like Truman and take these organized notes and then sit down and calmly spin them into prose."

"No?"

"No. I try to write. Stas and I would trot around with friends and pick up signs here and there of what is *beyond* the pleasure, *beyond* the fun—the insights—but I must not be able to apprehend them well enough for me to put them into words."

"That's a very specialized job, after all," said Truman.

"So is acting . . . !" said Lee.

"You have an innate gift for acting that involves insights," said Truman. "We're all better at some things than others."

"I guess so. I catch glimpses of lots of things I want to be better at, in the guides and caretakers we hire, and our friends who are curators and scholars and artists and poets; in the tuned-in-and-dropped-out former lawyers, and former investment bankers, and former corporate executives that we know; the hippies and mystics we encounter when we step off the boat on a Greek island. And I listen carefully to these people and respect them. But rarely, so rarely, do I wind up following them even a few steps down that path of dedication. Which is no crime, except maybe to myself."

"When I look at you, Lee, I see the artist," said Peter, "and the crime would be against the rest of humanity if you didn't try writing, or acting, or whatever you put your mind to."

"Hear, hear," said Truman. "You do get it, Lee—the truth about life. That's why I think you belong in front of an audience. That's why I want you to play the mother."

Lee explained to Peter that Truman intended to write an original screenplay for her.

"What's it about?" asked Peter.

"He hasn't started it yet," said Lee.

"I certainly have," said Truman. "But I won't know exactly what it's about until it's finished. That's what writing is."

"I understand that," said Peter.

"Another unfinished masterpiece," said Lee.

"Don't you make fun, you," said Truman. "I just have to figure out who lives and who dies in it. That's always the hard part."

One day, Lee showed some of her writing to me and asked for my opinion. We were in the library in New York. The memoir she had been contracted to write was not going as smoothly as she had hoped. Truman had been too busy to really sit down with her in a proper writer's work session, and even with the help of her editor from Rizzoli, there was little to show.

The passage was about visiting the Conca dei Marini and nearby towns on the Positano coast, and to me, it felt flat. She had the fishermen's nets, the orchards of lemon trees, the white houses set into steep rock cliffs, but her paragraphs read like tourist brochure copy. They lacked a soulful pulse. At the suggestion of her editor, she was using the Italian road SS163—the famously scenic Amalfi Drive—as a device to organize her thoughts and to say something big about that "timeless" part of the world: about the Mediterranean, the Romans, the Greeks, the way time and eras pass. But her account of travel along the Drive only itemized who was there in those towns for lunches and dinners, and what they wore, and what they ate and drank. Try as she did, she just could not capture anything more on the page. Where was that feeling that comes at the end of a day of adventure via a refreshing breeze on a sea-view terrace? And what did it mean? Where was the thrill of a sip of Fiano with hints of pear and almond, the delight in a briny bite of fried anchovy, or the mental clarity produced by a headful of mossy-lemony Ginestra, pure and fundamental? She told me she was frustrated because a proper description of the essence of her experiences—the eternity that she remembered inhabiting every moment—was eluding her. When I suggested she try writing about that—the frustration that some experiences might be beyond the reach of language—she laughed.

"That's something Truman would say," she said. She was the very picture of a lady author, sitting there at an antique writing table, surrounded by walls of books, in front of her a Smythson notebook, a Montblanc ballpoint pen, and a sleek new IBM Selectric II in black, humming almost imperceptibly while somehow expressing the power of a locomotive.

The lack of spark in her writing made her sad, Lee said, because she knew what a privilege it was for her to have been able to have those experiences—in Italy, during the 1950s, as well as some now in New York and London and a score of other places she wanted to include. She said she could remember moments very well, facts as well as feelings, but in looking inward, she found no fresh or particularly luminous way of expressing what they meant to her, let alone how they may have formed or transformed her—none, anyway, as luminous as those she read in Truman's work and the work of her other writer friends. She felt dejected that her writing seemed to be leading nowhere, just as she felt her acting did. Was there even really a creative Lee to emerge, now that she was on the edge of forty?

I wished I had been able to find something complimentary to say. Lee was an honest woman and did not expect people to be dishonest with her, including an employee. She was not one for flattery or empty praise, so I think my reticence only reinforced her sadness.

She told me about a recent exchange she'd had with Truman when they were discussing this memoir commission.

"Lee, what are you trying to prove with it?" Truman said.

"What do you mean? You're always telling me how creative I am," said Lee.

"That's not what I mean. I mean, what's this book trying to prove? What are you desperate to tell the reader?"

"Desperate? Well—that the Amalfi coast is so beautiful, historic . . ."

"They already know that. What else?"

"That . . . that I felt something there—this feeling of life, *all* of life, being contained in every split second . . ."

"Sweetie, that's true, but the Victorians were writing about it. What else?"

"I . . . don't know."

"What are you *desperate* to tell another person about your time on the Amalfi Coast? Certainly not that you were rich enough to afford to be there . . . ?"

"Of course not."

"Well, let me suggest you dig a little deeper," said Truman.

"So tell me, Truman dear," snapped Lee, "what are *you* so desperate to prove when *you* write? That you're smart?"

Truman grinned.

"Everybody knows that—anybody who has ever met me," he said. "No, what I'm desperate to prove is that I am worthy of love."

The declaration silenced Lee for a moment. She called it "starkly honest."

"I envy you," she finally told Truman. "I don't think I've ever been desperate that way, except maybe to look better on a horse than my sister."

My heart went out to Lee when I heard this. I suddenly saw that people with nothing to prove might have a hard time achieving that critical posture with life that critics say true creativity requires. In mentoring Lee, was Truman appealing to a quality that he thought and Lee hoped she must possess, but simply didn't?

Our conversation was interrupted by a call from Jackie, with the news that Diana Vreeland had been fired from *Vogue* and was planning to go to work at the Metropolitan Museum of Art, running the costume collection.

Lee was shocked. "Why was she fired?" she said.

Jackie said that Vreeland was thought to be spending too lavishly on photo shoots. The editor thought nothing of spending a million dollars to send supermodel Veruschka and fifteen trunks of sable, mink, and chinchilla halfway around the world to be photographed in the snow by Richard Avedon. Several friends who believed in Vreeland's vision of great style were coming together to endow her chair at the Museum, because "she has some fantastic ideas for shows." Lee said she would chip in. She agreed with Jackie that "this was something we must do because we *can* do it."

"Is nothing sacred?" said Lee, after hanging up. "Well, anyway, I'd better get back to work on this memoir—I should be able to come up with something, shouldn't I? I was there, wasn't I? Or else I'll have to turn completely into one of those committee ladies."

Meanwhile, though the buzz around *Answered Prayers* was building, Truman still had little to show for it. The way things were going with his partying, he was unlikely to meet the 1973 deadline he'd renegotiated for the book—let alone the two other books that he'd promised Random House in the new deal, which were now meant for a 1977 delivery. Yet in interviews, he tried to show confidence.

"I am the only person in this country who could write this book—the only person," he told one interviewer. "My whole life has been spent to develop the technique, the style, and the nerve to write this thing. It is the *raison d'être* of my entire life."

In truth, Truman was able to work less and less frequently, and for shorter periods of time. His concentration was often failing him. He was drinking more and more, taking tranquilizers, and, when going out at night with "supercool" friends, which was often, using more than a bit of recreational cocaine. Jack, when they were together, witnessed the drinking and warned Truman to take it easy, but I suspect that Jack saw little of the drug-taking and had no idea how bad things were getting in that regard. With a sense of pride that Truman had shown previously only for his literary achievements, he now exuberantly touted the pictures that were published in newspapers and magazines, of him in clubs and out in the Hamptons and Montauk with people like Andy Warhol and Bianca Jagger.

It was clear that Truman had achieved some of the fame and fortune of the people he liked to socialize with. In some corner of his soul, he had perhaps never fully embraced this as a possibility for himself, yet here it was. And the "dangerous" book he was working on, *Answered Prayers*, designed to judge the ethos of preening socialites, its theme announced as "a dark comedy about the very rich," was now applicable to his own ethos, as well. This may have added to the writer's block he was suffering due to the crippling expectation that his next book had to be a masterpiece.

I even wondered why, with so much on his mind and the vast socializing he was engaged in, Truman even bothered to meet with me. But I think our meetings were important to him as guideposts of normality. Neither a friend, exactly, nor an apprentice, I fit into his life as a caretaker, a mother confessor. It was in the latter capacity that I understood he was beginning to sink into infantilism, even as he was presented on television talk shows as a distinguished sage. I was happy to continue meeting with him under these circumstances because I was learning so much from him and had become so fond of him. That was a surprise for me. I don't think I had been "fond" of anyone before that. My work with him helped point my way forward, both as a writer and as a human being, and I remain so grateful for that.

"We tell ourselves stories in order to live," as he once told me Joan Didion told him. That's exactly what Truman and I did: tell each other stories. Only it worked better for me than it did for him. The formula wasn't good enough to save him. Nothing was.

"I wish I knew what was happening to me, Marlene," he once said. "I used to take such satisfaction in being paid well for my writing. Now the money makes me nervous and kind of dares me to do the work."

At our meetings, I would show him screenplays I'd been reading and hope to talk about them. Having read many of them, I liked the form and found it easy to come up with scenes that I thought might actually work. But Truman became too scattered to work with me on this level—and that scared me, since I had seen family members slip off the rails with booze and dope.

"I am still having trouble with the mother, Truman."

"How so?"

My manuscript was open to page forty-three. So far, the mother character was misguided, manipulative, and monomaniacal—a clumsy literary device rather than a flesh-and-blood character inadvertently harming her marriage and her children, because she herself had been harmed.

"She's too one-dimensional. Can I get your thoughts on this scene in the garden . . . ?"

He held up his palm.

"Not right now, please. Tell me instead."

"I have been looking through screenplays for monsters who are not one-dimensional."

"Good luck."

"They must exist. Noir films?"

"No—sure they exist. They're just hard to come by because they're hard to write. It's hard work for an author to create a monstrous person who also has a soul. Though of course, all people do have souls, even if they're vestigial."

"What should I do? No one's going to believe the mother if she's a cartoon."

"Listen to the character. She's you, so listen to yourself."

"Easier said than done."

"That's the path, my Serene One. I can't push you down it."

He was distracted that day by the fact that Jack had canceled a two-week stay they were to have spent together in Ravello, claiming poor health. But Truman felt like he was being punished.

"Somehow I have to spare Jack the anguish of watching me disintegrate. I just . . . it's so hard."

And then the frequency of our sessions tapered off, and they were replaced by coffee dates. Truman said that I should continue working alone on the screenplay—whether or not he would "ever be able to do anything with it as it stands."

The few smaller things he was tinkering around with were, he said, going nowhere. The *Rolling Stone* assignment, which in the past he would easily have been able to pull off, looked "monumental"—but it was too good to pass up. Large parts of

Answered Prayers were finished, he claimed, but "the story is shifting" and he needed time to develop it properly.

"I'm listening to my characters, you see, and they're yacking their heads off."

He repeatedly said he wanted to be "the Proust of our age," but was finding this goal increasingly elusive.

"Life is dragging me away from literature," he once said, as we were leaving the Mercantile Library. "Fine mentor I am to anyone!"

"We all mentor each other," I said.

He invited me for a drink that day at the Carlyle, but I was due back at Lee's. I had to prepare an informal dinner she was giving for Diana Vreeland and the women who would be supporting her.

When Truman returned to New York after being on the road with the Rolling Stones' *Exile on Main St.* tour, with Lee and Peter, he told me about hitchhiking with Lee in Dallas.

"The night before was . . . well, hanging out with the Stones after a concert. You can imagine."

"Wild?"

"They get the whole top floor of this Fort Worth hotel, right next to the arena where they're performing. Not a very fashionable place, mind you; the décor is very much a Texan's idea of a first-class international hotel in, oh, Frankfurt. Lee and I were staying at a much nicer place over in Turtle Creek. Anyway, everybody goes up there after the concert—very tight security, everybody needs passes, yet everywhere there are these pretty young things who are only groupies or party girls. All the rooms are open—the doors, I mean; even Mick's. He's in the so-called Presidential Suite, and that's where I am with Lee and some people, and Peter's off photographing something; and there's music and booze and drugs; and Robert Frank is running around shooting everybody—he's a filmmaker—and there are cameras he's put around the place for anybody to pick up and film people shooting up or getting blown or whatever; and the musicians are there and some of the crew and some of the locals; and there's another writer from the magazine whom I replaced, but he went along anyway; and yes, *wild* is the word for it—people going in and out of rooms, wandering through the hallways . . . Just wild.

"It's the energy of the concert, still vibrating. Fourteen thousand people were in the arena that night, screaming their heads off after 'Jumpin' Jack Flash' and '(I Can't Get No) Satisfaction.' And Marlene, every night on the tour there are riots over gate-crashing and forged tickets and marijuana possession; and stagehands being arrested . . . you know. Anyway, Lee and I are talking with Mick about the kind of physical stamina it takes to perform on an arena stage like that, and it's a relatively calm discussion, in a drunk sort of way, until this very slick, stoned-looking junior executive-type comes in with his arm around the waist of this fetching young woman in a slinky gown, whom we take to be the guy's wife or girlfriend.

" 'Great show, Mick,' says the guy, interrupting us.

" 'Thanks, mate,' says Mick.

" 'My girl and I, we think you guys are awesome.'

" 'Thanks. I appreciate it.'

"It's clear that Mick wants to keep talking to us, but the guy keeps interrupting.

" 'Can I offer you some . . .' he says, revealing a little bag of white powder.

" 'No, I'm good, man, thanks,' says Mick. 'Hey, listen, I'm talking to my friends here, so . . . have fun. There's some food and a bar set up in the suite across the hall.'

"Mick is already scanning the room to see if there are any security guys who aren't occupied with groupie girls.

" 'Man,' says the guy, showing some annoyance at being dismissed, 'and I come all the way up here to give you something . . .' And the guy proceeds to slip down a shoulder strap of his date's dress, exposing her left breast, which is barely covered by a skimpy pink bra. And the lady seems completely comfortable with this, like it's been rehearsed.

" 'C'mon, man . . .' says Mick, signaling a security guy. And security comes over and starts, with the phony politeness of law enforcement officials, to remove the offending couple, which of course turns into a melee involving other security men who materialize out of various rooms. And Lee and I decide to leave after a ceramic lamp is knocked over and explodes with a great pop.

"Anyway, we had plans the next day, just Lee and me, to go to Dealey Plaza and pay our respects—that's where Kennedy was shot. Mick had no interest at all in getting himself out of bed to do that, and Peter was scheduled to do a shoot with that idiot Keith Richards—Keith loathes me, for some reason; calls me 'an old queen.' So Lee and I go off. We're both hung over, dressed like spooks, all in black, with dark glasses. The limousine driver must have thought we were ghouls or spies or something."

I listened intently, not quite sure whether Truman was recollecting, or repeating something he'd written, or just gossiping. Not that it mattered, since everything about his language and expression was interesting to me. With Truman, I felt like I could learn something even from the small things he said, like the phrase *dressed like spooks.* There must be at least six other ways to express that detail, yet that one really "told," as he would have said. Sometimes, back then, when speaking with others, I even found myself emphasizing a word with a bit of a Southern drawl, as Truman often did.

"We drove past Dealey Plaza, and we were on Elm Street, the very road where Kennedy was shot, probably in the very lane, and from the limo, we saw the book repository where Lee Harvey Oswald was; and then we went over to the JFK Memorial, a block away. Philip Johnson designed a cenotaph—that's a kind of tomb without the body—quite an elegant and spare thing, an outdoor room without a roof. I gather it was Jackie's idea. Outside the cenotaph are the sounds of a busy city, street traffic and such, but inside, all that's muffled, except for the occasional helicopter flying over or echoing car horn.

"There is no bust or anything, only a low marble slab, meant perhaps to indicate consecrated ground—you feel like you're inside the Kaaba or something—and there's an inscription by Jim

Lehrer, the journalist—very plain, something about 'not a memorial to the pain and sorrow of death, but a permanent tribute to the joy and excitement of a man's life . . .'

"We were silent for a moment, and then I realized Lee was weeping.

" 'Poor Jackie,' she said.

" 'I know.'

" 'I don't know how she managed.'

" 'She had lots of support, including yours.'

"It was a very bright day, but the walls of the memorial are so high that it might have been shadowy inside, except for all this radiance pouring in from above. It was quite extraordinary. That Johnson is quite a magician.

"Lee said it was strange to think it was almost ten years ago. Anyway, and then the car got a flat on Turtle Creek Boulevard. We were on our way back to the hotel to meet friends for lunch, and we were late. And there we were on the side of the road, a kind of parkway, next to Turtle Creek trail, where people can stroll, and Turtle Creek itself, all lined with trees and bushes. And it's lunchtime and a very lovely setting, and no one's around except us and the driver and the passing traffic.

"The driver looked in the trunk but didn't find what he was looking for.

" 'No spare?' I said.

" 'I've got the tire but not the tool kit that's supposed to be there.'

" 'That's inconceivable,' I said.

" 'Sorry, sir. I'm going to have to radio for it.'

" 'How long will this take?'

" 'Hard to say—no less than half an hour.'

" 'Half an hour?!'

" 'Maybe more. I'm really sorry.'

" 'It's not your fault,' said Lee.

" 'Is it?' I said.

" 'No sir.'

"The trail looked so inviting—beautifully landscaped. 'Where does this go?' I asked the driver.

" 'Along the creek, and then it's actually a block from your hotel.'

" 'How far?'

" 'Oh, less than a mile.'

" 'So let's walk,' I said to Lee. I was starting for the trail, when I looked back and saw her at the edge of the road, at the rear of the limo, with her arm outstretched and her thumb out.

" 'What are you doing?' I said, stepping over to her.

" 'What does it look like I'm doing?' she said.

"And no, she was not showing leg, like Claudette Colbert does in *It Happened One Night*. She was in the pants suit, with black sunglasses and a little black scarf. Heels, too. I guess that's why she didn't want to walk.

" 'Come on, it will be fun,' she said loudly, over the traffic. 'We don't want to be late.'

" 'I'm afraid you've just lost your passengers, my friend,' I said to the driver. 'Have your boss call me at the hotel if there's any problem.'

"And I joined Lee. Two hitchhikers in dark suits and sunglasses, standing at the rear end of a black Lincoln with its trunk open. That must have been a sight.

" 'This is so representative of our lives,' I said.

" 'How so?' said Lee.

" 'Aren't we always on the side of some road, waiting for something to happen that somebody else controls?'

" 'It'll be a good story for your article.'

"I started to sing.

Oh, we ain't got a barrel of money,
We may be ragged and funny,
But we'll travel the road,
Sharing the load, side by side . . .

"The parkway was not particularly busy, and within a few minutes, a genial, white-haired businessman in a blue suit pulled over in a white Eldorado convertible.

" 'Could you folks use some help?'

"'We had a flat, but there are no tools,' I said. 'Our driver is taking care of the car, but we're due at the Turtle Creek Inn.'

"'That's right near where I'm headed. May I drop you there?'

"'That would be so nice of you,' I said.

"'Thanks so much,' said Lee.

"We both got into the front with him—I would say 'piled into,' but the front seat of an Eldorado is fully as wide as a living room sofa. This thing seemed bigger than our limo. Introductions didn't seem quite right, yet when he said his name was Stewart, I said we were Truman and Lee, which didn't appear to ring any bells.

"'It's not often you see a lady and gentleman stranded like that,' said Stewart.

"'No?' I said.

"'It's usually the hippies you see hitchhiking.'

"'Not on this beautiful parkway . . .'

"'Sometimes, sure. Why not? What are you folks doing in town, if I may ask?'

"'We came to see the Stones.'

"'The band—the Rolling Stones?'

"'The very same. Last night they were at the Convention Center.'

"'Yes, yes—I heard all about it. My daughter was there. She loved it.'

"'Did she?'

"'I'm more of a Dallas Symphony fan, myself.'

"'Marvelous,' said Lee.

"'And this morning, we went to see Dealey Plaza.'

"'Yes, they've really made that into something nice. Terrible tragedy. A big stain on our history—I mean both the city of Dallas and the country.'

"I think Lee was loath to get involved in a discussion of the assassination. I probably shouldn't have brought it up."

Lee chimed in. "'I can remember once hitchhiking with my sister from Lyon to Avignon, twenty years ago. When we got picked up, needless to say, it was not in a big car like this.'

"'No?' said the driver.

" 'It was more of a pickup truck.'

" 'Was it comfortable?'

" 'I don't remember. I only remember how exciting it was. The driver was a farmer. He laughed because our French was so formal.'

"Now, this man Stewart was quite a fox, Marlene—a Texan, but, you know, sophisticated. He flashed us this very wicked little smile.

" 'That's a terrific story, Princess,' he said. 'You should write about that—shouldn't she, Mr. Capote?'

"So he did know who you were, after all," I said.

"Absolutely," said Truman, always pleased to be recognized.

Chapter 19

Newish Beginnings

Why did I continue working on the screenplay alone? Because Truman had done nothing less than show me who I was, other than a socialite's housekeeper, and that probably was the nicest thing that had ever happened to me. Whether or not I was any good as a writer wasn't the point. Truman validated my habit of storytelling, which I had previously thought of only as a gritty survival tool, but which he reframed as a talent. I think he did something similar in his own life, with his own survival tools. Before that, I hadn't quite understood or believed in the difference between lying and storytelling, but through Truman, I was able to grasp it. How nonchalantly he would often pass off as his own a bit of wisdom from Mark Twain: "Never let the truth get in the way of a good story."

He inspired a big breakthrough for me in this regard on the last occasion we spent working together at the Mercantile Library. He was scattered and distracted that day, but there was always something wise in his utterances, even when they seemed flat and careless. The breakthrough followed my complaining that I was still having trouble with the mother—my fear that the character was one-dimensional.

"Why is that?" he said, trying to be patient.

"I was hoping you could tell me," I said.

"Well, let's see."

I nudged the manuscript toward him across the table, but he held up his palm.

"I meant that figuratively," he said.

"She's a monster," I said, pulling the manuscript back.

"Okay. We love monsters. They can be such great company for a reader. Ripley. Vautrin. Iago."

"But she is only a monster."

"Okay, well that's easy to fix. Humanize her."

"But how do you humanize a monster?"

"Oh, Marlene, I once saw a production of *Medea* that had her tenderly feeding the palace cats."

"Ha."

"Give her a boyfriend."

"A boyfriend."

"A love interest."

"I can't imagine that."

"Well, that's the issue, isn't it? You were so poisoned by the real events of your own life that you've blocked yourself."

"Have I?"

"That's the way anger works."

"Huh."

"Unblock yourself."

"How?"

"Wise advice that someone once gave me about a writing assignment—I now give it to you: Flirt with it."

I took a moment to think about this: *Flirt with it.*

"A boyfriend," I said. "That could work. But it must be someone who is a little questionable, no? Handsome but suspect."

"Now you're talking."

"Even monsters want to be lovable."

"That's it. Even monsters want to be lovable. Look around in the story and see who's available for the job."

We continued to meet for coffee, and as things got worse for Truman over the next decade, he seemed comforted to some degree by being able to reminisce with me or tell me without fear of judgment things that he knew others would find sordid, like watching people have sex in the discos he frequented. He talked about what "alley cats" some of his friends could be, and told me that it was his duty to witness their sins and crimes, large and small, and somehow capture in writing "the fear in all of it." Once, he confided that though he loved Lee, he was afraid of her, too—afraid of the power she had to cut him out of her life. Sometimes he'd reach me on my private line, in my room at Lee's apartment, or by mail or messenger, with envelopes addressed to me "Care of Princess Radziwill"—containing notes and letters often beginning with the salutation "Dear Serene Highness." Lee never asked what the notes were about, though I did make it a point once to mention that Truman liked to further my education by recommending books—and she seemed pleased with this as a very good use of both my and Truman's time.

It was a forty-five-minute helicopter ride from Manhattan to Montauk. Lee and Truman met in the tiny departure lounge of the Lower Manhattan Heliport, at Pier Six on the East River, on a warm, spring Thursday afternoon. Truman was dressed casually in white shorts and a long-sleeved, blue-and-white–striped Breton T-shirt, and carrying a Vuitton duffel bag. Lee was in white slacks and a white man-tailored shirt, carrying a canvas tote bag in orange-and-pink paisley.

"Why only soft luggage?" said Truman.

"It's a rule," said Lee.

"But I've been on helicopters with all my luggage, and baby, it's hard."

"It's the rule for this line, I guess."

The pilot-in-command introduced himself and walked them to the helicopter. While they strapped themselves into the passenger seats, he circled the vehicle, doing his pre-flight inspection, then joined them in the cabin and showed them how to use their headsets.

"Comfy?" he said, once all three of them were wearing headsets. "Can you both hear me?"

"Yes," said Lee, into her mic.

"Yes," said Truman, into his.

The sound was tinny but clear.

"Do we really need these?" said Truman.

"You will in a minute," said the pilot.

After the pilot delivered the prescribed safety announcement, during which Truman was repositioning his duffel bag for better leg room, there was some back-and-forth with the control tower about weather and air traffic, and then—"Bell 250-C20J cleared for takeoff, no delay, straight out departure approved"—the pilot commenced the flight.

Compensating for the steady, high-pitched roar of the helicopter's engine and rotors was the sheer wonder of the view. The first few minutes were the most astonishing, as they ascended swiftly and the towers of lower Manhattan went from looming above them to poking up from below; as the East River broadened into the Bay of New York; and as the hills of Brooklyn and the majestic Verrazzano Bridge gave way symphonically to the vast expanse of ocean horizon.

"We basically fly along the edge of Long Island the whole way," said the pilot, after he'd executed a turn toward the east. To the left was suburbia, flat and low, edged by wetlands and a ribbon of beach; to the right, a shimmering infinity dotted here and there with pleasure craft, and farther out, an occasional large vessel.

"We stay around three thousand feet," said the pilot. "Maybe a little lower for a minute over Fire Island, so you can smell the surf."

"Last time I was in a helicopter, the doors were open," said Truman. He was addressing Lee, but the pilot responded.

"We like to keep them closed," he said. "Makes the passengers feel more secure. And it's quieter, of course."

"Peter is out there already with the Warhol people," said Lee.

"Staying there, or at your place?" said Truman.

"Could be either."

"I see. All very cozy."

"He usually stays at my place."

"Makes it nicer if you and he want to . . ." said Truman in a tone somewhere between a whisper and a shout, before stopping himself. He pointed discreetly toward the pilot. "So he can hear everything we say? Sorry, sir?—uh, Captain?—I suppose we can all hear each other?"

"It's the rules, sir. I'm sorry," said the pilot. "I did mention it before we took off."

"Don't worry," said Lee. "They're very discreet."

"And so shall we be, too," said Truman.

Below them were the roomy, green landholdings of a rich, oceanfront town.

"It's funny," said Lee. "We were just in Mykonos, and then in the Yucatán. And now we're in Montauk for the weekend. Isn't it a little nuts, the way we keep bouncing around?"

"Nuts? Not at all," said Truman. "That's our job—righting bourgeois mores by bouncing from beach to beach, from man to man."

"Truman, I think you must be trying to be philosophical, but you're just being vulgar."

Truman laughed and gazed out the window. The weather was good, and there was little turbulence.

"Rather like being in a van," he said. "The CBS executive helicopter is much more luxurious, of course. Polished wood, real leather."

Landing was at the tiny Montauk airport—one runway, one helicopter landing pad, and a passenger terminal that in another location might have been mistaken for a gas station.

"It's finally coming apart," said Lee, in a taxi on the way to her cottage.

"You and Stas?"

She nodded.

"We spent my fortieth, last month in London, finalizing the divorce."

"Oh, baby. Happy birthday. Is it going smoothly, anyway?"

"Basically. I'm keeping the jewelry—the Radziwill pieces he gave me."

"Good."

"I offered to give them back, but a gift is a gift, he said, and

I might pass them on to Tina and any daughters she or Anthony might have."

"Very decent of him."

"I got the Fifth Avenue apartment, and some cash . . ."

"Thank God. A roof over your head."

"But we're selling Turville Grange."

"Ohhh, Lee. Do you mind very much?"

"I'll be fine."

"You're a survivor."

"No one wants divorce, but it's so much better than devolving into that mutual contempt thing."

"No."

"I think it was falling for Peter that helped me see the marriage more clearly."

"I love that you use that teenage word *falling*. You two have quite a thing going."

"I think so, yeah. I would only wish the same thing for you. These creatures you've been going around with—what's this new one? John something?"

"John O'Shea."

"It's obviously not unbridled passion, with these men."

"Not exactly. Though John is rather good-looking, in a respectable, small-town insurance broker sort of way."

"Brilliant young things I can understand," said Lee. "But these men . . ."

"They remind me of . . . oh, a type, from when I was a boy. A type I have always gone for."

"What *type*?"

"A type of masculinity."

"What good is that—if they don't work or have any manners?"

"Steady and dependable, like Jack."

"Jack, I understand. He's a writer, he was a dancer. But that child you brought to Buckingham Place last year . . . ? Please."

"John has a job."

"What does he do?"

"He helps manage a bar."

Lee sighed wearily.

"How did you meet?" she said.

"Don't laugh," said Truman. "At a bath house."

"Oh, Truman . . . !"

"He was in town on a job interview."

"In town from where?"

"From New Jersey, where he lives with his wife and kids."

"This is the man you took to Venice?"

"And on the Agnellis' yacht."

"Did you really?"

Truman giggled. "He was bored out of his brains and insisted on being let off," he said. "It was a bit of a scene."

"Poor Marella," said Lee.

"She did tell me plainly, afterwards, that she found the man very poor company. Yet, Lee, I took him to Verbier, and the Chaplins absolutely adored him."

"You didn't bring him home to Jack?"

"No, no. Jack was in Ravello. Charlie was a dear to him."

"He manages a *bar*?"

"He says he wants to be my business manager."

"What would you need a manager for? You have an agent."

"I happen to have funds that need managing, princess."

Lee's cottage, which she rented from Andy Warhol, was one of several on the grounds of Warhol's Cliff Drive estate, known as Eothen. Several members of Warhol's art factory or his magazine *Interview* might be in residence there at any given time, as might the artist himself and any of the celebrities he liked to invite there, including Mick Jagger, Bianca Jagger, Jerry Hall, John Lennon, Liz Taylor, Liza Minnelli, and Halston. Peter was at Lee's cottage to greet them, in the kitchen, wearing just a pair of shorts and his beat-up sandals.

"Andy will be out tomorrow, and I gather there's a big party, and of course we're all invited," said Peter, after the usual greetings.

"Fun," said Truman.

"Tonight, the cook's putting together some dinner for the

ones who have been out here all week," said Peter. "If we want to join, I should tell her."

"No need," said Lee, proceeding to pull several carefully wrapped food containers from her tote bag.

"And I thought you had clothes in there," said Truman.

"Marlene's roast chicken, with that barbecue sauce you like so much, Peter. Plus potato salad, cole slaw, and chocolate-walnut brownies. Also . . ."

She produced a tin of caviar, tucked into a plastic bag with some ice, and a neatly wrapped stack of blinis.

"I say we settle in a bit," said Lee, "Truman, you're right down the hall—and then have cocktails and a picnic on the terrace."

The kitchen was simple and old-fashioned, the high-end appliances and finishes dating from what looked like a late-'50s remodel. Truman said that even Warhol's main house was not particularly luxurious, only "solid." At the easternmost tip of Long Island, Montauk was not especially glamorous or much occupied then, wild and windy and quite empty, with a frigid, punishing surf that only the bravest surfers could handle. It was certainly not as glamorous as its neighbors closer to civilization: East Hampton, with charming houses and neatly landscaped grounds with ancient shade trees; and Southampton, with Gatsby-era mansions, even shadier trees, and exclusive bath, tennis, and golf clubs. Lee said she liked the Montauk cottage because it was so different from the Bouvier estate in East Hampton, Lasata, where she and Jackie had spent happy times during their childhood: a magnificent six-bedroom mansion with a pool, tennis court, stable, and formal gardens. Andy's compound, by contrast, was located on a treeless, weather-swept hill, all scrub and wild grass, separated from the raging ocean and boulder-covered beach by rocky cliffs whose rough paths were arduous and dangerous to climb up and down.

The "terrace" of Lee's cottage was more of a back porch, with a 180-degree view of the ocean beyond. The porch's furniture was made of heavy wood—less likely to be blown away during storms. It was around seven when they converged for their picnic. Lee warmed up the blinis and brought out a few bottles of a white Sancerre from one of the cases she'd had delivered to the cottage.

"What are you working on?" Truman asked Peter.

"Andy asked for some candids of his people on vacation," said Peter.

"Nude?"

"Sometimes, yeah. Whatever they want. It's supposed to be very informal."

"Will he put them in the magazine?"

"You never know, with Andy."

"Do you paint on these photos, too?"

"Sometimes."

"And glue things?"

"Sometimes. There are at least four kinds of prairie grass on this hill alone."

"It's extraordinary, the difference between Montauk and the other towns out here," said Lee.

"You grew up out here, didn't you?" said Peter.

"East Hampton," said Lee. "We found it thrilling, Jackie and I, to learn all about the rocks and trees here, even things like soil and drainage. The gardener we had told us all about the massive glacier that dropped all the sand and rock here, when it melted tens of thousands of years ago. Long Island is what they call a glacial moraine—an accumulation of rubble. Jackie and I thought we were so clever when we announced, one night at dinner, that our house was built on a pile of rubble. Our father laughed, but our mother was horrified."

"Four kinds of grass?" said Truman.

"I'll show you tomorrow," said Peter. "Nature walk in the morning?"

Lee and Truman both nodded eagerly.

"What's in that sauce?" asked Peter, after they'd finished eating.

"I think smoked paprika," said Lee.

"Honey?"

"I think she said maple syrup."

"And mustard," added Truman. "Definitely some mustard in there."

It was dark, and Lee had lit lanterns. Since it had gotten colder, both Lee and Truman had fetched a wrap from inside—Truman, a colorful Gucci pullover, and Lee, an almost floor-length cashmere sweater-jacket in plum. Peter remained shirtless and didn't seem in the least uncomfortable. In front of them, the ocean was invisible in the dark, and the sound of crashing waves had gone a bit softer.

"That's a splendid robe, or whatever it is," said Truman.

"It's Halston," said Lee. "Isn't it sweet? I love the color."

"He's doing some clever things, isn't he?"

"The thing is, there's a matching floor-length dress. It's meant to be for an evening, the ensemble, but his things are so easy to wear—like sportswear—and he told me I should wear this like a sweater any time and any place, and he was right."

"It's couture beachwear," said Truman, impishly.

"I am thinking of getting a set in pumpkin, too."

"Peter, Lee knows this already, but there's a story behind my sweater, too."

"Oh?" said Peter.

"Poor Monty," said Lee.

"I knew Monty Clift pretty well, from Hollywood," said Truman. "We had a mutual friend in Elizabeth Taylor. After that car accident—did you know that Elizabeth saved Monty's life, by sucking the teeth out of his throat?—he was pretty zonked on painkillers, and he'd always been a lush; and one year, before Christmas, he was in New York and said he'd take me to lunch at Pavillon if I'd help him do some Christmas shopping. I said sure, and we'd had several martinis at lunch, and then we were in the Gucci shop, looking at sweaters; and he was a little incoherent, but he got that way sometimes, with his medications. Anyway, while I'm buying a sweater—this very one—he suddenly scoops up an armful of them, walks out of the shop, dumps them on the sidewalk, and starts kicking them around. I run after him, and then the salesman comes out and asks Monty, very politely—

and mind you, he doesn't seem to know who Monty is—'To whom may I charge the sweaters, sir . . . ?' "

"Poor Monty," repeated Lee, shaking her head sadly.

"And Monty says, 'My face is my charge card.' "

It was not a punch line, so there was no laughter. Then there was a knock on the kitchen's screen door, from the inside.

"Hello," said a blond girl of around twenty, in shorts and a sweater. "I'm sorry—the front door was open."

"Oh, Barbara . . ." said Peter.

"Of course—that's all right. Come on out," said Lee.

"Lee, this is Barbara Allen, one of Andy's people."

"Hello, Barbara," said Lee.

"How do you do, Princess?"

"It's Lee."

"Truman Capote."

"Mr. Capote."

"Truman, please."

"Barbara, join us for a glass of wine?" said Lee. "Maybe a brownie?"

"Thank you very much, Lee, but no. I just wondered if you . . . if any of you were interested in some surfing tomorrow morning—Peter? Anyone?"

"I'm sitting it out tomorrow morning," said Peter. "But thanks."

"Sure."

"Isn't it awfully cold in that water?" asked Truman.

"We mostly wear wet suits," said Barbara.

"Oh, I see."

"Okay, thanks," said Barbara. "Well, then, have a good evening, everyone. It was a pleasure to meet you."

"I'm sure we'll see you again soon," said Lee. "Andy always surrounds himself with the most interesting people."

After Barbara left, it was wordlessly clear among the three of them that the party was not in need of being rounded out with a fourth.

"She's a good kid," said Peter, as if to excuse what might have looked like a dismissal. "She's involved with *Interview* and she does a little modeling."

"Oh, there's that old story," said Truman. "Magazine editing and modeling."

"Apparently, she just got married to one of Andy's backers, a horse breeder or something, but him, we rarely see around here."

"So young to be married," said Lee.

"I suppose she's from a very good family," said Truman.

"Not really," said Peter. "Army brat, or something like that."

And a few months later, near the end of a summer that looked idyllic for Lee and Peter, at least from the outside, it was over between them. Truman was in Palm Springs when Lee called him, distraught. He was with John, in a house that Truman had rashly bought because he "didn't want to keep imposing on friends all the time."

"I found him in bed—in *my* bed—with that girl," said Lee.

"The girl we met?"

"From *Interview*. The horse breeder's wife."

"How?"

"What do you mean, 'How'? I had just arrived, and there they were. I wasn't even early. He knew exactly when I'd be arriving."

"I mean when—today?"

"Just a few hours ago."

Truman took a deep breath, then exhaled.

"I'm so sorry, kiddo," he said. "Men are terrible."

"He's probably still at Andy's," said Lee. "I can see the station wagon from the guest room."

"You kicked him out."

"You bet I did. And I've just ordered a car, to take me back to the city. I'm going to let this place go."

"Good for you. But . . . you seem relatively calm."

"I'm furious, Truman—betrayed. But no, I don't rage."

"Very sensible."

"It's just never been me."

"It's no fun being dumped."

"No, no—he's not dumping me. *I'm* dumping *him*. I'm sure he'd be perfectly willing to go on, if I cared to continue—which I do not. The gall of that man!"

Within weeks, Lee had bought a place in Southampton, then invited Truman to come and stay with her and the children in Lyford Cay, at the exclusive club that she and Stas used to visit as a family. Once there, installed in Lee's private villa on the beach, Truman gave himself permission to put off the book once more and, as he explained afterwards, "have the opportunity to gain some perspective on my career." Though he needed money badly, he had withdrawn from the *Rolling Stone* assignment.

"I just can't concentrate," said Truman. "My mind goes blank."

"Good thing they sent the other writer, too," said Lee.

"Do you think they planned that? Was he my understudy, in case I broke my leg?"

"Who knows?"

After a morning of swimming, they were having lunch on the veranda of Lee's cottage, looking across the sparkling green waters of Old Fort Bay. The children were off at a tennis lesson.

"Think what a magnificent monster an ocean is," said Lee. "How seductive the waves are here, compared with that fierce surf in Montauk."

"Lee—forget about him."

"Mm-hmm. You're right."

"Anyway, that guy did exactly the kind of reporting that they apparently want now—and that was definitely not the kind of piece that we'd discussed. What I promised them was a more social piece—what it means to an American city when the Stones blow into town. That bit when we hitchhiked would have been perfect—much more interesting than police fights with drunken fans."

"You don't necessarily want to report on other stars, darling, because you are such a star yourself."

"Well . . . yes. That's right. Besides, the crimes associated with rock and roll have become so cliché—drugs, sex, violence. No surprises there. Now, if Keith had killed Mick or something . . ."

"Oh, Truman."

"No, really. Mick told me that Keith once pulled a knife on Brian Jones—the day Brian died. It was after they'd all had a big fight. There have been serious rumors of murder ever since."

"About Keith? I can't believe that."

"Or by some contractor who claimed Brian owed him money."

"Nonsense. Why do I listen to you?"

"Because I'm amusing, of course. And because I know things. Did you know, for instance, that they buried Jones ten feet deep? Mick told me."

"I don't understand."

"You're such a princess. Fans will dig you up if you're only three or four feet down."

"Oh, lord."

"Actually, the law in the United States is at least four feet. In the United Kingdom, I'm told, there is no law about it, but the recommendation is minimum one meter, which is interesting . . ."

"You and true crime. Are you still working on the piece about that Charles Manson murderer—what's his name? Bobby something."

"Bobby Beausoleil."

"The one who Peter photographed."

"Yes, yes. That's long done. I turned it in months ago, and they love it. It's one of my best interviews ever. Sometimes I feel quite at home in San Quentin."

"Peter said you were very flirty with the guy."

"Is that the word Peter used—*flirty*?"

"I believe so."

"Well, Bobby was flirting with me. He used to be a child actor, you know, and there's something of a child's need to be liked about him. He offered me a stick of gum."

"Did you take it?"

"Of course I did. It would have been rude not to. Do you know what his Manson family friends call him? 'Cupid.' "

"Peter said he was good-looking."

"*Cute* is the word I'd use, in a hustler-ish way—though *cute* don't butter any hay with me, as you well know. I think he contrived to be shirtless for the interview, to be honest, and I believe that's the way Peter shot him, too . . ."

"Yes."

"He's a defective human being. You'll see that in the article. I believe he's the reason why the Tate-LaBianca murders took place."

"How so? Peter said he killed another person entirely and is in jail for that."

"He did, he is," said Truman. "His so-called 'family' thought they could make his murder conviction look false if they committed another murder in the same manner, while he was locked up. That was Tate. Writing *pig* on the wall in blood—they were copycatting Bobby."

"But it didn't work."

"Of course not."

"Why are you drawn to such people, Truman?"

He thought about that for a moment.

"Because of the way they explain and defend their terrible actions," said Truman. "They exist completely detached from morality. It's terrible, but fascinating."

"I see."

"And with so many parallels in our own little world. That's what *Answered Prayers* is about."

"Mmm."

"He was fascinated that I'd met Lee Harvey Oswald."

That startled Lee. "What?" she said. "I never knew that."

Truman shifted in his seat. "I met him in Moscow—and now, of course, I remember why I've never told you about it," he said. "I'm very sorry to bring up such a painful memory."

"It's just . . . an odd thought, your knowing him."

"I wouldn't say I *knew* him. I met him through a correspondent friend who wanted to interview him. He was bursting with anger—for the Russians, for the Americans, for the American ambassador—because they wouldn't let him stay in Russia."

Truman told me later that he was startled, himself, by the slip. He wondered if alcohol and drugs were weakening his memory in addition to his ability to concentrate. He was always quite proud of his ability to keep his stories straight, when he told different versions to different people. And he said he wondered, that day in Lyford Cay, if the same memory lapse would have allowed him also to mention that on that same visit to San Quentin, he met with Sirhan Sirhan, Bobby Kennedy's murderer.

"Excuse me, Princess, a message for you," said a butler in a dapper white, short-sleeved shirt and shorts, who appeared on the footpath next to the veranda. He delivered a note and withdrew.

"Bill Paley called while we were at the beach," she said, after reading the note and tucking it under her bread-and-butter plate. "Good news about the show, he says."

"What show?"

"This talk show idea that David had. I told you about it. He's discussed it with Bill, and they want to talk about it for CBS."

"That's exciting."

"I'll phone him later," she said.

"Remember, I'm your first guest," said Truman.

"What do they say about one door opening up when another door closes?"

"That's what they say, all right—but let's find a fresher way of saying it, shall we?"

After the divorce, Lee more or less based herself in New York. And though she had always been involved in projects, I'd say that this was when she started working more steadily—I might even say "working for a living," since that's exactly what Jackie was about to do, as a fledgling editor at Viking Press, and make working seem suddenly chic. I think there may have been some of that sisterly envy involved, too, as there had been when Jackie married a billionaire. For Lee, the new job was "Conversations with Lee Radziwill," a series of half-hour conversations with

Lee's celebrity friends in a residential setting, which Bill Paley agreed to create for her at CBS and make available to the network's news programs. I remember Lee calling it her "dream job." The hope was that the series would lead to the development of Lee's own syndicated show, but though she interviewed such luminaries as Gloria Steinem, Peter Benchley, and Halston, the project was canceled after only six episodes. It never worked out for Truman to appear.

Life was bumpy for him, too. John O'Shea had begun to manage Truman's financial affairs, which served to widen the gap between Truman and Jack. Moreover, Truman associated Verbier and Sagaponack with *In Cold Blood*, so for *Answered Prayers*—when he could bear to work at all—he retreated to Palm Springs, where he had pretty much set John up in the house he'd bought. Jack, whom I came to know better in the following decade, as Truman needed more and more help, took the Palm Springs foray as "an undeclared but deeply felt estrangement," and bitterly referred to the house there as "Thirst's End"—in reference to the sybaritic lifestyle that Truman could indulge in in the luxurious desert resort town. "There's something terribly wrong with his life," said Jack. "He is like someone trapped in a hellish nightclub, who can't find his way out."

Some say that that moment was the beginning of the end for Truman. Suddenly, Truman was being seen everywhere with John, and people started whispering that this uncouth figure was nothing but a hustler—a judgment that was validated when John sent a letter around declaring that he was now Truman's "advisor and manager," and that all communication with Truman should go through him.

Lee tried to remain loyal to Truman—as she would do even after the "La Côte Basque" debacle that was coming—but she had her limits. When she invited Truman to the private launch of her book *One Special Summer*, a project that emerged out of the ashes of her memoir book, which never really congealed, she made it a point not to include John.

"Truman, we're using the same method to invite people to

this little party that you used for your ball," she said by phone from New York to Palm Springs. "One invitation per person, with his name on it, nontransferable."

"I understand perfectly," said Truman slowly. "Very reasonable." He was reclining on his sparsely landscaped pool patio, already quite intoxicated, though it was only two in the afternoon. From the low, flat eaves of the house, which surrounded the pool on three sides, came a curtain of cooling mist, a sliver of which, caught by the sun, glinted in all the colors of the spectrum.

"You should come out and visit," he said. "We make our own rainbows here."

"Maybe after the holidays," said Lee.

"I know you don't like John. Nobody does."

"We're just concerned about you."

"I know that some people don't want to invite me, because of him."

"Honestly, he can be a headache."

"He means well."

"He made fun of a Jasper Johns, for goodness' sake. He said a kid could have done it."

"You heard about that?"

"When Jasper was right there in the room."

"That was awkward."

"That's not fun."

"I know."

"That's not wit."

"I know."

"See you at the party."

On the night before the public launch of *One Special Summer,* the publisher, Delacorte, hosted a private, black-tie dinner to celebrate the book and its authors in the Grill Room at the Four Seasons. The book, beautifully produced and now credited as "written and illustrated by Jacqueline and Lee Bouvier," had morphed into a kind of scrapbook of the sisters' "magical" 1951 jaunt around Europe—a collection of the notes, poems, and almost-too-whimsical illustrations they had made on the spot, supplemented by snapshots and passport pictures. Lee was kind enough to invite me that night, and *charming* was the word I heard repeatedly on people's lips.

Jackie had made an early appearance at the party and had gone on to another event by the time Truman arrived—alone, as requested, and drunk, as usual. He caused little annoyance until he came upon Lee and Rudolf Nureyev standing together in front of a floral arrangement as big as a refrigerator, having their picture taken. She was in a simple ecru gown with a transparent silk chiffon jacket; Nureyev, by contrast, wore a Halston snakeskin Nehru jacket in shades of green, a pair of crushed velvet trousers in bright purple, and paisley-patterned boots in green and purple, with conspicuously high heels. And at close range, it was clear that Nureyev, though only in his mid-thirties, was heavily made-up.

The ballet star had been the guest on Lee's first episode of "Conversations."

"I see Rudy made it onto the show," said Truman, after Nureyev started talking with a *Time* magazine reporter and Lee stepped over for a private word with Truman.

"We tried to book you," said Lee, "but you said you were busy—no, actually, I'm told it was your new manager who said you were busy. And then the show was canceled."

"You should have called me yourself."

"I certainly would have done, if the show had continued."

"Why'd the bastards cancel?"

"The local hard news producers didn't want it, because it was soft."

"Bill should have positioned it better for you."

"It's done, and that's it."

"*Désolé*," said Nureyev, rejoining Lee and slipping a hand around her waist. "I had to give a quote about my new Don Juan. *Salut*, Truman—good to see you."

"Good to see you too, Rudy," said Truman. "Are you choreographing *Don Juan*?"

"Is a new ballet by John Neumeier."

"Well, you certainly look the part—and ready to leap onstage."

"Truman, really," said Lee.

"I see you two have been going around quite a bit together," said Truman.

"Yes, certainly," said Nureyev.

"Rudy performed at the Met when you were out of town," said Lee.

"Lee's the greatest company, isn't she, Rudy? And now we have her back again."

"Who does not love Lee?" said Nureyev. "You know, the interview she did with me on her show was the best prepared ever. Even culture writer, like this boy from *Time* I just talked to, is not so . . . Lee, *bien informé* . . . ?"

"Well informed, knowledgeable," said Lee.

"That's good to know," said Truman. "It's also good to know what I know and you know and eleven other men in this room know and are thinking about, as they make party talk, whether or not they are married—which is that that boy reporter you were talking to has a nine-inch cock, and I hear that's your thing."

There was a trace of a devilish smile beginning to appear on Nureyev's face as Lee took his arm, said "Good evening, Truman," and led the dancer away to a group of guests.

That's when I stepped over and said hello to Truman. I had overheard the incident and observed sadly that it was a new low in Truman's public vulgarity.

"Did you see the book?" I asked.

"It's charming," he said. "She could have dug deeper, but it's a nice little volume."

I knew Truman was proud of Lee's achievement, but there was a note of snideness in his praise that he didn't bother to conceal or wasn't even aware of. I recalled a bit of wisdom that Lee once shared with me. "Never refer to someone's book as *little*, even if it's short." She also taught me—I suppose as she had been taught by her mother—"Never say someone is an *old* friend. Always say that they're a *great* friend."

"I know that's damning with faint praise—or something," said Truman. "If anyone asked me when my little book will be done, I'd smack 'em in the kisser."

"People ask me about the book and I never know what to tell them," I said.

"Tell 'em nothin'," said Truman coyly. "There's nothin' to say. The book itself will say it all, when it comes out."

"Don't Repeat This" —by Lila North
Monday, October 14, 1974

. . . Spotted last night emerging from the new revival of *Candide*, at the Broadway Theatre, were socialite Lee Radziwill and ballet star Rudolf Nureyev, holding hands. Now that Lee's divorced from her prince, is she angling for a dashing dancer who often plays one onstage? • Speaking of the princess, whatever happened to the CBS show, "Conversations with Lee Radziwill"? Rudy was one of several notables who appeared on the show—but it seems to have evaporated. • And while some of us are reveling in entertainment, others are struggling to reclaim family values in this country—even forcefully, if necessary. A wave of moral momentum began back in March, in Kanawha County, West Virginia, when a brigade of concerned parents closed down their schools in protest against un-Christian, unpatriotic textbooks. Now an elementary school in the area was firebombed and dynamited, allegedly by some of the more radical protesters . . .

Chapter 20

Answering Prayers

"Truman! Truman! Truman . . . !"

Just as he was approaching the restaurant's front door, Truman heard the squawking, over the din of West 55th Street traffic, and turned to look behind him.

"Oh, Lila, it's you," he said.

She was out of breath.

"I've been chasing you for half a block, from Fifth," she said.

"Well, what is it?" said Truman. "I'm late for a lunch date."

"One of your swans?"

"My agent, if you must know."

"I saw the picture in *People*—you and Diana Ross. You're putting on weight, Truman."

"You *would* chase me half a block to tell me that."

"Were you happy with the shot?"

"I wasn't unhappy. And Diana looked marvelous, didn't she?"

"Truman, I . . ."

"You know, Lila, if I weren't so fascinated by humanity, I'd find your questions annoying."

Lila smiled. "Oh, I . . ." she began.

"No, no, that's not meant as flattery. I just want you to know why I never walk away from you. You remind me of a woman I once interviewed on Death Row. She had strangled her mother with a dishtowel, but she was so curious about everything and asked me so many questions—about my typewriter, the kind of paper I use. It was as if *she* were interviewing *me*, which is always nice."

"What happened to her?"

"She got the gas chamber a week later. Now, what do you want? I'm late."

"It's about the Onassis estate. I hear that Ted Kennedy is helping Jackie negotiate for a hundred million dollars, because she was only left ten million in the will. Do you know anything about it?"

"I know nothing at all, Lila."

"Any comment?"

Truman shook his head.

"I'm sorry you had to run down the street for so little," he said. "Now, if you'd like to know what I thought of your column on Wednesday, I'll tell you. It's an absolute disgrace the way you defend this madman who bombed those schools in West Virginia . . ."

"Marvin Horan."

"That's right. Bombing schools because textbooks tell the truth about Black people and the Civil War has nothing to do with family values or Christianity or whatever it is you're peddling."

"It's not . . ."

"Now if you'll excuse me. Run off and ask someone else about Ted Kennedy. Better yet, why not call Ted Kennedy himself? He's been saying lots of things about public schools and integration. You two should have a lot to talk about there."

Onassis had died in Paris in March, and was buried on Skorpios. A month later, Lee told Truman that she had been preparing to attend the funeral when Jackie called and asked her not to come.

"*Asked* you?" said Truman.

"Told me," said Lee. "We had quite a row about it."

"Why?"

"Because she was the star, of course. It was her show. And already she would have to share the stage with Ari's daughter."

"Whose face was built for mourning."

"Any comfort I may have been able to provide would have been more than overshadowed, in her view, by mumblings from the press about my affair with Ari. So that was that."

They were in a broad, display window–lined hallway in New York's D&D building, on Third Avenue, where many of the city's top décor, design, and supply firms have their showrooms. Lee was actively heading toward interior décor as her next career, and had been given the assignment of redecorating several rooms in hotels of the Americana chain, including the Americana Bal Harbour, in Florida, and El Presidente, in Acapulco, Mexico. If the project went well, Lee said, it could boost her visibility as a designer and supplement the career-building initiative she had launched by discussing possible partnerships with celebrity designer friends like Mark Hampton and Mario Buatta.

Truman was on the lookout for "a little brass lamp for the kitchen counter," and they had stopped into some furniture and accessory showrooms to look around, but the holy grail that day was just the right kind of blue-green tile that Lee had in mind for a bathroom scheme she was creating.

"Here's the place I meant—Mario swears by it," said Lee, in front of a lavish-looking tile showroom whose windows tastefully displayed samples of tile, trim, and mosaics as if they were high-end jewelry.

They entered and started browsing, and instantly, a salesperson was with them, listening to Lee's description of what she was looking for. When Lee was done, the salesperson repeated what he had heard.

"Vitreous ceramic. For an upscale hotel with a residential feel, modern but not futuristic. No metallic or Day-Glo. The color of the Caribbean at noon—Old Fort Bay. Do I have it?" he said.

"Yes, you do," said Lee.

"Let me show you to one of our worktables."

They had already visited two other tile showrooms and had had some things put aside as possibilities. To an outsider, these establishments, set up with cute retail-like displays to look more like luxury boutiques than industrial showrooms, might stimulate a gift-buying impulse. Bits of product were interspersed among worktables, seating areas, sales desks, and floral displays. But really, in this building, it was all business. Once the aesthetic choices were made, it was all about square footage, job locations, prices, discounts, shipping, and delivery dates.

Seated on stools in front of a country-Vermont-style antique pine table, they examined several bluish-greenish samples that the salesperson brought over for Lee's consideration.

"So—another Peter," said Truman, as Lee peered at a sample of one-inch-by-one-inch "Saint Tropez" recycled glass tiles mounted on a washcloth-size square of fiberglass mesh, by Mediterranean Mosaic.

"He's fun," she said.

"Another maverick?"

"Peter Tufo is hardly a maverick."

"Oh, I see him in the papers, crusading for this and that."

"He's got a very respectable law practice, in addition to all the public service."

"He looks handsome enough."

"He likes books and ballet, and skiing—we're thinking about getting away to Klosters."

"Okay. So just as athletic as Peter—Peter Number One, I mean . . ."

"Peter Number One was something of a perfect storm," said Lee thoughtfully. "That's not likely to happen again. We're still friendly, but we move on."

"What does mama think of the new one?"

"What does that matter?"

"Oh, I see—'not quite our sort, dear.' "

"Well, maybe. If I ever asked her, which I won't."

"I'm sure she's quite satisfied to see both her girls now with such good jobs."

Lee made a sour smile.

"When do we all have a drink, with this new man of yours?" said Truman.

"You've met him," said Lee.

"But I should inspect him more closely for you, shouldn't I?"

"We'll see."

Lee continued to examine the sample, then put it down and turned to Truman.

"This is not a lark, you know—working, seeing men socially," she said. "It's harder for women to support themselves, even today, even women in my position. I have children, Truman. I have to think about them."

"I found this for you, Ms. Bouvier," said the salesperson, placing another sample on the table.

"Oh, no, no," said Lee immediately, declining even to touch the sample. "That's quite wrong. You said 'variegated,' but that looks positively striped to me. A bit too garish, I'm afraid. But thank you. I think it's between these two, for the moment."

Lee had selected "Kimaada," by Lattitude, a one-inch-by-three-inch glass subway tile in celery, and "Quartz," by Kellani, a .75-inch-by-.75-inch glass mosaic tile in aqua.

"The Lattitude is a floor tile, but it should work beautifully on a wall," said the salesperson. "It's just made for heavier wear."

"Right," said Lee, "and that's priced by the box."

"Yes."

"And the Kellani is by the square foot? So can you work up a price comparison for me?"

"Of course. I can do that right here," said the salesperson, producing a pocket calculator. "Let's see, now, the Lattitude is thirteen dollars and forty-five cents per box, and that covers four-point-eight-four square feet, so that works out to . . . three dollars and thirty-five cents per square foot. That actually includes a nineteen percent discount. And the Kellani is two dollars and seventy-eight cents per square foot, so that's a bit cheaper."

"And my discount is on top of either," said Lee.

"That's right."

"Okay," said Lee. "Truman, these are better than what we've already seen today, aren't they?"

"They're beautiful," said Truman.

"But better?"

"Yes, better."

"Alright," said Lee, pulling out a spec sheet she'd prepared and giving it to the salesperson. "I have five rooms in Florida and five in Mexico. Here are the measurements and the dates. May I ask you to price out both jobs, including shipping and delivery, and phone me tomorrow by noon?"

"Of course. Thank you, Ms. Bouvier."

"You look tired, Truman," said Lee at the elevator.

"I have a lot on my mind," said Truman. "Taxes."

"You should get away."

"I just came from away."

"Did you want to look at a lamp? I know a wonderful place on the fifth floor."

"Afraid I can't now, kiddo," said Truman, checking his watch. "I have a drink with Gordon Lish."

"*Esquire*? What are you doing with *Esquire*?"

A gleeful grin came over Truman's face.

"You'll see," he said. "Cooking up a little trouble."

"Tru, you look like shit."

"Why are people always telling me that?"

"Maybe you need to get away."

"Maybe I will, with the money you're paying me."

Truman and *Esquire* magazine's fiction editor Gordon Lish were installed in a quiet corner of the cozy, wood-paneled lounge of the Warwick Hotel. They had been exchanging small talk. It was cocktail hour, and across the room, a pianist was playing soft jazz.

"Why here, Gordon? The Oak Room is more your thing, isn't it?"

"My instinct is that when these pieces appear in the magazine, it will be a surprise, and I want to preserve that quality."

"More like a bomb."

"In the best sense of the word, hopefully."

"Well, no one will see us here," said Truman, scanning the

room. "Only car distributors in town for a big General Motors meeting."

Through Truman's agent, Lish had bought the right to publish four excerpts of Truman's notorious novel-in-progress, to run in upcoming issues of *Esquire*: "Mojave," "La Côte Basque," "Unspoiled Monsters," and "Kate McCloud." The first would be "Mojave," set for June.

"Look, I thought we should talk, no agents, no publishers, no lawyers," said Lish, leaning into the conversation. "I know the deal stipulates that we don't get the *clef* to the *roman à clef*, but I thought, between us, if I knew . . ."

"Knew what?" said Truman.

"Who was who."

"Why would you need to know that? That's the whole point. It's literature, not a guessing game. As a writer yourself, you should know that better than anyone."

"Yes, of course," said Lish, "and I see what you're doing between so-called reality and the page, and I think it's marvelous, very exciting—something that American culture can really offer the world, building on the European. But . . ."

"But what?" said Truman. "You got a problem wit' reality lit?"

"It's just that I feel I'm the one who needs to know."

"That's rather monomaniacal of you."

"Come on, I don't want to be at a cocktail party—and you know this is going to happen . . ."

"Oh, I know it will."

". . . and someone brings up Lady Coolbirth and I don't know who it really is."

Truman harrumphed and ordered another round of bourbons, with a wordless gesture to the passing waiter; then he continued.

"First of all, Gordon, you will look more innocent if you know nothing," said Truman. "And second of all, these characters are more composites than anything else. They're inventions."

"Gloria Vanderbilt, Katherine Anne Porter, Princess Margaret . . ."

"Okay, those are real people."

"Which only makes a reader think that the other characters are real, too—just with different names. Kate McCloud . . . ?"

Truman described how he had come up with the character of Kate—the stages of development she had gone through and how she functioned in his tale.

"She is half a dozen breezy girls I have known, here and there. A tomboy *fatale*. Holly Golightly, but grittier. Fun but a little dangerous."

"And in 'La Côte Basque, 1965,' Lady Ina Coolbirth: Slim Keith?"

"And at least six others—Gloria, Pamela, and the rest."

"I am also worried about libel."

"That's all been cleared, and you know it."

"I'm not speaking about the law. I'm speaking about decency."

"Are you saying I'm indecent?"

"No, but what about a gentleman's code?"

"Ha. It's very hard to be a gentleman and a writer."

Lish sat back as the waiter delivered the fresh bourbons.

"Don't try to pass off Maugham as your own, Tru," said Lish with a wink. "Cheers."

"Cheers, Gordon."

The tension of the conversation lessened a bit.

"Jackie and Lee get off easy," said Lish. " 'A pair of Western geisha girls,' in 'Côte Basque.' "

"They'll get a huge kick out of that," said Truman. "They all will—don't you see? They'll be thrilled to think that they've been cameoed in a great piece of writing. I've always told them exactly what I'm doing. There's not one of them who doesn't know what it means to have a writer in their midst."

"You sure about that, Tru?"

Lish explained that he was most worried about "La Côte Basque, 1965." In it, Lady Coolbirth tells the tale of one Ann Hopkins, a wealthy woman who shot her husband in the face with a shotgun, claiming she thought he was a burglar, and got away with it because of the support of her social pillar of a mother-in-law. It was a tale very like the true-life story of socialite Ann Woodward, who had never openly been called a murderer. Lady Coolbirth also tells of the one-night stand between a powerful Jewish, New York executive, Sidney Dillon, and the wife of a former New York State governor, a WASP, whom Dillon wants to one-up. The deed takes place in Dillon's own bedroom, and his wife, Cleo, returns home afterwards to find her husband in the bathroom, scrubbing out stains of menstrual blood from the sheets, in the bathtub.

" 'Flogging away like a Spanish peasant on the side of a stream,' " said Lish. "That's good."

"Thank you," said Truman.

"The bloodstains were 'the size of Brazil.' "

"Mmm. 'France' didn't work. The French are too bloodless. 'Italy' was too obvious, tonally, and its shape and size didn't properly connote the blotch I had in mind. 'The Iberian peninsula' was a possibility, but too many syllables. 'Brazil' had the louche quality I was looking for . . ."

"Dillon's place is at the Pierre."

"Yes."

"The Paleys live at the St. Regis."

"What's your point, Gordon?"

"You're friends with the Paleys."

"We're good friends, of course."

"Aren't you worried about . . . repercussions?"

"The repercussions, my friend, are that I can pay my property taxes on three U.S. residences."

"Then I am worried for you, Truman."

"I think I'll be okay."

In June, "Mojave" appeared—a fanciful tale of rampant infidelities among three interrelated clusters of characters. *Esquire*'s sales that month were heavy, but though some praised the author's beauty of language, most critics noted that what seems to have been intended as a surprise ending wasn't much of a surprise. Lila North wrote in one of her columns about "the sad drift away from decency in Truman Capote's writing."

Truman was angered by Lila's comment. He mentioned the comment and her praise of school-bombing fundamentalists to her newspaper's editor, Peyton Highlander, when he and Highlander found themselves at the same clambake at a mutual friend's house on Nantucket, that month. The other guests at the clambake included the usual writers, editors, chief executive officers, chairmen, senators, doctors, and lawyers who usually summered on Nantucket.

"I don't mind so much for myself, Peyton, but I'm embarrassed for the newspaper. To be publishing that kind of reactionary bullshit . . ."

"I know,' said Peyton. "But it's a column, Truman, not news. It's opinion—and she's entitled to hers."

"But the paper is liberal, isn't it? Besides, even the quality of her gossip is third-rate—you know that. She never has scoops, because she doesn't have access."

They were standing at the bar—a wheeled cart that had been parked a few yards from a skinny, fifty-foot-long dining table—actually, four tables lined up—with forty place settings that stretched across a broad lawn between the pool and the dunes. The sun was going down, and the cool breeze from the ocean was strong. Party lights were switched on, strung up around the tables on six-foot-tall wooden tripods and flapping in the wind. Clumps of people dotted the lawn, talking and laughing; every now and then, there was a rush of running children. It was that moment at a beachside summer party when the gentlemen were glad they had brought those madras blazers and the ladies were glad they remembered to pack a cotton sweater in their raffia tote bags.

"I read the *Esquire* piece, by the way," said Peyton. "Great stuff."

"Thanks," said Truman, who'd had several vodkas laced with grapefruit juice and rose water. "Wait 'til the next one. It's a doozy."

"July?"

"No. They're saving it for the November issue."

"Must be big."

"Big enough."

"Can you tell me what it's about?"

"It's a secret—but I can tell you, if you promise to do something about North. She's a nuisance and an embarrassment, Peyton."

"Look, Truman, there's a story behind it," said the editor, looking around to make sure he couldn't be overheard. "Back in dim prehistory, Bernie—you know, Bernie Epler, the paper's publisher—when Bernie was still back on accounts, he and Lila, you know, had an affair."

"I think I heard that."

"Bernie was married—still is, same girl, nice girl—and Lila threatened to expose the whole thing. Apparently she felt she had been promised something."

"Oh?"

"Bernie had only been married a year, the way he tells it. And he hadn't promised Lila anything. He was just a horn dog, at that point, and she was . . ."

"Available."

"Oh, more than available. Apparently she was something of a nympho. Really slept around. Anyway, then she told him she was pregnant . . ."

"This just gets better and better."

"And so Bernie paid her off—five thousand dollars; a one-time-only payment to hold her tongue—but she also insisted on being guaranteed her column until she decided to retire."

"Which explains why she went from page four, to page six, to page ten, without being fired."

"Right."

"So she wasn't married."

"Never married. And . . ."

Truman was laughing.

"And," continued Peyton, "she gave the kid up for adoption—a girl. And Lila's very Catholic, I understand, so it was off to the nuns."

"I get it, I get it," said Truman, utterly amused. "And *this* is the voice of decency and family values!"

"Dinner's on," hollered a senator.

Up the narrow boardwalk from the beach, where the pit was, came a parade of the bake master's helpers, bearing trays of clams, lobsters, potatoes, and corn, headed for the buffet table, which was already set with big bowls of salad and baskets of bread. From another direction came platters of steaks from a portable grill.

"Can you sit with Sarah and me for dinner?" asked Peyton. "You can tell me all about the *Esquire* piece."

"Only if you don't tell a soul," said Truman.

Is it hindsight for me to say that in the summer of '75, it felt like big changes were quietly looming in the friendship between Lee and Truman? Or did I simply register the different needs and desires that were arising in each of their lives, around love and work, which couldn't help but rebalance the connections they'd enjoyed for a decade and a half? To tell the truth, each was drinking more heavily than was usual for them, though for Lee, any resulting behavior was mostly private, and for Truman, it was often spectacularly public. When he missed his most recently renegotiated deadline for *Answered Prayers* and had to forfeit a big bonus that had been attached, it was a blow to his pride and self-respect as a man of literature. He alternated during our coffee meetings between claiming that the novel was finished and "resting in a safe place," and confessing that little more of the book existed than the excerpts—"the fun parts"—he had sold to *Esquire*. His conversation was increasingly studded with excuses and doubts about his work. Once he claimed that part of the manuscript had been stolen by his partner/manager John "in a fit of jealousy"—though that made no sense to me. Qualms arose in my mind, and certainly in the minds of those who were interviewing him in the media, that Truman had lost his way. And Truman himself had qualms. He told me once that though he felt his literary mastery was as strong as ever, as defined by the old rules of writing, there were suddenly new rules, and in society "new conditions of truth I don't understand." This was crippling, he said, for any artist, but especially so for a so-called social novelist.

Around that time, he gave an obviously boozy interview to *Playgirl* magazine, in which he first publicly told the story that Lee had told him confidentially, about Gore Vidal and the 1961 White House party that Vidal may or may not have been thrown out of, drunk. It didn't take long for Vidal to file suit, claiming he hadn't been drunk or thrown out, and charging that Truman had libeled him and given him great mental anxiety and suffering. Depositions were taken. Truman decided not to lower himself to countersuing.

"I don't believe in that, I just don't," he said. "Writers and artists should not be suing each other. It's very childish."

Lee was obviously upset by this betrayal of a confidence, but she took it in stride. Maybe she started being a little more careful about what she said around Truman. It would be a few years, as the suit dragged on, before Truman found out that Lee had been subpoenaed and gave a deposition herself, affirming Vidal's version of the story.

"Don't Repeat This" —by Lila North
Monday, October 13, 1975

Want to know how much Jackie Onassis is making in her new job—yes, I said job!—as an editor at Viking Press? Two hundred dollars a week. Now, isn't that a nice wad of pin money to supplement the ten million she received via Ari's will? • Guess who got married—again?! Liz and Dick, while on holiday in Botswana. The marriage was conducted by African District Commissioner Ambrose Masalila and witnessed by two employees of the Chobe Game Park Lodge. • And speaking of married couples, if you aren't watching glitzy gospelers Jim and Tammy Faye Bakker on their new talk show, *The PTL Club*, out of Connecticut's WHCT-TV, you don't know what you're missing. Songs, jokes, skits—and all of it *wholesome*! (By the way, "PTL" means "people that love.") • What world famous

> American author, who has been postponing the pub date of his next book for years, just spent a month drying out at an exclusive sanitarium in California's Rancho Mirage? We keep hearing about this guy coming unglued in interviews and at parties. What's next? Slapping a lady's face in public? To be honest, we're not expecting to see that book anytime soon . . .

Then, in late October, "La Côte Basque, 1965" appeared in the November issue of *Esquire*. The story was basically a long string of gossip tidbits between Lady Ina Coolbirth and narrator P.B. Jones, a proxy for Truman, uttered over a lunch of soufflé and Cristal. It was a masterpiece, said Truman in an article in *People* magazine, which went on to repeat his admission that the story, while naming real people in the restaurant on that fictional day, like Lee and Jackie, also contained real people thinly disguised as characters, such as, possibly, Slim Keith, Gloria Guinness, and Pamela Harriman. The article failed to note that doormat wife Cleo Dillon and her philandering, conglomerateur husband Sidney Dillon, stars of the story's tawdriest episode, about the bloody sheet, might be Babe and Bill Paley. Other articles and commentators, however, did note this possibility—and suddenly, everyone was asking why Truman Capote was committing social suicide.

One critic wrote that, in contrast with Truman's previous work, "La Côte Basque, 1965" was stupid stuff, with "turgid action, pedestrian description." None of the people depicted or their "childish and venal" actions would be remembered in a generation. One passage in particular, centering on a snapshot of Sidney Dillon, even caused readers to speculate about Truman's attraction to his swans' husbands. The character P.B. Jones says, "I remember once picking up a copy of what was, after the Bible and *The Murder of Roger Ackroyd*, Ina's favorite book, Isak Dinesen's *Out of Africa*; from between the pages fell a Polaroid picture of a swimmer standing at water's edge, a wiry well-constructed man with a hairy chest and a twinkle-grinning tough-Jew face; his bathing trunks were rolled down to his knees, one hand rested sexily on a hip, and with the other he was pumping a dark, fat mouth-watering dick. On the reverse side a notation, made in Ina's boyish script, read: Sidney. Lago di Garda. En route to Venice. June, 1962."

Instantly, doors that had always been open to Truman were slammed in his face. Overnight, he was dropped by dozens of friends and acquaintances. People were aghast at his displaying their or anyone else's dirty laundry in public. They clucked and squawked about common gossip parading as fine literature. And the story also had a more terrible consequence. Ann Woodward, the model for the socialite murderer Ann Hopkins, committed suicide three days after its publication.

Truman and John were on the road when all this hit—an actual road trip across Canada, for sightseeing, that would end with their getting home to Palm Springs. Truman told me later that at first he was annoyed over the "ridiculous" reaction to his story.

"I wanted to show how venal the husbands are," he said. "Horny like adolescents. Bullies. Macho assholes. I meant the wives to be the heroes—tolerant, forgiving, stoic."

But of course, most of the victims of Truman's poison pen didn't see it that way. Several telegrams reached him at the Banff Springs Hotel, a venerable, old castle-of-a-railway-hotel in the Rockies.

THE STORY A HIT. BIG SALES. BUT SERIOUS CONSEQUENCES. PEOPLE HOPPING MAD. CALL ME ASAP. —GORDON

PEOPLE ARE TERRIBLY HURT BY YOUR STORY. THE LEAST YOU CAN DO IS APOLOGIZE TO THE P'S. CALL ME WHEN YOU CAN. —LEE

THE STORY ILL ADVISED. WE'VE WORKED WITH BILL SO THIS MUST BE FIXED. CALL ME IMMEDIATELY. —SUSSKIND

From one of the hotel's original oak-paneled telephone cabins, with cut-glass window panels in the doors, Truman tried to reach the Paleys.

"Marta, this is Truman Capote. May I speak with Babe, please? Oh, she isn't? Do you know where I can reach her? I see. Is Bill in? Oh, I see. Well, will you please tell them that I called. I need to speak with them. Thank you—it's important. For the next twenty-four hours, I can be reached at the Banff Springs Hotel—that's in Canada—Room 1411. That's 'Banff' with two *F*s. Then at my home in Palm Springs. Thank you, Marta. Please say that I need to speak with them as soon as possible."

He decided to get back to Palm Springs without further sightseeing. And he tried again several times from the road, on the way, but of course, he didn't reach the Paleys. They simply didn't want to speak with him.

Incredibly, I thought, Truman didn't process the furor through an emotional or personal lens, but through a literary one. After all, he said, he was just depicting society's truths in the manner of a proper nonfiction novel—and dealing deftly with literary issues concerning the artistic transformation of real facts into a semi-fictional narrative. What was wrong with that? Yet I saw a deeper dilemma at the center of this story that Truman was telling himself, and I didn't know if it was my place to tell him about it, so I didn't. It was the difference between the true and the real. Civilized people have always touted Truth—in art, in culture, in business. But what had happened during the '60s and '70s was the ascendency of Reality—which I thought might one day result in degraded, reality-based forms of art and entertainment. And *voilà—Real Housewives*. The essential truth that Truman had always been chasing had eroded, without his being fully aware of this; so his attempts in his work to keep dancing seductively between the True and the Real were doomed.

And who knows? Perhaps mine are doomed, too. In remembering and recounting these events, which are as true or real as I can make them, I fear I may be giving the listener less than enough reason to care about what happens next.

Babe continued refusing to take Truman's calls. I am still not sure whether he expected to explain something to her or apologize for something. From a distance, my heart went out to her. It must have been an immense blow—the more so for representing a demotion from her position as Chief Swan. I know the blow made at least one other swan think seriously about the difference between the spotlight Truman was offering and the one he so eagerly sought, and the kind of friendship that each entailed.

Two weeks later, after Truman had returned to New York, he was having lunch with his agent one day in Quo Vadis, when he spotted Babe entering the well-populated room. She saw him, too, of course, and had to walk right past his table in order to reach hers, where some friends were waiting. Impeccably dressed, always a lady of good manners—and, as Truman described the scene later, tearily, "a girl of rare sweetness"—she uttered a dutiful "hello" when he rose as she passed. It was a greeting that Truman suspected she was roundly criticized for, by her smartly dressed luncheon companions, who, he was certain, would rather have seen her cut him dead.

Chapter 21

Friends Forever

Perhaps predictably, I was of two minds about the "Côte Basque" debacle. I cared very much about supporting both Lee and Truman, yet I was in no position to help either of them alleviate the awkwardness that had come between them. On one hand, as someone who had experienced adversity and been the target of life-and-death threats in my life, I judged the incident more of a kerfuffle than a crisis. On the other hand, in my world—or if I may use the phrase "*our* world" to describe my spot in Lee and Truman's orbit—it was Pearl Harbor. A battle was on, yet the homeland remained unscarred. People smiled impassively and went about the usual holiday shopping and partying, though no one was happy about the silent perturbation that was unbalancing social doings that were usually so smooth and *tenus pour acquis*.

Why did Truman publish this story? Why had he written it? Why hadn't he taken greater pains to fictionalize the characters and events? Part of the answer, I think, is that his ideas about knowing and telling the truth were formed early in his youth. He was quite proud of what he'd once described to me as a certain "tribal devilishness"—a particularly Southern blend, he explained, of honesty, wit, and childish obstreperousness—and he accepted the sin-and-repent pattern engendered by this trait as some kind of noble fate to be borne. For years, especially after becoming famous, he tried to use each period of repentance as a moment when the self-importance he knew was growing inside could be ameliorated. Then, possibly under the weight of accumulated sins, amelioration slipped out of the process. He sadly confessed that he'd found it impossible one day to feel repentant anymore and asked if I thought that that meant he was somehow beyond redemption. I didn't know what to say, so I said nothing.

The mess with Babe may have inspired defensiveness in Truman's public behavior, but privately, with Lee, he spoke about it regretfully. When he made a point of promising to remain loyal to Lee, he seemed practically abject, which touched her heart, though of course, she was hearing from all sides that she should have nothing more to do with "that little bastard." I think it was in the hope that Truman might eventually understand and be able to fix the mess he'd made that Lee cautiously agreed to meet up with him in Milan, where she had an appointment with a young fashion designer whose work was in sync with her taste for minimalist *luxe*, Giorgio Armani. A few days in Milan would be good for Truman, she said, because it was far from many of the friends who were snubbing him, and because it was such a "sober" city. And indeed, when they got to Milan, the weather was gloomy, cold, and rainy—typical for December—though they did find a bit of social buzz. They saw some of Lee's friends for lunch and dinner, while Truman remained on best behavior, at least until their visit to the Armani studio.

Despite the rain that morning, they went on foot to the studio, since it was so close to the Grand Hotel.

"I love a hotel breakfast buffet, don't you?" said Truman, as they walked.

"They can be nice," said Lee.

"Six kinds of fruit juice, all lined up in crystal dispensers with silver spigots—now that's what I call luxury."

"I'm more of a room service girl, when I travel alone."

"All those grim business travelers, reading *Die Zeit*, or *Le Monde*, or *Corriere della Sera*. There's a certain kind of hush in a hotel breakfast room, isn't there?—an absence of the conversation one craves at lunch and the performance one expects at dinner."

The luxury shops of the Via della Spiga were still closed that morning, and the walkway—really, a glorified alley—was practically empty. Walking through a light drizzle, Lee and Truman were both carrying umbrellas and, though the sky was gray, wearing sunglasses. Suspended above them every few yards, between the sober-looking buildings facing the walkway, were holiday decorations in the form of garlands and wreaths of faux greenery. The sound of their footsteps echoed softly on the wet stone pavement.

Yes, Lee was one of the few women in the ladies-who-lunch crowd who'd stayed loyal to Truman, if loyal meant that the pleasure of Truman's company was now clearly bounded by wariness. Yet Truman was "a difficult habit to shake," and Lee admitted that he had always been particularly good company on travel adventures. I remember Truman wanting this to be his "driest visit to Italy ever"; he knew that alcohol was somehow damaging his mind. Happily—well, hopefully—he had agreed with Lee's request that he restrain his drinking during their stay there, and he was eager to show that he could comply.

"I'm glad we're doing this," said Truman, as they walked.

"I really think Armani is one to watch," said Lee.

"I mean getting together. I really appreciate it. I've been feeling very misunderstood."

"I'll be honest with you, Truman. Jackie advised me to see less of you."

"Well, sure, *Jackie* . . ."

"She doesn't want you to do to me what you did to poor Babe."

"Nonsense. I did nothing to Babe."

"You really can't keep saying that. Have you spoken to her yet?"

"She won't take my calls. Neither of them will."

"Let's hope what they say is true—that time heals all wounds. Good friends don't grow on trees."

"Now I'm wondering whether we really *were* friends."

"*You're* wondering? That's a laugh. I'd say that Babe's the one to be doing the wondering here. Really, Truman."

A brass plaque on one side of a wide, stone portal read

ATELIER ARMANI. After starting out as a department store window dresser and then designing menswear for other fashion houses, Giorgio Armani had just opened his own house. In a small office and studio located in a stolid, palazzo-like building on the edge of Milan's central fashion district, Armani was beginning to develop his own style and serve a small but growing clientele. A decade later, when Lee went to work at Armani as a kind of brand ambassador, after the house had grown rich and famous, she would chuckle to recall the difference between "Giorgio's little two-room place on the Corso Venezia, where there were, alas, no frescoes," and the House of Armani's ultimate home in the magnificent Palazzo Orsini, one of Milan's most beautiful historical palaces.

"Thank you for coming on such a dreary day," said Armani's studio director, Ettore, a handsome, highly polished man in his early forties, with a soft voice and unyielding smile. "Giorgio begs your forgiveness, but he has been unavoidably delayed. He will join us shortly."

"What a pity," said Lee, as an assistant took her and Truman's things.

"He is eager to meet you, of course," said Ettore, "but he knows your time is valuable, so he suggests, with your permission, that we begin immediately. We have some coffee for you."

He gestured toward a small seating area positioned opposite a tiny runway delineated by a stretch of off-white carpet.

"That is, if you would like to look at things . . ." said Ettore.

"Of course we want to look at things," said Lee.

"Excellent," said Ettore. "We have Sofi and Dilyana with us today."

Lee and Truman made themselves comfortable in two of the squarish, leather armchairs.

"I can also offer you some Ramazzotti," said Ettore.

"What's that?" said Truman.

"A *digestif*, a kind of health tonic, made here in Milan for two hundred years. It's very good for a cold day like today."

"No, thank you," said Lee, emphatically, before Truman could speak.

While Lee and Truman sipped macchiatos and nibbled tiny, sand-colored macaroons designed to look like beach stones, two beautiful, dark-haired young women, one with green eyes, one with blue, modeled exactly nine looks, emerging from and then disappearing into an adjacent room. The showing consisted of three short dresses, two pants suits, and four long dresses. The color palette was narrow—from cream, to beige, to gray. The mood was relaxed; the pace, unhurried. The mode of the models' presentation was markedly prosaic, not like that in most other fashion shows: they walked and posed in quite a plain, flat manner. Continuing to stand, Ettore described the cut and fabric of each look.

Lee moaned in pleasure when she felt the hem of a cashmere gabardine pants-suit jacket that Sofi was wearing.

"The silhouettes are as strict as Ellsworth Kelly," she said.

"Thank you," said Ettore, modestly.

"And yet it moves as if it were alive."

"Giorgio is called a minimalist, yet he lets the clothes have a great deal of life."

As the models moved about and conversation with Ettore continued, Lee was making quick sketches in her Smythson notebook. Truman remained quiet, though he shifted a few times in his armchair. At the conclusion of the showing, Sofi and Dilyana said thank-you and withdrew, and Ettore took a seat with his guests so they could all chat comfortably. An assistant refreshed the coffee service.

"You know, I think I will try a spot of that health tonic," said Truman.

"Truman, are you sure?" said Lee. "It's eleven in the morning."

"Eleven forty-three," he said, checking his watch. "Practically lunchtime."

After Truman was served, Ettore explained more about Armani's new business.

"We're showing spring/summer '76 here, like this," he said, "and then in March, we join fashion week to show fall/winter."

"Is that what they're calling it—Italian fashion week?" said Truman.

"Just so," said Ettore.

"That's a huge step for Giorgio, isn't it?" said Lee.

Ettore grinned and nodded.

"Good for him," said Lee.

"Tell me about the structure, Ettore," said Truman, who had been observing the studio director as carefully as he had been watching the clothing. He also signaled for the assistant to refill his glass. "And please excuse my inquisitiveness. It's just that I am always so interested in learning what causes the effect of great beauty."

Ettore made a gracious gesture to indicate Truman's question was no problem at all. Perhaps there was a hint of flirtation in that gesture.

"As you know," he said, "Giorgio did menswear for many years. He wanted to soften the image of men, so he dressed them in fabrics usually used for women's suits. Then, as he started to design for women, he saw that they were changing, so it made sense to harden the image of women."

"I see," said Truman. "Now, you use the word *minimalist*. Is that what the seventies mean for Giorgio Armani—minimalism?"

"To be honest, it is the 1980s that we are thinking about here in the studio," he said.

"Ah—the future."

Truman smiled wanly as Ettore continued speaking a bit about art and fashion, and the expression of minimalism in those fields. The names of several contemporary Italian and Japanese architects were also mentioned.

"Let me ask, Mr. Capote, is there minimalism in contemporary writing?"

The question struck Lee as amusing.

"If there is," she said, "Truman doesn't want any part of it."

"It's quite true," said Truman expansively, now on his third Ramazzotti. "I do like some flourish. But tell me, Ettore: Another so-called minimalist whose fashion show Lee and I attended recently had a much different approach to presenting the clothes—Halston. He had his models twirling around all over the place like Loie Fuller, yet you had Sofi and her charming counterpart walk before us in such an uninflected manner. Is this part of your vision?"

" 'Uninflected'?"

"Matter-of-fact," said Truman, with an ever-so-slightly exaggerated Southern drawl. He was growing animated—not drunk, but clearly tipsy.

"Ah. Maybe the Armani woman is not so much like a butterfly," said Ettore. "So Giorgio takes from men what women today want and need—power. *Sicurezza. Certezza.*"

Ettore made hand gestures to indicate "assuredness" and "certitude."

"And yet these clothes are not asexual, are they?" said Lee.

"No," said Ettore. "They are simply designed to let the clients supply a new kind of sexiness."

"And we all know who has *that* quality in spades, don't we . . . ?" said Truman.

"That's interesting," said Lee, who wanted to keep the conversation on track. She was, after all, shopping, which required focus. "I understand that this new idea of a woman was suggested by Giorgio's sister."

"Ah, yes—Rosanna," said Ettore. "She is an actress. Very . . . modern. Giorgio wanted to offer her a new way to look, a new way of being."

"Well, now," said Lee, "the suit you showed with the longer jacket. You showed it without a blouse. Do you think that's something I could get away with?"

"Oh, most certainly," said Ettore. "It's a very sexy way for a powerful woman to look in 1976."

Lee seemed tickled by the thought. "Truman—could I?" she said.

Truman winked. "You know very well you could."

"Princess, the design is such that an inch up or down for the décolletage will still work," said Ettore. "As the client wishes. We see what works, what is comfortable."

Truman seemed determined to remain the center of attention.

"Why is it," he said, "that fashion people always think they're inventing 'new kinds of sexiness,' when sex is the oldest thing in the world—eh, Ettore?"

It was an ungracious remark—clearly critical, somewhat aggressive. The studio director, though, smiling politely, remained focused on his celebrity client.

"Princess?"

"Okay, I want it," said Lee. "When can we do measurements?"

"Right now, if you like," said Ettore, rising. "We can begin, and then Giorgio will be with us, I am sure."

During the rest of their stay in Milan, another two nights, Truman did continue drinking, though he managed to keep it under control. Yet afterwards, he said that his bad behavior at the Armani studio made him feel "fatally unworthy." At any rate, Lee began seeing him less frequently after that, and she didn't include him in plans she made to spend the holidays in Sardinia with the children. Truman accepted this in stride, saying it might be interesting to experience the holiday season "like a leper." When he returned to New York two weeks before Christmas, Lila North called him, wanting details of the "Côte Basque" incident, and he decided to talk to her. He felt he needed all the help he could get, in explaining his position and the personal and literary thinking behind it. If there had been any fallout for her from the conversation he'd had with her editor, Peyton Highlander, she didn't show it.

"So you haven't spoken to Mrs. Paley since the publication?"

"No."

"Not a word?"

"Come to think of it, yes, one word, but only a word. She walked past me in Quo Vadis a few weeks ago and said 'Hello.' "

"Did you speak?"

"You mean, did we have a conversation? No. Just one word. She said 'Hello' and continued walking to her table."

"She didn't want to cause a scene."

"Probably."

"And she hasn't tried to reach you?"

"No."

"You haven't heard from any lawyers."

"Lila, that's not very likely. This was a work of fiction."

"You know she's ill."

"Yes, I've known that for a while."

"I hear rumors of cancer."

"So do I."

"Can you confirm it?"

"No, I can't. But I can confirm that I still love her and hope that we can repair the friendship. Please print that."

"What is your reaction to being shunned by people you thought were your friends?"

"Oh, I still have plenty of friends. There's maybe only one who still won't speak to me."

"And who is that?"

"Well, I'm not going to tell you, out of respect for her."

A week before Christmas, Jack Dunphy reached me at Lee's, to ask if I were free to join him and Truman for a drink on Boxing Day, the day after Christmas, at their place in UN Plaza. Lee was away, so I didn't hesitate to say yes.

"Feel free to bring someone," said Jack. "The more, the merrier."

But I had no one to bring except Judy—and given Truman's natural inquisitiveness and the possible clash of stories about my background, I decided that that was not a good idea.

"Thanks," I said, "but everyone I know is out of town."

"'Tis the season," said Jack flatly.

Jack sounded grim. In the absence of any holiday party and getaway invitations for Truman, Jack was trying his best to keep Truman's spirits buoyant. I knew that Jack thought I might be complicit in this desire, and he was right. Though I doubt I would have received the invitation if the doors of any of Truman's fancy friends had still been open to him, I was still happy to see him.

I asked how Truman was doing.

"So, so," said Jack. "He asked me to call Babe and see if she'd speak with him."

"And?"

"She said she'd have to speak with Bill about it."

"Oh."

"She said she'd call back, but she never did."

Lila, in her column, speculated that Truman was lashing out against the plutocracy that had used him for entertainment. She said that he had written his duplicitous partisans into "a literature of revenge," and described Truman's recent prose as café society gossip, not literature. But she did give Truman a chance to speak back to those of his society friends who felt betrayed. She quoted him as telling her, "They knew what I was doing. I'm a writer, for goodness' sake."

The whole affair made me sad, and the spiritless stroke of holiday decoration that greeted me in the lobby of UN Plaza at 2:00 p.m. on Boxing Day—an aggressively scaled-up wreath of multicolored glass balls, suspended against the window wall in back of the reception desk—did little to improve my mood. I tried to stay positive as I rode the elevator up to the twenty-second floor.

"We meet again," said Jack, showing me in and taking my coat. We hadn't seen each other since the ball.

Truman was in the living room, sitting at one end of a showy, medallion-backed Victorian sofa.

"Welcome, welcome. Come and sit down," he said, without getting up. He was lighting a cigarette.

He looked tired and was heavier than I'd ever seen him. Dressed in a green velvet smoking jacket and crisp white shirt, he was unshaven and seemed unsteady in his handling of the cigarette lighter. On the coffee table in front of him was a crystal low-boy glass of scotch or bourbon.

"Truman, give Marlene the twenty-five-cent tour, while I fetch the champagne," said Jack. "Show her where you keep the emeralds."

The apartment was not particularly large or grand. The parlor-like living room was cozy, with a nice mélange of antique and contemporary furnishings, including surprisingly kitschy knickknacks, like china cat and dog figurines, and a variety of mismatched throw pillows—several with needlepoint dog portraits and printed butterfly fabrics, some made of fur, two in the shape of toucans, and one with Truman's own face in needlepoint.

"Maria Dewey made that one for me," said Truman, pointing to an embroidered red-and-green pillow with a fringe the color of dried blood. "She's the wife of the detective in Kansas who caught Perry and Dick, Alvin Dewey."

The room also featured a great red-lacquered Chinese secretary and an ornate girandole lamp whose glass shades were fringed with crystal drops. In the bookcase-lined dining room, which doubled as the library, a group of Christmas angels blowing horns, made of straw and balsa wood, topped a round, brass-inlaid dining table.

What *was* grand were the views of the city and of the East River.

"Dusk is the best time of day here," said Truman, looking east, out into the infinity of Queens. "Some of the bridges have green lights, which look like strings of emeralds."

We installed ourselves in the living room, and Jack served the champagne. With what felt to me like forced blitheness, Truman commented on what a festive season it was and how all the clubs were full of the most exciting, creative people ever—"celebutantes," as Jack had described them to me. Jack disapproved of this crowd. They were a mix of notables and nobodies with a common interest in alcohol, drugs, and sex, he said—which was nothing terrible unless, as he feared was the case, there was nothing else of importance in their lives. If Truman understood what a coarse parody of his former society friends the worst of these celebutantes were, Jack said, he didn't mention it. In fact, I had already gotten the feeling that Truman was now drifting indiscriminately from party to party, without a plan. Plan A, befriending society's true swells, was no longer working for him, and there was no real Plan B.

Both Jack and I tried to keep the conversation light—we must have spent at least ten minutes on the amusing egregiousness of Sixth Avenue's corporate holiday displays; and a few on the ludicrous antics of Truman's self-identified business manager John, whom Truman had finally fired—though soon enough, the subject of Babe and Bill came up.

"I was supposed to be in Jamaica with them right now," he said. "Had a new plaid bathing suit and everything."

"Just as well," said Jack.

"She was the only person I ever liked everything about," said Truman. "And I believe I was the only real friend she ever had."

"Maybe she'll see that," I offered.

"I'm old, is the thing," said Truman. "That's what this whole thing has revealed to me."

"Nonsense," said Jack. "You're barely fifty."

"Not in years," said Truman. "I don't mean I'm *aged*. I mean I'm past my prime. I've never been past my prime before. I am no longer someone who does this or that, but someone who *once did* this or that. I have to start describing my life in the past tense—acknowledging that I've become irrelevant and then playing that awful game of waiting for contradiction and watching this description of myself go unchallenged."

"Truman . . ." said Jack.

"It takes some getting used to, this shift, let alone the actual weakness of the flesh and the spirit. At least we have champagne."

Truman raised his glass and took a sip, and so did Jack, and I thought it best only to smile and let them enjoy the moment's little toast without my joining.

"Well, look," said Jack, "what's done is done. Whether you want to admit it or not, you were attracted to their money and power, and you did use it for your own purposes."

"What you say may be true," said Truman distractedly. He was softly stroking a crocheted baby blanket that was displayed as a throw, over the sofa's arm. He'd told me that it was made for him in 1930, by his beloved cousin Sook. "How different this Christmas is from all the others."

"Truman, you like reading, don't you?" said Jack, suddenly. "I know you do. Will you honor us with a bit of 'A Christmas Memory'? Right now? Please?"

"Well, I . . ." said Truman.

"Oh, please . . . !" I said.

"Oh, lord. Well . . . alright," said Truman. "For Marlene. Because she and I have talked so much about tone and voice."

Truman went into the dining room and came back with a volume that looked like part of a decades-old set.

"I've decided on something else instead—Dickens," he said, reseating himself. "This is a passage that's actually quite dear to me, and I think it says lots about tone and voice."

"Perfect," said Jack, happy to have engaged Truman.

"Remember, you asked for this," said Truman, clearing his throat. "And then we'll have more champagne."

> "A merry Christmas, uncle! God save you!" cried a cheerful voice. It was the voice of Scrooge's nephew, who came upon him so quickly that this was the first intimation he had of his approach.
>
> "Bah!" said Scrooge, "Humbug!"

"They're at Scrooge's counting house," said Truman in an aside. "The weather outside is 'cold, bleak, and biting'—that's what Dickens says. People are wheezing and 'beating their hands upon their breast.' Okay?"

Jack and I nodded.

> He had so heated himself with rapid walking in the fog and frost, this nephew of Scrooge's, that he was all in a glow; his face was ruddy and handsome; his eyes sparkled, and his breath smoked again. "Christmas a humbug, uncle!" said Scrooge's nephew. "You don't mean that, I am sure?"
>
> "I do," said Scrooge. "Merry Christmas! What right have you to be merry? What reason have you to be merry? You're poor enough."
>
> "Come, then," returned the nephew gaily. "What right have you to be dismal? What reason have you to be morose? You're rich enough."

Scrooge having no better answer ready on the spur of the moment, said "Bah!" again; and followed it up with "Humbug."

"Don't be cross, uncle!" said the nephew.

"What else can I be," returned the uncle, "when I live in such a world of fools as this? Merry Christmas! Out upon merry Christmas! What's Christmas-time to you but a time for paying bills without money; a time for finding yourself a year older, and not an hour richer; a time for balancing your books, and having every item in 'em through a round dozen of months presented dead against you? If I could work my will," said Scrooge indignantly, "every idiot who goes about with 'Merry Christmas' on his lips should be boiled with his own pudding, and buried with a stake of holly through his heart."

As Truman read, he might have been the kindly nanny, entertaining her charge. He looked up often from the text and seemed happy that his listeners were paying close attention. He used a kindly voice for the narrative passages, then morphed into the disgruntled Scrooge and good-natured nephew as masterfully as an actor. And in his Scrooge, I thought I could detect a hint of sad confusion, as if both the character and the reader were perplexed to find themselves as such odds with the world.

"Uncle!" pleaded the nephew.

"Nephew!" returned the uncle sternly, "keep Christmas in your own way, and let me keep it in mine."

"Keep it!" repeated Scrooge's nephew. "But you don't keep it."

"Let me leave it alone, then," said Scrooge. "Much good may it do you! Much good it has ever done you!"

"There are many things from which I might have derived good, by which I have not profited, I dare say," returned the nephew; "Christmas among the rest. But I am sure I have always thought of Christmas-time, when it has come round—apart from the veneration due to its sacred

> name and origin, if anything belonging to it can be apart from that—as a good time; a kind, forgiving, charitable, pleasant time; the only time I know of, in the long calendar of the year, when men and women seem by one consent to open their shut-up hearts freely, and to think of people below them as if they really were fellow passengers to the grave, and not another race of creatures bound on other journeys. And therefore, uncle, though it has never put a scrap of gold or silver in my pocket, I believe that it has done me good, and will do me good; and I say, God bless it!"

Truman closed the book and placed it on the coffee table. I had to collect myself for a second, as the performance had brought me close to tears. It was lovely to see how much optimism Truman put into the words of the nephew. Of course, I heard the resonances with the seven-year-old narrator of "A Christmas Memory."

"Marvelous," I finally uttered.

"Still got it," said Jack. "Bravo."

"Do you know the story?" Truman asked me. "The story, not the movie."

"Of course I do," I said. "And what's so great is that it's a ghost story, and there's a little friction there between the ghost part and the Christian part."

Truman nodded in satisfaction.

"Yes, indeed," he said. "Very good. See, Jack? I told you she was a clever girl."

"Lionel Trilling has nothing on you," said Jack as he leaned over to top up my glass.

When "Unspoiled Monsters" was published in *Esquire*, the following May, Truman was pictured on the cover as an assassin, holding a stiletto. *Women's Wear Daily* dubbed him "The Tiny Terror." He was pleased. The explosion of juicy publicity seemed to reduce any qualms about the high cost of it. I remember hearing from Lee that "people up and down Fifth Avenue" were relieved that the story admitted no apparent poison-pen details. But the end of their friendship was nonetheless near, and Lee was forcing herself to concentrate on new interests. She had officially launched her own design business by then, Lee Radziwill Inc., under the guidance of her friend Mark Hampton; and after a spread on her work in *Architectural Digest*, she'd begun attracting new clients, including the California hotelier Newton Cope, whom she had met at a dinner party given by wealthy rancher and vineyard owner Whitney Warren, a friend of Lee's mother.

"Mother approves of Newton," she told me. "In fact, I think she set the whole thing up. And Truman seems to like him more than he does Peter Tufo. So I guess that's something."

In fact, within a few years, Lee would promise to marry Newton and get as far as planning the wedding trip with him. Then it all fell through, in what I gather was a perfectly civilized way.

So much felt like it was falling apart that year—particularly the American innovation machine that had revved up in the 1950s and '60s, bringing post–World War II optimism to a head. The machine ran out of steam. By 1976, defeat in Vietnam, the Watergate scandal, and the energy crisis had paved the way toward conservatism of the most poisonous, flag-waving sort. American public culture was fragmenting into self-fueled factions and constituencies; and nostalgia—for a past that was either real or imagined; it didn't matter which—became the feel-good emotion that replaced optimism in the nation's heart.

About this wave of nostalgia, Lila made a fool of herself, according to Truman, by demonstrating her lack of scope, understanding, and talent as a writer by publishing a few clumsy sentences—nominally hooked to the movies *King Kong*, *A Star Is Born*, and *That's Entertainment, Part II*—that failed to comprehend the origins and depth of this wave.

"It's obvious she wants to have a big thought about it, but she can do little more than actually type the word *retro*," he said. "All I can think about when I hear that word is *retrogressive*."

And in New York, even the lunch scene was falling apart—rather, evolving. There was a whole new group of trendy places that Lee and her friends started exploring, as red velvet and rustic charm gave way to beige suede and eclectic chic. Instead of the pomp of Le Pavillon, they wanted the spectacle of Le Cirque and the fresh bounciness of Mortimer's.

Stas's death in July was difficult for Lee, of course, and her refusal to let Truman console her at close range shocked me in revealing how far the relationship had deteriorated. Several times, she declined his offer to visit her. Several months earlier, when he had written glowingly about her for a *Vogue* spread, saying that she was lovelier than Audrey Hepburn, she'd been surprisingly indifferent.

"He seems to think that everything is the way it used to be," she said. She also felt his image was morphing rapidly from respected author to public buffoon—an opinion bolstered by his inept appearance that year in a spoofy whodunit movie called *Murder by Death*.

The last time they went out together, that I know of, was an event called "The Craft of Time," held at the New York Public Library—a display of historic, innovative timepieces by the venerable Swiss firm Patek Philippe, featuring the launch of the firm's newest line of watches, Nautilus. It was an evening I was to hear about in detail from each of them.

From Truman, there was a lot of lecture in his comments.

"I know so many people under thirty in the clubs who are happy to live in an eternal present," he said. "They are completely ahistorical. And when I tell them that ignorance of history is condemnation to repeat it, or that failure to achieve anything means that you will be forgotten by history, they shrug and say 'So what?' And I have begun to say 'So what?' too, about *them*. Let these people be forgotten. Let their lives mean nothing in the long run."

He said how much he admired the fact that Lee was grounded in actual history—she was proud that her ancestor had fought in the American Revolution—and that *I* was, too—a king of Spain, a line of Cuban *marquésos*, a different revolution . . . And this thought, he said, was provoked simply by his account of walking through Bryant Park and thinking that most people there had no knowledge of William Cullen Bryant, let alone of Samuel J. Tilden, John Jacob Astor, and James Lenox, who helped fund and fill the New York Public Library in the previous century. He laughed wickedly to guess how little many socialite husbands knew about anything but their own businesses, and how many socialite wives knew vastly more but were encouraged to smile quietly and "trophy it up." Not Lee, though, he said—then observed that "the poor girl" hadn't ever been able to stick with a man for very long.

"Sadly, some of these women enforce their own invisibility," he said. "Even when they are featured in the magazines. Forgotten by history—that's what I am afraid will happen to most of them. I can't witness it—I really can't."

Lee's account of the evening centered more on architecture—the Library's "marvelous" marble-paneled Room 80, crowned with a lyrical glass and cast-iron dome—and on horology and the new watch itself.

"We met the gentleman who designed it," Lee told me. "This man was one of the great watchmakers of the world, a master craftsman of the highest order. Just think of what he knows! Think of those skills! But Truman was unimpressed, distracted. He was more interested in grabbing a glass of champagne from a passing waiter.

"'The Craft of Time' is such a wonderful name, isn't it?" continued Lee. "There were watches on display dating back to 1842—all the most advanced technology of the time. The Nautilus is made of steel, you see, which has always been seen as a lesser material compared to gold. But this is what they call a 'luxury sports watch'—isn't that interesting? It just drips with all the adventure of the divers and aviators who need these very technically advanced timepieces in their work.

"Monsieur Genta—that's the designer—seemed to have the fire of an artist inside him—almost a maverick. A little like Truman, I thought. 'Watches, to me, are the opposite of freedom,' he said. 'I am an artist, a painter; I hate time because it is a constraint. I find it annoying.'

"I turned to Truman and was going to say something about hating time, and all he could say was something about liking gold watches and not seeing the point of steel. Talk about annoying."

It was easy to see in their accounts of that evening how differently each was looking at life at that point: Lee still curious and enthusiastic, Truman a bit brittle, perhaps stuck in some groove that once was glamorous but seemed much less so now. And what was similar about their accounts—their enthusiasm in being caught after the event by a well-known paparazzo on the 42nd Street entrance to the library—made me sad for both of them, since it exposed the vein of mutual exploitation that had run through their friendship and kept it going until this last minute. Ten years after Truman's ball, they had each wanted a trophy date for this Thursday night luxury watch launch, and for the last time, they had that in each other.

"Good evening, Gene—good to see you," said Truman.

"Hi, Truman. Hi, Lee," said the paparazzo.

"Hi, there," said Lee.

He was a man in his early thirties, with long fair hair and a straw fedora—a man much more decorous and likable than Ron Galella, the paparazzo who'd several times broken his restraining order to stay fifty feet away from Lee's sister Jackie. Over the years, Gene had caught Lee and Truman together for many memorable shots.

"Here, let's get the two of you," he said, and launched into a very quick series of darts and crouches in front of them, accompanied by the rapid clicking of the camera. "Looking great tonight—thanks very much."

"Thank you, Gene," said Truman.

"You guys look as brilliant tonight as the first time I caught you—I think that was in front of the restaurant."

"That's very kind," said Lee.

"My gosh, when was that?" said Truman. "I think Woodrow Wilson was president."

"You're timeless," said Gene. "We don't say that about everyone, in my profession."

"I don't know about timeless," said Truman. "But Lee and I do go way back, don't we, princess?"

"That's wonderful," said Gene.

"And we're friends forever," said Truman—and in an instant, Gene had raised his camera and gotten the shot of Truman looking adoringly at Lee.

"Can I quote you on that, Truman?" said Gene.

"Why not?" said Truman.

Chapter 22

Do I Wake or Sleep?

"Don't Repeat This" —by Lila North
Wednesday, June 8, 1977

. . . Who or what is the "Son of Sam"? That's what a new task force of elite New York detectives wants to know, after the April murders of 18-year-old Valentina Suriani and 20-year-old Alexander Esau. The .44-caliber killer of Suriani and Esau, who were kissing when they were shot in their parked car near the Hutchinson River Parkway, left a note at the scene of the crime identifying himself as "Son of Sam." The detectives, who are spearheading a task force called "Operation Omega," are working overtime to catch this monster before he strikes again. • And from "Son of Sam" to "Save Our Children": Now the gays are calling for a boycott of orange juice, to protest Anita Bryant's success in getting the Dade County anti-discrimination ordinance repealed by a margin of 69 to 31 percent. Poor Anita was already blacklisted in February, when the Singer sewing machine corporation withdrew its offer to sponsor a new weekly variety show that was being planned for her. Singer's move destroyed what Bryant called "a dream I have had since I was a child, to have a television series of my own." • The glitterati continue to mob the doors of the new disco Studio 54. Some people describe the place as "heaven" and "Oz," but we hear that with all the club's open drug use and public sex, it's more like "Sodom and Gomorrah . . ."

After Truman and I started seeing each other again regularly, in a little maid's room he rented in his building, I heard lots and lots about his visits to Studio 54, and about his new friends, and indirectly about all the alcohol and drugs he was consuming, which he described in a way that he seemed to think was devilishly entertaining, but I found pitiable.

"I've been to a lot of nightclubs in my life, but this is the best," he said. "Bianca Jagger riding in on a white horse, on her birthday . . . !"

"Really? Naked?"

"No, not naked. Why do people have such dirty minds? I'm only teasing, Serene One. No, she was wearing a red dress."

"Okay."

"Well, actually, that's the way it was reported—'she rode in.' Better for the story, don't you think? But Bianca made it a point to say afterward—in a letter to the *Financial Times,* no less—that she didn't ride in on the poor beast, but simply mounted it, out of politeness. She was very well-raised, you know. Steve Rubell had arranged to have the horse there, as a kind of birthday surprise; but as an environmentalist and animal rights defender, she had to make sure that readers of the *Financial Times* knew that she understands the difference between 'riding in' on a horse and 'mounting' it.

"Do you see how complicated life has become, Serenity? Studio is wonderful, of course, but sometimes I do miss the way things were when I arrived here from Alabama and was just settling into the city, and my girlfriends and I would go all the time to El Morocco and the Stork Club, and just have a ball. We knew the head waiter at the Stork Club, "St. Peter" we used to call him, because he guarded the holy gate to the Cub Room, which was absolutely *it* back then. The owner of the club would give us lunch for free, because we were such decorative young people. We were just teenagers, you know, and the place was open for lunch—a lot of people don't know that now . . ."

Truman was going out to Studio 54 two or three nights a week, at that point. He said he liked to watch the crowd from the DJ booth, above the crowd. I gathered he was doing lots of cocaine and drinking heavily. Jack heard about this but saw little of it, as he pretty much kept to himself in Sagaponack. Truman mainly went with a young writer friend, Bob MacBride, whom I never met, as a "club buddy," because Lee was not particularly interested in the disco scene, and Babe was by now too ill to go out.

The maid's room, seventeen floors below his apartment, was one of several such rooms that UN Plaza offered its residents with live-in staff. It was simply a single eight-by-fifteen-foot shoebox, with that signature glass wall at one end and an entryway and modest bathroom at the other. Truman furnished it with a desk, a bookcase, and a sofa and chair, but little else. The desk was always neatly crowded with piles of notebooks and open manuscripts; a bulletin board was pinned with three-by-five cards and assorted notes. There was a typewriter, but Truman didn't use it for early drafts, preferring, he said, to be "slowed down" by the effort of writing by hand.

I stopped by maybe once a week, and we made little pretense of working on the screenplay. In fact, he rarely mentioned it, and instead used me as a sounding board for whatever he was working on at the time—magazine articles and short stories that would eventually be published in *Music for Chameleons*. I thought one of them, "Handcarved Coffins," particularly good, since it seemed to show Truman in his best true-crime, *In Cold Blood* mode—though he did once interrupt his reading of a section of the story to admit that "I am fibbing a bit here and there, but don't tell my publisher." He was sometimes shaky, holding a manuscript, or he slurred his words, but he was an awfully good reader, captivating, a natural storyteller. When he was reading, he seemed to inhabit all the characters vividly, and appeared sure and strong and confident, like the old Truman. I felt that it was chiefly my job during these sessions to simply witness this, without judgment, even without the questions we used to talk about when we first started meeting.

Rarely did he mention *Answered Prayers*, and rarely did I ask about it. I would have liked to discuss the book with him, but as confidante of last resort, and far from a social equal, I felt constrained to do what was best, not necessarily what was right. In truth, I was far from serene during those sessions, because I felt, in that little shoebox, as he read to me and rambled on, that we were inside a nuclear reactor: Truman was the plutonium, and I was like those rods they insert to keep the reaction under control.

The notion of social equality came up once. I as much as said that unlike his swans, I did not live in as large a world as they did. His response was immediate.

"You're as big as you think you are. Anybody is. Remember that."

I said I'd seen so little of life. Oddly, within a second or two, this simple declaration brought Truman close to tears.

"Poppycock," he said. "Revolution? A life ripped away? Poor, poor girl, you."

I wanted very much to keep his mind settled, occupied. I couldn't imagine what an emotional explosion might be like, or, if one occurred, what I should do about it. Quite consciously, for a second, I imagined my having to dash for the door and down to the lobby, to get help from the concierge.

"I don't hate the revolutionaries, and I didn't especially love Batista," I said impulsively. "Anyway, none of that meant much to a twenty-year-old. I was thinking about buying a Fiat and driving to Turkey to join an archeological dig with two friends from school. I wasn't thinking about my country—even if I should have been. I guess I wanted to spend money and see the world."

This scenario did interest Truman and appeared to calm him.

"You know," he said, "I've lived in Communist countries, and the people there are always extremely interested in money. I think they are more interested in money than we are. They are certainly interested in material things. The irony of that is that in Communist countries, there isn't much to buy."

"Here in New York, we're safe and sound," I said.

"Yes," he said. "As safe as can be, anyway."

Did people sue each other so much, or so frivolously, in Communist countries? Here in the U.S., among those in the class that I served, suing people was something of a pastime. And in the instance of Vidal vs. Capote, the fallout of such a pastime was the end of Lee and Truman's friendship, which, while coming for many years, finally arrived in a rapid cascade of public and private events.

The suit had been dragging on slowly and, I gather, invisibly for years, through the legal system. In 1971, when *Playgirl* published the story that prompted the suit—Truman's account of that 1961 White House party from which Vidal was kicked out for drunk and obnoxious behavior—he said he'd been told about it by Lee, who attended the party and spoke to Truman later that night by phone from the White House's Rose Bedroom, where she often stayed during the Kennedy administration.

"This was back in '61?" the interviewer asked.

"Yes, in '61," said Truman.

"That was ten years ago. How can you be sure?"

"I have always had a photographic memory. This is an established fact. But I also wrote it down, as I often do anything that seems important."

"Is it so important that Gore Vidal was thrown out of the White House?"

"The story isn't important because of Gore Vidal. It's important because it was the White House."

Truman insisted that should the case ever go to trial, he would expect eyewitnesses to the incident, like John Kenneth Galbraith, George Plimpton, Arthur Schlesinger Jr., and even Jackie herself, to support his claim.

Since they were no longer as intimate as they used to be, Lee didn't tell Truman when, in 1977, she received a subpoena to testify in the lawsuit and gave a deposition confirming Vidal's version of the story—that he was not thrown out, and did not put his arm around Jackie inappropriately or insult Jackie's mother. I knew that Truman didn't hear about the deposition at the time, or he would have mentioned it to me. This was when he was in and out of rehab at Smithers, in New York, and then Hazelden, in Minnesota—and often drunk again days after his release, and sometimes so drunk that he was falling down during speaking engagements, in full view of the audience. He confessed to me then that he sometimes thought about suicide—"not a little, but a lot." He mentioned this on television, too, a year later, on *The Stanley Siegel Show*, after a series of headlines about Truman's intoxicated behavior. Siegel asked, "Truman, with all the pills and booze, what's going to happen to you?" And Truman answered, "The obvious answer is that eventually I'll kill myself."

Babe's death, soon after that, didn't help. Not only was Truman despondent; he told me he felt that essential parts of his life were being ripped away from him irrevocably. And by then, people who knew or had heard of Truman were divided into two types: those who had sympathy for this great writer and sensitive soul who was going tragically mad; and TV hosts, journalists, and the common horde who were happy to poke the crazy bear and give him opportunities to make a fool of himself.

But when Truman finally did hear about Lee's deposition—from Tennessee Williams, who'd heard about it from a gloating Gore Vidal—Truman exploded.

In a long and tearful session in the maid's room, he told me how shocked and bitter he was. Truman called Lee and screamed at her, after which she stopped taking his calls. He asked me to intercede with her, so he could straighten things out, but that was impossible.

"I wish I could," I said, "but I think you know I can't."

He sighed, exhaustedly.

"You're a good friend anyway," he said.

It was hard for me to say no. I knew how ardently Truman was trying to get back into the graces of his famous friend, partly because he was being lionized in clubland by so many self-important nobodies hungry for what Andy Warhol called their "fifteen minutes of fame." I did the best I could to help—even lied and said how marvelous he looked when, during his increasingly short stretches of sobriety, he got a facelift, or started swimming every day, or lost some weight, all of which only drew attention to the departure of his youthfulness—though I now see that no one could have helped.

"I do not recall ever discussing with Truman Capote an incident or the evening which I understand is the subject of this lawsuit," Lee had told Vidal's lawyer. This was a direct contradiction of what she'd told Truman long before, in her call from the Rose Bedroom. I believe that account was true and was surprised to see Lee changing her story, but I assumed she was doing so by design. She must have decided it was better to leave the sordid details of the incident untold. She may simply have wanted to protect her sister's legacy, whether or not she particularly liked her stepbrother, Gore Vidal, whom I heard her once call "sinister." In any event, I doubt she was making an effort to harm Truman.

"Why is she doing this to me?" lamented Truman. "What have I ever done to her?"

Since I wouldn't help Truman get through to Lee, and Jack had failed to help him do so, he turned improbably to Lila for help. Lila was surprised to be hearing from Truman, but was almost instantly intrigued by the idea of helping him.

"What can I possibly do?" she said.

"Just call her and ask how her design firm is doing, for your column," said Truman. "Maybe she'll give you the names of some clients."

"For my column, huh?"

"You're always asking questions."

"Would she answer them?"

"Why wouldn't she? She's got a young business. Publicity helps. Please, Lila. And then mention that you were speaking with me, and how sad and dejected I am to have this unresolved thing between us."

"Lord knows, we can't have unresolved things lying around."

Lila agreed to do it, and called Lee that very morning. And later that day, as soon as she had filed her column for the following day, which included a quote from Lee, Lila called Truman back and told him what Lee had said about him and Vidal—except for a comment containing a certain word that Lee used, which Truman saw the following day in the newspaper.

"Well, you know what they are," read the quote. "They're

just a couple of fags, and this is just a fight between two fags. I think it's disgusting that we have to be dragged into it."

Which hurt and angered Truman even more. He immediately went public with his response, in a return to *The Stanley Siegel Show*. This was almost a year after his previous appearance.

"If the lovely Princess Radziwill has such a low opinion of homosexuals," he told Siegel, "then why did she have me for a confidant for the last twenty years . . . ? I would say that a majority of Lee's friends and Jackie's friends are homosexual."

He considered Lee's statement "treachery in the first degree" and declared that he was not a man to be trifled with.

"We all know that a fag is a homosexual gentleman who has just left the room. What I'm going to say isn't very gentlemanly, but she's described me as a fag, and fags are supposed to be bitchy. So let's go."

His remarks were rambling. And as with all drunks who think they look sober, it was ridiculous and slightly painful to watch someone so obviously impaired trying to look blithe.

"This morning, I woke up remembering something Stas Radziwill had said to me after I had helped Lee establish her own identity, when she first came to New York," he said. "I got her *Laura*. I got her a big advance on that book she did with Jackie. I helped her get started in decorating. I did all this for the dear Principessa Radziwilla. Stas said to me, 'Goodness, Truman, if you'd do all this for a friend, what would you do for an enemy?' "

On the *Siegel* show, Truman came across not only as drunk, but demented. He told me he'd meant to appear this way—that he was impersonating a "crazy, drunk, Southern queen that one would meet in a bar," that his appearance was meant as a piece of theater, that he'd carefully written and rehearsed his character—but I didn't buy that for a minute. The real Truman knew better about the way public appearances work. Also, his being actually drunk on camera didn't help at all.

"I know that Lee wouldn't want me tellin' none of this," he giggled, "but you know us Southern fags. We just can't keep our mouths shut."

Amidst his vengeance, Truman professed genuine sadness as he spoke about the woman he'd considered his best friend for almost two decades.

"I was placed in an impossible situation by this whole thing," he told Siegel. "It wasn't as though I sat down and decided to be vindictive. She simply didn't tell the truth."

In response, Lee made another public statement, repeating what she'd said in her deposition: "I do not recall ever discussing with Truman Capote the incident or the evening." Vidal weighed in with a statement, too, referencing Truman: "After the age of fifty, litigation replaces sex." To which Truman responded, "I'm always sad about Gore—very sad that he has to breathe every day." To which Vidal retorted, "Truman made lying an art form—a minor art form."

It was all such a childish mess—and so much of it was public. But what actually happened, though, with Lila's intermediation was slightly different, which I was able to deduce after hearing both Lee's and Truman's sides of the story. Both of them bent my ear privately about the affair.

From Lee, I did hear that Truman was a "bitchy fag," but, as she had done previously, she qualified her use of that word.

"Now, you know I don't mean that badly," she said. "I haven't a prejudiced bone in my body. I'm just so frustrated with that man."

From Truman, I heard, "She's just a mean lady, and that's the truth of it. She's mean to absolutely everyone"—the lament of a spurned lover echoing from inside a substance-fogged mind.

"Love is blind," he said. "I suppose I've been in love before with ghastly people."

When Lila agreed to help Truman by calling Lee, she didn't tell him that the next column after the one in which she'd publish Lee's remarks would be her last. She'd been fired, and she suspected that it was Truman who'd gotten her fired, and wanted to get back at him. So, happily and on purpose, she strategically colored her account of her conversation with Lee, and made Lee's use of the word *fags* sound more insulting than intended, by not qualifying it.

I know this because I was there when Lila called, and I heard Lee's end of the conversation. Lee used the word *fag* as she often did in private: not so much pejoratively, but in an attempt to sound colloquial, hip. She thought the word *homosexual* too clinical and uptight. As to whether or not she thought it was homosexuality itself, working through society's usual mode of repression, that was somehow fueling the Vidal-Capote squabble, well, I suppose we all knew that it was.

Truman heard later that Lee was tired of having him ride her coattails to fame.

"*Her* coattails?" he exclaimed to me, one day in the maid's room. "Who got her *Laura*?" And he proceeded to rehash everything he had told Stanley Siegel almost verbatim, as if he had rehearsed that, too. He referred to Lee as a cunt, but I felt that he was using the word exactly as Lee had called him a fag—in a terribly childish and vulgar way, yet somehow not without forbearance, since they both came from a world in which bad behavior was routinely overlooked or indulged.

Lila didn't admit in her final column that she'd been fired. Nor were her readers particularly surprised to hear that her column was ending, after seeing its position in the paper slip backwards over the years, heading toward the back door. Aside from the shame of holding a double standard, her little secret about her affair and her illegitimate daughter—that domestic drama that had quietly been disfiguring her point of view—would have meant nothing to her readers or to the rest of the world.

"Don't Repeat This" —by Lila North
Monday, November 19, 1979

> . . . This is my final column for this newspaper. It's almost twenty-five years now that we've been speaking like this, and I am grateful to all of you for it, but I find now that I must go in a new direction. You know well of my thoughts on the decadence of contemporary society, and I have been conferring about this with my confessor, the Archbishop of New York, Terence Cardinal Cooke, who as you know played a crucial role in helping

defeat New York City's pro-gay antidiscrimination bill, a few years back. His Eminence, who recently hosted both the Dalai Lama and Pope John Paul II in our fair city, assures me that the wicked antics of all these fruits and pansies will have no more long-term influence on American culture than those of the obscene rockers and witless "pop" artists . . .

". . . And then the bitch retired," said Truman. "End of story."

"Why do you even care?" said Cecil.

"Because she was always trying to be a player, but never was one. Isn't that sad? Isn't it sad that in a New York media career, you can get by for thirty or forty years as a total mediocrity?"

"Let it go, Muzzy."

They were sitting, champagne flutes at hand, at a small table in the Crush Bar of the Royal Opera House in Covent Garden, during intermission of a first-night performance of the New York City Ballet. They had just seen one of the company's newest works, a ballet to Prokofiev called *Opus 19/The Dreamer* by Jerome Robbins, starring Patricia MacBride and Mikhail Baryshnikov. In attendance that night, as everyone in the house knew, was Princess Margaret, a confirmed balletophile and, as patron of the Royal Ballet, a kind of emissary/host to the American troupe. The hall's main gathering spot for intermission drinks and conversation, the Crush Bar was packed as usual with a glittering crowd, swanning beneath soaring white-and-gold neoclassical pillars and crystal chandeliers.

Most of the ladies were in long dresses; the gentlemen in either black tie or white tie. The men in white tie were older, and several wore medals, while the ladies accompanying them wore tiaras.

"I see at least two women in tiaras with men wearing black tie," said Truman. He was in a black Dunhill tuxedo; Cecil was in a midnight-blue dinner suit by Huntsman & Sons.

"It'll be tweed suits and tin pie-pan crowns by 1980, mark my words," said Cecil.

After the room filled and people found their drinks and their territory, there was still a bit of carefully navigated promenading, with a miraculous minimum of bumped elbows and splashed champagne. Several stately-looking couples nodded graciously or said hello to Cecil as they passed. Cecil had been knighted not long before and had had a stroke, and was now getting about with a cane. It was also common knowledge among those who cherished this national cultural treasure that he had been forced by necessity to sell most of his photographic inventory—with the courtly exception of his pictures of the Royal Family—and was living on the proceeds. He was now avoiding most public events, yet a first night at the ballet still seemed essential to him, especially if on the occasion he could help out an old *frère de sang*. Truman had mentioned that Lee was expected to attend at night, and that a "casual encounter" with her might be helpful.

"I don't see her," said Truman, taking a moment now and then to survey the crowd.

"Sad business," said Cecil.

"It'll pass."

"You should have apologized immediately."

"I tried to."

"If I know you, you didn't. You did that other thing."

"What other thing?"

"You purred and postured, and gave *her* an opportunity to apologize to *you*."

"*Oh* . . ."

"You know I'm right."

The sound of two hundred conversations required them to speak loudly, though they were sitting side by side.

"Acapulco will be fun," said Truman.

"I told you, dear, I can barely walk," said Cecil.

"Good evening, Cecil," said a gentleman, who was passing the table with his wife.

"Good evening, Sir George," said Cecil.

"Good evening, Sir Cecil," said the lady, pointedly using the photographer's new title.

"Uh, quite," said Sir George.

"May, you look lovely," said Cecil.

"Anyway, I can send a plane for you," said Truman, as the couple moved off.

"You can't afford it," said Cecil. "Besides, I already have an invitation for Christmas."

"Hello, Cecil," said a handsome young man who was passing with a practically duplicate handsome young man, both in stylish suits.

"You know very well I'm not speaking to you," said Cecil, wagging a finger impishly, then relenting. "Enjoy the show, boys. Martin, see that you call me tomorrow."

"Adorable," said Truman.

"Trouble," said Cecil.

"Oh, good."

"I'm sorry Eddy couldn't join us tonight. She always loves this."

"Robbins?"

"Everything—the ballet, this room. This is our world."

"This is our world."

Half the people in the room were titled.

"Isn't this the real show?"

They raised their glasses and sipped.

"Do I wake or sleep?" said Cecil.

"Shelley?" said Truman.

"Keats, of course."

"Oh, right—'Nightingale.'"

"He keeps journeying on, this boy in the ballet, looking for The Other—it's a feverish quest, yet tender . . ."

"So ethereal."

"What will Misha do with ABT, I wonder?" said Cecil.

"A whole new era," said Truman.

"I hope so. Though I fear I may not see much of it."

"Good evening, Cecil," said an older gentleman, passing the table with an owlish young man and a vivacious-looking middle-aged woman.

"My goodness—Johnny! I thought you were in Florence. Clarissa, Michael . . ." said Cecil. "You know Truman Capote."

It was the art historian Sir John Pope-Hennessy, and his much younger companion Michael Mallon, with Clarissa Churchill Eden, the widow of Prime Minister Anthony Eden.

"No, I'm here to look at a Renaissance bronze for the V&A," said Sir John. "And Lino and Clarissa wanted to look at Baryshnikov, so . . . *qui siamo*."

"*Bene. E tu cosa ne pensi?*" said Cecil.

"*Meraviglioso!*" said Michael.

"Quite marvelous, yes," said Clarissa.

"Enjoy yourselves," said Cecil.

"That girl is a kick in the pants, as we say in Alabama," said Truman, after the trio had stepped away.

"You know Clarissa?"

"Lee introduced me once," said Truman. "Lee said she reigned like a queen over Downing Street but hated Chequers."

"Quite right," said Cecil, shuddering. "Hideous place, Chequers."

"There she is," hissed Truman.

On the other side of the room was Lee, in a white gown, with that golden starburst ornament of hers in her hair, standing with Nureyev. The dancer was dressed in one of his colorful tunic jackets, this one in ruby metallic brocade.

"Will you go over?" said Cecil.

"Will *she* come over *here*?" said Truman.

"Don't be childish."

Then, with a glance Lee made in Truman and Cecil's direction, they saw that she'd already spotted them. There were scores of people in between, but Cecil raised his glass to Lee, and she, from afar, graciously smiled, nodding her head. Then she went back to her conversation with Nureyev and some admirers.

"There, she saw us," said Cecil.

"She won't come over," said Truman.

"So be it. One can't push these things."

Then a collective hush fell over the room, as conspicuous as a football stadium cheer. Princess Margaret, the Queen's sister, had entered, escorted by a friend of Cecil's, a theater director, and attended by some sort of equerry or bodyguard. The crowd parted, packing themselves together even more tightly, so the royal party could proceed smoothly. Most of the ladies curtsied.

The Princess was in a gown of arresting sapphire blue, with a grand tiara of aquamarines and diamonds. As she swept past the table where Truman and Cecil were sitting, she smiled and winked at Sir Cecil, prompting him to grab his cane and try laboriously to rise. In response to her gracious notice, he bowed.

"What's she doing in here?" said Truman. "I thought there was a private retiring room attached to the royal box."

"Are you kidding?" said Cecil. "Not on a night like this. Madame Darling loves nothing more than to cause a fuss. Did you see the way the crowd parted for her? She lives for that."

"Oh, my," said Truman.

"Absolutely lives for it. So much more important to her than anything on the stage."

"Look where she's stopping," exclaimed Truman.

Princess Margaret was talking with Lee and Nureyev.

"Princesses do like to stick together," said Cecil.

Truman and Cecil, while continuing to cluck, watched Lee and Margaret converse and laugh for ten minutes, until the bell was rung to signal the end of intermission. Then Margaret and her escorts swept out, past their table, after which Truman and Cecil rose to begin making their way back to their seats. As they did, Lee and Nureyev sailed past, with a simple nod of acknowledgment from the lady and a slightly surprised look from the dancer, who found himself being steered onward steadily, without a chance for any greetings.

PART IV

Chapter 23

The Next Party Begins

Back in my room at the Lowell, after the funeral, I took a moment to check my messages.

"Can we invite you here tomorrow night?" texted Judy.

"That would be nice," I said.

Better than a restaurant, I thought, and also nice to see the place again that I once called home.

"Just the three of us," she continued. "Though of course, if there's anyone you'd like to bring, just let me know. Say seven?"

There was no one. I did find myself thinking, though, like a girl in grade school, what it would be like to bring Vincent along—even if he and I were nowhere near as close as we would need to be to jointly accept an invitation, and who knows if we will ever be in that position.

There was also a phone message from Vincent.

"I just wanted you to know that I'm thinking about you. I hope you're having a comfortable stay, and I'm looking forward to seeing you when you return. If we can have that drink on Wednesday night, it would be great."

And there was an email from the producer I was meeting the following day.

"Confirming our appointment for tomorrow at 11:30. I'm looking forward to meeting you. We'll have lunch, if you have the time. Your name will be at the desk in the lobby."

My hotel room was decorated in shades of ecru and warm gray, with touches of celadon in a lamp and a throw pillow.

In addition to the generously proportioned bed and end tables, there was a desk and chair, a proper dresser, and an overstuffed armchair with footrest and side table, all in a commodious, contemporary style. The upholstery and wallpaper patterns were understated; the textures and finishes, subtle. Was there a pot of phalaenopsis orchids in every room of the hotel, or had the management placed one in mine specially, for some reason?

Settling into the armchair, I realized that all three messages I received represented some kind of shift taking place in my life; somehow being in a hotel—traveling, on the road, away from home—allowed me not only to sense the shift more fully than I might have done otherwise, but to feel okay about letting the shift happen, even if I couldn't predict exact results, which I normally try to do. Maybe I have been too rigid and too overprotective of myself for too long, I thought. Maybe the mental armor I'd had in place for sixty years was no longer necessary, and there was some room in my life for development in the areas of friendship, love, and career. I recalled the "fabulous possibilities" that Lee spoke of, once when she was showing me some designs for hotel rooms that she was creating. The rooms were supposed to make people feel comfortable and adventurous at the same time, she said—environments that made people feel *safe enough* but also stimulated and aware of their own curiosity, which perhaps hadn't had the chance to flourish back home, where "too many variables under our control were in the way." Is that why they say that travel is broadening? Sure, when you arrive at your destination, there are all sorts of marvelous new things to see and do, but isn't it the act of leaving home that primes our brains subconsciously to rethink our list of basic safety requirements, and once that's done, to take in the new possibilities, the new challenges . . . ?

I had settled into the chair thinking I'd take a moment and ponder my lunch options. But I must have closed my eyes, because I woke up an hour later and decided to wait until teatime to eat.

* * *

After their friendship broke down, Lee and Truman adopted the delicate social tango that former friends do when they occupy basically the same social circuit and attend many of the same public events. They may want to avoid too much contact with one another but not appear ungracious, or worse, vindictive. Private events were usually easier to manage, as hostesses and other friends either took sides or took care not to invite the squabblers to the same dinner table. However, Truman paused the tango periodically when he went on television, because, I think, the medium always overexcited him. By this time, though, his ability to appear suave in front of the cameras was failing him, and he was coming across like a deluded, irritable old man. And, as I learned one day when he asked me to accompany him to a television studio for an interview segment he was doing on a talk show, producers and show hosts understood his irritability very well and knew it could result in what they thought was good TV.

Truman was in makeup, in front of a mirror, his shirt collar protected by tissues while a makeup artist fussed about his face with a little sponge, while I went to fetch him a fresh can of soda. I happened to overhear the show's executive producer talking quietly with the host, at the edge of the set.

"Get him to talk about how well he thinks he did in rehab," said the producer. "He's lost weight. Get him to talk about that—you know? He's proud but slurring his words, for chrissake. Then ask about the swans who have cut him. *Bang*! The contrast should be pretty good."

The producer and host looked confident if not smug.

The show got under way, and Truman tripped while stepping onto the dais. The host came around from his desk to help. Everyone kept smiling, but it was not a felicitous start.

"You've just come back from rehab, I understand."

"Yes. Don't I look fabulous?"

There was applause and some laughter from the studio audience. To judge from a monitor in view, the director was sticking with a preponderance of close-ups on Truman, possibly because

Truman was sweating and often playing directly to the audience rather than to the host, which made him look slightly desperate.

"How do you feel?" said the host.

"I feel marvelous," said Truman. "How do *you* feel?"

"I went for a nice long walk today."

"Isn't that fascinating? This must be the kind of repartee that people talk about when they call you the best host on TV."

The show cut to break early, and a staff member took the opportunity to mop Truman's brow.

"They can't let him go on like this, boss," whispered a grip to a cameraman.

"Of course they can," said the cameraman.

In the next segment, Truman tried to explain the alienation of his friends.

"People who live by their wits develop killer talents," he said.

The host appeared to find the ambiguity of this statement puzzling. Was it an excuse? A rationale?

"Speaking of your talents," said the host, "I understand you can read upside-down."

"It's not magic—just something I can do," said Truman, "like remembering long speeches almost verbatim. How about that!"

A little demonstration ensued, to great effect, as Truman read from a prepared sheet that the host produced.

"'For all her chic thinness, she had an almost breakfast-cereal air of health, a soap and lemon cleanness . . .' Well, for goodness' sake, I should know those words. I wrote them."

"Your description of Holly Golightly," said the host.

"That's right—from *Breakfast at Tiffany's*."

Applause.

"How does the rest of it go?"

"The whole book?"

"The description of Holly."

"That's all you've got written down on this sheet."

"Don't you remember?"

"If I knew this was to be a quiz, I would have studied up."

Laughter and applause.

Truman looked oddly unfazed. Then the host asked more pointedly about Truman's society friends.

"All a writer has for material is what he knows," he said. "And what I know is *this* world, *this* milieu. They're all I've got. I'm not doing anything that Proust didn't do."

"I know so little about French literature, but did Proust call anyone the c-word, as you did Lee Radziwill?"

Truman sighed.

"You know, she calls herself a princess," he said, "but as far as I know, she ain't no daughter of a king and queen."

In the third segment, Truman announced that he had once more renegotiated his contract for *Answered Prayers*—a deal that the host clearly knew all about in detail, since he reminded Truman that the full amount promised him by Random House—now one million dollars—would be payable if, and only if, *Answered Prayers* were delivered in 1981, which was two decades after he had originally promised the book.

"You're so good with figures," sniffed Truman.

I was surprised when afterwards, in a cab back to his apartment, Truman told me he thought the show had gone well.

"I got everyone to laugh," he said.

"Well, yes . . ." I said.

"I did that little stumble on purpose—did you see?"

It had looked like an accident to me.

"I'm glad you didn't hurt yourself," I said.

"Oh, no. It was just to get the crowd on my side. That host is a smart cookie. I'm glad we talked about the book."

I was probably one of the few people who still had regular contact at that point with both Lee and Truman. Lee was good enough not to bad-mouth Truman to me, because she knew that he and I had something of a friendship. In fact, I rarely heard her bad-mouth Truman to anyone. In the years to come, she even spoke of him quite generously and acknowledged the loss of a great friend. Truman would sometimes, when we'd meet for coffee, ask me how Lee was, but usually avoided saying anything too insulting about her, since he knew that would put me in an awkward position. Yet his tongue remained sharp when it came to the likes of Lila North, who reappeared in print around that time, in a free, weekly city newspaper that featured coverage of politics and culture, but rarely of high society, let alone gossip. Lila's new column was entitled "Do Repeat This" and featured a remarkably unflattering portrait of the author at the top, in grainy black-and-white, consistent with the paper's low production standards.

"Never doubt that there is always a lower rung for you to sink to, in the New York media world," said Truman, when I told him that she had mentioned him in her new column. Following an overheated item on Sunny von Bülow's coma, Lila told of Truman's misstep during his TV interview and went on to describe his "making the scene" at Studio 54—being photographed by paparazzi and smiling endlessly, but unable to work anymore because "one of our greatest writers spends his days and nights in a drug-and-alcohol-induced haze."

"On the brink of the 1980s," wrote Lila, "too much is clearly not enough for Truman Capote."

"No news there," snapped Truman. "How about this for a headline about her new column: 'Untalented Hack Now Enjoys a Dramatically Smaller Audience'?"

Random House did manage to publish a collection of the short fiction and nonfiction works that Truman had been working on, *Music for Chameleons.* It was the first book of new material to be published by him in fourteen years, and it quickly became a best seller, which was almost unprecedented for a collection. Most of the proceeds went toward settling old debts.

Random House had sent a galley to Lee for a blurb, and she declined, though she did read the book and told me that parts of it were "marvelous—just as good as the old Truman."

This was a time, at the beginning of the 1980s, when Truman was going in and out of hospitals and sanitariums often, trying to break the habits of drinking and drug-taking. He seemed to be declining with accelerating speed. In March, it was widely reported that Truman was found comatose in his UN Plaza apartment and had to be carried out by ambulance workers. It was also reported, with some glee, that an offer Truman made to write a column for *Vanity Fair* had been rejected. Yet opposite the pack of media people intent on taking advantage of Truman's weakened state, there were many doing what they could to help him. I was part of the latter, as was Jack, and there certainly were others. And I think that Lee, despite the insults and injuries she'd received from Truman, was basically on his side, hoping for the best—whatever that meant.

Since our Boxing Day visit, I had stayed in touch with Jack, who was living at the Sagaponack house. In our role as caretakers, he and I spoke frequently. After years of acquiescing reluctantly in Truman's de facto withdrawal from their relationship, in response to bad affair after bad affair, Jack was falling back into the role of dutiful husband. He once mused on the dilemma of biography writers who had words like *husband*, *partner*, *companion*, and *lover* to contend with.

"Will I be called any of those things in Truman's obituary, do you think?" he said.

"'Dear friend'?" I suggested.

"They don't use words like 'dear.' Christ. I pity whoever at the *Times* is freshening up Truman's obit right now. What will he call the other ones—Newton Arvin, George Davis, John O'Shea . . . ?"

Truman had been thinking not only about death, but what would be left of him after death, Jack told me.

"Not just his literary legacy," said Jack. "With or without *Answered Prayers*, that will endure. He's thinking a lot about his stuff—the objects he's acquired so passionately over the years: antiques, books, mementos . . . the meaning of all *that*, good and bad, seems to obsess him. Did you know he got rid of that portrait of him by Fosburgh?"

"Why?"

"I don't know. But the pillow that that detective's wife made for him? He was weeping the other night over what might happen to that, after his death. 'It has no value, it has no value,' he moaned, 'but it means everything.' He said he thought people might be reading *In Cold Blood* in a hundred years, but this bloody dog portrait I once bought for him, which he loves—'What's going to happen to that?' "

Jack looked distressed.

"He made me promise to give you a book of essays from his library that he treasures," he said.

"What book—can you say?"

"A Cuban author. I forget the name."

"Poor soul. That's very sweet of him."

"And Lee! For some reason he's obsessed about all of the things she's accumulated."

"Whatever for?"

"Lord knows. Maybe it's because he's been so envious, over the years, of all the very fine things that Lee and his other swans could acquire. His own collection is a shadow of that."

"I see, yeah."

"One day he was wailing about Lee's things. 'Will there be an auction someday?' he said. 'Will people pile into Sotheby's or Christie's for the preview, friends and strangers and gossip columnists alike, and walk through galleries of her furniture and artwork and beautiful *objets d'art,* gawking while carrying tiny plastic glasses of wine?' "

"Dark. And funny."

"Right? That's Truman. 'Will some queen pay five thousand dollars for her Chanel sunglasses? Or will the reality of us pass into oblivion like the Hindenburg?' "

In one of our calls, Jack read me part of a letter that Truman sent him.

"Somewhere there must be a place for me, a place that will take my problem away, and leave me free to do as I please again—and as I deserve. After all, who have I hurt? Nobody. Not really. Or anyway, not much."

"That makes me sad," I said.

"He doesn't understand," said Jack. "His mind's been affected. I know exactly when it began. It was when they executed Perry Smith."

I asked if there were anything else I could do to help Truman, besides listen to him ramble.

"No one can help," said Jack. "I decided long ago that I wasn't going to be Truman's governess."

Nevertheless, I thought that work could somehow provide Truman with some patches of painlessness, so I brought up our screenplay once again. At one meeting, I gave him a copy of its present form, and at the next, I tried to discuss it with him, using a second copy I'd brought with me, since I knew he probably wouldn't have it. But our conversation quickly devolved into the general ramblings du jour. I doubt he'd even looked at the manuscript, which disappointed me, because I thought I'd made some real improvements in it, according to principles we'd been discussing over the years. Every now and then, I'd get his permission to read him a bit, just so it was in his ears, and he approved, which thrilled me.

"You're a natural," said Truman. "You just get it. You might just be able to write yourself out of servitude one day."

Emboldened by his encouragement, I took it upon myself to bring the screenplay up with Lee, when after I'd returned from a meeting with Truman, she asked me how he was.

"The same," I said.

"Poor soul," she said.

"He asked me to show you something."

"What?"

"A piece of writing. The screenplay he's been writing for you."

"Oh, I know all about that. I passed. Why is he going through you?"

"He's shy about bothering you directly."

"Shy?! That man doesn't have a shy bone in his body."

But Lee was at least partly intrigued.

"What's it about?" she asked. "He never really said. Only that I would be playing the mother, not the girl, and I was supposed to be happy about that."

"It's about a girl seeking independence from her mother. The setting is the Cuban Revolution."

"Oh, lord, Marlene. That's not for me."

"There's a great part in it for you—he says."

"He should show it to someone else. Really. It shouldn't go to waste. Did you help him with local color, as it were?"

I supposed she meant Cuba. "I did make a suggestion or two," I said.

Going through the screenplay again, I was pleased to remember how much of it was my own work. I was proud of it: the once-glamorous matriarch; the property deeded by the King of Spain; the matriarch's brother, the last *marqués*, who'd died without an heir; the matriarch's daughter, a big fan of Elvis Presley and James Dean, rebelling against a crushing family tradition and maybe a little glad to be freed of it when the revolution strikes; the other daughter, the "good" one, dead from pneumonia; the matriarch's choice between leaving Cuba with nothing or remaining on her land, with her grand memories; the empty mansion; the nationalized sugar mills; the overgrown mausoleum of the last *marqués*.

It was I who invented almost every detail of the story. After the first few scenes, over which Truman and I explored ideas about plot, character, tone, and the rest, I found myself able to keep going alone. Even though we'd more or less discontinued working on it together, I was still concerned about byline and credit issues. When I brought this up timidly at one of our coffee meetings, he simply said that he had "to think about it more"—though I doubt he was thinking about it at all. There were much more important matters on his mind, of course, yet I wanted clarity. I guess it was then that I was first coming to see myself as a real writer and wondering if maybe I could do something with this screenplay—show it to someone, maybe a producer.

He was found comatose a second time, and again, he was carried out of his apartment, after which he went off to Los Angeles to be nursed by Joanne Carson. But the fire inside him was not so easy to extinguish. When Truman found out that Lila North had called me asking for details of his collapse, he called Lila from Joanne's home in Bel Air and, to use his phrase, "ripped her a new one."

"Look, you," he said, "keep the kid out of it. Understand? Or

I'll have you not just demoted but defenestrated. That girl has no idea what to do with someone as nasty and pointless as you. While I, on the other hand, could use a nice, gothic story about a dried-up old scribbler who dyes her own hair in the kitchen sink and stalks her twenty-five-year-old trainer. Ha ha—I hear things, Lila. How'd you like to read them in *Esquire*? I don't just write about rich and famous people, you know. I also write about poor, pathetic ones."

By then, Truman was spending a lot of time in L.A., with Joanne. She'd already designated one of the rooms in her house as Truman's writing room. As far as I could tell from my calls with him, Joanne was trying to help him avoid the worst excesses of Hollywood party life, and it's true that under her influence, he probably drank less and snorted less cocaine. He chuckled when he told me he'd heard that Andy Warhol told Joanne that Truman should have "better" boyfriends.

"'Can't you find someone younger for him?' said Truman, mimicking Warhol's soft drone. "Isn't that funny? I don't think Andy ever liked Jack. Or maybe they never met—I can't remember now. Anyway, he told Joanne that I'm always getting involved with these old guys. 'They're not very attractive and they're so dull.' I guess maybe that's true. Andy said that it was quote-unquote scary how mad I am at Lee. But I ask you, Serenity, how could I ever be scary to anyone? He said that if Lee was drinking before the feud, she was probably a lush by now."

I knew what Truman was going to ask next.

"So . . . is she? Drinking? More than usual?"

Truman knew me well enough to know that I wouldn't answer. I paraphrased a statement of Jack's: "I'm not her governess."

She *was* drinking, a bit more at that point. At least, I saw her at home several times in a state I'd call drunk. One time I had to get her to bed after finding her sleeping upright on the sofa in the library, next to a half-full bottle of Balvenie, a crystal tumbler lying empty on its side on the carpet. She was also seen visibly tipsy at a reception at the Metropolitan Opera and falling out of a cab one night when out with Peter Tufo. Actually, when Lila called me, it was primarily to ask about Lee's drinking and only incidentally about Truman. But I didn't tell Truman that, since his being upstaged by Lee in the eyes of even so small a creature as Lila North might have set him off. Lila wanted to know if I could confirm that Lee was attending AA meetings, and I said I couldn't confirm it, though of course, I knew she was attending them. Once she even took Jackie to a meeting.

But Lee was the very picture of a high-functioning alcoholic. Dauntlessly, she kept up her busy social schedule. In fact, the next phase of her life as a career girl resulted from her attendance at a glittering, star-studded Armani fashion show that was mounted at the skating rink at Rockefeller Center. As a loyal Armani customer, she was given VIP treatment—being greeted by Armani and seated next to Hamilton South, then one of the public relations directors of the Armani company. Lee wore one of the first outfits by Armani that she'd ever bought, a black-and-white–striped top with prominent shoulders and a long black skirt.

There was more light at that event than anywhere in the solar system but the sun, Lee said. Architectural lighting on the buildings themselves was cranked up to full intensity. Those massive structures gleamed. Special theatrical lighting was brought in and mounted on four towers, to focus on the runway area—specially built over the skating rink—on the golden statue of Prometheus, and on the audience itself, which included movie and pop music stars, socialites, and fashion leaders.

"Marvelous event," Lee told South. "It's very exciting the way you've used the entire space."

With the RCA building towering seventy stories above them, glowing in the light like the edge of a glacier, and with music from a hundred speakers echoing among limestone façades, Rockefeller Center felt more alive, she said, than it did even at Christmas.

"Teamwork," said South. "And a vast amount of money, of course."

Lee laughed. "That helps," she said.

"We'd love to work with someone like you, creating events for us," said South. "Would you ever consider such a thing? You'd get lots of great clothes out of it . . ."

At that point, Lee was still calling herself an interior designer, though her business wasn't really building, and she was finding the acquisition of new clients endlessly exhausting.

"Hmm. Did you have something specific in mind?" said Lee.

"Like an ambassador for the brand," said South. "That's exactly the term that Giorgio used this morning, for you. Imagine creating events to take place at the Louvre, at the Metropolitan Museum . . ."

"I like the sound of that."

Within months, Lee had joined the Armani team as Director of Special Events.

Chapter 24

Lee and Her Memories

Andy Warhol's party for Michael Jackson occupied all three floors of Danceteria, the superhot music and dance venue housed in an old, twelve-story building on West 21st Street. Celebrating the new issue of *Interview* magazine, which featured Jackson on the cover, and previewing the musician's about-to-drop album, *Thriller*, the party was exactly the kind of trendy A-list event that both Truman and Lee would be invited to, and Andy invited both. He discovered that Lee was in Sardinia at the time, but welcomed Truman after the author had been shown up to the more exclusive of the party's two VIP lounges.

Truman had once referred to Andy as "a sphinx with no secret," but according to Lee, who'd known the artist for a long time, Andy did have a secret, and it was not the doublethink of celebrating and denigrating American mass culture beguilingly at the same time. Everyone knew Andy could do that. The secret was his talent for creating new epicenters of cool on the edge of previously celebrated centers of cool, in both aesthetic and social spheres.

"Why did the doorman call this 'the secret VIP room'?" asked Truman, seated on a long, low banquette with Andy and members of the artist's coterie.

"There's another one, on the other floor," said Andy.

"Everybody will try to get into that one and maybe get in," said Andy's assistant, a pretty young man in dramatic eye makeup, seated next to him. "And if they do and think that's the real VIP room, that's where they belong."

"This one is quieter," said Andy. "You can talk. And I can tape."

Andy was, in fact, recording his conversation with Truman on a small, hand-held tape recorder, while the assistant prepared a duplicate recorder by inserting a fresh cassette tape.

Lighting in the room was low, and included colorful projections on the wall and ceiling. The DJ on that floor was playing tracks from the new album, which felt considerably darker and more urgent than Jackson's previous work, mixed in with a stream of 1982's other edgier pop music, while the DJ on the floor below was floating a brighter vibe, including older Jackson 5 tracks from *ABC*, *The Third Album*, *Destiny*, and the like. On the floor below that was a mix of strictly bouncy, danceable hits from the current and previous season, by the Talking Heads, the Clash, Grandmaster Flash and the Furious Five, Grace Jones, Kraftwerk, Siouxsie and the Banshees, and others.

"I heard you lost a million dollars," said Andy, dryly.

"That's the way it goes," said Truman. It was widely reported that he'd missed the Random House deadline and forfeited his seven-figure payday.

"That's cool. You have to really be something to lose a million dollars."

"Are you recording?"

"Uh-huh."

"There'll be plenty more where that came from," said Truman.

"What's the delay?" said Andy.

"Writing is hard. It takes time."

"You should have people do it for you."

"Ha. Like at the Factory?"

"Yeah."

"I did have a girl I was working with. She was good."

"You should call her Truman Capote, too."

"Hi, Andy," said a blond girl in a man's suit jacket, black

leggings, black boots, and a bowler hat. She was wearing one earring dripping with several crosses.

"Wow, you look great," said Andy, from the banquette.

The girl leaned in to share a kiss with the artist.

"Madonna, you know Truman Capote," said Andy.

"Hi," said Madonna, brightly.

"A pleasure," said Truman.

"Andy, we're doing our thing here next month," said Madonna, not joining them on the banquette but swaying a bit to the music. "A song called 'Everybody.' It's pretty good. You should come."

"Great," said Andy, sticking the recorder in front of Madonna's face. "What do you think of the new album?"

"Michael's new album? It's great," said Madonna. "He's a genius."

"She's fantastic," said Andy, after Madonna went off.

"I don't know her stuff," said Truman.

"Tell him about the new series," said the assistant.

"Oh, yeah," said Andy, "you should do it."

"We're working with a writer who's also a medium," said the assistant.

"A psychic medium?" said Truman.

"She talks to the dead."

"Okay."

"We're signing people up so if they die, we can contact them and do an interview," said Andy.

"Isn't that fabulous?" said the assistant.

"I might die anytime now," said Truman, with a hoot.

"You never know," said Andy. "So we're signing up people now who we think will be great."

"Sure, sign me up," said Truman.

"Her name is Blanca, and she's supposed to be here tonight," said the assistant. "If I see her, I'll introduce you two, so when the time comes, you'll have already spoken. That will be so much smoother."

"We'll wait until you're dead," said Andy. "Fully dead."

"I imagine that's the only way it works," said Truman.

It made sense to Truman to be talking about death in a club.

He told me about the party a day or so later. He said that a club's lighting and shadows and soundscape gave the space a sense of infinite possibilities, whereas the actual Danceteria building, constructed in 1907 for merchants in the garment trade, was no more than fifty feet wide and undoubtedly looked drearily finite in normal lighting. What dance club design and décor was meant to bring an old stone-and-steel edifice was what Mahler brought to symphonic form: amplitude defined by as much of life as we could know and as much of death as we could imagine. This is why Truman had started going to clubs so much, he told me—for the oceanic vista of existence.

"Michael, come and say hi to Truman," said Andy abruptly, having spotted the guest of honor coming their way with a small group in tow.

"Hi, Andy," said Jackson, in his soft voice. "Hi, Mr. Capote."

"Wonderful party," said Truman. "I hope the album's a smash."

"Thank you," said Michael.

Andy scooted over a bit, as did his assistant, so Jackson could take a seat between the artist and the writer. Andy had the tape recorder in his lap, in front of all of them.

"Great party," said Jackson.

"The album is fabulous," said Andy, raising a finger, to signal that a track from *Thriller*—"Beat It"—was playing at that moment.

"Thanks," said Jackson. Then he turned to Truman. "I'm a big fan, by the way."

"That's nice of you to say," said Truman.

"I read *In Cold Blood* twice," said Jackson. "You have no idea how much it affected me and gave me ideas about my own work."

"Really?"

"I loved that it was real and that you were in it."

"Thank you. That was very difficult to pull off."

"But you did it. And that's exactly what I was thinking about when I went in the direction I did with *Thriller*."

"Did you?"

"Everybody thinks American life is so harmless."

"And that's not so, is it?"

"Not at all. I tried to think about the whole album as a kind of crime story."

"That's interesting . . ."

The assistant tapped Andy on the shoulder.

"Are we getting this?" said the assistant.

Andy nodded.

"Yeah, it's fantastic," said the artist.

From the deck of the lavish villa that Giorgio Armani rented in Sardinia, on top of a limestone cliff near Capo Caccia, the vista was of the voluptuously beautiful Bay of Alghero, whose waves crashed thunderously and continuously on the beach nearly a thousand feet below. On the beach itself, situated on a private cove that was part of the villa's property, was a mock-rustic hut for bathers and a nearby dock whose land-end led to the base of a funicular that ascended steeply to the house. Though the villa was of futuristic-modern-with-touches-of-age-old-local-vernacular stone design, the funicular's carriage was fashioned in a fanciful classical Venetian manner, with Baroque scrolls and scallops in pink and gold. Lee was part of a house party that included, besides Armani and his boyfriend and business partner Sergio Andreotti, the designer's muse Sofi and her brooding but sometimes amusing boyfriend Andrej; the designer's sister Rosanna and a fellow actor, Clive, who was starring with her in an upcoming project—Lee later described the actor as "mathematically handsome and quite aware of the fact"; and an aging, overtanned French novelist named Marcel, who referred often to the intellectual talk show he hosted on French TV.

After a week of marketing meetings in Milan, during which Lee proposed a variety of promotional events and potential clients, the party had sailed from Genoa to the Sardinian town of Alghero, where Armani moored his yacht. Though there was a road around the bay and up to the villa, the party had been ferried over from the marina to the dock by a local fisherman, then ascended to the villa, which consisted of the main house and two *villinas*. Compared with other house parties Lee had told me about, this one was relatively unstructured, with no planned excursions to points of local interest, few compulsory group meals, and "refreshingly few occasions"—her phrase—in which people were expected to come together. There were as many staff as there were guests, working silently in the background to keep everybody comfortable. Lee said she liked this arrangement, rather than a more structured house party, where there was the constant need to be "on" for other people. The library of the main house was well-stocked with books pertaining to the Mediterranean, and Lee used the time to dive into *The Count of Monte Cristo*—because obviously, she said, it was the thing to read when staying in a fortress at the top of a cliff, overlooking the sea.

And she also found herself thinking about Truman, remembering the fun times they'd had together—those bouncy parties in New York hosted by the likes of Babe Paley and Diana Vreeland; those yummy afternoons at the Colony and, yes, at La Côte Basque; that splendid afternoon with the Duke and Duchess of Windsor, and then getting caught in a political demonstration; hitchhiking in Dallas while traveling with the Rolling Stones . . . With no one else in her life but Truman—not Newton Cope, not Peter Tufo, not even with Peter Beard—Lee had been swept along in such a whirlwind of thrilling adventures. But she couldn't abide Truman's slide from unpredictable to erratic. She liked Michael Jackson and had wanted to attend the launch party hosted by Warhol; that was the kind of party that one flew into town for, if one were away. But the idea of encountering Truman there, and the radical uncertainty of his possible behavior, made her attendance untenable.

"These things happen," said Janet Auchincloss, one day when Lee was lamenting the loss of the friendship. "Relationships can fade as people change."

"It's over, Mother, and I accept that," said Lee. "But I do find myself missing him so much."

"You can't choose friends based on who is the most exciting."

"Can't I?"

"Solid is what to look for."

"Do you mean predictable?"

"Isn't predictable good? Do you want surprises—unpleasant ones?"

"No. But I keep thinking about him."

"Of course you do. That's natural—the way we sometimes think about people who have died. We mourn them."

Under the Sardinian sun, Lee spent hour after hour on the breezy terrace reading Dumas, in a pair of Chanel sunglasses and a headscarf, as fearsome waves crashed onto the rocky beach below.

"How are you finding the book?" asked Marcel, who appeared on the terrace one morning while Lee was reading.

"Good morning," said Lee. "Oh, it's thrilling."

"Ha, yes. A comedy of manners, with lost love and vengeance."

"Comedy? I suppose that's one way of looking at it."

"Is it a particular favorite of yours?"

"I've actually never read it. I've been meaning to tackle it since I was a girl."

"Where are you now in the story?"

"Dantès is in prison. The abbé is speaking about knowledge and wisdom."

Marcel smiled generically.

"The real Isola di Montecristo is two or three hundred kilometers that way—did you know that?" he said, pointing out over the rocks in back of them.

Lee was eager to keep reading but didn't want to appear rude. "Are you working on something?" she said.

"This is a break for me," said Marcel. "The show is *relâche*." He glanced down from the terrace toward the cove, his open white shirt and white Speedo looking impossibly white, possibly brand new. "Do you care for a swim? The waves on the other side of the cliff are actually quite gentle."

Lee feared that Marcel might have been invited especially for her benefit, but she was not interested in him at all. "Too pompous," she told me later.

"Maybe tomorrow," she said.

Marcel nodded and went off.

Lee even copied out into her notebook the passage from Dumas she referred to, which spoke to her, she said, of the life she had shared with Truman:

> "You must teach me a small part of what you know," said Dantès, "if only to prevent your growing weary of me. I can well believe that so learned a person as yourself would prefer absolute solitude to being tormented with the company of one as ignorant and uninformed as myself. If you will only agree to my request, I promise you never to mention another word about escaping."
>
> The abbé smiled.
>
> "Alas, my boy," said he, "human knowledge is confined within very narrow limits; and when I have taught you mathematics, physics, history, and the three or four modern languages with which I am acquainted, you will know as much as I do myself. Now, it will scarcely require two years for me to communicate to you the stock of learning I possess."
>
> "Two years!" exclaimed Dantès, "do you really believe I can acquire all these things in so short a time?"
>
> "Not their application, certainly, but their principles you may; to learn is not to know; there are the learners and the learned. Memory makes the one, philosophy the other."
>
> "But cannot one learn philosophy?"
>
> "Philosophy cannot be taught; it is the application of the sciences to truth; it is like the golden cloud in which the Messiah went up into heaven."
>
> "Well, then," said Dantès, "what shall you teach me first? I am in a hurry to begin. I want to learn . . ."

What was the tone of this passage in the original French, wondered Lee. She was sure she had a French edition somewhere in one of her libraries. Did the original make the adventure of learning sound quite so dramatic? Why do people condescend to melodrama, anyway? Why do they insist on putting books into such restrictive categories?

The last year of Truman's life was characterized by malaise that was made deeper by the July '83 death of Mona Williams—otherwise known as Mona von Bismarck, a Kentucky girl born Mona Travis Strader in 1897, who grew up to be a socialite included on the original list of the World's Best Dressed women, captured in a portrait by Salvador Dalí, photographed by Cecil Beaton, and said to be the model for "Kate McCloud" in Truman's *Answered Prayers*. Truman had lost Tennessee a few months before that; Billy Baldwin, that same year; Cecil in '80; and of course, Babe in '78. And among those still living were many who were not speaking to Truman: Marella Agnelli, Pamela Harriman, and Slim Keith, in addition to Lee. A fall in Sagaponack had put him in the hospital in Southampton, then New York Hospital; an episode in Verbier had led to a hospital in Geneva; a broken nose from a fistfight in Miami had landed him in Larkin Hospital there; and there had been further more-or-less voluntary stays in psychiatric hospitals and rehabilitation centers.

Yet Truman was anything but gloomy the last time I saw him, in the fall of '83—and of course, I never dreamed it would be the last time. Funny how those things work. Had I known that that lunch would be the last—with him and Judy at Neil's Coffee Shop, the little place where Judy and I would sometimes meet on the Upper East Side—I would have paid attention to every word, made it a point to show every bit of affection and gratitude I felt for him. When I retired in 2005 and said goodbye to Lee, I thought *that* might well be the last time I would ever see her or New York, and was prepared for it. And then, of course, I saw her again when she asked me to come back for the Sofia Coppola shoot; and that experience was nice and didn't feel particularly freighted. That time when I left, we said we might get together in Palm Beach "sometime," and yet that *was* the last time I ever saw Lee.

Now that I think of it, Neil's Coffee Shop was as good a place as any for an unsuspected farewell scene. On the corner of Lexington and East 70th, Neil's was the quintessential New York coffee shop-with-a-soul—not a diner or part of a chain, but a small and family-owned kitchen that since the 1940s has been one of the definitive Upper East Side havens for catch-up lunches, hangover breakfasts, and post-doctor-visit cups of tea with friends and neighbors. Whereas the feel of La Côte Basque was "pretend fishing village" vernacular, and that of Le Pavillon was "pretend French haute bourgeois" vernacular, the feel of Nick's was "hometown neighborhood vernacular," which on New York's Upper East Side meant a wide mix of classes, from patrician to upper-middle to solid-working, where the performance of class and financial status seemed unnecessary for the hour or so that you were there. The décor was determined strictly by what was practical and serviceable. On the counter, under glass, near the entry, was a display of pastries and desserts; on the walls were framed pictures of celebrity customers; on the tables, with paper place mats, were pieces of stamped, stainless-steel silverware, and heavy, well-worn, white ironstone china plates rimmed with burgundy bands. The booths, once one settled in, with bags tucked away, felt like comfy mini-forts.

It was more than just a catch-up for me and Truman, this time. Pointedly, I told Judy yes, when she asked to come along and finally meet my great friend, the distinguished author. I figured, why not? I sensed my story with Truman was coming to an end, and though I had no particular plan in mind for when they met, neither did I have any fear about their meeting and discovering awkwardly that their stories about me didn't quite match up. I had no fear, because I knew that each of them accepted me unreservedly, even if in slightly different ways. And the odd thing is that those stories didn't come up at all during lunch. The hour and a half we spent together, in our little booth, over salads and burgers, was all about culture and literature and the adventures of the mind—the imagination.

"It's essential you have a big idea about yourself," said Truman.

"You mean confidence?" said Judy.

"No, I don't mean confidence, or a well-developed set of preferences, or anything to do with accumulated wealth and possessions. I mean you need to feel the space you take up in life—you need to take up all the space of your own life, all the time."

I knew what he meant: not narcissism or self-importance, but a kind of spiritual effulgence.

"You need to shine," he said.

"I see," said Judy, not quite seeing.

"And the point is that there is always more shining to do," he said. "You don't just discover or achieve this quality and then you're set, turned on. Rather, it's a function, a constant responsibility."

Truman spoke brilliantly. He was animated and seemed clear. He asked remarkably little about Judy and nothing about me, which was uncharacteristic, given the endless curiosity I had known him capable of; and then, it was over. After a while, he slumped, as if someone had pulled the plug. He said it was time for his nap.

And outside the coffee shop, Judy and I shared ladies-who-lunch-like air kisses with him, then watched him as he set off down Lexington at a slow, stooped sort of pace, a diminutive, receding silhouette of rumpled safari jacket and khaki pants, topped with a Panama hat.

"That was wonderful," said Judy. "Thanks for inviting me."

"He's quite a guy," I said.

"Now I see why you've changed so much, over these, what, two-and-a-half decades."

"Have I? I'm just trying to learn a bit about writing."

"I think he's giving you so much more than that. It's like there's something about his personality—his philosophy of life—that's rubbing off on you."

"Hmm. Is that what it is? Maybe."

It was an unusually warm fall day—hazy, the way New York can get on an Indian summer afternoon, when you can almost believe that the earth's axis might have started to tilt in a new way and we might finally be able to have summer all year around.

* * *

Trust Lila, though, to dwell on the negative. And trust the lowest-common-denominator world of New York newspaper publishing to give it prominence. That fall, Lila wrote what I found to be a nasty item that mentioned both Lee and Truman, though the end of their friendship was hardly news anymore.

"Do Repeat This" —by Lila North

. . . I ran into so many amazing New Yorkers at last week's Big Apple Polisher Awards luncheon, hosted by Hizzoner Ed Koch at the newly renovated Grand Hyatt Hotel on 42nd Street (which some of you will remember as the venerable Hotel Commodore). There was Chrysler chief Lee Iacocca, who is heading the commission to rehabilitate Ellis Island. There was artist Willem de Kooning, whose massive bronze sculpture, *Seated Woman*, has been on view outside the Seagram Building. There was talented young Black filmmaker Spike Lee, whose *Joe's Bed-Stuy Barbershop: We Cut Heads* is the first student film to be screened in the prestigious New Directors/New Films series. Bravo! • Then there were those who were honored, it seemed, more for their fame (or notoriety!) than for any accomplishments, notably Lee Radziwill and her ex-best-friend Truman Capote. Both of them—seated separately and far apart, on different sides of the Grand Hyatt's Manhattan Ballroom—looked ready to bolt for a *real* lunch at any of the city's finer restaurants. • After the luncheon, I got to speak with that amazing young real estate tycoon in back of the new Grand Hyatt—Donald Trump. Only 37 years old, he bought The Commodore, stripped the building down to its steel frame, and revitalized it with a gleaming skin of reflective glass. The hotel's new bar, cantilevered daringly out over the 42nd Street sidewalk, is the city's hottest rendezvous. I asked The Donald—that's what his people call him!—about his new hotel venture. "I think we've done a marvelous job, I know we have," he said. "It's better than anything else in New York—the Mayor just told me so. We have great things in store for this city and maybe even for the country . . ."

The gratuitous mention of Lee and Truman made me seethe. I was infuriated by the meanness of it, and by the obviously shabby strategy of substituting meanness for wit. I called her to complain, but got nowhere.

"This is why no one reads you," I said.

"I've got more on both of them, much worse, and I'll print it if I have to," said Lila.

"Why would you ever 'have to'?"

"Some weeks are slower than others."

"Your insinuations and half-truths hurt people, Lila. I know you've heard this before."

"Let me worry about my craft."

"I want you to stop writing about them."

"Or what?"

"I might have something for you, about myself."

"What could you have, after all this time?"

I hesitated, then spoke calmly. "I have a personal secret that I could trade for your silence about them."

That made Lila laugh, which I found insulting. She replied dismissively. "What could you possibly have?"

"Oh, it might be interesting," I said—and I proceeded to tell her everything.

It only took a minute or two to give Lila the basic gist of my personal story—the *real* story, and the subsequent lies. And she didn't have to think too much before she replied, with a chuckle.

"Oh, that's rich, dear—very rich," she said, "but I doubt anyone would be interested. It's certainly not what I'd call a bargaining chip. But feel free to call me back the next time your employer or her sister invites one of their beaux to spend the night."

Not long after that, I was surprised to hear from Jack that Truman had gone back to California to stay with his friend Joanne Carson.

"It's to be indefinite," said Jack.

"Indefinite?"

"He feels comfortable with her. I think there's a motherliness there."

"Will she continue to bring him around to parties to show him off?"

"I think he's beyond that now."

Truman hadn't said a word about this to me. Lila reported that he had done the equivalent of what many older Hollywood actresses do when they retire definitively from public view: they "close the door" to all but family and trusted intimates, as a way of preserving the integrity of their public image. Lila openly dismissed the hope of anyone ever seeing *Answered Prayers* completed, despite what she reported as "the author's loony-sounding claim that the completed manuscript is locked away safely in a vault and will be discovered there when the time is right."

Then, on an August morning, Lee came into the kitchen to tell me that she'd heard that Truman had died the night before, at Joanne Carson's home.

"It was natural causes," said Lee. "Joanne called me."

We looked at each other for a moment, and then, almost in unison, said "I'm sorry" quietly to each other.

"The news will be made public within hours," said Lee.

"I know it's a cliché to say so, but at least he's at peace now," I said.

"Poor soul. Are you okay? Do you want me to call anyone?"

"There's no one to call."

"You and Jack are in touch."

"Yes."

"Please feel free to take a few days for yourself. Joanne says that there'll be some kind of ceremony out there, so please feel free to fly out. I'll manage here. Just let me know when."

"Thank you, Lee."

We embraced lightly, for a moment.

"The last time I saw him, it was at that silly award ceremony," she said. "I wanted to say hello. It wouldn't have hurt me to say hello."

Joanne Carson made it a point to call me directly, later that ay. She told me the news and said how welcome I would be at e funeral ceremony.

"He spoke of you so often," she said. "He called you his se. Isn't that sweet?"

flew out the next day. While waiting for a cab at the Los Angeles airport, I overheard a young man making fun of the famous author who had just died. He pronounced the last name *ka-POAT.*

"Just a drunk little fag," said the guy, to his friend.

I had to butt in. "Excuse me," I said, "but you are talking about one of the great literary artists of our time. And even if he did have some personal problems, he deserves some respect for his work."

Chastised, the guy was silenced.

The funeral took place at the Westwood Memorial Park in Los Angeles. Attendees included John Dunne, Joan Didion, Christopher Isherwood, and Don Bachardy. The music ranged from Mozart to Billie Holiday's "Good Morning Heartache." The niche in Westwood's memorial wall where Truman's ashes would be interred was near those of child star Heather O'Rourke and singer Mel Tormé.

Afterwards, at a private reception, Joanne Carson gave me the draft of a letter of apology that she said Truman had been writing to Lee. She said she thought I might be the best one to know if the letter should actually be delivered to Lee or not. Even in its unfinished state, it might mean something to her. I said I'd take a look at it.

She was kind enough to spare a moment to reminisce with me about "our mutual friend." I confessed that I had learned a great deal about art and life from him, chief of which was the wisdom to accept fate and make it work on the page. That's when Joanne brought up the screenplay and said she'd be glad to look it over.

"I'm always looking for good material," she said.

I let the idea drop.

She also said that she had read three, new, "very long" chapters from *Answered Prayers*, entitled "And Audrey Wilder Sang," "Yachts and Things," and "Father Flanagan's All-Night N****r Queen Kosher Café." She said that on the morning before Truman's death, he had handed her the key to a safe deposit box that he claimed contained the completed novel, stating that "the chapters will be found when they want to be found." When she pressed Truman for a precise location, he rattled on about a number of familiar places that he had considered, including Manhattan, Palm Springs, Los Angeles, and New Orleans. She said he grinned enigmatically when she asked for further details. I smiled to recall this teasingly fabulistic side of Truman's imagination. I had seen it often, and I had seen through it often. I doubted there was more to *Answered Prayers* than what the public had already seen.

After the funeral, I realized that I was in an odd place with the screenplay. Should I claim it as my own and try to get it seen and maybe even produced? Should I more properly credit it to Truman and try to offer it to the world posthumously? How would the idea of a previously unknown collaboration sit with the literary critic and historian and biographer types? I needed some time to think about this—and indeed, I spent the years since 1984 considering it, before mentioning it to my class and agreeing to let one of my students, a woman of almost my age, tell her Oscar-winning film producer daughter about it.

"*God is happiest when he's playing with us*," I remember thinking, on the plane up to New York. It's something Truman used to tell me as a way of explaining his woes. "*Life just feels like that. We are his favorite toys. A talented writer with a naughty streak hits it big, then unravels. A girl from Cuba whose life was undone by revolution finds an unexpected role for herself in New York. A member of one aristocracy winds up working for the wife of a member of another aristocracy. Who can explain these things? We are lucky if we can even* tell *another human being these things.*"

CHAPTER 25

THE LADY OF THE WHITE ROSE

Truman left the bulk of his estate to Jack, but stipulated that some funds be used to establish an annual prize for literary criticism—a prize that is now administered by the Iowa Writer's Workshop at the University of Iowa. Most of Truman's ashes also went to Jack, which Jack said he planned to spread over the wetlands near their place in Sagaponack, where Truman liked to walk; though Joanne kept some of the ashes for herself, and apparently displayed them in an urn at her Bel Air home before enshrining them in the niche at Westwood Memorial. Gore Vidal kept silent in the media about Truman's death, but was reported to have told Random House's Jason Epstein, in a phone call, that he thought it "a brilliant career move."

I decided to recommend that Joanne not show Lee the apology that Truman had been working on. Lee's wound from the breakup had healed somewhat, and I saw no use in possibly reopening it. As far as I could tell, from the sad and relatively calm way I saw Lee talk to friends about Truman's death, she had achieved some peace with the memory of her former dear friend. She told me, in fact, that she forgave him—and then laughed quietly about how easy it was to forgive the dead. After Truman's death, she and I enjoyed a closer rapport than ever before, probably because of the sheer bulk of experience that we shared; that is, the time we spent together—almost fifteen years; and maybe also because of the new self-assurance I saw in her, as she watched great friends like Truman and Cecil, and ex-husbands and former boyfriends, pass into history. I think she was proud of her place among such people, and knew that they, like herself and the rest of the swans—people with more access and experience and taste than anyone else in the world—could not simply be re-manufactured. They were products not only of their circumstances but of their times, and those times had passed into eclipse. By the end of that decade, for example, the whole lunch scene was morphing into something else, largely due to the extinction of ladies who lunch. The new great women were too accomplished and too purposeful to sail through the world as mere swans—women like Diane Sawyer, Geraldine Ferraro, Anna Wintour, and Oprah Winfrey, who were following in the footsteps of Kay Graham, the first woman CEO of a Fortune 500 company, and many others. They ate lunch where men ate lunch. Today, of that antediluvian crop of the midday watering holes, only La Grenouille and Le Cirque survive, the latter in its third and slightly anachronistic incarnation on East 58th Street.

When Lee started seeing Richard Meier, the glamour of his cultural stardom quickly gave way to her feeling that the architect was stuffy and "old-mannish," and she found herself wondering, *What would Truman think of Richard—not so much as an architect, but as a suitable companion for me?* Indeed, she told me she often thought about what her dear old friend would think of all the fabulous events that kept right on happening after his death—the glittering parties, the exclusive openings, the society weddings and funerals, the exciting new books and plays . . . She and I both, it seemed, were fighting the feeling that the richness of the world and its energy in continuing to spin forward was at odds with the loss of an apparently necessary engine of global cohesion like Truman Capote.

By then, Lee had sold the duplex at 969 Fifth Avenue, which had been photographed by *Architectural Digest* in 1976, and was living in a beautiful penthouse on Park Avenue, which the same magazine photographed in 1982. It was there, on Park, on top of the dresser in a staff bedroom that was considerably nicer than the one I'd had on Fifth, where I displayed the Victorian rosewood box that Lee had given me on the twentieth anniversary of my hire. In the box, I kept what I thought of as Truman's legacy to me: all the little notes he had sent me, many of which began with the salutation "Serene Highness," a witty endearment I treasure as much as I do the content of the notes—mostly short quotes taken from books that Truman thought I should read. I also kept the screenplay that Truman and I had been working on in the box. I tucked it in there shortly after his death, in my grief, and didn't work on it again until I retired, thinking of it less as a potential asset than as a memento of a marvelous time of my life that was now gone forever.

Yet I did ask myself, when I pulled the screenplay out again, years later, *was* it an asset? Was it any good? Good enough to find a public—that is, to *sell*? I knew the story was melodramatic, even corny, but was it "the right kind of corny," which Truman often said was a quality that he admired in great Southern writing? Our story was not set in Yoknapatawpha County, of course, but in Havana, and it had morphed, in my effort to give it a bit of historical sweep, from a family drama into a tale of revolution, as in the Pasternak novel we'd once discussed, *Doctor Zhivago*. In our final months of working together, Truman had been too out of it to offer any thoughts on the *enlargements* I was making with the Russian tale in mind. If only I could have gotten him to concentrate long enough to give me a thumbs-up or thumbs-down on even the first few pages.

```
THE LADY OF THE WHITE ROSE [WORKING TITLE]
Written by Truman Capote
With Marlene Béatrice Marguerite Marie-
Thérèse Barón y Gavito
```

Y para el cruel que me arranca
el corazón con que vivo,
cardo ni ortiga cultivo;
cultivo la rosa blanca.

And for the cruel person
Who would want to break my heart,
I cultivate neither thistles nor thorns,
I cultivate a white rose.

—From "Cultivo una rosa blanca," by José Martí (1853–1895)

EXT. RESIDENTIAL GARDEN—TWILIGHT

A private, formal garden attached to a massive Colonial-era mansion in the Vedado neighborhood of Havana, Cuba. It is November, 1958. Numerous royal palm trees tower over ceiba and sea grape trees. Well-tended flowerbeds frame a white marble monument in the form of a grieving angel at the foot of an obelisk; the monument's bronze plaque is inscribed "Gonzalo Barón y Gavito, Marqués de Leganés (1921–1952) Requiescat In Pace." MARGARITA, a dark-haired woman in her early thirties, dressed in a simple black cocktail dress, stands opposite the monument, praying. Only a few of the season's last white mariposas are in bloom.

MARGARITA (praying quietly)

Ave Maria, gratia plena, Dominus tecum. Benedicta tu in mulieribus, et benedictus fructus ventris tui, Iesus. Sancta Maria, Mater Dei, ora pro nobis peccatoribus, nunc, et in hora mortis nostrae. Amen.

She makes the sign of the cross, then notices a servant has entered, followed by FIDEL, a handsome man in his early thirties, with a strong nose, luxuriant black beard, and wavy black hair.

SERVANT

Excuse me, Doña Margarita, he is here.

MARGARITA

Thank you, Rosa. Leave us now.

The SERVANT departs. For a moment, FIDEL simply beholds the lady and her garden.

FIDEL

It is my dream, you know, to make a national garden, with specimens from all the regions of the island.

MARGARITA

I'm sure it will be beautiful.

FIDEL approaches respectfully and, with a slight bow, kisses her extended hand.

FIDEL

Tesoro.

MARGARITA

You have a beard now.

FIDEL

Yes.

MARGARITA

It suits you.

FIDEL

I hope so.

MARGARITA

Though I do miss the handsome boy I knew at university.

FIDEL

He no longer exists.

MARGARITA

They said you were in the mountains.

FIDEL

I was. We enter the city tomorrow. Some of us are already here. I wanted . . . to say goodbye.

MARGARITA

The Americans have abandoned the president?

FIDEL

Ambassador Smith has already left the island.

MARGARITA

What happens now?

FIDEL

The future, *querida*. But this garden will remain as it is, if you like.

MARGARITA

My husband will leave. He is making arrangements even now.

FIDEL

And you?

MARGARITA

My place is here, on this land, with my ancestors. If it is allowed.

FIDEL

I will see to it.

MARGARITA

(looking at him closely)

But you are saying goodbye. Even though we are both to be in Havana.

FIDEL

"Y para el cruel que me arranca el corazón con que vivo . . ." It is my destiny.

MARGARITA

I will pray for you, then.

FIDEL

Pray for all of us, Rita. Pray for the people. We will need it.

Thirty-five years later, I was on the balcony of my condo in West Palm Beach when Carole Radziwill called with the news. I like to have coffee out there in the morning, before the day gets too hot.

"It was quiet and peaceful," said Carole.

"We can be thankful for that," I said.

"The funeral will be private, of course, but we'd love it if you were there, if you can come."

"Of course. I'd like to be there. Thank you."

"She loved you so much, Marlene. She could always depend on you."

My balcony looks over a little garden, which is adjacent to the swimming pool. I could see one of my neighbors doing his customary morning laps.

I should make it a point to use the pool more, I thought.

After Carole's call, I spent a brief moment in quiet tears, remembering the employer who was always unfailingly gracious and generous with me; then, I phoned the creative writing program office and rescheduled my classes. I regretted having to postpone the next session of the "Autobiography as Seeing" class I was teaching, since one of my students had just had a piercing breakthrough: "It's not so much about my mother. It's about *me*!" she had exclaimed, and I was so thrilled to hear it. Since starting the classes, shortly after I arrived in West Palm Beach, in 2005, I had found it deeply satisfying to be able to help other adults and seniors develop their writing abilities—not only as recreation or professional training, but as a form of psychotherapy.

Remembering Truman's description of the grandeur of arriving in New York by train at Penn Station, I was tempted to go north by Amtrak. It was Vincent, a frequent traveler by train in Europe, who convinced me to fly instead.

"American trains are barely in the twentieth century," he said. "Even the private rooms are laughable, unless you're in your twenties and find travel hardships thrilling. Do yourself a favor, Mar, and fly. Maybe someday we will do a proper train trip in Europe or Asia."

He drove me to the airport, parked the car, carried my bag to baggage check, and saw me to the entry of the security checkpoint in the terminal's departure concourse.

"Is it okay to wish you a good time?" he said.

"Wish me a good stay," I said. "That's different."

"You writers!"

"You're sweet to see me off."

"It's my pleasure. Just trying to be helpful."

"I'll text you tonight or tomorrow."

"Tonight *or* tomorrow?"

"Yes. I can't promise exactly when."

Vincent has been very patient with me, and I am not quite sure why he continues to be interested, though I have become happier with the fact that he is.

His hair is silver-white and kept quite short, and his body is thick though athletic. He swims every day and tries to play tennis twice or three times a week. I hadn't been on a tennis court at all until a few weeks ago, when he got me to agree to a few volleys and then started explaining some of the fundamentals of the game. I think he thinks I can be molded into a tennis partner—and I do have to admit that tennis is fun.

"I don't want you to be late," he said. Morning light was pouring in through the skylights, making the terminal's blue-gray structural steel elements look silver. Beyond a screen of glass panels etched with images of palm trees, in front of which were pots of real palm trees, was security. Echoing from somewhere above, inside the terminal, was the happy sound of birds chirping.

"Would a little kiss be alright?" he said.

We'd hardly touched at all until then—maybe just a tap on the arm or two, for emphasis, during discussion.

"Sure," I said, feeling glad he'd asked but slightly silly, especially at my age, to suddenly be enacting a public parting scene.

As I stood as I was, upright, he took half a step closer, slipped his arm halfway around my waist, and leaned in for an affectionate peck on the cheek. The moment was both warm and chaste at the same time.

What would Truman think of Vincent? I wondered as I was waiting to have my briefcase X-rayed. *What would Lee think?* Having to face this question alone, after decades of having the benefit of both their thinking, still felt like a new thing for me. And I didn't feel guilty at all about my habit of consulting my memories of these two strong figures when trying to make sense of the world right now. One of Lee's favorite quotes, from Buñuel, was "Without memory, there is no life." This is the same thing I tell my class now.

An unaccompanied elderly woman, well-dressed but obviously confused, was sitting in my "comfort-plus" seat when I boarded, and it took a very patient cabin attendant to get the woman into her own seat, which happened to be in first class.

Does derangement always creep in, eventually? On the smooth, two-and-a-half-hour flight to JFK, I found myself recalling all the events I witnessed after Truman's death, while still working for Lee, and then the events I heard about or saw in the media after I retired and moved to Florida: Lee's marriage to film director and choreographer Herb Ross, in 1988; the death of Lee's mother, in 1989; the death, in 1991, of Lila North and the end of her frothy column items (like "Pop Star Sells Pop"—Madonna makes an ad for Pepsi-Cola; "The Queen of Mean Dethroned"—Leona Helmsley goes on trial for tax evasion; "The Hunk, Esquire"—JFK Jr. passes the bar on his third attempt; "Love at Eighth Sight"—Liz Taylor weds Larry Fortensky at Michael Jackson's Neverland Ranch); Jack Dunphy's death in 1992; Anthony Radziwill's marriage to journalist Carole DiFalco in 1994; poor Jackie's death of cancer in the same year (and Lee's surprise at having been left no money by her sister); Lee's attempts throughout the '90s to write a memoir and her occasional regrets about not pursuing acting (especially when Faye Dunaway movies like *Chinatown*, or *Mommie Dearest*, or *Barfly* appeared on television); Anthony's untimely death in 1999; Lee's divorce from Herb in 2001, and his death that same year, as well as the sale of the East Hampton house; Lee's move from the Park Avenue penthouse to the lovely place on Lexington where she lived for the rest of her life, which I visited in 2013 to help with the Coppola shoot; the publication of Lee's *Happy Times*, a slim picture book with reminiscences of her and Jackie's early years . . .

And I found myself recalling, too, so many of the other moments during which I would ask myself, "What would Truman think about Palm Beach today?" "What would he think about the décor of my condo?" "What would he think of my hair color, carob brown, by Matrix Biolage Plant-Based Hair Color?" "What would he think about the short stories I've written, and the fact that some of the principles and practices that I teach have come directly from him?" "What would he think of Carole Radziwill's memoir, *What Remains: A Memoir of Fate,*

Friendship, and Love, or her first novel, *The Widow's Guide to Sex and Dating*?" "What would he think of Lee's picture book, *Lee by Lee Radziwill . . .* ?"

Keenly I wanted Truman's take on the death of Judy's longtime husband, John, and her conclusion that John had never acted on his gay feelings, and how sad that was, while at the same time magnificent, to have stayed devoted as a husband and father. Keenly I wanted Truman's take on Lila's death and the fact that she never revealed the personal secret I shared with her. Keenly I wished I could ask Truman—whom I trusted more than Lee did, because there was far less at stake for me—if a secret like mine, which I had come to think of as a magnificently florid lie, were of so little value. Was it a decent thing that Lila did for an innocent woman in her early forties, who could have gotten into trouble with her employer over this lie? Or was Lila just too dense to understand the value of such a crazy-good story and write it up somewhere?

Chapter 26

Society with a Small "S"

The comment Vincent Scully made after the demolition of Penn Station, which Truman quoted to me once in the '60s—"One entered the city like a god. One scuttles in now like a rat"—could well be paraphrased to describe one's arrival today via JFK: "We were once received in great halls, like honored voyagers. Now we're marched past racks of merchandise, like common shoppers." I must have walked through half a mile of mall before I found baggage claim and emerged to meet Judy.

When I arrived at the hotel, it would have been perfectly easy for me to text Vincent immediately. I wasn't so busy that I couldn't put thumbs to phone. I just didn't know what to say. Announcing the fact of my safe arrival should require a context, as far as I was concerned, and "daily witness," an important aspect of serious relationships, was not yet established between Vincent and me, though I could feel him trying to inch closer to it. As it happened, hours later, after I'd strolled over to Madison and bought a little thank-you gift for Judy, enjoyed a bath, and had a relaxed, early dinner in the hotel restaurant, I did text Vincent; and he was smart enough to understand that only one exchange was necessary.

The flight was smooth and I got here safely. Thanks again for the lift.

Glad to hear it—thx. You're very welcome. See you soon . . .

Then, in a little while, there was a knock on my door, and a bellboy delivered a box of large, waxy tulips in the most beautiful shade of apricot, from one of Lee's favorite florists, Renny on Park Avenue—or rather, Renny and Reed, as it is now known. They were from Vincent. SEE YOU ON WEDNESDAY? read the card.

It was good to see that Vincent was also smart enough to know where to get his flowers. Renny was one of the few floral and event designers that Lee would trust to create weekly and occasion-specific arrangements of exuberant beauty. Lots of the most important hostesses on Fifth and Park used him, and for them, he acquired the rarest and freshest flowers that came into the city on any given day. My dozen tulips might well be one-third of the only shipment of those particular high-quality tulips available to anyone in the city that day. Mrs. Newhouse might well have gotten the other two-thirds for a pink-and-orange-themed luncheon she was giving that week, using a set of Sevres or Ceralene that Renny and his chief designers would know well, because part of their job was to be familiar with the pots, vases, cachepots, centerpieces, décor preferences, and entertainment styles of all their clients. I made a mental note to stop by Renny's on the day after the funeral and pick up a little bouquet of whatever looked great, to bring to dinner that night for Judy.

The tulips triggered a memory of Lee and Truman's life together—involving one of those moments that I heard about from each of their points of view. Lee used to drop into Renny's shop all the time, to inspect newly arrived bunches of flowers that were gathered in pails and glass cylinders and such, displayed in color-coordinated groupings in the front of the shop, on a gaggle of antique tables. The place was an indoor garden, framed by pink walls featuring painted trelliswork in pink, green, and white, and an array of fanciful antique mirrors. One morning, when Lee was there ordering arrangements for an upcoming dinner, she mentioned to Renny that afterward, she was off to lunch with her dear friend Truman Capote.

"Does Mr. Capote wear a boutonnière?" asked the florist.

"I guess he does," said Lee.

Lee thought that Renny might offer her a little lagniappe to bring Truman—maybe a tiny white rose. But Renny did one better. Selecting three tiny white blooms of different types—perfect specimens, but with stems too short to be used in any arrangement; refuse, really, in a shop like Renny's—he added a sprig of green and tightly wrapped the stems together with a bit of wire and a few twists of green floral tape, curling the end into a sweet little tail. It took only a minute to do. The result was a miniature buttonhole firework that was miles better than the common carnation of a Hollywood stock department-store manager.

With a leaf of tissue paper, Renny packed the thing deftly into a tiny cardboard box.

"Maybe he'd like this, with our compliments?" said Renny, presenting the box to Lee. "Or I can send it over to the restaurant right now, if you prefer."

"It's a tussie-mussie!" exclaimed Truman, when he opened the box in his and Lee's booth at La Caravelle.

Over time, Renny made Lee several of these boutonnières to give to Truman, and Truman would gratefully tuck them into a buttonhole or carry them like a nosegay, or once even hook the stem around the bow of his glasses, for a clownishly tropical effect. Lee once referred to them as "nothings," but Truman insisted adamantly that, far from nothings, they were miniature compositions by a great designer, comparable in some ways to the floral compositions seen in seventeenth- and eighteenth-century Dutch Master paintings, equivalent in effect to an ethereal string quartet by Fauré. I have always hoped that Truman hung onto these creations. Maybe he let them dry and put them away carefully somewhere? Maybe Jack found them after Truman's death and bequeathed them to some young writer or scholar or aesthete, who now displays them lovingly in a tabletop vitrine in his Brooklyn Heights bedroom? Though, of course, no one wears boutonnières anymore, let alone ones that could be compared to chamber music.

And it made sense to me, after the funeral, to dine that evening at the restaurant where Truman and I first met on our own, the Four Seasons. The place is much changed, as I have described. The restaurant's restoration was meant to be true to the original, yet there was no Picasso, no quenelle-like crab cakes, no customers in the Grill Room, where I chose to be seated that evening, whom I recognized as noteworthy. Yet in a way, the place was better than before. Halfway through dinner, I realized how foolish I was to think of myself as someone who knew the restaurant well because I'd first stepped through its doors fifty years before. Neither I nor it was, or could be, the same as before. If I needed any evidence of this, it was simply the ease of my dining alone in public as a woman. Back when Truman brought me to the Four Seasons, in the early '60s, it was not usual for a woman to dine alone in a nice restaurant, especially at dinner. If anything kept me from wistful nostalgia that night, it was that thought.

"God is happiest when he's playing with us."

When Truman said this to me, it was a joke, off the cuff. It was one day when we were working together, toward the end of his life, in a moment of lucidity. Maybe it's because Lee's funeral was still on my mind, but as I sat there in the Grill Room, I thought how funny it was that they were dead and I was still alive for another few years. Wasn't that attitude better than nostalgia and regret? Surviving even a much beloved friend is, itself, a kind of divine jest. When Truman originally made that crack about God entertaining himself, he went on to say that God also means for us to be entertained by being played with.

"And that, dead or alive," said Truman, "is why I will always be in the audience, in Row F, center."

My meeting the following day was in Tribeca, in a renovated, six-story building at Hudson and North Moore that had once been a grain warehouse. "Oats & Barley Productions" read a directory in the lobby. The same name, along with an image of a Midwestern grain field, was etched on a glass wall on the fifth floor, at the entrance to the producer's suite of offices.

A receptionist greeted me warmly by name and showed me into a conference room, where a platter of fruit and pastries had been laid out, and asked me what I might like to drink. I said coffee, and before she returned, the producer entered, a woman in her forties with very short hair, wearing a pair of stylish heels with her jeans and T-shirt.

"I'm Avis," she said. "It's so nice to meet you. Please sit."

"Thank you for taking the time, Avis," I said.

"My mother says you're a genius."

"Well—that's nice of her to say. She's a very fine writer herself."

The room was luxurious but simple in design, with horizontally aligned panels of a grainy, reddish wood and a black steel conference table and chairs. Two Oscar statuettes and an Emmy stood on a credenza, over which hung an abstract painting in broad slashes of black and white.

"You're in town for a funeral, I understand."

"Yes. Lee Radziwill. She was my employer."

"I was sorry to hear about her death."

"She was a wonderful woman."

"So I gather. Those women gave themselves a lot of freedom. I admire that."

It wasn't clear to me whom Avis meant by "those women." That generation?

We chatted a bit about life in West Palm Beach—Avis visited her mother there often—then we began speaking in a very relaxed manner about *The Lady of the White Rose*: how I met Truman, how he and I came to work together, how it had been his original intention to write something for Lee to act in that would be better than *Laura* was.

"So it was *for* Lee, but things, you know, evolved," I said. "Lee was no longer interested in acting."

"We tried to get hold of her *Laura* remake, just for fun, but so far no dice," said Avis.

"They have it at the Paley Center."

"Ah."

"I believe you need an appointment to screen it."

Avis had a pleasantly direct and focused way of speaking. I knew how busy someone like that must be. I'd done my research and knew that her production company had several projects in the works, yet I didn't feel this meeting had been given to me simply out of courtesy.

"And you attended the ball?" she said.

"Truman's ball? I sure did. What an experience."

"Celebrity central!"

"Oh, yes."

"Now that was history."

"Indeed."

"Lee dancing with Jerome Robbins."

"Right."

"Ballet is a particular love of mine. I'm on the board of New York City Ballet. Robbins was one of the greats."

"Yes, I know."

After some chat about the Miami Ballet, the conversation finally came back around to the screenplay and to the characters of the matriarch and her rebel daughter. Avis said that she liked the story but thought that it would be difficult for her to do anything with it, "in today's climate."

"How so?" I said.

"Just the usual politics."

"Politics?"

"Mother says you're of Irish extraction."

"Well . . . yes."

"Okay . . ."

In fact, I had indeed told my students the bare bones of my own story—the true version. I owed them that as the teacher of a class called "Autobiography As Seeing," and also because there was no audience left for the elaborate fiction I had constructed. Now that Lee and Truman were gone, let alone dear Mrs. Hawkins, there was no one else who cared about it; and the reason I had invented it in the first place, self-protection, was now too far in the past to feel as compelling as it once did.

I was born in Woodside, Queens, and raised there until I was a teenager, in a Black Irish family. It's true that I was illegitimate. My mother was a housekeeper in a fancy New York hotel and was raped by one of the guests. My mother's husband, a drunk and a lay-about whom I never called Father, always resented me, as did my older half-brother, crazy and violent, who came close to raping me several times, until the day I bit him and then bolted. They all argued all the time, often viciously and sometimes about me. Even my mother resented me, yet some mistaken understanding of Christian charity impelled her to keep me around for years, treating me worse and worse as time went on, as I slipped in and out of school. For sheer sanity, I buried myself in fiction and poetry, made up characters, and sought out high-falutin' ideas—until after my half-brother's assault I finally ran away and found myself in the East Village. This was the late '50s, and the East Village was a wonderful place to get lost from the world—filled with poor but by no means desperate people, a live-and-let-live mix of old immigrants and young folks lumped into the "beatnik" category. I was taken in by an informally constituted family of characters whose chief lives were on the street—not exactly criminal, but making a basic living by activities that were probably not recorded as part of the city's official economy: selling marijuana, though not the hard stuff; performing at cafés—music, dance, poetry; running errands and deliveries for local shopkeepers. The family was held together by a poor but elegant woman with an Eastern European accent who seemed both dutiful and resentful about the maternal responsibilities she assumed, like paying the rent and providing food and shelter. And she was not afraid of expelling any family member who behaved badly or otherwise betrayed her values—no theft or drugs or prostitution, please!

The woman's name was Zorka, and she claimed to be descended from the royal family of Montenegro, which we all assumed was a fairy tale, though she did have some lovely pieces of antique clothing and jewelry, and some wonderful black-and-white photographs of ladies in long dresses and enormous hats, and gentlemen in uniforms with medals. None of us was able or willing or allowed to be very close to Zorka, except as a flock of beneficiaries. It was an odd arrangement, I admit, but it worked for me at the time. After a while, I sent a note to my mother, telling her where I was but begging her not to share the information with her husband or my half-brother—yet none of them ever came or reached out to me, which was fine with me. What could any of them possibly have offered, anyway? No one reached out to me at all until one day I came home to find Zorka sitting in the kitchen with a soft-spoken elderly gentleman in a black suit, describing a kind of school and employment agency that he worked for. Zorka said I should pay attention.

"We offer free training—and free room and board—and then we place the students in a suitable household, in a staff position," said the man. "It's purely voluntary. They are free to leave whenever they want."

"Do you hear that, Mary?" said Zorka. "You can go to school and then get a job."

Me? I had been happy enough earning a few dollars and free soup at a nearby café, by reading the little poems I was making up, but was beginning to think about where all that might lead, so I was interested.

"But why do you come here, specifically?" I said. "Why us?"

"We are a private foundation, and someone in the neighborhood told us about Madame Zorka."

"Who?"

The man paused for a second.

"Well," he said, "it was the owner of the newsstand, Mr. Rzewski, I believe."

Really?

"What do you think, Mary?" said Zorka.

My life was a Dickens novel, anyway, I thought.

"I guess," I said.

The three of us spoke a bit more, and within a month, I had been taken into a small institution in Riverdale called Merton Hall, where five of us, all girls, were tutored in the basic subjects, and taught manners and such. For two years, I was happy with that, coming down to Manhattan every now and then, but rarely returning to the East Village and certainly never going out to Woodside. It was then that I started making up the story of my Cuban background, for the amusement of my four classmates, based on a novel that we were reading in English class.

The other students both believed my story and knew better—which was a valuable thing to learn, in itself. When I was placed with Mrs. Hawkins and asked to entertain her, I was gratified to see how delighted she was with my story. She praised these so-called tales from my family's past and encouraged me to keep developing them. She said I had a wonderful way of telling them—a talent I had honed, I suppose, in those cafés.

And when Lee came along, I asked Mrs. Hawkins's daughter—Judy's mother, Sandy—to say a bare minimum about my background, the Cuban version, when recommending me, as I wanted a fresh start, and she kindly complied. Yet without realizing quite how deep a lie I was getting myself into, I wound up expanding the story a bit for Lee and much more than that for Truman, because it felt much nicer than my "real" story; and using it seemed a good way for me to settle into a safe, quiet social niche far, far away from my awful childhood. I wanted nothing more than to be invisible, to keep my head down, and to do a good job for Lee.

For a while, I felt terrible about lying to Truman especially, yet I also rather cherished the fact that the great author believed the story I created and the details I kept adding to it.

"The thing is, Mary," said Avis, "the marketplace right now just doesn't allow an Irish-American woman to write a main character who is so strongly grounded in another culture."

"*Half* Irish-American," I said, partly in jest. "We don't know the other half."

Avis snorted lightly.

"Be that as it may," she said. "Besides, in the last thirty years, everybody's horse sense about narrative has sped up about a thousand percent. We know where this thing with Fidel is going."

"So—the fact that it's well-written . . ."

"That's all great," said Avis. "Absolutely. But here's the thing—why I was so eager to see you. You've had this great experience, these great friendships—this fascinating life. You've been witness to history and collaborated with one of America's most important writers of the twentieth century. Now *that's* a movie. I'll be frank with you: that's how this could work. Poor white girl, smart, wounded—maybe kind of a grifter, but with a heart of gold, just trying to survive—finds her way among the rich and famous during New York's go-go sixties and seventies, and outlives them all to tell the tale. Who wouldn't want to hear about *that*?"

"Huh," I said, never having looked at things that way before.

"Can't you see yourself as the hero of your own story?"

I took a moment to consider this question.

"A grifter?" I finally said.

"Okay, well, let's say a pragmatist."

What would Truman do? I could almost hear his voice: "Flirt with it."

I also had Vincent to think about. I had never told him much of the Cuba story, but neither had I gone very deeply into my real background, either. If I were to explore the idea of writing about my real life, it would be a big commitment that might affect both him and my teaching. And it was odd to be thinking about someone else in my life who wasn't Lee or Truman. As Judy often said, I'd always put them first.

"I think you're becoming special to me," Vincent had said, when we were driving to the airport. "And I don't quite know why."

"That's nice to hear," I said. "And I don't quite know why, either. I've never been that special to anyone."

"You must've been special to your parents."

I smirked. "Least of all them," I said. "You know I don't come from a normal family. What happiness I have, I've made up."

"That's a great gift."

My life is a Dickens novel, anyway . . .

Was it possible, finally, to put myself first? True, it would require using a mental muscle that I'd really never used—to own my own, real-and-true story—yet why should that be so difficult for someone now resigned to accepting the physiological realities of advanced age? The experience of attending Lee's funeral and vividly recollecting my years with her and Truman had somehow put my whole life into a different perspective—

like a movie you understand only after watching it a second time. I knew the facts of my youth and the nature of my lies, yet suddenly, unexpectedly, with a push from Avis, I'd arrived somewhere new in my own story.

I took a sip of my coffee, which the receptionist had served to both me and Avis in antique china cups with saucers.

"I have to admit that the idea intrigues me more than so-so," I said.

"I thought it might," said Avis. "Mom says you're a guru with autobiography. Audiences will want to know about what you saw during your life with these two people—what you came to see. Why didn't Lee ever find the love she deserved? Why couldn't Truman come through on *Answered Prayers*? What the hell ever happened to ladies who lunch? You were there, so tell us. But we also want to know, how did all of that affect *you*?"

"You're giving me a lot to think about, Avis."

"Glad to hear it. I was hoping you'd say that. And speaking of lunch, I'm glad you didn't touch the croissants. How does a bite sound to you? Are you free? There's a Korean place around the corner that's quite good . . ."

I arrived at Judy's apartment at seven, as requested. The building is among the grandest on Park Avenue, and the lobby was almost exactly as I remembered it: a sturdy reception desk at the end of a broad hall; comfortable seating areas on either side, each with theatrical torchères in a Renaissance Revival style. The dark wood paneling was the same. Only now, hanging on the walls, instead of seascapes, were two large, framed mirrors.

"Yes, ma'am," said the receptionist, when I gave him my name. "Elevator on your left."

He discreetly indicated the direction with an elegant hand gesture.

"Yes," I said, resisting the temptation to add the information, immaterial to him, that the apartment I was headed for had been my home for two years. In fact, all of the homes of my adult life until I retired—here, with Judy's family, and at three different addresses, with Lee—were within ten or fifteen blocks of each other. For all the much-vaunted high standard of living of the neighborhood, life on Manhattan's Upper East Side was awfully parochial.

The elevator, fitted with a little bench upholstered in green velvet, was still attended by a uniformed staff person.

"Mar, wonderful, wonderful!" said Judy when she opened the door. "Come in."

From the vestibule, I stepped into the apartment's spacious central gallery. Odd that I never knew that the room had been decorated by Dorothy Draper. It had been kept basically in its original shape since the 1930s, when it was commissioned by Mrs. Hawkins. The scheme was a dramatic but sensuous study in simple contrasts. It was basically an empty white room defined by a symmetrical arrangement of neoclassical pilasters and two great arched windows, with a stark black-and-white floor and doorways to the library, living room, and dining room framed in neoclassical moldings and pediments. At the center was an octagonal table surrounded by four, footed ottomans, upholstered in a vivid floral-patterned fabric; on top of the table was an oversized white china cachepot crowded with white lilies, on a carved wooden stand.

"I brought these," I said, handing her the parcel of pale orange ranunculus I'd picked up for her at Renny's, while Judy's husband took my coat.

"Oh, splendid," she said. "Aren't they beautiful? Mar, this is Burt."

"Very glad to meet you, Burt," I said.

"Very glad to meet you, Mar," he said. "I've heard a lot about you."

"Also this," I said, handing Burt a small parcel. "Judy said you both cook."

He opened it gracefully.

"Wonderful," said Burt. It was a jar of single-origin peppercorns from Kerala, India. "Perfect!"

He was an intelligent-looking man with thinning gray hair.

Immediately I sensed a nicely cooperative energy between him and Judy, who were, after all, practically newlyweds.

"The place looks terrific," I said.

"We're making little changes here and there," said Judy.

"She doesn't want me to feel like I've moved into a museum," said Burt.

The house was filled with the delicious smell of something roasting. We settled in the living room, and Burt poured drinks. That room, too, had been decorated long ago, but by someone other than Draper—in a style that was intended to look undecorated and was by now, after updates and replacements, markedly comfortable and, except for some of the modernist artwork, aesthetically undemanding. Counterpointing the ample, overstuffed sofas and chairs, and unadventurous window treatments, were paintings that had been collected by Judy and her deceased husband John: works by Twombly, Rivers, Johns, and others, in addition to the Warhol "Marilyn."

"This was your home, too, I understand," said Burt.

"I lived here, in back, for almost two years," I said. "I was on staff—a companion for Judy's grandmother."

"I hope you'll come and stay as often as you like."

"Thanks. This is my first visit to New York in five years—no, six."

We talked about New York, Palm Beach, and my meeting with Avis, though I decided not to give too much detail about the screenplay project. Burt told us about a start-up he had invested in; then discussion turned to the Philharmonic, then to a few of the more innocently amusing stories I could share about Truman. Since retiring, I had more or less stuck with the practice of not divulging too many personal details about Lee or Truman's lives—out of respect for their memories, I guess.

"We'll sit down shortly," said Judy. "Burt has a quick call, so why don't I show you what we've done with the rest of the house?"

As at the Four Seasons, everything was the same but different.

"Granny's paintings weren't all that good," said Judy, in the library, "so little by little, John and I sold them, as we collected new things."

"Did Burt have a lot of his own things?"

"He said they reminded him of Ellen—his wife. So he let his kids take what they wanted and sold the rest."

I somehow hadn't remembered the house as being so palatial. "So much room," I said.

"It is," said Judy. "But his kids come and stay, James and Kelly come and stay . . . we like being a hotel."

"Nice."

Slowly, we walked through the bedroom hallway, peeking into rooms.

"So this man you're seeing . . ."

"Vincent. And I wouldn't say I'm *seeing* him."

"Pre-seeing."

"Exactly."

"What's he do?"

"Financial services—with two partners."

"A widower, you said."

"His wife was an obstetrician. There's a son living in London."

"And how lucky that you just happened to wind up as his teacher."

"I suppose."

"That's great."

"He really does have some talent. And the thing is, I take teaching very seriously. They have every right to expect that, all my students—adults who are really committed to getting something out of it. I just feel . . . funny pursuing the social scenario with one of them."

"Oh, Mar, you're not children. You can be a responsible teacher and still have a drink with the guy. Or more."

"I know."

"So it sounds like it could be something."

"It could be. We'll see. I do find the situation . . . interesting."

"That's good. Very good."

"Good that I'm perhaps beginning to feel something for

the first time that other people feel when they're teenagers? I guess so."

"You know what they say: Better late than never. Sorry—I shouldn't be using clichés with the writer."

"Or ever."

"Or ever, right."

"I'm going to have a drink with him this week, I guess, and see how that goes."

"I mean, that's really all you can ever do, isn't it? Take a step and see where it leads. And there's no optimum time to do that. Except maybe right now."

"As someone said, it's either at once or at last."

The staff wing comprised two small bedrooms, a sitting area, and a bathroom. Judy's current cook-housekeeper, Mrs. Pasmore, occupied the larger of the staff rooms, and the one that I used to occupy was now an office.

"Burt uses this for business," said Judy. "It's quiet, and he says working in the library makes him feel like J.P. Morgan or something."

"It's nice," I said.

Instead of the bed, dresser, and drapery I remember, there was a built-in desk and bookcases in blond wood, all sleekly modern, with two computers and a flat-screen TV. On the window was a white, semi-sheer, pull-up shade.

So little had happened to me in that room that I felt no sadness in seeing it so changed. I chiefly remember it as the place where I could continue the reading habit I had picked up at Merton Hall. In that room, I went through much of Dickens and Eliot and Trollope, and lots of other books that Judy's mother, Sandy, encouraged me to borrow from their library.

"You guys seem very happy," I said.

"Yes," said Judy. "It's very different, but *happy* is definitely the word I'd use."

I wondered if Judy now, with a second husband, had been inclined to reevaluate any aspects of the marriage to her first husband, John—especially in terms of romance, in view of John's homosexual impulses. It was the writer in me, I suppose, that wanted to know this; but I didn't feel the time was right to ask such a question.

Truman had met John once and understood him instantly. Judy, John, and I ran into him at the theater one night in 1976. It was intermission of the show *Oh! Calcutta!* and Truman was drunk. I didn't know the man he was with—someone distinguished, probably someone from Random House. We all spoke briefly in the crush at the back of the theater, about the legal issues involved in depicting sex onstage; then, the lights summoned us back to our seats. As Judy and John went ahead, Truman pulled me back.

"They're very nice," he whispered. It was gin that I smelled on his breath. "Not that it matters, but he's as gay as a three-dollar bill."

"Truman, I . . ."

"Don't tell her."

"Of course not. I don't even know if . . ."

"They can be very happy anyway."

People were squeezing to get past us; some were staring at Truman.

"We'd better get back to our seats," I said.

"Everything is an arrangement," said Truman. "Remember that."

Through a door in the servants' hall was the pantry and kitchen.

"I just want to check on dessert," said Judy. "Come with me and meet Mrs. Pasmore."

The kitchen had been radically renovated and was now all white, and it made me chuckle to think that with its massive island and capacious eat-in area and expansive prep areas, the kitchen was as large as my entire apartment in West Palm Beach.

Mrs. Pasmore, the cook, greeted us warmly and walked us over to the second of two refrigerators. Inside was the dessert she'd made, sitting regally on a pedestal cake plate: a dome-shaped thing covered in gold-tipped meringue peaks.

"Beautiful, Mrs. Pasmore," said Judy.

"Thank you," said the cook.

"Is that what I think it is?" I said.

"Venetian Rum Cake," said Judy, triumphantly.

"'Delight'!" I said. "Venetian Rum *Delight*! How marvelous!"

"Of course—*Delight*," said Judy.

"Thank you! That's so sweet of you. We used to have this in the Village, when we were girls, Mrs. Pasmore."

"Yes, I heard," said the cook. "It was fun to make!"

"The little fruity bits were glacéed right here in this very kitchen," said Judy. "Mrs. Pasmore is a magician."

Across the kitchen, an assistant was at the oven, basting a chicken that looked almost done. I had a momentary flashback to the kitchen's previous incarnation, where I was so nicely treated from the very first day I began working at the house, when I was given tea and a piece of apple pie.

"You know," I said to Judy, "it dawned on me yesterday at the funeral that I was very lucky that you were the closest thing to family that I've had in my life."

"Oh, Mar . . ." said Judy, obviously touched.

"I know we only lived here together for a couple of years, but you never treated me like a servant—none of you did. It was more like having a sister."

"Yes, I feel that."

"Your grandmother was like a grandmother to me, too—not just someone I was working for. And you and I have stayed in touch all these years. It means so much to me, even if we haven't been particularly close during those times. The thing has endured, which is its own kind of intensity, the kind that sisters sometimes have."

"You're right."

"As you know, I certainly haven't kept up with my mother, let alone with her horrible husband and son. For all I know, those people are long dead. So you were a bit like family, and I'm so grateful."

"I feel the same way," said Judy. "In fact, can we sit for just a second?"

We installed ourselves at the far end of the kitchen table.

"Well, then, this thing I wanted to tell you the other day . . ." continued Judy. "I might as well tell you now, since it's kind of in line with all this."

"What do you mean?" I said. I had forgotten that moment in the car, on the drive in from the airport, when she said she had something to tell me, and I demurred.

"Well—my grandmother. You were more important to her than you probably realize. In fact . . ."

"I had a great deal of affection for her. I would say that I loved her, and I hope she liked me . . ."

"Oh, she did—she did, Mar. She loved you. She said so often. And, uh, in a way, she's partly responsible for how your life went after you left home—you know, as a teenager . . ."

It was more Judy's manner of saying those words—almost portentously—than the words themselves that caught my attention.

"How so?" I said.

"Okay. The thing is, your biological father was her husband."

I had to re-parse the sentence in my brain after hearing it.

"What?"

"My grandfather was attending an event at the hotel where your mother worked. He was the one who attacked her. Granny found out about it afterwards."

"Your grandfather . . . what?"

Judy put her hand on my wrist and told me the whole story.

Merton Hall had been founded in the 1890s by Mrs. Hawkins's mother and some of her society lady friends, as a home and school for what were then called wayward girls. In turn, Mrs. Hawkins became a patron of the home, and when she learned about the rape, during a conversation she overheard one day between her husband and a private detective who came to the house, she hired her own detective to determine who the victim was and offer some financial help. The victim refused, but when Mrs. Hawkins learned the victim was pregnant, she vowed to help the child. It wasn't hard for a woman as rich and clever as Mrs. Hawkins to keep tabs on the girl and the child through the 1940s and '50s; she took it as her cue to act when she was informed that the child was so unhappy at home that she'd run away to Greenwich Village. That was when Mrs. Hawkins sent a gentleman to Zorka, with more or less the truth about the opportunity presented by Merton Hall.

"He was one of their board members," said Judy. "Apparently, the only man on their board. Mother said that they all liked him a lot. He was from a very old New York family. Knickerbocker stuff."

"I remember him as quite courtly," I said.

"A bachelor gentleman."

"Oh, I see."

"You didn't think it was odd—to have this stranger show up out of the blue?"

"Not really. It felt like anything could happen in the Village back then. Were the other girls . . . victims, too? I mean, of your grandfather?"

Judy shook her head.

"Just needy girls," she said. "Now Merton Hall is run by the Episcopal Diocese of New York."

"I heard. But you didn't take it on? Like you took on the Philharmonic?"

"It was too much, with the kids. That kind of charity work was of another generation. Those women were powerhouses."

I was stunned, of course.

"So in a way," I said, "we are actually, what, half-sisters? No—your mother and I would be that . . ."

"I don't know what that makes you and me," said Judy, "except family."

But the revelation wasn't particularly shocking, though I did find it slightly staggering how someone could suddenly discover something so important yet unsuspected in their life. At least now I knew who my father was.

"I'm afraid he wasn't very nice," said Judy. "They didn't divorce, because people didn't do that very much then, but they wound up leading very separate lives. You'll recall that we didn't talk about him all that much."

"I remember."

"After Granny died, Mother and I talked about how and when to tell you, or even *if* we should tell you at all. Then Mother died, and I really didn't know what to do, until now."

"So you always knew?"

Judy nodded.

"Mother explained it to me, before you started with us," she said. "She said that it was our duty to help you, but that it must be done in just the right way. I hope that my delay in telling you isn't a problem."

"No, no. Not at all . . ."

I was thinking—replaying long-past scenes in my head, reinterpreting them in the light of this revelation. My mind flashed on the last time I saw dear Mrs. Hawkins, shortly before her death. It was in her room up at Shady Hill, in the early '70s; she was ninety-two or ninety-three at the time. She was sitting in an armchair in the room's seating area when we arrived. A nurse was reading to her.

"We brought your great friend, Mom," said Sandy, as we walked in.

"Marlene!" said Mrs. Hawkins.

"This is Mary," said the nurse gently, alert to any issues that might be important, including episodes of memory loss. Then Sandy explained that her mother was only being playful.

"I know who it is," said Mrs. Hawkins. "Come and let me kiss you."

"How are you, Mrs. Hawkins?" I said, approaching and leaning over for a kiss.

"Very well, my dear. Seeing you is such a tonic!"

I was delighted that she seemed pleased I'd come, and I was gratified to see that she was being so well cared for. The room was lovelier than any in a luxury hotel, I imagined. Impeccably decorated, bright and cheery, it boasted several items that I knew Mrs. Hawkins had long treasured, like a silver bud vase and a pair of paintings of narrow houses on Amsterdam canals.

The three of us sat down next to her. To give us some privacy, the nurse settled with a copy of *Reader's Digest* on the other side of the room. Mrs. Hawkins was dressed in a pink-

and-white–striped housecoat with a Peter Pan collar. Her white hair was neatly done in a slightly smaller-scale version of the shortish hairdo that she'd always worn, probably since before I started working for her. During our conversation, she kept her hands chiefly in her lap, occasionally raising the right one for emphasis, clutching a crumpled facial tissue.

After exchanging the latest news with Sandy and Judy, Mrs. Hawkins turned to me.

"And you, dear?"

"All is well, thanks."

"They read me stories here, but it's not the same."

"What kind of stories do you like these days?"

"Anything that takes me away. Althea, what are we reading today?"

"*Mother Carey's Chickens*," said the nurse.

"It's very good," said Mrs. Hawkins. "A classic! But I miss my tales of Marlene."

"That was a lot of fun, wasn't it?"

Glowing in her eyes was the same curiosity mixed with acceptance that I remember noting on the first day I met her, more than ten years before. In fact, this quality seemed to have mellowed into a Buddha-like contentment—or seemed especially so now that Mrs. Hawkins's relative immobility meant that most of her expressiveness radiated from her face. Compared with all the titled individuals I have known or observed in my life with Lee and Truman, Mrs. Hawkins was possibly the most naturally aristocratic, in the best sense of that word, incorporating the ideal of *noblesse oblige*; and she managed to pass on this quality, whether by nature or nurture, or both, to her daughter and granddaughter.

"I hope you're inventing a world for someone else to dream in now," said Mrs. Hawkins.

"Well . . . thank you for opening the door to all that," I said.

If Judy and her mother shared a private look of fulfillment at that moment, due to a secret they shared, I didn't notice it. Dear Mrs. Hawkins died within months of our visit.

"You sure you're okay with this?" said Judy.

"Of course," I said, snapping out of my reminiscence and focusing on my friend in the here-and-now. "Thanks, Jude. I'm fine. Really I am. I'm happy with the news and happy that you told me. And I'm glad that you're not *un*happy that you told me when you did. It's just a bit to take in."

As we paused for a moment, Mrs. Pasmore stepped over.

"Sorry to interrupt, but dinner is ready to be served," she said. "Shall I keep it ready, or did you want to sit down?"

"Do you feel like some dinner, Mar?" said Judy.

"Absolutely," I said.

"Then thank you, Mrs. Pasmore. We'll sit down in five."

Judy and I rose and began making our way to the dining room.

"So that gentleman who found me . . . ?"

"Family friend. Shipping money—tons of it. Apparently, once as an eligible young heir, he'd escorted King George V's daughter, Mary, the Princess Royal, to a ball in London."

I shook my head, marveling.

"He played his part brilliantly," I said.

"As it happens, he had a background in amateur acting, too," said Judy.

"*He* must have been something!"

"Mustn't he? Mother once told me that Granny adored him and had wanted to marry him. But she was maneuvered into marrying Grandfather, because that was a more 'appropriate' match—and we all know how *that* turned out."

One end of the dining room table was set with three places. On the table were the ranunculus I had brought, arranged prettily in an urn-shaped crystal vase.

"I'll go fetch Burt," said Judy.

"Does he know?" I asked.

"Not the part I just told you. That's not my story to tell anyone but you."

"Not that I'm ashamed of it or anything."

"Of course not."

"In fact, it's kind of cool."

"I was hoping you might think so."

"Sure. And I may—who knows?—use it in something I'm thinking of writing, about myself."

"Are you? Good for you. A short story?"

"Maybe. Or maybe something bigger, like a novel or a movie."

"About your life? Wow—that would be fantastic. We can talk more about it anytime you like, though I'm pretty sure I don't have any more revelations to add."

"Mmm, roast chicken," said Burt, entering the dining room. "Yum, yum."

"And here you are," said Judy. "Burt's been looking forward to dinner. I think he has a million things to ask you about New York in the sixties and seventies. He's from Ohio."

"Now, now . . . !" said Burt, affectionately.

"You'd better slip me a safe word in case you want me to shut him up," said Judy.

"I can fend for myself, you know," I said.

"Right."

"Besides, I'm sure Burt could also get some of the same tales from you. You're a New Yorker, too."

"Oh, no. I have to pass. You're the one who hobnobbed with celebrities. You're the one who attended the ball. Unless you want to hear more about start-ups, you're the entertainment tonight, my dear. I'm afraid that's the price of having lived an interesting life."

AUTHOR'S NOTE

I am deeply grateful to my editor/publisher, John Scognamiglio of Kensington Books, for approaching me through my agent, Mitchell Waters of Brandt & Hochman Literary Agents, with the idea for this book. Having worked previously with John and Mitchell on my novel *Now and Yesterday*, I count both of them as friends and trusted colleagues. Instantly I saw that John's idea had terrific possibilities, and I am thankful to Mitchell for helping me develop it.

My sincere thanks also go to others with whom I discussed the book and its ideas during the writing process: Victor Bumbalo, Doug Fitch, Edouard Getaz, Craig Hensala, Lesley Horowitz, Matthue Keck, Eric Latzky, Morgan Millogo, Kate Orne, MaryEllen and John Panaccione, Adam Snyder, Matt Wagner, Simon Watson, and David Winn. And I will be forever grateful to David Anthony Perez and Dr. Martin Nash for suggesting, one day in 2019, that we all meet at Christie's in New York, to see the preview of the auction of items from the estate of Lee Radziwill. Thanks, too, to Sarah Waring for an astute pre-publication read of the novel.

I owe much to the creative legacy of the two individuals whose friendship this novel is based on, Lee Radziwill and Truman Capote. The novels, short stories, and articles written by Capote, and the books and articles written or edited by Radziwill, are important parts of cultural history that both inspired me and brought me closer, I hope, to the true natures of these extraordinary individuals. While not a historian, I was thrilled to immerse myself in the details of their privileged lives. Gratefully I acknowledge the thoughtful work of Radziwill's and Capote's biographers, respectively: Diana DuBois, author of *In Her Sister's Shadow: An Intimate Biography of Lee Radziwill*; and Gerald Clarke, author of *Capote: A Biography*. I was also lucky to be able to rely on several other books related to my story, notably: Jack Dunphy's *Dear Genius: A Memoir of My Life with Truman Capote*; Greg Lawrence's *Jackie as Editor: The Literary Life of Jacqueline Kennedy Onassis*; George Plimpton's *Truman Capote: In Which Various Friends, Enemies, Acquaintances and Detractors Recall His Turbulent Career*; and Tison Pugh's *Truman Capote: A Literary Life at the Movies*.

The vast majority of dialogue in this novel is invented, but a small portion is based on actual quotations of Radziwill and Capote as reported in the books listed above, as well as in the work of the scores of media workers—authors, magazine and newspaper writers and interviewers, television hosts and producers, and filmmakers and photographers—who covered these figures. Having worked in the media myself, I greatly admire the journalistic care these media workers took in gathering and presenting quotations from Radziwill and Capote. Respectfully in this regard, I acknowledge Max Abelson, Richard Avedon, F. Lee Bailey, Peter Beard, Cecil Beaton, Eric Boman, Tina Brown, Bill Cardoso, Johnny Carson, Igor Cassini (as Cholly Knickerbocker), Dick Cavett, Henry Clarke, Heather Clawson, Bob Colacello, David Patrick Columbia, Rebecca Cope, Sofia Coppola, Edward Cotterill, Reggie Darling, Deborah Davis, Michelle Dean, Tate Delloye, Gioia Diliberto, Anne Taylor Fleming, Ron Galella, Megan Gorman, Benno Graziani, Michelle Green, François Halard, Caroline Hallemann, Larry Harnisch, Nancy Hass, Karen G. Jackovich, Kristopher Jansma, Chris Jones, Jon Kalish, Sam Kashner, Judy Klemesrud, Lorna Koski, Albin Krebs, Laurence Leamer, Lisa Lockwood, Aileen Mehle, Martina Mondadori, John Otis, Mitchell Owens, Sally Quinn, Nancy Schoenberger, Nock Scott, Mark Shaw, Stanley Siegel,

Mario Sorrenti, Kate Storey, David Susskind, John Swaine, J. Randy Taraborrelli, Norman Vanamee, Charles A. Van Rensselaer (as Cholly Knickerbocker), Mary Vesoa, Stellene Volandes, Sally Quinn, Stan Wan, and Andy Warhol.

Finally, I am grateful to those individuals who, over the years, invited me to social events attended by Radziwill and/or Capote, as well as to the publicists who, when I was editing and contributing to style and culture publications, invited me to promotional events attended by these two. It was always exciting to be in the same room with them.

A READING GROUP GUIDE

SUCH GOOD FRIENDS

ABOUT THIS GUIDE

The suggested questions are included to enhance your group's reading of Stephen Greco's *Such Good Friends*!

Discussion Questions

1. Have you read any of Truman Capote's books or stories? If yes, how would you describe his writing? If not, did this book inspire you to read any of Capote's work? Which books or stories, and why?

2. How much did you know about the private lives of Lee and Truman before reading this book—and where did you learn about them? Which of the other historical celebrities in the story did you already know about—the ballet dancer Rudolf Nureyev? The billionaire Aristotle Onassis? First Lady Jacqueline Kennedy Onassis? Of all the characters in the book, who would you most like to have known and why?

3. The book portrays events of the 1960s and '70s: space shots, assassinations, political demonstrations, etc. What do you think were the most significant aspects of these decades in American and world history?

4. Think about Marlene's job as a cook/housekeeper: Do we still use the word "servant" to identify someone like that who does domestic household work? Why or why not? In the novel, does Marlene identify as a servant?

5. Why do you think Marlene's story about being a Cuban aristocrat was so important to her? Would you call this story a delusion, or a fantasy, or something else? Why do you think Marlene's screenplay was rejected by the producer?

6. Do you think Lee and Truman shared the same definition of friendship? What do you think were the most important aspects that attracted each to the other? How does your own definition of friendship compare with those of Lee and Truman?

7. What are your thoughts about the breakup of Lee and Truman's friendship: Did you find it sad or tragic? Do you think it was inevitable, and if so, why? Do you believe that Truman was telling the truth when he claimed that Lee told him about the Gore Vidal/White House party story? Why or why not? Why would Lee have told Truman this story if true, but then deny it?

8. In what ways do you think that Lee and Truman thought similarly about wealth? In what ways might they have thought differently about it? What about fame: How similarly do you think Lee and Truman thought about being famous? How do you think that their fame affected their relationship? How do you think celebrity during the 1960s, '70s, and '80s compares to today's celebrity culture? Would you say that Lee and Truman and their friends were the influencers of their time?

9. How would you describe Truman's relationship with drugs and alcohol? Would you call him an addict? What do you think he was after, with his drinking and drug-taking? Do you think the rich and famous have any better chance of falling into, or battling against, substance abuse than the rest of us?

10. Thinking specifically about fashion and style, how do you think the role of fashion designers and fashion brands has evolved since Lee and Truman's time? Lee and her friends were known for a certain elegant, put-together look; do we still value looks like that—why or why not?